The Circle of Reason

The Circle of Reason

by

AMITAV GHOSH

VIKING

VIKING
Viking Penguin Inc.
40 West 23rd Street,
New York, New York 10010, U.S.A.

First American edition
Published in 1986

LIBRARY OF CONGRESS CATALOGING IN PUBLICATION DATA
Ghosh, Amitav.
The circle of reason.
I. Title.
PR9499.3.G536C57   1986   823   85-40785
ISBN 0-670-80984-5

Printed in the United States of America by
R. R. Donnelley & Sons Company, Harrisonburg, Virginia
Set in Caledonia

For my parents

Acknowledgements

For their help and encouragement, I would like to thank, among many, many others, Mukul Kesavan, Hari Sen, Radhika Chopra, Supriya Guha, K. Jayaram, Felix Padel, Veena Das and my sister Chaitali (who helped more than she knew).

Part One

SATWA: REASON

Chapter One

Heads

The boy had no sooner arrived, people said afterwards, than Balaram had run into the house to look for the Claws.

There were plenty of people gathered outside the big house to vouch for it – boys in buttonless shorts, toothless, shrouded widows, a few men who had not found work for the day, squatting and scratching. Toru-debi threatened and scolded, but not one of them budged. It was not every day that someone new arrived in Lalpukur. Especially in such unusual circumstances (everyone knew them, of course).

Years later – thirteen to be exact – when people talked about all that had happened, sitting under the great banyan tree in the centre of the village (where Bhudeb Roy's life-size portrait had once fallen with such a crash), it was generally reckoned that the boy's arrival was the real beginning. Some said they knew the moment they set eyes on that head. That was a little difficult to believe. But, still, it *was* an extraordinary head – huge, several times too large for an eight-year-old, and curiously uneven, bulging all over with knots and bumps.

Someone said: It's like a rock covered with fungus. But Bolai-da, who had left his cycle-repair shop and chased the rickshaw which was bringing Toru-debi and the boy home from the station, all the way to the house on his bamboo-thin bandy legs, wouldn't have that. He said at once: No, it's not like a rock at all. It's an *alu*, a potato, a huge, freshly dug, lumpy potato.

So Alu he was named and Alu he was to remain, even though he had another name, finely scriptural – Nachiketa. Nachiketa Bose. But Alu was all that he was ever known as, and nobody could deny its appropriateness.

It was remarkably apt, as Bolai-da said – a little too apt, if anything – that Balaram, who had for so many years spent all his spare time measuring and examining people's heads, should have a nephew who had the most unusual head anybody had ever seen. No wonder he had run inside as soon as he set eyes on the boy (though he could have waited a bit since the boy was, after all, coming to live with him).

People were sorry for the boy, of course. It was barely a week since he had lost his mother and his father (Balaram's brother) in a car accident. It was hard after a shock like that to go away to live with an unknown aunt and uncle.

It was common knowledge that the boy had not met Balaram, his own uncle, ever before. Balaram and his brother had never so much as exchanged a letter since the day, fourteen years before Alu arrived in Lalpukur, when Balaram took his share of their inheritance and moved to the village – without so much, as his brother shouted after him, as a thought for the floundering family business. Later, with that vicious prescience peculiar to close relatives, he had even left instructions in his will that Balaram was not to be told of his death, nor asked to attend the funeral. But, as people told their children, nodding wisely, death chooses its own ironies: in the end it was to Balaram that his orphaned and more or less destitute son had to go.

And after all that to be faced with an unknown uncle bearing down on you with what looked like gigantic eagle's talons!

Actually, it was only Balaram's Claws. The villagers through long familiarity knew it to be harmless; but, still, they also knew it was little less than terrifying when seen for the first time. It was a kind of instrument, with three arms of finely planed and polished wood, each tapering to a sharp point at one end and joined to the others by a calibrated hinge. Balaram had designed it himself, soon after he discovered Phrenology. It had been made for him in Calcutta, at considerable expense. But, for all that, it was a simple instrument; merely a set of calipers, for measuring skulls. Only, at first sight, it looked as though it had been specially designed for gouging out eyes.

As Balaram advanced with the Claws held out in front of him, the boy shrank back, his knees shaking beneath his starched black shorts. Luckily for him, at that very moment Toru-debi turned towards the house after paying off the rickshaw. One look at the Claws and she knew exactly what was happening. She bounded up the four steps to the door with a cry, and snatched the instrument out of her husband's hands. He dropped his head, crestfallen, and ran his fingers through his thick white hair. Again? she cried, herding him into the house. You've started again? And on your own nephew, even before he's stepped into the house?

She came back to fetch the boy only after she had shut Balaram safely into his study. The boy was standing on the steps in front of the door, staring silently with his large wondering eyes, at the people gathered outside and the swaying coconut palms and fields of green rice beyond. She took him by the hand and led him into the house, and with one last angry gesture at the people outside she barred the door behind her.

But once he was inside the house she panicked. Tugging him across the courtyard towards the smoky, soot-blackened kitchen on the other side, she shouted: Nonder-ma, Nonder-ma.

Nonder-ma hobbled out of the kitchen mumbling toothlessly, bent almost double, no more than a few withered bones, with her widow's white homespun wrapped so carelessly around her that her dugs flapped outside, hanging down to her shrunken waist. Give him milk, give him milk, Toru-debi cried. She remembered that children are said to like milk. Muttering and complaining, Nonder-ma handed him a brass tumbler; and then, thrusting her face forward till he could see the grey flecks in her eyes, she examined him minutely. Liverish, she muttered. Look at his eyelids. Probably constipated, too.

The boy put the tumbler down and looked away. Be quiet, Nonder-ma, Toru-debi said, and handed it back to him, clucking her tongue in encouragement. But he would not touch it again.

What *did* he want? What do boys of eight do? What do they want? Childless herself, Toru-debi knew nothing of children. Children inhabited another world. A world without sewing machines. They neither hemmed, nor chain-stitched, nor cross-stitched, nor quilted. What *did* they do?

She had spent the whole morning worrying. How would a boy of eight, brought up in the clamour and excitement of Calcutta, like Lalpukur, she had wondered, as the cycle-rickshaw, honking with flurries of its rubber hooter, took her down the red-dust lanes of the village; past the great vaulted

and pillared banyan tree with the tea-shop and Bolai-da's
unrepaired cycles nestling in dark niches in its trunk; past the
rickety shed of the pharmacy, where the young men of the
village gathered in the evenings to read newspapers and play
cards and drink toddy; past the ponds mildewed with water-
hyacinth and darkened by leaning coconut palms, through
velvety green fields of young rice, to the little red-brick station
three miles away.

Once she was at the station she forgot her greater worry for
the more immediate one of finding the right boy. And when at
last she saw him, potato head and all, with a few bits of luggage
and an impatient relative beside him, the Singer which had so
long and so securely colonized her heart wobbled precariously.
For a moment. Ten years earlier she might perhaps have
pushed the machine away altogether, but at middle age it was
too difficult to cope with the unexpected. Besides, the Singer
had been part of her dowry; she had seen it for the first time on
the morning after the traumas of her wedding night; it was her
child in a way her husband's nephew could never be. On the
way back to the house she began to explain to the boy that his
uncle had not come to meet him because he was busy (which
was a lie: the truth was that Balaram had been afraid – he had
not been able to summon the courage to meet this offspring of
his brother in the impersonality of a railway platform), but he
showed no interest, so she talked to him happily of the clothes
she would make him on her sewing machine.

That was how it was to be with Toru-debi and Alu. After he
arrived her courtship with her machine was to be forever
punctuated by bouts of concern for the boy. Had he eaten? Had
he bathed? Where was he?

But actually the daily chores of bathing him (for it was
clear that he had never seen a well before) and feeding him
fell to Nonder-ma. She complained, of course; but, then,
Nonder-ma had always complained, ever since the day
Nondo, her first-born and only son, left her tyranny behind
him and ran off to Calcutta with all that she possessed (which
was very little), leaving her only the life-long curse of his
name.

Everything in this house, Nonder-ma often muttered, falls
to me – the cooking, sweeping, washing, everything, and now

the boy, too. And all for what? A few rupees, hardly enough for a sari a year.

Lying, ungrateful woman, Toru-debi would rail. I do nothing but give you money all day long, do everything for you, and still you go on and on. D'you think I've got a money tree?

And in any case it was little Maya Debnath, no bigger than Alu, who actually did most of the washing and sweeping, walking over every day from her father's huts beyond the bamboo forest. Besides, Toru-debi would say, what *do* you have to do for the boy anyway? But that she would say a little uncertainly, for her idea of what had to be done for the boy was by no means clear.

The truth was that Nonder-ma did not really have to do very much for Alu even in his first year in Lalpukur, for when he was not at school he was busy exploring the house.

It took him a long, long time, for the house brimmed over with rooms. The plan was simple (Balaram had designed it himself): there was a large square courtyard in the centre, shaded by the overhanging branches of a huge mango tree. There were rooms all around the courtyard, built on a high foundation a few feet off the ground. A cool open veranda ringed the courtyard, joining the rooms. A red tile roof, held up by bamboo struts, sloped low over the veranda, so that the sun never reached the rooms. It was always cool inside, and green, for the light was filtered through the innumerable lemon and banana trees and coconut palms which grew around the house.

The kitchen and the store-rooms fell on the far side of the courtyard, opposite the front door. A path snaked out from a small door next to the kitchen and led to a well and, beyond it, a pond surrounded by thickets of bright yellow bamboo. One side of the courtyard was Toru-debi's and the other Balaram's, each with four rooms. The fourth side, which faced out towards the dusty red lane, was kept for receiving visitors. That was the only part of the house which had two floors: there was one small room directly above the front door, joined to the courtyard by a ramshackle wooden staircase.

In those early days nobody could be sure where Alu disappeared. Sometimes he would be found in Toru-debi's room with its perpetually burning electric lights, its heavy mosquito-netted bed, its hillocks of trunks and discarded cloth,

its sewing machine, and its incense-blackened images of Ma
Kali, Ma Durga and Ma Saraswati piled high on the trunks (you
had to be an athlete to pray in that room, Balaram used to say);
and sometimes they would find him in the huge room which
faced out, with its clutter of dust-laden furniture, carefully laid
out for guests who never came; or in rooms pungent with
pickles in stone jars, or rooms piled high with old newspapers
and English magazines and cut-out sewing patterns, or others
stacked with grain and alive with rats' squeaks and the quick
slithering of snakes, or others half-full of firewood and coal, or
others still, empty of everything but dust, built in who knew
what unspoken hope?

And of course there was Balaram's study in one corner of the
courtyard.

For a long time Balaram could not persuade Alu to come
near his study, and he bitterly regretted the rash impulse
which had sent him looking for his instruments the day the boy
first arrived. It was little less than a torment to him to have to
watch that extraordinary skull at a tantalizing distance, just
beyond examining range.

Balaram did not know that when he was away, or when he
had to work late at the school, Alu would often slip into the
dim, dusty room and perch on Balaram's immense easy chair
and arrange its folding arms at right angles like the wings of a
plane. And when he tired of that he would prowl around the
room breathing in the smell of yellowing paper and staring at
the rows of books in the tall, glass-fronted bookcases.

It was not till many months had passed that Alu would enter
the room while Balaram was in it, and even then he would only
stand at the door and look in, often for hours, while Balaram
read reclining in his easy chair. Balaram kept his patience, and
it was well worth it, for when at last the boy trusted him enough
to let him run his fingers over his skull for the first time he knew
at once that it held material enough for a lifetime's study.

At first, as Balaram admitted to himself, he was baffled. The
boy's head confused him utterly and for entirely unfamiliar
reasons. Most heads were puzzling because they were so even.
Often there was nothing, not the slightest undulation or bump
to mark the major faculties and organs. Most heads, in a word,
were dull, even boring.

With Alu it was another matter altogether; it was like sitting down to a wedding feast after years of stewed rice. His head abounded with a profusion of bumps and knots and troughs, each more aggressively pronounced than the next and scattered about with an absolute disregard for the discoveries of phrenology. The array of bumps and protuberances grew cheerfully all over his head and showed no signs at all of dividing into distinct and recognizable organs. It was all very confusing and very exciting – a wealth of new stimulating material. In time it prompted Balaram's paper on the Indistinctness of the Organs of the Brain (he sent it to the Bombay Natural History Society and to the Asiatic Society in Calcutta, but unaccountably it was never acknowledged).

Later, when Alu was old enough to understand, Balaram often said to him: You'd have to change your head if you read Spurzheim or Gall – wouldn't be able to live with the confusion.

Take, for instance, that big spectacle-shaped lump which covered a large part of the back and sides of Alu's head. Starting a little above the hair-line, it stretched across the skull, but stopped short of the ears. To put it more precisely, it covered the squama occipitus and grew over the lateral areas of the lambdoidal suture, covering symmetrical parts over the asterion. It looked harmless enough, though hardly pleasing, but for Balaram it meant a fair number of sleepless nights. It was large enough to contain a multitude of organs and yet its boundaries were too shadowy to say which. And the worst part was that it was right on the trickiest part of the skull, for the founders of the science of phrenology were all agreed that the organs which govern the lowest and least desirable propensities all grow on the back and sides of the head. For all Balaram knew, a witch's brew could be bubbling in that lump – Destructiveness perhaps, mixed with Amativeness or Secrecy and peppered with Combativeness or Acquisitiveness. And if he could find no way of identifying and combating those organs it would be just a matter of time before they drove the poor boy to some hideous crime.

But eventually it all turned out well, for Balaram discovered that the lump cloaked nothing more serious than the organs of Philoprogenitiveness or the Love of Children, Adhesiveness or

Friendship and, regrettably, Combativeness. There was even a possibility of Vitality at the base of the skull but, on the whole, Balaram was one of those who argued against rather than for the existence of the Organ of Vitativeness.

Seen as a whole, it wasn't altogether encouraging, but still Balaram could not but be grateful that the lump so neatly avoided Destructiveness and Secretiveness and Acquisitiveness and all the other moral quicksands which lie around the ear. It was only much later, when Alu was older, that Balaram noticed Amativeness or, to put it bluntly, the Organ of Sex blossoming tumescently just above the hair-line. He jotted it down in his notebook with horrified embarrassment; no doubt it had something to do with Self-Abuse. Ever after he did his best not to look at it.

As for the rest of Alu's head, it took Balaram years before he could even begin to make sense of certain protuberances, and some were to remain puzzling for ever. But in a general way he was more or less sure that there were distinct depressions over the organs of Self-Esteem, Vanity and Cautiousness. On the other hand, there was a pleasing undulation over Benevolence, just below the crown. To Balaram's great relief the crown itself with its collection of religious organs was absolutely flat. And the two pronounced horn-like protuberances on both sides of the crown probably held Firmness, Hope and Wonder, while the depressions at the temples almost certainly spelt the lack of Poesy and Wit (over neither of which was Balaram likely to shed any tears). But the strangest part of that strange head was the forehead, for it was enigmatically flat exactly where all the higher Perceptive and Reflective faculties ought to have been, except for a mysterious bump in the centre, where the hair began. That bump could be anything – Language, Eventuality, Cause. . . .

Many, many years were to pass before Balaram discovered its function.

Balaram often wished there was something to be learnt from Alu's physiognomy, but the boy's face gave very little away. It was a compact face, of what Kretschmer called the shield-shaped type: that is, straight at the sides with a rounded jaw and chin – with large eyes and generous lips. The nose was of the kind which the Barbarini manuscript names Lunar – short, with a rounded end. But those were mere classifications; there was nothing to be learnt from them. Looking at his face, nobody could have called the boy handsome or ugly. If there was a word for it, it was *ordinary*. In fact, with his stocky build and being as he was, neither tall nor short nor dark nor fair, Alu would have been nothing other than ordinary to look at if it were not for his head.

When Alu was much older and had to sit on the floor because he had grown too heavy for the arms of the easy chair, Balaram often used to wonder aloud, patting him gently on Benevolence, at how the two of them came to be so unlike each other. After all, they were blood relatives and there ought to have been something to show for it, something in the skull. There could no longer be any doubt, he used to say, that the skull and therefore the character are to some degree hereditary. Wasn't that why Lombroso was so celebrated – for demonstrating the hereditary nature of character? Wasn't that why the American laws of 1915 prescribing sterilization for confirmed criminals were enacted?

But, laws or not, there was no discernible resemblance between Alu and Balaram. Balaram's head was long, narrow and finely modelled. It was almost flat at the back and sides, and, except for two barely perceptible undulations over Vanity, it betrayed not the slightest trace of a Lower Sentiment or Propensity. But it had not always been so. When Balaram first began to read about phrenology, he had discovered a few signs of liveliness on his Amatory Organ. Balaram was, and always had been, extremely prudish. Such was his embarrassment at his discovery that in a few weeks he managed to rub a fair-sized depression into the back of his neck.

Balaram's physiognomy reflected his cranium perfectly. He had a thin, ascetic face, with clean lines, a sharp ridge of a nose and wide, dreamy eyes. His high, broad forehead rose to a majestic dome, crowned with a thick, unruly pile of silver hair. It was an astonishing forehead: it shone; it glowed; it was like a lampshade for his bulging Higher Faculties – Language, Form, Number, the lot. It was a striking face even in repose. Sometimes, when he was animated, it was lit with such a bright, pointed intensity that it imprinted itself on the minds of everyone who saw him in those moments.

After he began thinking about heredity and character
seriously, Balaram often wondered what a child of his would
look like. Once, on one of his frequent visits to Calcutta, he put
the question to Gopal Dey, his oldest and dearest friend. They
were walking in the ornamental gardens of the National
Library at the time (it was a beautiful garden in those days
when B. S. Kesavan was the director of the Library, not an
overgrown, bureaucratized swamp as it is now). Gopal was
tired. He had spent a long hard day at the High Court, and after
hours of ploughing through briefs he was in no mood to
speculate about the children Balaram might have had. In any
case, it was a difficult question. If Balaram had had children,
they would in all likelihood have been Toru-debi's children as
well, and, in contrast to the lean ascetic Balaram, Toru-debi,
with her soft woolly cheeks and dimpled face, was a bundle of
pleasantly unruly plumpness, even though her eyes, somewhat at odds with the rest of her face, had been honed into
pin-points of concentration by her years at her sewing
machine.

Toru-debi had never permitted Balaram to examine her
skull, and never would, but for years Balaram had carefully
observed her head in the mornings when her hair clung to her
head after her bath, and as far as he was concerned he knew it as
intimately as one of his plastic demonstration skulls. It was a
large head, with a not inconsiderable cranial capacity; more or
less evenly rounded, except for well-marked protuberances on
the median over the bregma, on the religious organs, and
another on the occipital bone. That was an odd one: once upon
a time he would have had no hesitation in entering it under
Philoprogenitiveness, or a remarkably well-developed Love of
Children. But over the years he had watched it slip sideways,
towards the asterion, until it became something else
altogether. Sometimes he interpreted it as Constancy, but the
suspicion always lurked somewhere in his mind that actually it
was the yet unclassified organ of Tenacity (or, not to mince
words, plain bloody Obstinacy). As for the rest, he could guess
at a luxuriant growth on Constructiveness or the Mechanical
Sense (for even sewing needed a mechanical sense of a kind),
but he had never been very sure about the exact location of that
organ. And then, of course, there was that swollen lump above

the ear meatus, which he had no alternative but to interpret as Destructiveness. It was certainly true that her face, usually so tranquil (mainly because she hardly seemed to recognize the existence of a world outside her sewing room), was quite transformed when she was angry. In a rage she was capable of doing anything at all.

If you and Toru had a child, Gopal said sharply, it would probably be quite ordinary.

Oh? said Balaram, disappointed, and turned away to look at the extravagant stucco façade of the National Library.

Gopal had not really believed in phrenology or physiognomy or Balaram's theories of heredity ever. And over the years he had developed a positive hostility to them. That may have been because in one of their earliest arguments on the subject Balaram had said to him, in a long-regretted flash of temper: You ought to be preserved in methylated spirit. You're a discovery. You're the only person alive with a Phlegmatic organ.

Gopal had little vanity. Even in those days, well before middle age, he knew himself to be short and paunchy. He knew his broad face with its childishly rounded cheeks to be pleasant, but nothing more. But he was not phlegmatic; anybody who cared to look at his eyes, shining behind his gold-rimmed glasses, would know that at once. But the trouble with people like Balaram was that theories came first and the truth afterwards.

Take, for example, Balaram's theory about Dantu.

Dantu, their friend and ally through all their most difficult times in college, had vanished soon after his final examinations (in fact he had had very little to do with Balaram after the Accident, but that's another story). A year after college they heard that he had found a good job with a tea company. But soon after he vanished again. They often wondered what had happened to him, but this time he really hadn't left a trace. But then, one day, more than twenty years afterwards, with the help of his new-found theories Balaram declared confidently that Dantu had become a sadhu; that he had abandoned worldly life and was wandering around the country with a begging-bowl. Why? Simple. Because of his sharply domed head, of course, and his thin, hollow face and those two long, peeping front teeth from which he took his name. It's his bregma, said Balaram. I can see now that it was Veneration that had pushed his skull up so sharply. Besides, he always had the look of a saint.

Nonsense, said Gopal, but only to himself, for he knew how touchy Balaram was about his theories. Nonsense; politics interested Dantu much more than religion – it's just that your theory doesn't allow for a Political organ.

And, sure enough, a year or so later he came upon an article in a newspaper about a Shri Hem Narain Mathur (which was only Dantu under his real name) who had been arrested somewhere in north Bihar for organizing the landless labourers of the area to agitate for fair wages. He snipped the article out and showed it to Balaram later, but he didn't say, as he had planned to: Veneration is a long way from leading strikes. What about your theory now?

That was just it, the reason why phrenology was rubbish – all theory and no facts. He had said so, as he never tired of repeating, since the very first time Balaram had shown him the copy of *Practical Phrenology* that he had discovered in a secondhand bookshop in College Street.

As it happens, we know exactly when that happened. It happened on 11 January 1950 at 4.30 in the afternoon. We know the date because that was the day Madame Irène Joliot-Curie, Nobel Laureate in physics and daughter of the discoverers of radium, Pierre and Marie Curie, arrived in Calcutta ablaze with glory.

Balaram was thirty-six at the time. He was working as a sub-editor on the *Amrita Bazar Patrika*, which was still, at that time, Calcutta's best English newspaper. He had been working there for close on fourteen years, ever since he left college, so he was fairly well known in the office then. That was probably why he was allowed to go to the airport with the staff reporter that day.

Of course, Balaram had planned for the day ever since the papers had announced the date of the Joliot-Curies' arrival in Calcutta on their way back from the Science Congress in Delhi. There were other scientific stars scheduled to arrive on the same day: Frédéric Joliot, Irène Joliot-Curie's husband, with whom she had shared her Nobel; J. D. Bernal, the English physicist later to win the Nobel himself; Sir Robert Robinson, distinguished chemist and president of the Royal Society.

But in that whole gathering of luminaries there was only one person Balaram wanted to see and that was Madame Irène Joliot-Curie. He had read about the Curies since he was thirteen. Radium had powered the fantasies of his adolescence; he had celebrated Marie Curie's second Nobel with fireworks. For him Irène Curie was a legend come alive, a part of the secret world of his boyhood, an embodiment of the living tradition of science. He would have gladly given up his job only to *see* her.

On 9 January, two days before she was scheduled to arrive, Balaram went to the news editor and asked permission to go to the airport with the staff reporter. It'll help, he said in explanation, with the subbing of the story and the headlines. The news editor, always busy, hardly looked up: Yes, of course, do what you like. But on the tenth Balaram went to him again, just to make sure. Yes, yes, the news editor snapped, didn't I say so?

The eleventh was bitterly cold by Calcutta's sultry standards; the coldest day the city had had in years. Balaram wrapped himself up carefully in two sweaters, an overcoat and a new muffler. At Dum-Dum airport two of his childhood heroes were pointed out to him in the waiting crowd, the physicists Meghnad Saha and Satyen Bose. But Balaram, busy scanning the skies, hardly noticed them. When he spotted the silvery Dakota with the Star Lines emblem painted on its wings, he hopped about flapping his overcoat, almost beside himself. The staff reporter, long accustomed to the famous, said quite sharply: Can't you stand still for a moment?

Madame Joliot-Curie climbed out first, wrapped in a grey overcoat, with a cloth bag in one hand. She was taller than he had expected, with clearly drawn jowls, grizzled hair and bright, sharp eyes. Her husband came out next, smiling, his tie tucked into his crumpled trousers. And then came J. D. Bernal, dapper, elegant, hat in hand, exuding ease and grace. Balaram tried not to look at him. But of course it wasn't his fault. The difference between him and Irène Joliot-Curie was not the difference between two individuals. It lay outside either of them; it was a geographical difference, a spatial difference, the difference of two opposed traditions – one which produced Louis Pasteur, battling himself into paralysis, and Marie Curie's revolutionary fervour, and another which turned out these clever, passionless, elegant sleepwalkers. (He was wrong about J. D. Bernal, of course, but he didn't know it then.)

Balaram pressed forward with the reporters, towards the three figures standing by the plane on the runway. Faintly he heard one of the reporters remark to Professor Joliot that they looked tired.

We flew over high altitudes, Professor Joliot said in answer, over 9000 feet, and this has somewhat told on us. He turned to his wife and smiled. She nodded, running the back of her hand across her forehead. With an electric thrill of excitement Balaram saw that she was looking straight at him.

Balaram knew that he had to say something. He knew Professor Joliot was wrong; 9000 feet wouldn't tire a Curie. The Curies lived in the highest reaches of the imagination.

Balaram strained eagerly forward, brushing a shock of his springy black hair off his eyes. But, sir, he said loudly, hardly aware of what he was saying, are you not accustomed to keeping high altitudes?

It was only a silly impulse; he knew that the moment he said it. It meant nothing. But it was too late. There was a moment's awkward silence and then everyone, led by Professor Joliot, burst into laughter. Even Madame Joliot-Curie smiled.

For Balaram each peal of that laughter carried the sting of a whiplash. He turned, humiliation smarting in his eyes. They were all the same, all the same, those scientists. It was something to do with their science. Nothing mattered to them – people, sentiments, humanity. He pushed his way through the crowd and ran and ran till he reached Dum-Dum village.

Back in Calcutta he wandered down the roaring traffic of Dharmotolla, away from the buses and trams of the Esplanade. He could not bear the thought of compounding his humiliation by going back to the office or facing Toru-debi at home. He went where his feet led him, and inevitably they took him to College Street. Soon, chewing acidly on his humiliation, he was back among the familiar crumbling plaster façades and the tinkling bells of trams; the students pushing their way to bus-stops and the rows of stalls piled high with secondhand books. A little way from the wrought-iron gates of Presidency College he absent-mindedly picked up and paid for a tattered old book. It was called *Practical Phrenology*.

He walked down to the Dilkhusha Cabin in Harrison Street, found a quiet table and ordered a cup of tea. After a while he opened the book and desultorily skimmed over a few pages. Then, with gathering excitement, he began to read.

At four o'clock he took a tram to the High Court. Gopal was busy in his chambers, but Balaram dragged him out to a roadside tea-stall run by a Bihari, in the Strand. Look, he said, handing him the book. Look what I've found.

Gopal was not particularly pleased at being pulled out of his chambers at a quarter past four in the afternoon, especially since he had an important tax suit coming up the next day. He fingered through the book, looked at the photographs of typical criminal types with distaste and handed it back to Balaram.

Balaram, he said warily, you've never studied science. You know nothing of anatomy. People like you and me just don't know enough about these things. We should leave them alone.

How does that matter? said Balaram. There are ideas in science like anything else. Do you ever tell me to stop reading history? Do I ever tell you to stop reading novels?

Gopal looked at his watch. It was four-thirty and he was late. To me, he said, this looks like rubbish.

Don't you see? said Balaram, stuttering with excitement, eyes blazing. Haven't I always told you? What's wrong with all those scientists and their sciences is that there's no connection between the outside and the inside, between what people think and how they are. Don't you see? This is different. In this science the inside and the outside, the mind and the body, what people do and what they are, are *one*. Don't you see how *important* it is?

I think, said Gopal stolidly, that if you must keep on with this science business you'd better to go to hear Madame Curie this evening when she opens the Institute of Nuclear Physics. And now I have to go.

Balaram did go to hear her, and so did Gopal. They stood far back in the crowd, behind cheering groups of schoolchildren and college students, and watched her cut the tape. She looked incongruous, surrounded by ministers and governors and petty pomp – a simple housewifely figure in a plain dress. Balaram listened intently as she began to speak of the importance of nuclear physics and the new chapter in the prosperity of mankind it had opened.

But then Gopal dug him in the ribs and winked, unkindly reminding him of a little defeat. Once, about three and a half years ago, a harassed chief sub had asked Balaram to compose a banner headline. After a good deal of hard thought he came up with: Nuclear bomb dropped – Hiroshima disappears. The chief sub had not thought it fit to print. 'A-bomb', he said, was better than 'nuclear' (it was some years before the paper worked out a house style on the matter). And anyway Balaram had chosen the wrong type-case. It rankled absurdly for years.

Balaram looked hard at Madame Curie and, soon after, he left without a word to Gopal. Next morning, he was on his way up to the newsroom when a man stopped him. He was a youngish man, not past his late twenties, Balaram judged, dressed in grey trousers and a blue sweater. Could you tell me where the advertising department is? he asked nervously. His Bengali had a slight but distinct rural slur.

Why? Balaram said, and smiled.

Reassured by his friendliness the young man invited him out for a cup of tea. Balaram went, glad of an excuse to put off his entry into the newsroom. When they were sitting at the tea-stall the young man showed Balaram his advertisement. He wanted a teacher for a primary school in a village called Lalpukur, about a hundred miles north of Calcutta, near the border.

It was a very new settlement, the young man explained. Most of the villagers were refugees from the east. His was the only family which owned land in the area.

And where are you from, sir? he asked Balaram.

I'm from East Bengal, too, Balaram said. From Dhaka.

I see, he said. A few of the villagers are from there as well.

Anyway, he went on, after finishing with his bachelor's degree in science he had trained as a schoolteacher. Now that the time had come to find a job, he had decided to start a school of his own instead – in Lalpukur where it was really needed and where he could keep an eye on his land. It would be both an income and something worthwhile. Besides, why work for someone else when you could work for yourself?

But he needed another teacher – he wouldn't be able to handle it all on his own. He looked at Balaram, his eyes shining with enthusiasm: You'll never believe how eager those children are to learn.

When Balaram left the young man and went up to the newsroom, he was greeted with slow handclaps and broad smiles. He discovered that a number of that morning's papers had carried his question to Frédéric Joliot – and the answering laughter – in their reports.

He applied for a day's leave at once and walked out of the office. He walked down to the Hooghly, hugging his sweaters around him, and watched the boats sailing languidly down the river. He stood there all afternoon and then went down to the High Court.

Gopal was patient with him that day, for Balaram's terrible distress was stamped large on him. They went for a long walk across the green expanse of the Maidan. Halfway across Balaram stopped and waved a hand at the tall buildings and snarling traffic of Chowringhee. In a place like this, he said, people can't think about the difference between what they are and what they ought to be. Nothing can change people here. Not science, or history, or reason. Nothing. Nothing could ever be taught here. Not really; not so that it *changed* anything.

But what makes you think, said Gopal, that you could teach?

I've been reading the book I showed you, Balaram answered. Look – he ran his hands over the upper parts of his temples and the sides of his head – look: Hope, Wonder, Ideality *and* Firmness. What could make a better teacher?

He went back home and for ten days he battled with Toru-debi. A week later they were in Lalpukur. He only learnt the young man's name when they reached the village. It was Bhudeb Roy.

How different Bhudeb Roy was then! His squama occipitus, even though not quite flat, was certainly not the knobbly tribute to Progeniture it became after the birth of his fifth son. Nor did he then possess those distinctive egg-like growths on Combativeness and Destructiveness above the asterion and the ear meatus.

Balaram often admitted that a good deal of his reconstruction of the young Bhudeb was mere conjecture. A long time had passed after all, and he had only just discovered phrenology when he first met Bhudeb Roy. But he had a good memory and, thinking about it later, the reason why he had taken such an immediate liking to the shy young man was obvious to him: their heads were remarkably alike at the time; almost mirror images of each other. It would have been impossible to distinguish their parietal regions, with Conscience and Hope, from each other without instruments. And he was absolutely certain that on that first day, in the tea-shop outside the *Amrita Bazar Patrika* office, he had seen distinct signs of a swelling on the middle of Bhudeb Roy's frontal bone, in front of the coronal suture, right over Benevolence, and another striking growth over Ideality at the temples.

But, then, as Balaram used to say to Gopal later, a science can only tell you about things as they are; not about what they might become.

Ideality withered on Bhudeb Roy's temples because he never really believed in anything. Even afterwards, when the organ of Order under his eyebrows bloated and grew into a bent for straight lines, he never had *real* passion. Balaram would have forgiven him anything if he had. But he hadn't. Those obscene little swellings, Balaram claimed, were just funguses feeding on the dead matter of his head.

Nor, in Bhudeb Roy's youth, were those bits of his skull immediately over and outside the obelion as distended and hideous as they were to become later.

But wait, Gopal would interrupt Balaram. You only noticed Vanity and Self-Esteem *after* he began hanging up his portraits all over the school.

But it wasn't easy to interrupt Balaram once he had started on the subject. Just look at the skin around his squamous suture, he would say. It's a monument to Acquisitiveness and Secretiveness. There Gopal would stop him firmly. He knew for certain that Balaram had begun to talk of Bhudeb Roy's Acquisitive organ, on the upper edge of the front half of the squamous suture, only after he discovered that Bhudeb Roy was taking fifty rupees for himself from the parents of each child he admitted to the school. And as for Secretiveness, on the posterior part of the squamous suture, he had no doubt that Balaram had noticed that long after he heard that Bhudeb Roy had another steady trickle of money flowing in from the police station in the next village, in exchange for secret monthly reports on almost everybody in Lalpukur. It's only natural, Balaram explained to him once. Lalpukur is a border town and the police are given money from their headquarters to get information. If they didn't spend it somehow, the funds would lapse and they'd have to go without their own cuts. Besides, it has to be said of them that they've proceeded on sound phrenological principles in choosing Bhudeb Roy to be their informer: his cranial capacity is enormous – there can't be any doubt that he's as clever as a fox – and he has exactly the right kind of squamous suture.

But, Gopal objected, you only noticed his squamous suture *after* you heard about his links with the police. What comes first, then, the act or the organ?

Balaram did not give him a proper answer. Instead he said: But tell me, is any of it untrue?

And then Gopal was reduced to silence. He had met Bhudeb Roy on his first visit to Lalpukur, soon after Balaram had moved there. He had looked like a fairly ordinary young man then, with thinning hair and a large pleasant face. He was stout even then but far from fat, and in his starched white dhoti and kurta he had even possessed a certain kind of grace.

When Gopal saw him years later he had flinched, as anybody would on seeing for the first time that huge slab-like face nodding upon the rolls of flesh of a massively swollen neck. The sockets of his eyes had bulged forward as though to startle a hangman, but curiously the eyes themselves had shrunk into tiny, opaque, red-flecked circles. His mouth had grown into a yawning, swallowing, spittle-encrusted chasm, stretching across the entire width of his huge jaw. His upper lip had shrunk away altogether, while his lower lip had looped upward almost to the tip of his nose. His head was bare and shiny, except for a few limp hairs which he combed vainly over the gnarled swellings on the sides of his head. His ears stuck out of his head at right angles and waved occasionally like banana leaves in a breeze. His body had changed, too – his legs had become two dimpled pillars of flesh and his arms had shot forward till they dangled at his knees. And above it all, for Bhudeb Roy was usually prone, rose his stomach, surging turbulently above him in an engorged, hairy mass, straining at the thin cotton of his kurta.

It was not till he discovered criminology, Balaram claimed, that he found a science adequate to Bhudeb Roy. And even Gopal had to admit that there *was* a remarkable resemblance between Lombroso's photographs of voluminous jaws and peaked zygomatic arches, of razor-like upper lips and sadly delinquent beetle eyes, and parts of Bhudeb Roy's physiognomy. No wonder, Balaram said, the police chose *him*.

But Balaram's discovery was to become a dilemma. Soon after he showed those photographs to Gopal, Bhudeb Roy arrived in his house one evening to ask a favour of him. There was nothing unusual in that. Balaram had always been polite to Bhudeb Roy for the sake of the school. And Bhudeb Roy, for his part, had always had a great respect for Balaram's learning, a respect he never lost. At that time he even had what Gopal, for one, took to be a deep affection for Balaram. But Balaram himself thought otherwise. No, he told Gopal once, all his attempts at kindness, all those little things he always does for me, have nothing to do with *me*. They're just a part of his regret for his own lost youth.

Bhudeb Roy came to Balaram's house because a sixth son had recently been born to him. The astrologers had already seen the boy, he confided to Balaram swaying his gnarled head forward, but their prognostications were not good, and he was worried. The palmists would be no use until the boy's hands grew a bit. In the meantime, he said, drawing his rubbery lower lip back in a smile, I may as well have phrenology. After all, it's scientific, and I'm a man of the future. Let it not be said that Bhudeb Roy hung back when the opportunity to have the first phrenologized baby in Bengal, perhaps in Asia, was at hand.

Balaram answered him with vague mumbles. His first instinct, knowing what he did about the hereditary nature of the criminal physiology, was to refuse. What would he say to Bhudeb if his son was exactly like him?

And just then Bhudeb smiled again and said reassuringly: You'll like the little swine – he's just like me.

But at the same time Balaram was flattered. It was the first time he had been consulted like a doctor or a surgeon. In a way it was more than a triumph for his science – it was a personal victory. Besides, Bhudeb would be terribly offended if he refused.

So he agreed (later he was to hit himself so hard on his troublesome Vanity that his scalp bled).

The next day, without telling Toru-debi, Balaram packed his instruments in a bag, along with a copy of Combe for reference, and walked over to Bhudeb Roy's house, a little way down the path which ran past his own house. Bhudeb Roy was lying flat on his back on a mat under a mango tree in his garden. His stomach billowed above him like a sail in a high wind, while he fanned it gently with a palm leaf. He struggled to his feet when he saw Balaram. Followed by his five sons he led Balaram into his newly built, peacock-green house.

Balaram knew the worst as soon as he saw the child in its cradle, shrieking with rage at being woken from its evening sleep. Somehow he found the heart to go through the motions of a perfunctory examination. It was difficult, for the child, thoroughly resentful at being handled by a stranger, screamed and clawed at him with an ominous strength. Finally he wetted Balaram's shirt, and Balaram almost dropped him. He stopped then and washed his hands and put away his instruments. He had seen enough.

Well? said Bhudeb Roy as he led him out, smiling indulgently. What do you think? Then he saw Balaram's grim face and stopped short.

What's the matter? he cried. Balaram-babu, tell me quickly, what's the matter? Balaram walked straight on, without a word. Wait, Bhudeb Roy shouted after him, Balaram-babu, wait. Have some tea, biscuits, fish, dinner, anything. . . .

Balaram walked straight on, down the garden, towards the dirt path, frowning. Bhudeb Roy hurried behind him waddling, pulling up the folds of his dhoti. His five sons ran out behind him. Wait, he cried again plaintively. Tell me, Balaram-babu, what is it?

Balaram stopped only when he was halfway to his own house. When Bhudeb Roy caught up with him, panting in great shuddering sighs, Balaram said: Bhudeb-babu, I don't know how to tell you this. I beg that you will not misunderstand. The exhibit, that is to say your son, has distinct protuberances above the asterion and over the temporal muscles above its ears. Furthermore, his mandible and zygomatic arches are already developed to so extraordinary a degree that I can only tell you, with the utmost regret, that he reproduces almost exactly the structure of the Typical Homicidal. With careful nurture you may perhaps be able to hold him down to mere felony, but no further, I fear, no further. Pray, Bhudeb-babu, for I know you believe in prayer, pray that you may not be his first victim.

Balaram turned, lean and erect, his cloud of white hair lifting in the breeze, and walked away while Bhudeb Roy sank to the dust with a punctured cry.

Next morning Toru-debi woke to find that six of their coconut palms had been axed and all their lemon trees uprooted during the night. Nonder-ma, who always knew, told her the whole story.

When she had heard her through, Toru-debi went to the middle of the courtyard. She stood, legs apart, holding a huge stone pestle above her head, and shouted: Listen, you. If I ever hear again that you've gone out of this house with those instruments, there'll be nothing left in your study. Those books have cursed you, and now you're trying to drag me down with you. But I won't go.

Balaram did not leave his study or even acknowledge that he had heard her. There were times, he knew, when Combativeness ruled her so completely that argument was futile. Those were the times when it was best to do as she said.

After that Balaram's evening walks around the village with his Claws and his bag of instruments ceased. The notebooks of observations of over three hundred of the village's living heads that he had so carefully compiled in a decade's painstaking work were frozen. Balaram's study became a prison and his evenings would not pass.

On those long evenings, Balaram tried to see the matter rationally, but he could not find it in himself to forgive Bhudeb Roy. But there was little he could do: reason is not a good weapon with which to wreak revenge.

What Bhudeb Roy made of the incident was a mystery.

When Toru-debi made Balaram go with her to his house a month later to offer condolences after his baby son had died of double pneumonia, he was as courteous to Balaram as he ever was. But Balaram was not deceived. He saw Combativeness growing on the back of Bhudeb Roy's head like a new potato, and secretly he was afraid.

About a year later Alu arrived in Lalpukur.

So, in an odd way, Bhudeb Roy was partly responsible for the surge of enthusiasm with which Balaram greeted Alu. The moment he saw him Balaram knew his evenings would never be empty again.

Though a long time passed before the boy would let Balaram examine him, once they started he grew to enjoy his sessions with Balaram almost as much as Balaram did himself. To eliminate all taint of the haphazard, Balaram worked out a timetable for the examinations. Since Alu was in the fourth class of the Lalpukur school then, Balaram scheduled his examinations early in the morning, before school, three times a week, and after school another three times a week, with holidays on Sundays. The timetable, with the days shuffled around for variety every week, was pinned up on the door of Balaram's study late every Sunday evening. But neither he nor Alu paid it much attention. Alu was always somewhere in Balaram's study in those days – rummaging around in the bookshelves, leafing through books in some dusty corner, or often just dozing, leaning against the easy chair's clawed legs.

Balaram could not have hoped for a better subject. But still something worried him.

It may be his bregma, he told Gopal. He's so completely impassive. Nothing, nothing at all, seems to make an impression on him.

They were sitting at a grimy marble-topped table in Nizam's Restaurant, behind the New Market in Calcutta. The waiters in their lungis were making so much noise running between the tables and the kitchen outside that Gopal had to lean forward to hear Balaram clearly.

He's still just a boy, Balaram, he said, prodding a kebab with his forefinger. You can't expect him to be as enthusiastic about phrenology as you are.

But Balaram was still worried. It wasn't natural for a boy of ten to be quite so impassive. Alu betrayed no emotion about anything at all. It was obvious, for instance, that in his impassive way he hated school – if there could be such a thing as an impassive hatred. He never opened a school-book, never wrote so much as a word in his hard-bound exercise-book. He went off to school obediently enough, but always hanging back, as though waiting for a miracle to strike the school off the fields of Lalpukur.

It was already a matter of deep embarrassment to Balaram, and it would be worse if his own nephew, studying in the very school he was teaching in, were to fail in the examinations. Bhudeb Roy, whose sons somehow always won all the prizes the school offered, never let Balaram forget it. Not very bright, that boy Alu, he would say, is he, Balaram-babu? Perhaps you should beat him a bit?

Balaram would look straight at him until his opaque little eyes shifted.

The trouble was that he *was* bright, even if it wasn't immediately apparent. There could be no doubt about it. He had to have some intelligence to read as much as he did.

How much he read! Far too much, in fact, for a boy of ten. He would read almost anything he happened to come across in Balaram's study: history, geography, geology, natural history, biology. . . . Anything at all. And not just in Bengali. It had taken him amazingly little time to learn English. And then Balaram had tried to teach him a little French the same way he had learnt it himself, from a grammer and a pocket dictionary. Alu had proved so quick in learning that Balaram had decided not to teach him any more for fear of confusing him. But then one day he had found him reading a French primer on his own, with the help of the pocket dictionary.

He had learnt to speak a number of languages, too. Cycle-shop Bolai, who had once served in the Army somewhere in the north, had taught him Hindi. And he was fluent in the villagers' dialect, which Balaram, after sixteen years in Lalpukur, could barely understand.

Most of the people of Lalpukur belonged originally to the remote district of Noakhali, in the far east of Bengal close to Burma. They had emigrated to India in a slow steady trickle in the years after East Bengal became East Pakistan. Most of them had left everything but their dialect behind. It was a nasal sing-song Bengali, with who knew what mixed in of Burmese and the languages of the hills to the east? Many of them had learnt the speech of West Bengal, but it had only made their own dialect more dear to them – as a mark of common belonging and as a secret weapon to confuse strangers with. It was their claim that it was impossible for anyone born outside Noakhali to understand their speech when they spoke fast. And yet after only two years Alu spoke it so fluently that the whole village had learnt to be careful not to talk about Balaram when he passed by.

But always impassive, never betraying so much as a trace of emotion. Perhaps, said Balaram, ruminating, I could try massaging him on the occipital bone where the emotions and sentiments are.

Balaram! Gopal exclaimed. You leave his occipital bone or whatever alone. You're imagining things. Toru told me herself when we were last in Lalpukur that he's had trouble in school because of his devotion to you. That's an emotion. Gopal put his glass of water down and looked accusingly at Balaram. Balaram nodded reluctantly.

Once, on his way out of the school in the afternoon, Balaram heard shouts and wild laughter in a classroom. He stopped, for the school was meant to be empty at that time of the afternoon. It was soon apparent that the noise was coming from his own classroom. As he was walking back, it grew from scattered shouts into a high-pitched schoolboy chant: Balaram's dog, Balaram's dog. . . .

The boys in the classroom scattered as soon as he entered. He saw four of Bhudeb Roy's sons tumbling out of the windows. But the fifth, a squat, paunchy boy with a sprouting moustache, stood his ground in the middle of a pile of overturned benches and looked straight at him, with a curling smile. Then he turned and sauntered out of the room, whistling. Balaram saw that he had a deep gash across his cheek.

Then Balaram saw Alu, sprawled on the floor, tied to an upturned bench. His chin had split open and his nose was dripping blood. Balaram had to cut him free with a blade. As they came out of the school, Balaram heard a shout: Balaram's dog – follow him home. He turned, but all he saw was a flash of feet disappearing into the bamboo.

But, said Balaram, the strange thing was that even then he didn't say a word. He didn't cry or even complain. The whole thing seemed to have no effect on him at all.

Maybe, said Gopal meditatively, maybe he's still trying to get over the shock of losing his parents.

Balaram dropped his kebab in astonishment. He stared at Gopal. I hadn't thought of that, he said at last.

No, said Gopal. You wouldn't.

When Balaram got back to Lalpukur that evening, Alu was sitting in a corner of his study reading. Once he was comfortably settled in his easy chair, Balaram called out to him. Alu came up to him and proffered his skull. He was a little puzzled because it was Sunday, and a holiday.

No, said Balaram, not today. He patted the arm of his chair, and Alu jumped on to it.

Alu, said Balaram shyly, one mustn't brood on the past. One ought to think of the future. The future is what is important. The past doesn't matter. One can do anything with the future. One can change the world.

He scanned the boy's face. Alu, he said, don't you want to change the world? The boy looked at him steadily, his eyes larger than ever, saying nothing.

How can one change the world, Balaram said, if one has no passion?

The boy did not respond. Suddenly Balaram felt himself strangely touched by the boy's wide-eyed silence. He felt his throat constrict, and in embarrassment he reached for the copy of Vallery-Radot's *Life of Pasteur* which always lay beside his chair, and began to read him the chapter about that turning-point in the history of the world – 6 July 1885 – when Louis Pasteur took his courage in his hands and at the risk of his reputation and his whole professional life (for he had never lacked for enemies) filled a Pravoz syringe and inoculated poor, hopeless ten-year-old Joseph Meister, only that day savaged by a rabid dog, with his still untested vaccine.

When he stopped and put the book down he saw tears in Alu's eyes.

Perhaps I was wrong, Balaram said to Gopal a week later. Perhaps his occipital bone is all right. Still, I must make sure.

He never did make sure. He forgot for a few days, and after that he couldn't have even if he had remembered. But by then he would probably not have thought it necessary anyway.

That was the week of the autumn harvest. Bhudeb Roy, who had planted a new high-yielding seed, had a magnificent harvest that year. It was a very cheap harvest, too, for three classes of schoolboys did most of his harvesting, on pain of being failed in their examinations. There was a good reason for it, he explained, when Balaram protested feebly. It was a part of the botany practicals – the Lalpukur school had always believed in a judicious mixture of practical and theoretical knowledge.

Otherwise, too, it was a good year for Bhudeb Roy. He didn't have to spend any money on the school's annual prizegiving because his five sons shared the prizes between them. He had had another son, and this time the astrologers were quite encouraging.

So good was his fortune that a twinge of superstition led him to announce to the school that in thanksgiving he – in other words, the school – would hold an exceptionally lavish Saraswati Puja that year. What could be a more appropriate festival for a school than that of the Goddess of Learning?

But, Balaram discovered, Bhudeb Roy's motives were not wholly spiritual. He also intended to invite and suitably impress the district's Inspector of Schools. If he was successful, anything was possible – a grant, an appointment. . . .

And so Bhudeb Roy set about organizing his triumphal feast. A six-foot image of Ma Saraswati, with spinning electric lights behind the eyes and a silver-foil halo, was commissioned in Naboganj, the nearest large town. Bolai-da, who had once been on a kitchen detail in the Army, closed down his cycle-shop and took charge of the cooking. Two goats and a pondful of fish were fattened for the feast. A large multi-coloured tent, with a low platform for the image, was erected in the schoolyard, and the most learned pandit in Naboganj was hired to preside over the ceremony.

So splendid were the preparations that Bhudeb Roy did not have the heart to restrict his special invitations to the Inspector of Schools. Eventually he sent invitations to all the important officials in the district: the District Magistrate, the Superintendent of Police, and even the Block Development Officer. He had a vision of a sparkling row of official jeeps parked outside the school.

Of course, he had to invite Balaram, too, for the sake of propriety (and the Inspector of Schools was bound to ask to meet the other teachers in the school).

Bhudeb Roy was a little disappointed when the day came. Only the Inspector of Schools arrived, and that, too, by bus and covered with dust. But by then he was enjoying himself too much to let a minor reverse upset him unduly. He showed the Inspector of Schools to a special chair and busied himself herding cowering groups of scrubbed schoolboys into the tent. His five sons, who had been armed with bamboo poles for the occasion, were equally busy outside, keeping the villagers – all but an approved few – out.

When the lights were switched on, a few people noticed that Ma Saraswati, usually so serenely beautiful, seated on her white swan, with her eight-stringed veena in one hand and a book in the other, looked a little pained. But no one dared say anything and, in any case, in all that bustle no one had time to give it much thought.

Balaram left his house late. Toru-debi was busy with a new design for seamless petticoats, and she had flatly refused to go. Balaram had no wish to go, either, or so he said, but duty prodded and he had had no alternative but to respond.

The ceremony had started when he arrived at the school. Standing outside the tent, he could hear the pandit droning inside. He took a deep breath and stepped in.

For a breathless moment he stood frozen, his eyes riveted to the image. Then he raised his hand and shouted: Wait!

The startled pandit stopped in mid-mantra, his mouth open. In the crackling silence everybody turned and followed his pointing fingers to Ma Saraswati's head, brightly lit from the inside. There was no denying that she looked distinctly migrained. (It was simple really: Bhudeb Roy, unable to resist the temptation to save a few paise, had refused to pay for special insulation for the lights inside the image's head, and as a result the clay had buckled when the lights were switched on.)

But everybody's eyes were on Balaram now. He shouted again: Wait! Then he ran across the tent and, with dirty, defiling sandals still on his feet, he leapt on to the platform. The pandit fainted away from shock.

Balaram paused for a moment, his hand poised over the image's head. Then he ripped the dyed cotton hair off the head and laid the clay skull bare. He pointed to the peeled head with the light still bravely flickering inside and turned around. This, he said to the electrified crowd, is not Saraswati.

This is not Learning, he said, knocking the clay with his knuckles. This is Vanity.

The scraping of the Inspector of Schools's chair tore through the silence. He stalked out without so much as a glance at Bhudeb Roy. Bhudeb Roy called off the ceremony, and people said that he didn't swallow a morsel at the feast afterwards.

You were taking revenge, Gopal accused Balaram later. So you deserved what happened next.

No, Balaram protested. It was just the truth. It was Vanity, precisely where it ought to be, outside the obelion.

But, at the time, even truth was no consolation.

The morning after the ceremony Toru-debi went down to their pond for her morning bath and found it covered with poisoned fish. At almost exactly the same time, Alu, who was eating in the kitchen, heard screams in the bamboo forest behind their house. He pushed away his brass thala and ran out of the house by the back door.

A path ran from the back door past the well, through dense stands of bamboo to three solitary huts nestled in a dip, a long way off. Those were the huts in which Maya Debnath lived with her father and her brother. She walked down that path every morning, on her way to Balaram's house.

Alu raced down the path trying to make as little noise as he could. He heard the voices again. One of them was Maya's, shrill with fear. Alu left the path and circled round, through the bamboo, towards the sound.

Then he saw them: Maya was standing in the middle of the path, surrounded by Bhudeb Roy's five sons. The youngest, barely six, was clinging to his oldest brother's shorts.

Maya was eleven then, a few months younger than Alu, but a good head taller and sturdily built. She had a red sari wound

around her, covering her budding breasts. It was an old
shrunken piece of cloth, and it fell well short of her ankles and
left her shoulders bare. She had a six-foot length of bamboo in
her hands. Her firm, rounded face and her gently slanting
eyes were dark with anger. She had the pole steady in her
hands, pointed at the oldest boy. But he could see that she
was afraid: sweat glistened on her chin and her bare
shoulders.

Bhudeb Roy's oldest son, circling outside the range of the
pole, said, threatening her with his bunched fists: Don't make
trouble. Listen to me. Don't go to that house again. If you do,
there'll be trouble for you and your father.

Maya spat back: Why don't you try to stop me? All you'll
have is a hole in your babu shorts where it hurts.

Alu stopped only for a moment. Then he ran, throwing
himself through the bamboo thickets, towards the three huts
where Maya lived.

Maya's family were weavers. Her brother, Rakhal, was only
sixteen, but already among the tallest in the village, and known
everywhere for his skill with the bamboo pole. He had a special
one for serious fights, studded with nails. He had made it
himself, after a fight in which his cheek had been opened with a
knife. He still bore the scar. Usually it was hardly visible, for
Rakhal was by nature a gentle, dreamy boy. But when he was
angry the scar would open up and glow an unearthly bloody
crimson.

Alu found him sitting at his loom, tugging at the strings of the
shuttle in mechanical boredom. Alu pulled him up and pointed
to his fighting-pole beside the loom. He tried to speak but,
panting, couldn't find his breath. Rakhal looked at his wild eyes
and he needed no telling. He leapt up, gathering his lungi
around his waist, threw his fighting-pole over his shoulder and
ran, with Alu close on his heels.

From a distance they saw Bhudeb Roy's oldest son snatching
at one end of Maya's pole. They saw the other boys throw
themselves on Maya and they saw her go down, struggling
under their weight. Then Rakhal roared and his pole flailed in
the air, whistling like a kite-string in a gale. The boys looked up
and they saw him, bearing down on them with his pole in his
hands and his livid scar shining like a pennant, and the next

moment they were running and Maya was picking herself slowly off the dust.

Rakhal, balked, stood looking after them as they crashed through the thickets of bamboo, and spat into the dust. He glanced at Maya to make sure that she was unhurt and turned back towards their huts, leaving Alu alone with her.

Alu, suddenly overcome with embarrassment, dug his hands into his shorts and began walking quickly towards their house. Maya followed close behind. When she was a step behind him, she laughed: Why did you have to call *him*? Were you afraid? Alu's steps quickened, but she was right behind him. Were you afraid? Why don't you say, little babu? Alu, walking stiff-legged, almost running, could not bear it any more. He broke into a run and disappeared into the house.

When Maya reached the house, Toru-debi, only just returned from the pond and its carpet of dead fish, was standing in the courtyard listening to Nonder-ma. She saw Maya dishevelled and covered with dust and beckoned to her.

After she had heard the whole story, Toru-debi went to the well and bathed. She oiled and combed her hair and dressed herself in a new sari. And then, armed with all the powers of cleanliness, she marched into Balaram's study.

Without a word to Balaram she began tipping his books out of the bookshelves. Balaram did not even try to stop her. He stalked silently out of the study and shut himself up in his bedroom.

Even with Maya and Nonder-ma's help, it took Toru-debi a long time to carry the books out into the courtyard. But she did a thorough job. At the end of it the study was as empty as a dry eggshell. Not a leaf of paper nor a scrap of binding remained to remind Balaram of his library.

Then, after sprinkling kerosene over the huge mound of books in the courtyard, Toru-debi struck a match and set them alight. Alu, standing behind a door, watched the crackling flames dance around the mound. Then he spotted something and darted forward. Toru-debi saw him, and shouted: What have you got in your hands?

Alu backed away, his hands behind his back, as she bore down on him. She lunged, but he managed to sway out of her reach. Then he heard Maya's voice, close to his ear: Give it to me. A sari rustled and he felt the warm, sweet firmness of her breasts against his shoulder.

When Toru-debi caught up with him his hands were empty. Maya had disappeared.

That night, when all that was left of Balaram's books was a pile of ashes and a few charred bindings scattered around the courtyard, Alu crept into Balaram's room. Balaram was sitting crumpled in his easy chair, his fingers in his hair. Alu climbed on to the arm of his easy chair and slipped a book out of his shorts into Balaram's lap. Then he put his arms around his neck.

It was the *Life of Pasteur*.

This time the tears were Balaram's.

Chapter Two

A Pasteurized Cosmos

Eventually, Assistant Superintendent of Police Jyoti Das heard about it all. Bhudeb Roy told him about Balaram's doings at the Saraswati Puja in the course of a rambling and slightly nostalgic account of Balaram's life in Lalpukur. Though ten years had passed, he remembered the incident graphically.

It was the first sign, Bhudeb Roy said, of Balaram's deterioration. He said it a little regretfully, for even then, after all that had happened, he could never speak of Balaram without respect. But he remembered that he was talking to an AS of Police and why, so he added: But he was always like that – confused. A confused extremist. It took me many years to find out, and by that time it was too late. He was set in his dangerous ways. An extremist; no respect for order. A terribly confused extremist.

ASP Das was tired and a little bewildered after all that had happened that day. It was the first time, as he told his mother afterwards, that he had drawn his gun in earnest, meaning to kill. Of course, they had all been trained to deal with situations like that at the Police Academy. But it was different somehow when it actually happened. With un-officerly embarrassment he had noticed his wrists shaking long before he had fired a shot, and despite himself he couldn't help being glad that he had not actually had to use the gun. He had hardly expected that one flare would do the whole job for him. He noticed Bhudeb Roy's huge face again with a start and sat up. But, Bhudeb-babu, he said, if you thought so then, why didn't you do something? Why didn't you make him leave the village?

You don't understand, Bhudeb Roy said. You don't understand, Superintendent-shaheb (Assistant, Assistant, Jyoti Das protested). There was little I could do. By then he was part of the village. He'd been here sixteen years, and as a schoolmaster, too. He had a house here. What could I do? Who knows what the villagers would have done if I'd tried to push him out of Lalpukur? You know how they are – simple. . . .

Jyoti Das looked at that vast, bloated face with its little squinting eyes and clamp-like jaws and he flinched inwardly. He had had no alternative but to accept Bhudeb Roy's 'co-operation' and hospitality, but he could not bring himself to like the man.

Jyoti Das heard of the burning of Balaram's books quite by chance from Gopal Dey a few months later, in a small south Calcutta police station. He liked Gopal the moment he was led into the interrogation room. Gopal was very indignant at first and full of bluster. He quoted laws and sections and sub-clauses for a good five minutes after he was brought in. But once Jyoti Das shook his hand and offered him a cup of tea Gopal sat down quietly on a straight-backed wooden chair across the desk from him. Soon he began to talk. In a few minutes Jyoti Das knew he had nothing important to say, but he listened anyway, for he liked his flustered avuncular manner. And in any case there was nothing else to do but to go back to his grimy office and listen to his boss the Deputy Inspector-General, who was something of a horticulturist, talk of carrots and cauliflowers.

So he half-listened as Gopal's distraught mind wandered to the day Balaram had told him of his burnt books. It was 1967, and Alu was eleven then. Eleven. Jyoti Das had turned eleven in January 1964. On his birthday he was taken to the Alipore Zoo in Calcutta. His father, who was a minor revenue official, took leave from his office for the expedition (using up his last casual leave, he complained later to Jyoti's mother).

All morning they wandered listlessly from cage to cage, staring at grimacing baboons and mangy hyenas. Jyoti's father kept up a constant drone of complaint: about the jostling crowds and gangs of young thugs with their blaring transistors; about crawling beggars let in probably because they gave a share of their pickings to the gatemen; about the boys prodding the monkeys with sticks; about mismanagement and white tigers that had gone grey, and other miserable beasts whose increasing miscegenation was marked by names like those of ascending generations of computer chips – tigon, litigon . . .

litiligon, titilitigon. . . . Where would it lead? Where would it all end?

Leaving the white tigers behind, they wandered towards an area of relative peace on the far side of the lake which lay in the centre of the zoo. Jyoti's father spotted a snack-bar near cages of wattled cassowaries and Chinese silver pheasants, with tables and chairs laid out in the shade. He seated himself at a table and motioned to Jyoti's mother to sit. A moment later they were hit by a blast from a transistor and a group of young men danced past, holding hands and doing something between a twist and a bhangra. Two of them were fighting over a bottle of rum wrapped in a handkerchief. Inevitably, they tripped, howling with laughter, and the bottle exploded on the pavement.

Jyoti's father, glaring, nervously wiping his forehead, muttered: Chaos; that's all that's left. Chaos, chaos. The note of unease in his voice caught in Jyoti's mind, as it always did, churning up a drifting cloud of fears. He got up and ran down to the railing by the lake. There, with the chaotic surging of human life invisible behind him, he saw a shimmering, velvety carpet of ducks and cormorants and storks covering the lake. Somewhere in that mass of birds his eyes picked out a pair of purple herons with their long bills raised to the sky and their brilliantly coloured wings outstretched. He had been told that every year they flew across the continent to winter in that lake; in *that* lake and no other. Looking at them in the flesh he was struck with wonder, and as he watched them he gloried in the peace, the order, the serenity granted by a law on such a vast and immutable scale. He could have stayed there for hours, but soon his father's voice was behind him: Always day-dreaming, worthless boy. Never works. He'll never pass his examinations. . . . And he was led away by the collar of his birthday T-shirt.

They went home and Jyoti was sent to his desk to study as usual. But that day, while he was doodling with his pencil to pass the time, he saw the lines take a new, sinuous, muscular shape. He covered one sheet, threw it away, tried another, and another until he saw quite clearly a purple heron wheeling in the sky, its neck outstretched. Then his father was back again to check: Never studies. He'll never pass. Shame, shame for the family. . . . But Jyoti's drawing was already hidden away under an exercise-book. He knew it to be ordained for him to redeem his father's failures, to do even better than all his successful uncles, the engineer in Düsseldorf, the Secretary in Delhi, and to do it by sitting for the Civil Service examinations and becoming a Class I officer – of whatever kind, in the administration, in the police, in the railways, it didn't matter – but with his name in the Civil Service gazette and a genuine officer's dearness allowance to guard against inflation. But he knew, too, that acquiescence could buy safety for his own, real world – for neither his father nor the Civil Service could wage war against a clear winter morning's vision of purple herons.

Do you want the exact date? Gopal asked, for the young officer in plain clothes had straightened up suddenly. I could try to remember.

No, no, Jyoti Das said quickly. He smiled. I'm just writing a report, not a biography.

A biography?

Even Gopal, with all his love for his friend, would never have thought of writing Balaram's biography. Once, as a joke, he had suggested it to him: Balaram, so many odd things happen to you, someone should write your biography. Maybe I will.

Balaram had thought about it quite seriously. He had pushed his hair back, and for a whole minute he sat absolutely still, with his eyes shut. Then he had said, with absolute finality: You're wrong. Nobody could write my biography, because nothing important ever happens to me. There wouldn't be any events to write about.

Gopal, half-offended because Balaram had taken his joke seriously, had retorted: That doesn't matter at all. Think of Dr Johnson – nothing *ever* happened to him.

Balaram had smiled with total certainty, like a gifted child, and said: How could anyone write a biography of the discovery of Reason?

Gopal had said no more, but of course Balaram was wrong, and he knew it. Even Reason discovers itself through events and people.

Balaram's birthday, for example. Nobody knew exactly when it was. His parents had never told anyone because of

something their family astrologer had said after working out
the newly born infant's horoscope. All that Balaram knew was
that he was born in 1914.

It was a difficult year to choose from, for Reason was
embattled that year. Balaram could have chosen a date as many
of his friends in college would have, to mark one of the many
terrorist strikes against the British in Bengal. In distant Europe
there was always the declaration of the First World War, and
its assortment of massacres and butchery. Or there was the day
in early August when an American judge in San Francisco,
arbitrating on the second-ever application by a Hindu for
citizenship in the United States, took refuge in prehistory and
decided that high-caste Hindus were Aryans and therefore free
and white. And, equally, there was another day in August
when the colonial government in Canada rewrote a different
prehistory when it turned the eight thousand Indians on board
Kamagatamaru back from Vancouver, after deciding that the
ancient racial purity of Canada could not be endangered by
Asiatic immigration. Or, at much the same time, there was the
date of the launching of a drive by the imperial government to
recruit Indians for an expeditionary force to join Algerians and
Vietnamese and Senegalese in defending the freedom of the
Western world from itself.

But Balaram chose none of those dates. Even reading about
them he suffered, for he saw them as abysses tearing apart the
path of Man's ascent to Reason. Instead, he vacillated between
any one of several dozen days in May and June when Jagadish
Chandra Bose, in a laboratory in south London, demonstrated
to stunned audiences of scientists and poets and politicians, all
half-deafened by the ringing of sabres in Europe, that even a
vegetable so unfeeling as a carrot can suffer agonies of fear and
pain.

But, as Gopal said to him once, if it were not for an
astrologer's accidental remark, you wouldn't have been able to
choose your birthday.

Balaram was surprised at that. Astrology isn't chance, he
answered. It's quite the opposite.

Again Gopal let it pass. He knew Balaram to be dissimulat-
ing: if it were not for a chance whim of his father's, Balaram
would not have discovered science at all.

Balaram was born in Dhaka, then the capital of East Bengal, now of Bangladesh. His father, who had moved to Dhaka from the little village of Medini-mandol in the nearby district of Bikrompur, was a prosperous timber merchant. He owed his prosperity to obliging relatives in Burma, who provided him with a connection with the rich Burmese teak forests. He was also very conservative. Long after their neighbours in the old Kayet-tuli quarter of Dhaka had acquired electric lights, their house was still lit by kerosene-lamps. Then suddenly, in 1927, when Balaram was thirteen, his father changed his mind and festooned their house with bulbs.

That was the turning-point, and in a way it *was* an accident. Had Balaram been accustomed to those bulbs with their spiral filaments from his childhood, had they arrived a year before or after he reached the enchanted age of thirteen when the whole world comes alive for the first time, they would probably never have been touched with magic. His brother, for instance, who was ten at the time, hardly gave them a moment's thought. Not so Balaram. He was bewitched from the very first time he used one of those large, unwieldly switches. After that he couldn't find enough to read about electricity. He read about the Chinese and Benjamin Franklin, and Edison became one of his first heroes. In school he pursued the physics teachers with questions.

But it was already too late. His teachers had decided that he had a gift for history, and this new enthusiasm for science would pass. Balaram did everything he could, but his teachers – in those days in Bengal teachers knew everything – would not let him change his subject to the sciences. So instead Balaram read.

When, at sixteen, he matriculated quite by chance with a sheaf of distinctions, his teachers decided that he must go to Presidency College in Calcutta to study history. They told him of the legend of Suniti Chatterji, the Professor of Philology, and his mastery of several dozen languages, and of a brilliant young philosopher called Radhakrishnan, only recently appointed professor (and still decades away from becoming President of the Republic).

Balaram listened to them quietly, and they took his silence for acquiescence. But Balaram was not thinking of their

Calcutta at all, with its philology and philosophy and history.
He had his own vision of Calcutta. For him it was the city in
which Ronald Ross discovered the origin of malaria, and
Robert Koch, after years of effort, finally isolated the bacillus
which causes typhoid. It was the Calcutta in which Jagadish
Bose first demonstrated the extraordinarily life-like patterns of
stress responses in metals; where he first proved to a disbelieving world that plants are no less burdened with feeling than
man.

Balaram knew of Presidency College, too: it was there that
Jagadish Bose had taught two young men – Satyen Bose, who
was to appropriate half the universe of elementary particles
with the publication of the Bose–Einstein statistics; and
Meghnad Saha, whose formulation of the likeness between a
star and an atom had laid the foundation of a whole branch of
astrophysics.

And of course there was the gigantic figure of C. V. Raman,
whose quiet researches in the ramshackle laboratories of the
Society for the Advancement of Science, in Calcutta, had led to
the discovery of the effect in the molecular scattering of light
which eventually came to be named after him. In 1930, when
Balaram was ready to go to college, the newspapers were
already talking of Raman's candidature for the Nobel.

Long before his teachers spoke to him about it, Balaram
knew that he would go to Calcutta and to Presidency College.

But his father would not hear of it. He had been brought up
on tales of the wickedness of the city; and, besides, there was
the expense. Dhaka, he said, had a perfectly good university
and, if it was good enough for the whole of Dhaka, there was
no reason why it should not be good enough for his son (and it
was true that Satyen Bose was teaching there then). He didn't
understand Balaram at all. He could never have understood
that Balaram was launching on a pilgrimage, a quest to retrace
the steps of Jagadish Bose and Meghnad Saha from their
native district of Bikrampur to Calcutta and Presidency
College.

Balaram's father would not budge, not even when one of
Balaram's teachers threatened to bombard the local and
national newspapers with letters denouncing rich men who
wanted to deprive young India of talent. Then chance inter-

vened again. Riots broke out in Dhaka University that year. A
lecturer's house in their own neighbourhood was attacked by a
mob.

Balaram's father gave in at last, just in time. The day Balaram
arrived in Calcutta accompanied by an uncle, the newspapers
announced that C. V. Raman had won the Nobel Prize.

Balaram's uncle took him as far as the two gatehouses outside
the Eden Hindu Hostel, just off College Street, where he was
to live. He looked up at the heavy ornamental brickwork of the
façade, at the imperial baroque pilasters and the long rows of
shuttered windows, and with a hasty blessing he abandoned
Balaram.

Balaram was left to cope with his new world alone. His one
consolation was that Professor C. V. Raman could not have
been more than a few hundred yards away.

The interior of the Eden Hindu Hostel was even more
imposing than the façade. There was an immense quadrangle
in the centre with cascades of columns rising three storeys high
on all sides of it. Balaram made his way round the quadrangle
through a high, echoing corridor. It was terrifying after the
cheerful chaos of Dhaka's Kayet-tuli.

After wandering through the corridors for half an hour, he
found his room and unpacked his luggage. He arranged the
few books he had brought with him on the bookshelf and set
out the jars of pickles and sweetmeats his mother had sent
with him in a neat row on a window-sill. Then, pulling his
dhoti up to his knees, he tiptoed to the door and looked up
and down the corridor. It was empty. He stepped out and
walked quickly down the corridor, trying to keep to the
shadows. He slipped down the staircase and came to a corner.
He hesitated for a moment, and then, making up his mind, he
stiffened his back resolutely and went on. It was only after he
had turned the corner, when it was already too late, that he
noticed a group of students standing in the corridor. Two of
them wore European clothes – baggy trousers and collarless
shirts. The others were dressed as he was, in dhotis and long
kurtas, but somehow their kurtas were different, smarter.

He hesitated for a moment, but they had already noticed
him and he decided not to draw attention to himself by turning
back. As he walked on he saw there wasn't enough room in the

corridor to slip around them. He saw that they had stopped talking and were looking at him with pointed interest. He could feel his stomach churning with nervousness.

He decided to be brave. He stepped up to them and said: Excuse me. Could you tell me where I might get a good view of Professor C. V. Raman?

The young men looked at each other in puzzlement. One of them said politely: Could you say that again, please? He was in European clothes and he had gold-rimmed spectacles and lustrous, pomaded hair, parted down the middle. He shall remain unnamed, for he was later to rise to prominence in Congress politics and achieve renown for his venality. He may still be lurking in some Calcutta suburb today.

Balaram cleared his throat: I was only asking if you could tell me where I might get a nice view of Professor C. V. Raman.

The puzzlement on their faces deepened. It occurred to Balaram that they could not understand his Dhaka accent. Stammering with embarrassment he repeated himself, very slowly.

There was a snort of laughter. Middle Parting silenced it with a wave. He said to Balaram, gravely fingering his chin: But have you bought a ticket?

A ticket?

Oh, yes. And they're quite expensive. Anyway, why do you want to see C. V. Raman? Usually villagers want to see the High Court and the Museum first. I didn't know C. V. Raman had appeared on the programme.

I'm from Dhaka, sir, Balaram said.

Oh, I see, said Middle Parting. Same thing. Anyway, wouldn't you like to see the Museum and the High Court first?

Not right now, I think, Balaram said, edging away. Later perhaps. I was on my way to see. . . .

No, wait. Middle Parting caught his elbow. But you must, you must see the Museum. How can you be in Presidency College if you haven't seen the Museum? He winked at the others and turned back to Balaram: And how can you see the Museum without Museum practice?

There was a snort of laughter. Balaram looked at him in surprise: Museum practice? What is that?

Middle Parting rubbed his chin. We'll show you, he said.

Free, since you're new, though most people charge quite a lot.
I hope you're grateful.

Balaram found himself being led into the middle of the
quadrangle. Middle Parting lifted Balaram's right hand, palm
outwards, and explained: That's how you have to stand when
you look at the images of the Buddha. Naturally you have to
take your kurta and vest off as well. Now, please take them off.

Balaram tried to wrench his hand free. Later perhaps, he
said. Maybe some other day. Thank you for so much information, but now I must go.

Take it off, Middle Parting said again. He twisted Balaram's
hand a little. Balaram threw a desperate glance around him.
The others were standing in a circle around him. There was no
escape. Fumbling, weak-kneed with shame, he took his kurta
and vest off. His chest was pathetically bare and thin. He
looked at his feet, trying not to hear their laughter.

That's right, said Middle Parting, still grave. And then,
when you go into the Greek room, you have to take the rest off
as well.

There was a chorus of laughter and cheers. Balaram, horror-
struck, struggled to speak, but his throat was as dry as baked
clay. He managed to stammer hoarsely: I think I'll leave
Greece for next year. Thank you very much, and now, if I
may. . . .

For next year? Middle Parting pulled a face of mock-
surprise. How can you be in Presidency if you leave Greece for
next year?

Balaram began to back away. Middle Parting waved to the
others, and with cheerful whoops they lunged at him, snatching at his dhoti. Balaram lurched as the cloth was ripped away.
He fought off their hands with a desperate strength, struggling
to keep a few shreds around his waist. There was only one
thought in his mind: that his drawers were dirty and even death
would be better than standing in the middle of that great
quadrangle in dirty drawers.

It was lucky, he said afterwards, that there is so *much* cloth to
a dhoti.

Still, it was just a matter of time. He was losing fistfuls of
cloth every second.

It was at that precise moment, when Balaram was clinging to

his last few wisps of white cotton, that Gopal appeared. It took Gopal no more than a glance to understand what was happening. He ran across the courtyard and flung himself at Middle Parting and his friends. Heaving with all the strength in his shoulders, he pushed two of them aside and spread his arms across Balaram. He was very angry. He shouted, his spectacles tottering on the edge of his nose: Leave him alone. Why can't you leave these new students alone? Why don't you go into the streets if you want to fight?

Middle Parting, laughing, dusted his hands: All right, you can play Mother to him now. Take him to see C. V. Raman. But be careful. Don't leave him outside the laboratory. They might pour him into a test-tube. He threw his arms around his friends' shoulders and they went away, still shaking with laughter.

Balaram stooped and spread the few shreds of cloth left to him carefully over his drawers. Gopal turned to him eagerly: C. V. Raman? Are you interested in C. V. Raman's work? Balaram did not answer. He barely heard Gopal. He was too angry and confused.

But when at last his head cleared, and he understood Gopal's question and sensed his elation, he knew he had a friend.

Later that day, Gopal came to fetch Balaram to take him out for a cup of tea. With him was another new student, a slight, bespectacled, shy boy from Lucknow whose two prominent front teeth had already tagged him with the name of Dantu. They went down the road to Puntiram's sweetshop. Puntiram's was not then the neon-and-plastic marvel it is now: it was a small place, a little tumbledown, but quiet. A good place to talk.

They ate rosogollas, sweet and spongy as only Puntiram's could make them, and drank rich milky tea, and Gopal told them about a society he and a few others in the Eden Hindu Hostel had recently founded. Formally it was known as the Society for the Dissemination of Science and Rationalism among the People of Hindoostan, but usually they simply called themselves the Rationalists.

Balaram and Dantu pushed their dues – eight annas each – across the table the moment they had finished their tea.

Later, Gopal and Balaram were often to argue about the

circumstances of their meeting. Gopal claimed that it was an accident of sorts, a mere lucky chance. Balaram argued that it could not have been. It was too apt. They would have met anyway, for the hostel was divided into five wards and Balaram and Gopal happened to be in the same ward. But no chance encounter would have been able to capture the appropriateness of their first meeting. Wasn't the Rationalists' motto 'Reason rescues Man from Barbarity'?

A few days later Gopal lent Balaram a book he had recently bought at Chakerbutty & Sons in College Street. It was a copy of Mrs Devonshire's translation of René Vallery-Radot's *Life of Pasteur*.

He was to regret lending Balaram that book. A year or so later he could not have said whether he was more bewildered or hurt when the very Balaram he had rescued from barbarity, his closest friend, turned his own book, bought with his own carefully saved money, into a weapon against him.

That year Gopal was elected president of the Rationalists. He called a meeting soon after the election. It was an important meeting, for a Science Association had recently been founded in the hostel and many of the Rationalists had been tempted to change their membership. Gopal was anxious to meet the threat head-on.

The difference, Gopal told the Rationalists, between the Science Association and their own society was that they did not consider science alone, something people pursued in the seclusion of laboratories, important in itself. He himself was studying not science but English literature. Their aim was the application of rational principles to everything around them – to their own lives, to society, to religion, to history. It didn't matter what. That was what made the Rationalists unique.

It was to that task – of applying rationalism to everything around them – that the society now had to turn. And for that he had a plan.

As a boy, Gopal went on, he had been made to read through some of the Sanskrit scriptures with his father. Later, when he began to read about science, something – he didn't know what – had troubled him. Now that he had read much more, he had an idea of what it was: there could no longer be any doubt that there were certain very curious parallelisms between the ideas of the ancient Hindu sages and modern science. If that was true, and many very learned authorities believed it to be so, then it was definite proof that over the centuries those ancient and completely rational ideas had been perverted by scheming priests and brahmins to further their own interests. It was *urgently* necessary, therefore, that the society make known to the masses of Hindoostan how they were daily deceived and cheated by the self-styled purveyors of religion.

For example, it was certain that the pandits and brahmins had distorted the ancient Hindu idea of God, the Brahma, into their thousands of deities and idols, so that they could make money quicker. Just as a shopkeeper might open new counters, so each new god was a steady new source of income for the priests. As for the real Brahma, he was without attributes, without form, nothing but an essence, in everything and in nothing.

In fact, Gopal said in a sibilant whisper, the Brahma is nothing but the Atom.

Gopal stopped there and looked at his enthralled audience. There were a few inadvertent claps. He squashed them with a raised hand. And so, too, he said, it has been proved beyond all doubt that the Universal Egg of Hindu mythology is nothing but a kind of Cosmic Neutron.

He was met with a storm of cheers and claps. He smiled, luxuriating in the applause. When it had faded away, he began again: If we are to disseminate the truth we must begin here, in our own society. I propose, therefore, that we begin all our meetings hereafter with salutations and prayers to the Cosmic Atom.

There were nods of agreement all around the room. Then Balaram stood up. But you know, he said, atoms and suchlike are old-fashioned now. Ever since Professor Satyen Bose published his famous paper, all the elementary particles which obey his statistics have been renamed Bosons. Should we not, then, salute the Cosmic Boson instead?

There was a murmur of approval. Gopal nodded, a little apprehensively. Yes, he said, it's only right that we keep up with the times.

But, said Balaram, smiling slyly, as I'm sure you're well aware, all other particles obey Enrico Fermi's statistics and are known as Fermions. So shouldn't we, then, salute the Cosmic Fermion as well?

A hubbub of consternation eddied through the room. Only Dantu laughed and he was quickly quelled by a roomful of frowns. Everyone there had long since boycotted British-made and foreign goods, and many had publicly burnt every scrap of Lancashire cloth in their houses. Bosons, made in Calcutta, they could applaud; but salutations to Italian particles?

No, no, said Gopal. We can't salute everything. I think we'd better keep to Bosons. Now, sit down, Balaram.

Balaram sat down.

Their next two meetings began with the chant: Hail to thee, O Cosmic Boson. Gopal spent half of one meeting exhorting them to begin their letters home with *Hail, Cosmic Boson* instead of the sacred syllable *Om*. Then they went through the epics and tried to find rational explanations for various magical events, objects and creatures. It was decided, for example, that the sudarshan-chakra, the legendary wheel of fire, was actually an example of ancient fireworks, and Gopal was applauded for his ingeniously down-to-earth suggestion that the mythical clawed bird of the Ramayana, Jatayu, was no early phantasm but merely one of the last surviving pterodactyls.

Balaram said nothing at either meeting. He sat in a corner with Dantu and fidgeted.

At the next meeting Gopal urged the Rationalists to turn their minds to the business of finding a rational substitute for the superstitious incantations which Brahmins chanted at weddings. While others eagerly offered suggestions, Balaram's fidgeting grew till he was twisting and turning on his mat. Then Dantu prodded him sharply in the ribs and whispered: Go on; tell them.

Drawing in a deep breath, Balaram jumped to his feet. What does it matter? he shouted. What does it matter?

Gopal looked at him dumbfounded: What do you mean?

I mean what does it matter what the Brahmins say and the rishis say and the myths say? What does it have to do with science or reason or the masses of Hindoostan? What good will it do anyone if the masses start saying *Hail, Cosmic Boson* instead of *He Bhagoban*? Will it cure them of disease? Will it fill their stomachs? Will it get the British out of here?

Gopal said: Balaram, that's enough. Remember where you are. Don't shout; you're not in your right mind.

In astonishment Balaram exclaimed: *I'm* not in my right mind?

Gopal cast up his hands: All right, then, tell us what *you* would like us to do.

Balaram's slim face narrowed with intensity. He swept his hair from his eyes and looked straight at Gopal. It's not *what* I want to do, he said. It's *how*. This is nothing. Just talk. Empty talk. That's what Pasteur would have called it. Do you remember Pasteur? Do you remember the book you gave me – you, yourself?

Soundlessly Gopal sank on to a mat.

Do you remember how Pasteur first came to science? It wasn't by thinking about the Cosmic Atom. It was because his father was a poor tanner. Do you remember why he left his promising studies in crystallography? It was because the brewers of France came to him and said: What makes our beer rot? It was that question, asked by simple people, which led to the discovery of what he called the 'infinitesimally small' – the Germ, in other words.

Has anything changed the world as much as the discovery of the germ? Has there ever been a greater break in history than the moment when men were unburdened of their responsibility for their bodies and all disease was assigned to the treachery of the elements?

And how did it come about? Not through cogitations about the cosmic, but as an answer to the everyday problems of simple people.

Who did the silk farmers of Europe go to when disease struck their silkworms and whole provinces lay devastated and groaning in misery? Who did they go to with their children hungry at their breasts and their livelihood wasting in their fields? Who but Pasteur? They went to him and they said: Save us. And when he saw their wretchedness not all the powers on the earth could have kept him from answering.

That is why the world still has silk.

What was it that led him to struggle for years, at the risk of his own life, to rid the world of hydrophobia?

Nothing but the everyday suffering of helpless children and

their mothers. It was that which sustained him when all the world laughed and said: Pasteur is mad, bitten by his dogs.

Why? Why did he do it? What drove him?

It wasn't talk of reason, it wasn't the universal atom. It was passion; a passion which sprang from the simple and the everyday. A passion for the future, not the past. It was that which made him the greatest man of his time, for it is that passion which makes men great.

Gopal cleared his throat uneasily. All right, Balaram, he said. But what can *we* do? We're not scientists. We can't find cures for things.

Balaram paused. Slowly he said: I don't know. How can I say? All I know is that this is pointless. If all these things we talk about – reason, science and all the rest – are to mean anything, they must have the power to move people. Who can be moved by the Cosmic Boson? It is the everyday, the mundane things that happen in real life which move people. If we want to do anything at all, that is what we must think about. And we have to start here, in Presidency College, in the Hindu Hostel, with our fellow-students. If we can't make *them* change their lives, if we can't make *them* see Reason, what can we ever have to say to the masses of Hindoostan?

He stopped there and started as though he had only then noticed that everyone in the room was staring at him. He looked around once, in confusion, and then he ran from the room. Dantu followed him out.

As he watched Balaram go, Gopal had a premonition: a premonition of the disaster he would call upon himself and all of them, if ever he was allowed to take charge of the society. He decided then, with an uncharacteristic determination, that he would do everything in his power to keep that from happening.

After that meeting Gopal's standing among the Rationalists suffered greatly while Balaram's, with Dantu's quiet help, grew. Despite that, through the rest of that year Gopal struggled with all his resources to fight Balaram's influence in the society. He succeeded, though narrowly, and the Rationalists spent that year safely rewriting parts of the great epics. But Gopal had only that year left in college. At the end of it he was to leave to study law.

Through that year, perhaps because of their clashes over the future of the Rationalists, their friendship grew stronger than ever. The day Gopal was to leave the hostel, Balaram helped him tie up his luggage. Gopal could see that Balaram was no less saddened than he was. But he saw, too, that Balaram was charged with the energy of a new-found freedom, and he was filled with a terrible foreboding.

But there was no longer anything he could do to save Balaram from himself.

Four decades later, long after the vindication of that first premonition, Gopal was to know that same foreboding again.

One afternoon, about three years after Toru-debi sent Balaram's library up in flames, Gopal was busy with a client in his chambers at the High Court, when his peon interrupted to tell him that Balaram had arrived. Gopal was surprised, for it was not a Sunday, and Balaram rarely came to Calcutta on weekdays. But Gopal had to appear in court for his client that afternoon, so he told his peon to ask Balaram to wait in a room outside.

After the hearing Gopal came back to his chambers pleased with himself, for the judge had complimented him on his line of argument. He found Balaram pacing his chambers, frowning. Gopal dusted his hands briskly and lowered himself into the chair behind his desk. So, Balaram, he said, how did you spend the afternoon?

Does it matter? Balaram snapped.

Gopal paused. Balaram irritable was a matter of some surprise; it was rarely that he noticed the everyday vexations which irritate the rest of the world. So Gopal sent his peon to fetch some tea and Circus biscuits, and droned comfortably on about his client and his case. Balaram listened with evident impatience, pulling books out at random from the bookshelves.

Gopal stopped when he judged it right, and said: What's the matter, Balaram?

I'm worried about Alu, said Balaram, running his fingers through his hair. It's probably the asterion growing together with the sagittal suture. A disastrous combination: Firmness plus Combativeness. It could only spell obstinacy.

The boy had stopped going to school altogether. He still read when he could find books, and his talent for languages had grown if anything, but when it came to school the boy seemed quite determined. He never said anything – he simply wouldn't go. Everybody had talked to him and argued with him, but it made no difference. He never said a word.

He seemed to have made up his mind, and he had a determination unusual in a fourteen-year-old. It was that asterion. And there was no known remedy for it. But there had to be. There had to be an answer.

What does he do, then, Gopal asked, when he's not at school?

Nobody's sure, Balaram answered. But people say he spends most of his time in Shombhu Debnath's huts.

Shombhu Debnath? said Gopal. Who's that?

Oh, said Balaram, don't you know him? He has a remarkable glabella and frontal sinuses. I haven't examined him, and now I suppose I never will, but even from a distance anyone can tell. It's not just his glabella. The orbital edges over the trochleas are some of the best I've ever seen. It's unusual to come across so many Perceptive Faculties in one specimen: you know – Individuality, Size, Colour. He has an interesting forehead, too, and good temples. You'd probably like it – plenty of Wit, Hope, Wonder and Poesy.

Yes, said Gopal, but who is he, what does he do?

He's a weaver, Balaram said absently. He settled in Lalpukur years ago. You've probably seen his daughter Maya. She works in our house in the mornings. He has a son, too, called Rakhal. He's taught him weaving, too.

What does Alu do in a weaver's huts? Gopal asked astonished.

I don't know. Watches them weave perhaps.

Well, said Gopal, you must explain to Alu that if he doesn't go to school he'll never be able to get a job.

What? Balaram looked at him in stunned amazement. How could I say that? It would be wrong; it would be immoral. Children go to school for their first glimpse into the life of the mind. Not for jobs. If I thought that my teaching is nothing but a means of finding jobs, I'd stop teaching tomorrow.

Gopal looked at him wearily. Balaram, he said, as you grow older, you grow more foolish. Why *do* you think children are sent to school?

Balaram sank on to a chair, cupped his face in his hands and stared at Gopal.

Gopal decided that Balaram needed a diversion. So he suggested that they go to see a film. That year, to Gopal's surprise, Balaram had developed an enormous fondness for Hindi films. He saw one, sometimes two whenever he came to Calcutta. He often went to Naboganj, near Lalpukur, to see films, sometimes taking Alu with him. Gopal was hard put to understand his new passion. After suffering through a few at Balaram's insistence, he had decided that he could stomach no more. But that evening he changed his mind; even three hours of tedium would be better than playing midwife to Balaram's worries.

So he sent his peon home to tell his wife that he would be late and they caught a taxi to the Menoka, near the Lakes. The film was *Aradhana*. The queue for tickets stretched for more than half a mile. They had to buy tickets at ten times the rate, from a tout.

When they came out of the hall three hours later Balaram was smiling crookedly, his eyes mistily damp. But now it was Gopal who was irritated, resentful of his three wasted hours. He followed Balaram as he wandered to a bench in the park by the Lakes.

How can you bear these noisy melodramas? he burst forth at Balaram's back in annoyance.

Balaram turned to him angrily: Noisy melodramas?

So much predictable rubbish, said Gopal. No story, no plot, just hours of weeping and breast-beating. There's nothing remotely real even about the way they talk. It's just speeches all the time.

Real? Balaram cried. Is it real to be cut to size with a tape? What you heard is rhetoric. How can rhetoric be real or unreal? Rhetoric is a language flexing its muscles. You wouldn't understand: you've spent too many years reading novels about drawing-rooms in a language whose history has destroyed its knowledge of its own body. The truth is your mind is nothing but a dumping-ground for the West.

Gopal gasped at the injustice of it. *My* mind? he said. And what about yours? What about you, spending your life reading about Pasteur curing beer in nineteenth-century France?

What about all those books you read written by crazy Europeans about the shapes of skulls in prisons? How can *you* say *my* mind is a dumping-ground . . .?

Balaram's face was suddenly flushed. He jumped to his feet: Be quiet, Gopal. Don't say any more. You don't know what you're saying. Science doesn't belong to countries. Reason doesn't belong to any nation. They belong to history – to the world.

Balaram turned, flung a stone into the lake and stalked off. Wait, Balaram, Gopal called after him, listen. . . .

Balaram's voice came back to him from a distance – You're wrong, I'll show you – and Gopal was left alone with his sense of foreboding.

For eight months after that Gopal neither saw nor heard from Balaram. He sent three letters to Lalpukur in that time. None was answered. He sent a telegram: Cable welfare speediliest. There was no answer, and Gopal was seriously worried. He began to think of dropping his cases for a few days to make a quick trip to Lalpukur.

Then one day in mid-July, while Gopal was at home, drinking his evening tea, his wife heard the doorbell ring. She saw Balaram at the door and exclaimed with pleasure. Before he could step in she unleashed a volley of questions about Toru-debi and Alu. But he brushed past her, straight to the veranda.

He stood in the doorway, looking at Gopal, his hands on his hips. I have an answer for you, he announced. I've made Alu a weaver.

Gopal instantly forgot all his relief at seeing Balaram again. His mouth fell open with disbelief at the thought of an educated, literate man pushing his own nephew to manual labour.

Balaram, delighted at Gopal's surprise, said: Yes, it was the answer. The right thing to do. It took me a long time to reach it, but I did at last.

Gopal, in stupefaction, took off his spectacles and began to wipe them on his vest. But why? he said. Why?

It was the lump on his forehead beneath the hair-line. It had taken him all these years to discover its meaning. Spurzheim was wrong. The Mechanical sense was not on the pterion; it was not a mere propensity, to be lumped with Alimentiveness and Acquisitiveness. The Mechanical was the highest of all organs – the organ that made a mere two-legged creature Man, the seat of Reason. Where else could that organ be but on the crown of the forehead?

Once the organ was identified everything else became blindingly clear – Alu's huge hands, his squat stocky frame. Even the mysterious attraction that drew him to Shombhu Debnath's home. How could he cheat his destiny?

As soon as he knew the truth he had smuggled his instruments out of his house, under his clothes, and gone to Shombhu Debnath's house. For months he had spent his evenings measuring Shombhu Debnath's looms, the distance between the shuttle strings and the weaver's hands, between the pedals and the seat. He had worked until there was no room left for error. The calculations had taken even longer. When at last it was all done, trembling with apprehension, he had matched Alu's measurements with his calculations.

His intuition was proved right in every detail: Alu's body, his hands, his legs, his arms, not to speak of the Organ, corresponded exactly to his calculations of the proportions ideal for a weaver.

Only then, when Balaram knew he was right, did he take the boy to Shombhu Debnath and say: Take him to be your apprentice.

And the boy?

The boy was overjoyed. He wanted nothing better.

But why? Why weaving?

What could it be *but* weaving? Man at the loom is the finest example of Mechanical man; a creature who makes his own world as no other can, with his mind. The machine is man's curse and his salvation, and no machine has created man as much as the loom. It has created not separate worlds but one, for it has never permitted the division of the world. The loom recognizes no continents and no countries. It has tied the world together with its bloody ironies from the beginning of human time.

It has never permitted the division of reason.

Human beings have woven and traded in cloth from the time they built their first houses and cities. Indian cloth was found in the graves of the Pharaohs. Indian soil is strewn with cloth from China. The whole of the ancient world hummed with the cloth trade. The Silk Route from China, running through central Asia and Persia to the ports of the Mediterranean and from there to the markets of Africa and Europe, bound continents together for more centuries than we can count. It spawned empires and epics, cities and romances. Ibn Battuta and Marco Polo were just journeymen following paths that had been made safe and tame over centuries by unknown, unsung traders, armed with nothing more than bundles of cloth. It was the hunger for Indian chintzes and calicos, brocades and muslins that led to the foundation of the first European settlements in India. All through those centuries cloth, in its richness and variety, bound the Mediterranean to Asia, India to Africa, the Arab world to Europe, in equal, bountiful trade.

Think of cotton. It's easy now, but it wasn't once.

India first gave cotton, *Gossypium indicus*, to the world. The cities of the Indus valley grew cotton as early as 1500 BC. But soon cotton was busy spinning its web around the world. It had King Sennacherib of Mesopotamia in its toils by 700 BC, and before long it had found its way to Herodotus in Greece. It travelled eastwards more slowly, but its conquests were no smaller in magnitude.

Everywhere it went people had trouble thinking of it. Only the oldest of the Indo-European languages could think of it as a thing in itself and even then the thought was so difficult that across continents people hardly dared differ. In Sanskrit it was called *karpasia*, in Persian *kirpas*. In Greek it was *carbasos*, and in Latin *carbasus*. They gave Hebrew its *kirpas*.

But it couldn't last. Cotton changed the world too fast, made too many demands, called for too much subtlety. English is lucky. It has a word which can even begin to suggest cotton as a substance different from others. So many languages, like German with its *baumwolle*, are condemned for ever to the blinkers that bound Sennacherib and Herodotus to think of cotton as a misbegotten wool. But even the English were handed down their word, like so much else that raised them to civilization, by the Arabs, from their *kutn* (how fine an irony when several centuries later hundreds of thousands of Egyptian fellahin were tied in bondage to the demands of the cotton mills of Lancashire). But the Arabs took their own word from the Akkadian *kitinu*. And there they had lost the battle already, for that word came from *kitu*, in the same language, which meant nothing but dreary flax.

What does it say for human beings that they let themselves be ruled so completely by so simple a thing as cloth?

When the history of the world broke, cotton and cloth were behind it; mechanical man in pursuit of his own destruction.

Perhaps it began in the sixteenth century with William Lee in England, and his invention of a stretching frame for yarn. Then it was Arkwright with his spinning-jenny, and Kay and his flying shuttle.

The machine had driven men mad.

Lancashire poured out its waterfalls of cloth, and the once cloth-hungry and peaceful Englishmen and Dutchmen and Danes of Calcutta and Chandannagar, Madras and Bombay turned their trade into a garotte to make every continent safe for the cloth of Lancashire, strangling the very weavers and techniques they had crossed oceans to discover. Millions of Africans and half of America were enslaved by cotton.

And then weaving changed mechanical man again with the computer. In the mid-nineteenth century when Charles Babbage built his first calculating machine, using the principle of storing information on punched cards, he took his idea not from systems of writing nor from mathematics, but from the draw-loom. The Chinese have used punched cards to discriminate between warp threads in the weaving of silk since 1000 BC. They gave it (unwillingly) to the Italians, and the Italians gave it to the rest of Europe, in the form of the draw-loom. Basile Bouchon of Lyons, in 1725, added a roll of perforated paper to store the pattern in its punched memory. And in 1801 Joseph Jacquard invented his automatic selective device based on the same principle. Babbage took his ideas for his calculating engines from Jacquard's loom, and Holleville who patented the first punched-card machines took his ideas from Babbage. Once again the loom reaches through the centuries and across continents to decide the fate of mechanical man.

Who knows what new horrors lie in store?

It is a gory history in parts; a story of greed and destruction.

Every scrap of cloth is stained by a bloody past. But it is the only history we have and history is hope as well as despair.

And so weaving, too, is hope; a living belief that having once made the world one and blessed it with its diversity it must do so again. Weaving is hope because it has no country, no continent.

Weaving *is* Reason, which makes the world mad and makes it human.

Chapter Three

War

Wars keep people busy. As a rule the spectators are the busiest of all. Some keep busy helping armies with their business of murder and massacre, loot and rapine. Others are left with blood trickling their way and no choice but to join the flow or mop it up.

The people of Lalpukur could not help knowing that a war was brewing across the border; their relatives on the other side never let them forget it. Often they were drummed to bed by the rattle of distant gunfire. But on the whole the fighting was to pass Lalpukur by. And, unlike some of their neighbours, no one in Lalpukur had the energy to join in of their own will. The reason was that the people of Lalpukur were too melancholy. Vomited out of their native soil years ago in another carnage, and dumped hundreds of miles away, they had no anger left. Their only passion was memory; a longing for a land where the green was greener, the rice whiter, the fish bigger than boats; where the rivers' names sang like Megh Malhar on a rainy day – the Meghna, the Dholeshshori, the Kirtinosha, the Shitolokhkha, the majestic Arialkha, wider than the horizon. Rivers which bore the wealth of a continent to their land, from Tibet, from the Himalayas. Rivers overflowing with bounty, as wide as seas, their banks invisible from one another.

Lalpukur could fight no war because it was damned to a hell of longing.

The vocation of the melancholy is not anger but mourning. When in need they charge by the hour and sell a bitter sort of consolation. And all that Lalpukur had to offer was consolation of a sort – refuge. It could never be a battlefield; nothing but a dumping-ground for the refuse from tyrants' frenzies.

Long before the world had sniffed genocide in Bangladesh, Lalpukur began to swell. It grew and grew. First, it was

brothers with burnt backs and balls cut off at the roots. Then it
was cousins and cousins of cousins. Then it did not matter;
borders dissolved under the weight of millions of people in
panic-stricken flight from an army of animals.

Bamboo shanties soon luxuriated around the village. The
great banyan tree at its centre became a leaky shelter for
dozens of families and their bundled belongings. Lalpukur
burst its boundaries and poured out, jostling with the district
road a furlong away. Bhudeb Roy's rice fields sprouted shacks
of packing wood and corrugated iron. He didn't mind. On the
contrary, he was very helpful and even hired a few tough
young men to organize the shacks properly. He had discovered
that rents from refugee shacks yielded a better harvest than
rice. The tea-shop under the banyan tree diversified into
selling rice and vegetables, and Bolai-da began to stock
corrugated iron and sheets of tin beaten out of discarded
kerosene-containers. Soon cycle-repairing was the smallest of
his concerns.

Everyone was busy, and Balaram, though he did not know it
and would not have cared if he had, had good reason to be
grateful for it. Had people had time on their hands he may have
had to face a good deal of criticism and even straightforward
opposition over his decision to apprentice Alu to a weaver. And
despite everything people *did* find time to talk: what business
had a schoolmaster to take his nephew out of school and
apprentice him to a weaver (and that, too, when schoolmasters
didn't have to pay school fees)? What could it mean?

A few rumours took root under the banyan tree: Alu had
been thrown out of school for failing once too often; Balaram
was going to start a cloth factory in Calcutta with Alu as
foreman. It was something deep; that was for certain.

But then Lalpukur would be convulsed with growing pains
once more and people would be busy again.

As for Balaram, the only person he was really worried about
was Toru-debi. But Toru-debi was busy, too: she had perfected
her seamless petticoat and was hard at work on a scheme for a
buttonless blouse. Weeks passed before she heard of Alu's
apprenticeship. When she did she talked of it only once to
Balaram. The books weren't enough, she said resignedly.
There's nothing I can do about your head. But it doesn't matter

– you'll put an end to it yourself.

Balaram could hardly believe that he had got off so lightly. He sighed with relief; at last he was free to give his whole energies to the new problem that had so suddenly confronted him.

The fact is that, because of the extraordinary developments in the village, Balaram had almost forgotten about Alu. Soon after the refugees began flooding into Lalpukur, Balaram had gone to take a look at their shacks and shanties. He was appalled: he saw people eating surrounded by their children's shit; the tin roofs were black with flies; in the lanes rats wouldn't yield to human feet; there were no drains and no clean water, and the air was stagnant with germs, pregnant with every known disease.

Balaram could think of only one answer: carbolic acid. Nothing else would be remotely as appropriate. There was a kind of *historical* legitimacy about carbolic acid. The only alternative Balaram could think of were mercury-based disinfectants, and somehow he could not bring himself to use those. Weren't they created by the Great Adversary, Robert Koch, who had so tenaciously and falsely opposed Pasteur until he could no longer deny the truth? And weren't they invalid in a way, since Koch had come upon them almost by accident, believing their effects to be other than they actually were? Besides, they'd probably be too expensive anyway. No, it had to be carbolic acid, that masterly brainchild of Lister's, Pasteur's friend and Great Disciple.

So Balaram started a campaign. He went around the shanties, warning people of the swift death they were calling on themselves. He called meetings and urged them to contribute what they could to buy carbolic acid. People listened to him, for they knew he was a schoolmaster, but they hesitated. It was not till he started a fund with a bit of his own money that they threw in a few annas and paisas. Soon they had enough to buy a fair quantity of disinfectant. Then, very systematically, with the help of a few volunteers, Balaram began to disinfect every exposed inch of the new settlements.

Bolai-da said one day, watching him: This is a new Balaram-babu. It was true: Balaram, antiseptic and pungent with disinfectant, had never been so happy.

Bhudeb Roy, as he told ASP Jyoti Das later, did nothing to stop Balaram, because at the time he was one of the busiest people in the village. But he watched suspiciously because it was clear to him at once that Balaram was up to something. It had to be more than mere coincidence that he had started the business with disinfectants and apprenticed his nephew to Shombhu Debnath at the same time.

It was the link with Shombhu Debnath which really upset Bhudeb Roy. It worried him so much that he managed to find time to speak to Balaram about the matter.

One day Balaram was summoned to Bhudeb Roy's office in the school. He went reluctantly, for he hated the office. Five portraits of Bhudeb Roy stared out of its narrow walls. Two of them – one a photograph of Bhudeb Roy in a black gown, holding his BA degree, and another, a picture of him in Darjeeling, his massive bulk posed playfully against a railing with the Himalayas in the background – had incense sticks burning reverentially under them.

Balaram could not bring himself to sit in that room. He stood stiffly, holding the back of a chair, and said: Yes?

Sit down, Balaram-babu, said Bhudeb Roy. Balaram shook his head. As you please, said Bhudeb Roy, sticking a plug of tobacco into his jaw with his little finger. His jaw worked laterally as he chewed on it.

Balaram-babu, he said, your decisions are your own and I don't want to interfere, but I have to think about the good of the school. Do you think anybody will want to send their children to a school where they will be taught by a man who has apprenticed his own nephew to a weaver? Think about it, Balaram-babu. I leave it to you, but perhaps you should think about your future in the school, too.

Balaram turned and would have walked out, but Bhudeb Roy called out after him: Wait, Balaram-babu. Have you thought about what you're doing? You're putting his health at serious risk. People like us can't do that kind of work. He'll fall ill, and you'll be responsible. He'll have to drink water there, maybe even eat there. I don't believe in caste, as you know, but their food is dirty. Very dirty. Have you thought about that?

Balaram had not. He stopped worriedly. Do you mean, he said, their food may have germs?

Yes, yes, said Bhudeb Roy, germs.

But, Balaram said, thinking hard, their food must be cooked by Maya, and Maya cooks in our house, too, sometimes. There can't be much difference.

Bhudeb Roy's tiny eyes hardened. His voice rose: Balaram-babu, you're calling disaster on yourself. I warn you: stay away from that man Shombhu Debnath. Have you any idea what that man is like? Why, he's not even a good weaver.

Balaram had to turn sharply on his heel and walk out of the room. It would not have been correct to let Bhudeb Roy see him laughing.

You couldn't expect Bhudeb Roy to be dispassionate about Shombhu Debnath.

Once, a long time ago, there were a few toddy palms on a patch of land behind Bhudeb Roy's house. They were rented to a toddy-tapper, and they yielded a fair income every year.

But one year the toddy-tapper refused to pay rent any longer. His toddy-pots were empty every morning, he complained, and he earned nothing from the palms any more.

That was an eventful year. Bhudeb Roy married Parboti-debi and brought her to Lalpukur that year, and it was at about the same time that Shombhu Debnath first arrived in Lalpukur.

The toddy-tapper was a drunken old man, but shrewd. Bhudeb-babu, he leered, if you wanted some, why didn't you tell me? You'll hurt yourself climbing those trees.

Bhudeb Roy, red-faced: What do you mean?

The old man, nodding towards the curtains which had screened the consummation of Bhudeb Roy's nuptials, whispered conspiratorially: Bit dry, is she? He was hurled out of the house.

But no one else would rent the palms, either. It became common knowledge in the village that the pots which were hung up in the fronds to catch fresh toddy at night were usually dry in the morning. But there was nothing wrong with the palms – the nicks in the trunk oozed fresh milky toddy through the day.

It became a deeply shameful matter for Bhudeb Roy. He was bombarded with tips on wife-rearing. Everybody was full of sympathy: he was too soon married to be driven to drink by a wife. Bhudeb Roy could only gnash his teeth. It was true that he could not always understand his Parboti, but she was as gentle a woman as any in the village.

Bhudeb Roy decided to solve the mystery. He bought a huge torch in Naboganj and one night he waited up in his room, nervously holding on to Parboti-debi's ankle. He discovered something that made the blood stop cold in his veins.

Late at night, in the furry blackness before dawn, an eerie noise wafted out of the toddy palms and curled around the house. It was like a hoarse wail; a high, gliding, sobbing wail. Bhudeb Roy's joints melted. He jammed his mosquito-net tight under his mattress and put a pillow over his ears.

Parboti-debi watched him with a smile. It's like the night calling one, she said, isn't it?

Bhudeb Roy, astonished: Have you heard it before?

Yes, she said. I hear it every night. She smiled. At the time she was pregnant with her first son (he of the incipient moustache and old man's paunch). She was an imposing figure then, very far from the wispy, harassed woman, stooped with fecundity, that she became later. She was erect and tall (taller than Bhudeb Roy), fresh-faced, with hair which shone like painted glass. She had a low, rich-timbred voice, very pleasing. It was said that she used to sing once. But Bhudeb Roy had put a stop to it: No shrieking in my house; besides you need your strength for your children.

Why didn't you tell me about the noise? Bhudeb Roy said.

You didn't have a torch, she said, smiling limpidly.

After that Bhudeb Roy slept with two pillows over his head. One night he woke to find Parboti-debi gone from his bed. The room whistled with the jagged echoes of that distant wailing. Biting his knuckles Bhudeb Roy crept to a window and shone his torch out. It fell on Parboti-debi, in her white night-time sari, stock-still in the mango grove behind their house.

Bhudeb Roy decided that something had to be done. Wails were bad for pregnancies. So he decided to hire Bolai-da, who was on leave from the Army, to investigate the mystery with him.

It was a mistake. Bhudeb Roy discovered too late that Bolai-da's real love was gossip.

Bolai-da was thin and painfully bandy-legged even then, but

it was only much later that his face twisted mournfully sideways, like soggy cardboard. At that time, because he was the only soldier in the village, nobody doubted that he had the courage of a pride of lions. He could look a Sardar-ji in the eye, people said. A real one, with a proper turban and everything. He had once knocked over a seven-foot, mustachioed and bandoliered Pathan. The wails would shrivel, everyone agreed, at the very sight of Bolai-da.

The stories gave Bhudeb Roy courage. He armed Bolai-da with a wooden club and bought new batteries for his torch. Then he locked Parboti-debi into their room and told her to shut her ears and pray if the wailing started again. She looked very distressed, and Bhudeb Roy was flattered by her concern. But she said nothing.

Bhudeb Roy and Bolai-da wrapped themselves in blankets and went down to the mango grove to wait. With eerie punctuality, in the awful blackness of the last hours of the night, howls wafted through the mango grove. Bhudeb Roy pushed Bolai-da. Bolai-da pushed Bhudeb Roy. Coward, said Bhudeb Roy. I thought you'd knocked over a seven-foot Pathan?

To tell you the truth, Bhudeb-babu, Bolai-da said through chattering teeth, a bus I happened to be on did it.

They held each other's shoulders and crept forward, towards the palms. They were no more than a yard or two away when the wail suddenly soared and splintered into a comet of high notes. Bhudeb Roy leapt backwards. Somehow his feet entangled themselves in a creeper. He fell with a shriek.

The wails froze into silence. Then they heard a voice, a disappointing, all too human voice, slurred but perfectly comprehensible: Come up, come up before it finishes.

It was Bolai-da who recovered the torch and shone it into the palm. He spat on the ground and smiled at Bhudeb Roy. Bhudeb Roy did not see him, for he was crouching in the undergrowth, his head between his arms.

Bhudeb-babu, Bolai-da said, you can come out now. It's only Shombhu Debnath.

He shone the torch into the palm. Shombhu Debnath was clinging to the top with his knees. He had one arm wrapped around a fan-shaped leaf for support. In the other he held a toddy-pot. All he wore was a strip of a cotton gamcha around his thin, angular waist.

Bhudeb Roy's jaws worked convulsively. He coughed, for he had grass in his mouth. Shombhu Debnath? he spluttered. What's he doing here?

Drinking God's milk, Shombhu answered, and singing.

Bhudeb Roy exploded: What?

Raga Lalit of course, Shombhu said, surprised. What else could you sing at this time of the night?

Come down here with that pot, Bhudeb Roy roared.

Why? The toddy's fresher here. Closer to God. It ferments nastily when it gets down to earth with men and money.

Thief. Bhudeb Roy flung himself at the palm. Thief, thief, petty thief.

Next day he had all his palms chopped down. That was the only time he had ever destroyed a source of income.

It was generally felt that Bhudeb Roy was wrong. Shombhu Debnath was no thief. If he were, why would he sing while he was up in the palms? Besides, everybody knew that if they found a few emptied pots in their palms they had only to ask Rakhal to be paid their price (though, of course, only if Rakhal happened to have money that day).

People who had known Shombhu Debnath and his family in Noakhali used to say that he had always been like that: restless, unpredictable, fond of heights. A little mad, too: that was why he sang.

Only those who did not know him well were surprised when he first disappeared at the age of twelve from the quiet, reassuring huddle of his father's and uncles' and cousins' huts on the edge of the Noakhali mainland opposite Siddi Island, where the Meghna becomes the Bamni before flowing into the sea.

His family, like all the Debnaths, were weavers of coarse cotton. They wove thick white cloth, checked lungis, coarse cotton gamchas, and suchlike in great bulk. It was mere drudgery: throwing the shuttle one way and another for years without end until their spines collapsed. It was not much of a technique, and Shombhu mastered it while he was still a child. His mother was not at all surprised when he vanished. She had known; she had seen it in his hands. He had beautiful hands, long-fingered and strong, quicker than the eye, and always restless.

But even she had no inkling of his plans. Nobody did, for Shombhu had set out to do the impossible.

As a child Shombhu, like all the other children in his hamlet, had heard tales and legends about the Boshaks of Tangail, near Dhaka. Everyone knew the legend of the Boshaks: for centuries they had ruled continents with their gossamer weaves. But it was not only for their weaving that they were legendary; it was also for the secretiveness with which they hoarded the trade and craft secrets of their caste. A Boshak could no more teach an outsider than another man could give away his family's best land. The few outsiders who learnt from them disappeared into the fastnesses of their families – they married Boshak girls, lived in their houses, ate their food, and surrendered every memory of their lives outside. And if there was anyone against whom every glimmer of an opening in the Boshak defences would be clamped shut it was a Debnath – a despised weaver of coarse cotton.

Twelve-year-old Shombhu Debnath found a way of breaking the formation. He walked from his village to the ferry port of Shahebghata and found a boat to take him up the Meghna and down the Padma to Tangail. There, passing himself off as an orphan, he found a place in a Boshak master-weaver's family, in a hamlet outside the town. He worked with them for years, for nothing but his food and a few clothes. He learnt to size and to warp; with the master-weaver's sons he learnt the secrets of punching Jacquard index cards. He learnt the intricacies of their jamdani inlay techniques. He even learnt to make the fine bamboo reeds which were the centrepieces of their jamdani looms, the only ones which could hold fine silk yarn without tearing it. That was a skill few even among the Boshaks could boast of, for it was the preserve of a wandering caste of boatmen and bangle-makers called Bédé.

And he learnt their songs, melancholy, throbbing songs of love and longing. They all sang, he and the master-weaver's sons and everyone else, they sang as they worked in their tin-roofed shed, each at their own loom, taking their beat from the rhythmic clatter of fly-shuttles and the tinkling of needle-weights hanging on Jacquard looms.

Shombhu forgot his hamlet; he had no family left but the master-weaver's.

But it had to end. One day the master-weaver met a merchant from Noakhali. That day, tears pouring down his cheek, he confronted Shombhu with his secret. Shombhu fled that night, straight back to Noakhali, towards the safe circle of huts that had suddenly been resurrected in his memory.

But the master-weaver's tears had burnt his curses into Shombhu's flesh. Shombhu paid for his treachery – the dreadful, corroding price of a wasted secret.

He arrived in his hamlet with the gift of fire cupped in his palms and found that his world preferred its meat raw. We know what we know, they said when he tried to teach them the secrets of jamdani, and we want to know no more. A crow falls out of the sky if it tries to learn peacockery.

Shombhu, too, had his burnt books.

That was when Shombhu first began to frequent the branches of toddy palms. Soon he stopped working altogether. Then one day he disappeared again. This time his family were relieved.

He left the hamlet with a group of singers – wanderers who spent their lives journeying from one village to another, living on alms, dancing and singing of their love of Sri Krishna. They taught Shombhu what they knew of the rudiments of music: the moods and the hours, the ascending and descending scales of a few basic ragas like Bhairavi, Asavari, Desh, Yaman Kalyan, and Lalit. But the lessons never lasted very long. His teachers usually lost interest halfway. Technique was immaterial to them; all their bhajans and songs ended in the same ecstatic chant: Hare Rama, Hare Krishna; Krishna, Krishna, Hare, Hare.

Then one day, long after the convulsions of the decade had swallowed his family, Shombhu appeared in Lalpukur, with an ailing wife, and incurably and thirstily hoarse. Some people in the village recognized him and helped him a little for the sake of his vanished family. He cleared a patch of land and built himself a couple of huts, at a marked distance from the rest of the village. He even built himself a loom. His wife recovered long enough to bear him a son. But her strength failed her the second time, and she died bearing Maya.

Shombhu almost stopped working then. He wove barely enough to keep them alive. When Rakhal was about eight, he taught him to weave the coarse cotton of his ancestors, and let him cope as best he could. All the help he offered him after that was the encouragement of an occasional, hoarse Jaijaiwanti. Maya listened to him, and when she was barely knee-high, and already wise with poverty, she thought ahead to her wedding day and decided that a hoarse Jaijaiwanti for dower would fetch her no husband. So she decided to ask Toru-debi, for theirs was the house nearest to their own, for a job – anything at all.

Shombhu, wounded to the last ragged edge of his proud poverty, forbade her: Shombhu Debnath's daughter a servant? But her womanly courage and worldliness were proof against him, and she had her way.

In revenge, Shombhu Debnath thundered Bhairavi from the tree-tops and would not speak to Balaram.

But Balaram watched him, especially when he heard that he had stopped weaving. Balaram could only guess at the wealth of his skull, but even at a distance he felt a theory stirring. . . .

Balaram had not told Gopal the whole truth. Alu's was not the only organ he had identified. Alu was just one part of the pattern he had conceived. The other was Shombhu Debnath.

Shombhu Debnath was tall, spectrally dark and skeletally thin. He was usually nearly naked, with only a thin gamcha wound around his waist, displaying proudly the corded muscles he bore all over him as a legacy of his years of weaving and wandering. His face was his own hoarse crescendo in Bhairavi, a stumbling sweep, lush-lipped and full-nosed, pouring in a broken glade from ridged cheekbones at the corners of his eyes; the eyes blood-red but lustrous, the forehead soaring uneasily to a crown of knotted hair, coiled snake-like on top of his head. That was his own little bound rivulet, he liked to say, a pale echo of the Jatadhari's Ganga.

I know what you are, said Balaram after the interests of science and the discovery of Alu's mechanical organ had lent him the courage to force himself on Shombhu Debnath and his looms.

What? said Shombhu suspiciously.

You're a teacher, said Balaram. That's why you must take our Alu to be your apprentice.

Shombhu laughed: I haven't taught anyone except my Rakhal, and in Naboganj they display his cloth when they want a laugh. I haven't woven in years.

That's why you haven't woven, Balaram said, serenely sure. You're not a weaver; you haven't the right organs. Everything about you goes to prove that you're a teacher.

To prove that he was serious he pulled five ten-rupee notes out of his trouser pocket and slapped them into Shombhu's hand. There, he said, the price for your head – your first fees. Shombhu shook his hand, aghast, but the money clung to it. Static electricity, said Balaram. Sri Krishna's leela, said Shombhu. Divine play, but not for a mortal man to question.

That was how Alu had his wish and arrived in Shombhu Debnath's courtyard one morning, no more as a visitor, but an aspiring apprentice, spick-span, oiled and eager. But it was not to be as he had imagined: no welcoming embrace from the Master, no words of craftsmanly wisdom. Shombhu Debnath smiled to see him, a grimace of a smile, baring his hookah-blackened teeth, and said: No more peace here. Then he picked up his hookah and wandered gurgling into the bamboo forest.

Imagine Alu: fifteen now, stocky and broad-shouldered, in blue shorts, his head still huge but the bumps a little smoother, standing forlorn in a courtyard, listening to the fading gurgles of a hookah. The courtyard is not large as courtyards go, but tranquil, shaded by an overhanging jackfruit tree. It is a simple square uthon of beaten earth set between three huts. The huts are large, cool rooms, four walls of clay, covered by a thatch of bamboo and straw, arched over like upturned boats. One is Maya's, one shared by Rakhal and his father, and the smallest serves as a kitchen. At the far end of the courtyard is an open shed, a sloping thatch roof, held up by bamboo poles, under which Shombhu Debnath's two fly-shuttle looms are set in waist-deep pits. Rakhal is sitting at one of those looms. He sees Alu's disappointment and calls out sourly: Do you think he'll ever teach you? Do you think he knows how to teach? Look how he taught me. Go back while there's time. Don't waste your life here. Rakhal is thinking of his own youth and strength, wasted at the loom, when he could be at a kung fu class in Naboganj instead.

The forest did not yield up Shombhu Debnath that day or

the next or the day after. Eventually it was Maya who became
Alu's first teacher.

First, she taught him to starch yarn: tedious foul-smelling
work, days spent hanging yarn up to dry after dipping it in pots
of congealed rice starch. Then she taught him to wind the
starched yarn on bobbins, with a spinning wheel: children's
work – spin the wheel with one hand, hold the yarn taut with
the other, making sure that it winds evenly. Dreary, dreary
work. Even the speed with which Alu turned out perfect oval
bobbins – more than a hundred a day, many more than Rakhal
could use – was no consolation.

Where was Shombhu Debnath? Where was the Shombhu
who had once sat on the stoop of his hut and talked into the
night about the cloth he had heard of in the master-weaver's
shed in Tangail? Of abrawan muslins as fine as mountain
springs, invisible under the surface of the clearest water;
shabnam muslins, which when spread on grass melted into the
morning dew; cloth which was thin air, fifteen *yards* of it no
heavier than two handfuls of rice, and yet denser than the
thickest wool, with four hundred warp threads to the inch.
Shameless, shameless insubstantial cloth, nature's mirror,
carrying on its conscience the curses of the exiled princess
who, swathed in thirty *yards* of it, had stepped into her father's
court, for all the world to see, mother naked and beautiful.
Where was that Shombhu Debnath?

When, when would Shombhu Debnath begin to teach him?

Never, said Maya, rocking back on her heels as she squatted
beside Alu, watching him at the wheel. Rakhal's right; he'll
never teach you.

Alu's hand slipped, and next moment his fingers and the
wheel were wrapped in a tangled cat's-cradle of yarn. Morti-
fied, Alu began disentangling the yarn. Maya watched him,
sucking her lip. Then she hissed: What's the use of your
learning this? This is real work; you'll never be able to do it. Go
back to your school and your books.

Alu had most of the yarn wrapped around his open palm. He
bit through a knot and spat out the metallic sharpness of dye
and starch. Do you hear me? Maya said. Go back home; this is
real work. You'll never learn to do it.

Alu had the yarn disentangled and wound tightly around his

palm. He began to lay it out in loops so he could start again.
You're proud you can wind a bobbin, aren't you? Maya said,
dark eyes flashing. Do you know what this is? This is children's
work; children do it when they're eight. That's what you're
doing – children's work – even though you've got hair bursting
out of your clothes.

Unsteadily Alu ran a sweating palm over the rim of the wheel
and gave it a trial spin. Little boy, hissed Maya, playing with
toys. Why don't you get out of your shorts and back into your
cradle?

Alu, suddenly a child again, knocked the wheel aside. He
lunged forward and pushed her over. Trembling, he watched
her pick herself up and brush the dust off her worn red sari.
That's right, she cried. Hit me. You'll never be good for any
real work.

She spat into the dust. Alu saw her brush the end of her sari
across her eyes. She turned and ran into her hut.

Rakhal had left his loom. He was leaning against the shed,
watching him. It's true, he said. You're really in trouble.
You're caught between two madmen, and who can tell what a
madman will do or a goat will eat? Maya's right; you should get
out of this while you still can.

But at the end of that month, when Balaram punctually
handed Maya her father's fees yet again, she took the notes to
her father, and held them up in both hands: I'm tearing these.

But why? Shombhu said. His fees had fuelled a new fondness
for arrack. He was in no mood to have his money torn up.

Because it's stolen money, Maya said. He's paying you to
teach him weaving, and you've taught him nothing.

Shombhu snatched the money from her and stormed out of
the courtyard. That night they heard him giving vent to an im-
passioned, night-jarring Raga Kelenga on some distant branch.

Next morning he was in the courtyard, waiting for Alu,
sucking on his hookah.

Warping first: no weft without a warp.

Other weavers with only a loom or two usually had their
warps sized and wound by contractors. Not Shombhu Debnath. Somehow he had acquired a drum and frames for his own
warp beams.

So Alu learnt how to arrange bobbins of yarn on the

hundreds of spindles on the warping frames, so that they ran true to the warp drum; he learnt to conjure up patterns by arranging bobbins of different colours on different parts of the frames; he learnt to thread the ends of the yarn through a wooden board, like a racket, with hundreds of metal eyes, so that the yarn would not tangle on its journey to the drum; he learnt to wind the drum, so that it drew the yarn into it, like a lake swallowing a waterfall. And so on, often mere tedium, changing bobbins when they ran out, rethreading them through the board, twisting together the ends of broken threads.

Days of work, painstaking, eye-crossing work, to wind one warp beam properly. But sometimes there was a kind of music to it, when the drum was turning well, clattering on its hinges, and the yarn was whirling through the eyes of the board, like a stream shooting through rapids.

And then, one day, Shombhu at last led Alu to a loom. Alu, in his eagerness, would have jumped straight down to the bench, but Shombhu's hand was on his shoulder. He smiled his cracked, discoloured smile: You have to know what it is first.

The machine, like man, is captive to language.

So that was another month gone, a labour of a different kind.

Shombhu Debnath squats by the loom with Alu beside him. He points with his cane at a heavy beam. He opens his mouth, he would speak, but lo! the loom has knotted his tongue. So many names, so many words, words beaten together in the churning which created the world: Tangail words, stewed with Noakhali words, salted with Naboganj words, boiled up with English (picked up who knows where in his years of wandering). Words, words, this village teems with words, yet too few to speak of the world and the machine. Such wealth and such oppression: to survive a man must try twice as hard, pour out words, whatever comes his way, and hope. . . .

Kol-norod, Shombhu shouts, pointing with his cane. *Kol-norod* in Noakhali, *nata-norod* in Tangail, *cloth beam* in English.

Then his cane switches to the other end of the loom: *bhim-norod* in Noakhali, *pancha-norod* in Tangail, *warp beam* in English. Understood? All right now – his cane points back at the cloth beam – in Tangail?

Alu hesitates, and a fraction of a second later a weal is reddening on his back. Shombhu Debnath smiles: You have to study hard, you know. We sucked it all in through our mother's tits.

So many words, so many things. On a loom a beam's name changes after every inch. Why? Every nail has a name, every twist of rope, every little eyelet, every twig of bamboo on the heddle. A loom is a dictionaryglossarythesaurus. Why? Words serve no purpose; nothing mechanical. No, it is because the weaver, in making cloth, makes words, too, and trespassing on the territory of the poets gives names to things the eye can't see. That is why the loom has given language more words, more metaphor, more idiom than all the world's armies of pen-wielders.

And so it went on.

It was hard, but at the end of a month Alu, his back matted with scars, could name every nail and every join on the fly-shuttle loom. And so at last Shombhu Debnath could stop him no longer from climbing into the loom's pit.

Actually weaving is simple. All it is is a technique for laying a cross-thread, called the weft or woof, between parallel long threads, called the warp, at right angles. To do this, it is enough to part the warp threads so that the weft can be passed through, and then close them again so that they lock the weft in place. That is all it is and it rules all cloth (except bashed, beaten things like felt, which, despite dictionaries, is *not* cloth), in all times and in all the realms of the world. The machines change as dizzily as all appearances; there are dummy-shuttle looms and rapier looms and water-jet looms and circular looms. But the changes are merely mechanical, they have to do with speed and bulk and quality. The essence of cloth – locking yarns together by crossing them – has not changed since prehistory.

It's so simple, Alu said with a conqueror's elation. It took no more than a day to learn, just a matter of co-ordination: tug on the shuttle-cord once and the shuttle flies across with the weft, press the right pedal and the warp closes on the weft, push the reed once towards you and the cloth grows by another minute fraction of an inch, then tug the shuttle-cord again. . . . like a dance, one way, then another, hands and feet together.

Yes, said Shombhu Debnath. Plain white cloth, like you're

weaving, is simple. You'll find out how simple it is if you ever get past that.

Alu paid him no attention. He had his reward at last: a five-yard length of cloth. Maya cut it from the cloth beam for him. You'll never learn, she said, folding it. Go back to your books. But she smiled.

Alu walked sedately out of the courtyard, the cloth folded under his arm. When he reached the bamboos he began to run. He bounded into Balaram's study and shouted: Look, the first bit of cloth I've woven. But Balaram was away, dousing the village in antiseptic.

It didn't matter, for Alu was already in a dream. It took him barely a week to master the weaving of ordinary white cloth. At the end of the week the loom, rattling faster than it ever had before, had thrown out a waterfall of cloth.

But Shombhu Debnath curled his lip. He looked at the bale Alu had woven, and snorted: How old are you?

Fifteen, Alu said, sixteen soon.

Shame, said Shombhu. We used to do better than that when we were ten.

But, again, Maya smiled.

At the end of the week, Shombhu Debnath moved Alu on to coloured cloth. The simplest first, a weft of one shade and a warp of another – no different, really, from weaving plain cloth. Then real patterns: checks which needed two changes of shuttle for every inch; then bordered stripes and even bordered checks.

Alu learnt quicker than Shombhu Debnath could teach. His loom poured out rainbows of cloth with magical ease.

Fast, too fast, faster than Maya could wind bobbins. Maya had to appeal to Rakhal for help. But Rakhal, proudly, had no time. He was busy at last. He had saved enough money to join the Bruce Lee kung fu class (daily 7 a.m.; fees weekly) near the ancient banyan of Poramatola in Naboganj. He was working furiously himself, after his classes, to earn money for his bus fares and for fees for months and months ahead. So Maya, disappointed, had to hire bobbins out to families with lots of little children, so that Alu would have enough yarn for the maws of his loom.

And Alu wove still faster. His hands flew like pistons; the

shuttle became a wooden blur, its knocking, as it hit the sides of
the batten, merged and rose into a whine. Maya marvelled at
last; she had never seen such speed, and that night Alu
somersaulted all the way back through the bamboo forest.

Alu was peacock-proud. He longed to preen, to spread the
feathers of his skill. But Lalpukur was churning like cement in a
grinder, and Balaram was busy chasing its shooting boundaries
with buckets of carbolic acid, his hair wafting behind him, in
the germ-free air; Toru-debi was fouled in the tangles of her
buttonless blouse; and, as for Shombhu Debnath, he had taken
to disappearing again, all through the day, and in the chaos of
that churning no one knew where he went.

Alu had to be content with quantity. In two weeks he wove
seventy-five violently coloured lungis. It was something
tangible. After he cut the seventy-fifth from the cloth beam he
and Maya laid them out in the courtyard and waited late into
the evening for Shombhu Debnath.

But Shombhu Debnath was unimpressed when he arrived at
last, panting and damp with evening dew. He dismissed the
carpet of cloth with a wave: Simple patterns; a boy could do it.

Then, teach me better ones, Alu retorted.

Too fast, said Shombhu Debnath, you're going too fast.

But, still, between disappearances he taught Alu to tie the
heddle of his loom for grainy tabby weaves: two adjacent
strings of the warp, instead of the usual alternate, in a regular
series across the beam, crossed with two picks of the weft
instead of one. He taught him dizzying spectroscopic patterns,
spiralling combinations of eight, ten, twelve colours. He
banished the coarse yarn Alu had started with and warped his
loom with fine, delicate cotton instead – 80, 100, 120 warp
threads to the inch. Be careful, he said, this yarn tears if the
shuttle so much as touches it.

Alu's loom swallowed it faster than Maya and all her hired
bobbin-winders could feed it. In another two weeks Alu had
woven 120 lungis.

They stared at the pile aghast, as they might at the sulky rage
of a jackfruit tree bombarding the earth with heedless profusion, pouring down more fruit in a day than a district could eat in
a week. Who would buy so much cloth? There was enough to
crowd several shopkeepers out of their counters.

It was Rakhal who came up with the solution.

Listen, he said to Alu. I'll sell your cloth in Naboganj. I have to go there for my classes anyway, and I know Naboganj. I'll get a better price for you than you'd ever be able to get yourself. No one argues with me. But you'll have to give me a tenth part of the money I earn you, *and* you'll have to pay for my kung fu classes. You'll be able to afford it.

That's fine, said Maya. That's settled, then.

Rakhal leapt into the air. He bent his right leg back under him, while the other shot out, parallel to the ground, pointing forward. His palm opened stiffly, swung out sideways and crashed into one of the bamboo pillars of the loom-shed. A corner of the shed buckled and slumped over. The scar on Rakhal's cheek suddenly blazed crimson. A scream tore out of his bowels, sending a cloud of birds into the air, twittering with alarm.

He's pleased, Maya explained.

Yes, Rakhal grinned, I'm pleased. He struck another bamboo pole with his palm. Half the shed collapsed, covering his loom with straw. And I'll tell you a secret, he said. Soon I won't ever have to touch a loom again. I'm getting a job – of a different kind. I'm going to be rich.

Tell us, Alu and Maya chorused, tell us, Rakhal-da, tellustell-ustellus.

No, said Rakhal, narrow-eyed, mysterious. It's a secret.

They saw very little of him in the next fortnight. He left early every morning with a few lungis wrapped up in a bundle and came back late without them. But one evening he returned with a bigger, heavier bundle than he had taken with him that morning. No bundle of cloth, that was for sure. He carried it through the courtyard carefully, on his shoulders, and darted straight into his hut and hid it away under the thatch, ignoring Alu and Maya's stares.

The next day he did not go to Naboganj. At midday Alu and Maya saw him going into the bamboo forest with the bundle perched on his shoulders. Going into the forest so late, Rakhal-da? Alu shouted. Constipation?

Rakhal didn't deign to answer. So naturally Alu and Maya stole into the forest behind him.

They found him all but invisible in a copse, a small fortress of bamboo. He was sitting, legs folded, on a patch of grass. There were piles all around him: piles of old bottles and tin cans, of oriole-yellow powder, rusty nails and metal scraps, broken razor blades, torn rags, and other steel-grey and nondescript powders. He was working busily, filling bottles with powders and scraps, stuffing their necks with rags.

Rakhal heard a rustle in the bamboo and looked up. He saw them, four large, curious, wondering eyes in the bamboo. Get away from here, he growled. This is secret.

What are those things, Rakhal-da? Alu asked.

Get out, Rakhal shouted. But they were far beyond his reach and he had a half-full bottle on his lap.

What are they, Rakhal-da? Alu asked again.

Rakhal hesitated, drawing a finger over his lips. He could not help stiffening with pride.

They're bombs, he said. Bombs.

Bombs! they chorused.

Yes, he smiled, bombs. He looked anxiously at them. Of course, he added quickly, they're simple. Don't think I don't know that. This is just to begin with. They'll teach me the difficult ones later.

Alu and Maya looked at him in silence. You have to start somewhere, he said apologetically. I'll be doing better soon.

But, Rakhal-da, Alu said, what will you do with them?

Make money, he answered. There's a good market for them. Because of the war, you know.

What war? said Alu.

Not that one. Rakhal waved a dismissive hand at the eastern horizon beyond the bamboos. There's a war in the towns, too. They need bombs. You watch; I'll be rich.

They did not answer. Maya raised the end of her sari to cover her open mouth. Alu stared at the piles in front of Rakhal, biting his lip. All of a sudden Rakhal whipped around, picked up a bottle and threw it high into the air.

Alu and Maya, sprinting through the bamboo, heard it smash harmlessly somewhere behind them. They heard Rakhal call out, laughing: There's nothing in it. . . . But they did not stop running till they reached the safety of the courtyard.

Alu leapt panting on to his bench at his loom. He had no time for bombs. At last, after days and days of persuasion, argument and reluctance, Shombhu Debnath had promised to teach him jamdani weaving.

The first lesson was a disappointment. Shombhu Debnath handed him a six-inch steel needle with a hook at one end. Get to know it like you know your own tool, he said. Better; you'll use it more. That'll be your god now. Kamthakur. The god of work. The god of jamdani.

Not much of a god, said Alu, fingering the hook.

You'll find out, Shombhu Debnath smiled. You'll find out if you ever learn.

For a long time it seemed as though he never would. His hands, too long accustomed to brute speed, fumbled when Shombhu Debnath tried to teach him to use the kamthakur to insert bits of coloured yarn parallel to the weft, between the warp strings of a ground-cloth. Every slip meant a tangle of torn warp yarn and an hour spent twisting the frayed ends of the delicate yarn together again. So every tangle meant a swish of Shombhu Debnath's cane, and a stinging cut across the shoulder and a jubilant smile: I told you so. You'll never learn. It's not in your blood.

Then, when he ought to have thrown the shuttle lightly across to fix the inlaid yarn into the ground-cloth with the weft, instead, out of habit, he would slam the shuttle across and the reed after it, like a stonemason wielding a jack-hammer, and the painfully inserted strip of yarn would become a thin smudge, when it ought to have stood out proudly, like a bas-relief, on the cloth. More swishes, more weals, more triumphant You'll-never-learns.

Alu ignored his smarting back and struggled to steady his hands. It was a bitter fight: to have to be a child again after once having conquered the loom. The trick was patience. He warred on himself, with Maya urging him on, until his thirst for speed ebbed away. Slowly, with joint-numbing pain, his fingers grew in deftness and skill. Through the whir of Shombhu Debnath's cane he learnt to build patterns – small geometrical ones first – with the tiny lengths of coloured yarn. Bleary-eyed, squinting, he learnt to cover a whole six-yard sari with figured patterns after a fortnight's back-breaking work.

And Shombhu Debnath drove him still harder, leaning over

his shoulder as he sat at the loom, the cane poised over his
knuckles. He started him on the classic patterns, the butis of
jamdani: the simple star, the tara-buti, and the heart-shaped
pan-buti. He made him draw the patterns on paper first, and
taught him to hold the pencilled outlines beneath the warp so
that his kamthakur, sifting between thousands of fine warp
threads, would never vary in its precision by so much as a
frayed strand of cotton.

Alu's butis spun out of his loom: perfect, precise, without
blemish.

Shombhu Debnath stopped watching him and began to
disappear into the forests again. But every week he would
leave a carelessly drawn pattern on Alu's loom. From those
tattered messages Alu put together the lotus, poddo-buti, and
the intricate ghor-buti, row after row of figured houses,
abstractions of shelter and peace. For his labours he earned
tooth-rattling thumps on his back from Rakhal: the traders of
Naboganj were willing to pay half as much again over the usual
price for his cloth. Money at last; plenty of it.

And then, one morning, Shombhu Debnath in a final
challenge threw down a pattern which covered his whole loom.
Alu hardly slept for days on end. At the end of it his loom rolled
out six yards covered with the dazzling pointillism of the
hundred thousand diamonds, the lokhkhohira-buti.

Give me another, another buti, something harder still, Alu
begged, at the feet of the Master.

Shombhu Debnath turned his face away: I have nothing
more to teach you. The time has come for you to grow from an
apprentice to a weaver. Skill is not enough; you have all that
you ever will. Technique is just the beginning. The world is
your challenge now. Look around you and see if your loom can
encompass it.

Alu looked.

Bomb-buti? Too dull, too easy, bottles and scraps and hints
of blood. Refugee-buti? Too much corrugated iron and leaning
tin sheets. Some angles were impossible with a kamthakur.
War-buti? Too much chaos; the loom demands order. Antisep-
tic-buti? Buckets in the air?

Instead, Alu conjured up six yards of majestic howdah'd
elephants, trunks curled over villages, lords of the world.

Politics-buti; nothing more immediate in the world, for that very week Bhudeb Roy had answered the call of the People and mounted a caparisoned elephant and toured Lalpukur and the villages around it to announce his plunge, his nose-dive, his lake-emptying leap into politics. Hundreds of the People had followed him, racing after the elephant, pushing and jostling, fighting to get at its shit. Elephant droppings make good manure.

Nervously Alu spread six yards of politics-buti in front of Shombhu Debnath.

Shombhu Debnath's red eyes flamed. He snatched up the cloth and ripped it apart. He flung it on the earth and ground it into the dust with his bare feet. He spat upon it, blew his nose upon it, and tried to vomit. When he finished there was no cloth left. Five hundred rupees of cotton and sweat swallowed by the dust.

Filth, he said, filth; uglier than the man and filthier. He smiled at Alu, not in triumph, but sadly: You can never learn jamdani because jamdani is dead, with the world which made it. Beauty doesn't exist; it is *made* like words or forts, by speakers and listeners, warriors and defenders, weavers and wearers. That world has washed away. Jamdani is only a toy for the wives of contractors and mahajans now. Stop now: no one can make a thing beautiful alone. No one would understand him. Only a madman would try. Stop now, or you'll be nothing but a toymaker, piecing together your politics-butis with these elephants and the filth that rides on them.

Shombhu Debnath was suddenly leering at him; his mouth fallen open, baring teeth that dripped like fangs. No, he said. I can't allow that. Wait. Wait a moment. I'll get you a knife. You can cut your thumbs off and give them to me. I'll pickle them in mustard oil and chillis and hang them up for the village to see – Alu grown to manhood at last.

Alu turned and ran – away from Shombhu Debnath's red eyes, his dripping blackened teeth, and ashen knot poised on his head like a nesting cobra – straight back to the safety of his loom. He sat there for a day and a half, scratching on cloth with his kamthakur. And then, one morning, while the village shook with the thunder of planes flying eastwards, his shuttle began its knocking again.

By the time Maya came back from Balaram's house, he had two rows finished. He called out to her and pushed the heddle up so that she could see the figures fresh upon the cloth.

What is it? she said, gazing at the cloth: firm, tip-tilted, dimpled shapes, like green mangoes on a branch.

What do you think it is? said Alu.

I don't know, said Maya. What?

It's Maya-buti.

Maya-buti! The back of her hand rose to cover her mouth. She shook with stifled laughter.

What's the matter? said Alu. Don't you like it? She kept her face covered.

All right, said Alu. He picked up a blade and bent down to cut the pattern off the loom. Maya darted forward and caught his hand. No, she cried. Let them be.

Alu sank back to the bench, and she drew her hand slowly back. He turned away, his fists clenched. Maya, he called out.

What?

Do you think if I talked to Balaram we could get married?

Married? Maya whispered. She sank on to her knees beside him. How could we get married? You're only sixteen; barely out of shorts.

What do you mean? Alu said angrily. Half the boys of my age in the village are already married.

Yes, said Maya, but their uncles aren't schoolteachers.

That doesn't matter; I'll talk to him.

No, said Maya sadly. I can't get married. Not now. Not till Rakhal marries. She raised her voice and shouted above the drone of another flight of planes: Who would look after them? And then a voice burst upon them, a hoarse, piercing wail. Maya leapt back and turned away, and a moment later Shombhu Debnath staggered into the courtyard. He made his way across, weaving drunkenly, and leant against one of the poles of the loom-shed. He thrust his face forward at Alu, until it was so close that Alu could feel the toddy steaming off his own face. No time for your butis now, he said. The radio's declared war, real war, with armies and planes.

Shombhu Debnath was wrong; not about the war, but about the butis.

With the beginning of the war, the stream pouring over the

border became a deluge. The boundaries of Lalpukur began to outrun Balaram and his buckets of carbolic. Balaram ran out of money. The new refugees hardly had bodies; they hadn't even the strength to laugh when he tried to raise a collection.

Balaram gave up. He staggered, exhausted, back to his study with a bucket in his hands. He put it on his knees and stared into its dry bottom. He reached into it, wet his fingers with the last few diluted drops of antiseptic and anointed his forehead. Beaten, he said. Beaten by filthy money.

But that very day Rakhal handed Alu more money than he had ever earned before. The busy traders of Naboganj (who were as busy as ever, following laws no war could suspend) had fought grim internecine battles of their own, over Maya-buti, and money had poured out of their iron-clad purses. So Alu worked as he had never worked before and Balaram had money for a new antiseptic offensive.

How tortuous, said Balaram, taking Alu's money, is the path of reason.

Later it was a puzzle. Sub-Inspector Jyoti Das lost himself in that labyrinth of cause and effect. While writing his report he found a newspaper-cutting in the file; a yellowed scrap of paper, left there perhaps by some conscientious clerk. 'Teacher battles with germs,' it said 'saves thousands.' The report claimed that Lalpukur had stayed germ-free when thousands of other villages on the border were consumed by disease, because of the efforts of one Balaram Bose, a teacher, who had doused the village in waves of antiseptic.

Even cheap disinfectants cost money. How could he afford it? Jyoti Das wondered. After all, Lalpukur wasn't Calcutta with its fund-raising drives, women's clubs melting discarded jewellery, and eager schoolboys skewering flags into collars, pinning them to the war effort.

He was in school, too, then, but the phalanxes of fund-raisers had not claimed him. He had had to live with a different worry. What would the purple herons do that winter? Where would they go, with shrieking planes circling their retreat and the air thick with the dust of worriers and warriors? The herons proved hardier than he had imagined. They were in the lake at the zoo as they always were, supercilious, undismayed by human strife.

But the antiseptic?

Extremists have money, said the Deputy Inspector-General, chewing cryptically. It comes across the border. That's why they're extremists.

Jyoti Das was not wholly satisfied. He put the matter to Bhudeb Roy, not without a note of accusation, for the only reference to Balaram in Bhudeb Roy's reports of that period was a short note which claimed that Balaram had wilfully and maliciously destroyed his best cabbage patch by drenching it with disinfectant.

How is it, Bhudeb-babu, said Jyoti Das, that your reports mentioned nothing of this business of fighting disease and all that?

I was busy then, Bhudeb Roy smiled blandly, with political matters.

Jyoti Das persisted: But tell me, Bhudeb-babu, where did he find the money for the antiseptic?

Who knows? Bhudeb Roy said with a vague wave. There was so much chaos then, the war seemed to be right in the village.

Yes? Jyoti Das prompted.

But he never had an answer. Bhudeb Roy didn't wish to speak of it. The war was right on us then, he said abruptly. It fell on us.

It did. It fell after a day of fearful silence, when a mist hung about the village till midday, and a gathering expectancy snaked through the huts and houses and hung in the air, as real and prickly as knotted hessian.

It was a day when people huddled into their houses and shacks. Nobody wanted to let themselves out into the fingers of the fog, though nobody could have said why. Perhaps it was the silence; the sudden muffling of the usual far-away bursts of shooting.

It grew worse as the day wore on. Early in the evening the fog crawled out of the ponds again, and a still, fetid dampness clamped itself on the village. It reached everywhere. It crept into Alu's loom and dampened the warp yarn and made it stick. Alu had to work slowly, painfully prising the yarn apart. He would have stopped, but a consignment had been promised to a hungry merchant in Naboganj and the work had to be done.

As the murky twilight was fading away, Maya brought him a

kerosene-lamp, and hung it from a nail in the loom-shed. Where's Rakhal? Alu asked.

In Naboganj, she answered.

And your father?

She jerked her head at his hut. He's in there, I think, she said. Sleeping.

She went to the kitchen and put a match to a lamp's wick. It would not light. She shook it and tried again. At that moment the roar of a plane overhead broke clammily through the fog, shaking the courtyard. The lamp fell from her hands and smashed on the earth. The flames leapt up for a moment, on the spilt kerosene, and died away. Maya stood transfixed for a moment, looking down at the blackened oil. Then she hitched up her sari and ran across the courtyard to the loom-shed.

What's the matter? said Alu, looking up from the loom.

I'm afraid. She reached forward and put a hand on his shoulder. She stood there for a while, watching him. Then she slipped down to the bench and Alu felt her thighs beside his and smelt her smoky warmth. He put out his hand and touched her cheek. She turned all at once, and threw her legs across his, and sat straddling him, her face on his, bouncing with the rhythm of his legs as they pushed the pedals of the loom. Don't stop, she whispered urgently into his ear, he'll wake up if you do.

Alu jerked on the shuttle-cord again, and the shuttle shot across, while she tore at the buttons of his trousers, ripped them off and thrust her hands inside. Don't stop, she hissed again. Then, with a heave of her hips, she threw her thin sari up, past her waist. She flung her arms around his neck, pressed her knees to his ribs, and sank upon him.

Don't stop, she cried into his ear, faster, and the shuttle pounded through the parted, twitching limbs of the warp, and the cloth poured out, tangled and damp; gushed forth, in a surge of joyful abundance, till the sky burst, with an explosion which sent a gale tearing through the bamboos and seared the tips of the mango trees, and the fog flared scarlet over the village while hundreds of glowing sparks fell out of the sky.

The whole village was running, stumbling through the fog, before Alu and Maya were out of the courtyard. They picked their way through the murky darkness of the bamboo thickets, tripping on shoots and stumps, helping each other along. Then at the edge of the thickets they heard someone crashing through the bamboo. The noise grew louder and they stopped, holding each other's hand, and peered into the grey fog. They could see nothing but the swaying outlines of bamboo. Then the footsteps were upon them, and Maya screamed.

It's only me, Shombhu Debnath gasped, panting for breath.

Maya, stupefied: But weren't you at home, sleeping?

No, no, he said. He smiled crookedly. I'm going home now. Now, go. Run. Go and see. It's a plane, fallen out of the sky, on the school.

He stumbled off in the darkness, and they ran out of the bamboos, into the lanes, and with the rest of the village they poured down into the school, and craned over the shoulders of the crowd which had got there before them and caught a glimpse of a flaming fuselage, driven into the earth like a broken stake.

Beside it, sitting quite still, legs crossed, her face brilliantly lit by the flames, was Parboti-debi. She was staring up into the sky, oblivious of the crowd, all her haggardness vanished, smiling serenely, gratefully.

Chapter Four

Signs of New Times

The plane was like an exclamation mark fallen on Lalpukur from the sky. The war ended a few days after the crash, and not long after some of the refugees flowed back to the new country across the border, and the others wandered off to the cities or spread out over the country. Soon they were half-forgotten.

But nobody in Lalpukur forgot the crash.

The professional interpreters of portents split immediately: a proper fight had long been in the offing anyway, ever since the numerologists had ganged up with the astrologers against the palmists and sabotaged a move for a licensing system and a union to guarantee uniform rates for predictions irrespective of methods used. After the crash things took a new turn. The numerologists assumed the leadership of the End of the World Signalled camp and heaped scorn on the palmists and their theory of Signs of New Times. Whose palm do you read an aircrash on? they sneered. God's? The astrologers, warily neutral for once, took the conservative view that it meant nothing at all: crashes and tempests and earthquakes were normal in Kaliyug. What else could you expect in the Age of Evil?

But they're wrong, said Balaram, telling Gopal the story on his veranda in Calcutta. If it has no meaning, why would it happen? Of course it has a meaning, but the meaning must be read rationally – not with the hocus-pocus of these Stone Age magicians.

Balaram stopped and looked at Gopal with a hint of a challenge glinting in his eyes. Of course, he said, some people think it rational to believe that events *don't* have a meaning.

Gopal looked away and blew wearily into his cup of tea. With Balaram forty years weren't enough to forget an argument.

Balaram was lying in a chaotic, noisy general ward in the

Medical College Hospital, his legs encased in plaster, like
gigantic boiled eggs. He could have had a private room had he
wished. Dantu and the others who had rushed down from the
first-floor balcony to the flower-bed where Balaram lay writhing in agony had tried to persuade him to take one. They
knew his father could afford it. But even then, between
screams of pain, Balaram had managed to sob: No, my father
mustn't know. So Balaram had gone into the general ward and
Dantu had decided not to write to his father about the accident.

Accident, he called it. There were others at that fateful
meeting at the top of the stairs on the first floor of the
Presidency College building (led by Middle Parting and his
unremorseful friends) who called it the Fool's Fall.

Almost two days had passed before Gopal heard of it. One
evening Dantu, his hollow face haggard and strained, knocked
at the door of the room he was staying in then. Gopal, he said
pleading, sucking his teeth in distress, can you come with me
to see Balaram now? I can't face him alone – not with what I
have to say to him.

Come where? Gopal said in surprise.

To the hospital, of course.

Hospital? Gopal cried. What do you mean?

Dantu took off his spectacles and squinted at him: Don't you
know? And then he hit himself on the thigh. Of course, he
exclaimed, no one remembered to tell you about it. I was too
busy with Balaram in the hospital, and the other
Rationalists . . . well, there aren't any other Rationalists now.
Those who haven't gone over to the Science Association are
busy trying to keep out of sight.

Gopal caught his arm and dragged him into the room, and
later they almost ran all the way to the hospital. When they
reached the foot of Balaram's bed, Gopal saw him smiling
through the twin white mounds of his plastered legs and he
collapsed on to a chair.

Balaram surveyed them calmly: Well? There was no answer.
Gopal panted helplessly, staring at the white expanse of
plaster. In the end it was Dantu who broke the silence.

Balaram, he said abruptly, I've come to tell you that I'm
leaving the Rationalists, too.

Balaram nodded as though he had expected it; and Dantu,

who had braced himself for an argument, was suddenly
deflated. I told you, he said weakly, I told you it wouldn't work.
I told you it was a mad idea.

Balaram shrugged, smiling: But I had to try, didn't I?
Grimacing, Dantu began to drum on the rusty steel bedpost.

And you, Dantu? Balaram said. Are you joining the Science
Association, too?

Dantu snorted: You should know better than that, Balaram.
He began to say something else, stopped, and toed the floor
meditatively. Then with a long sigh he patted Balaram's plaster
casts. All right, Balaram, he said, I'll go now.

Quickly Balaram called out: Wait. He reached under his
pillow and drew out a book wrapped in a tattered brown-paper
cover. Give me your pen, he said to Gopal and, taking it, began
to scribble on the title-page.

When he had finished he held the book out to Dantu. Here's
something for you, he said gravely. Look after it; put it in that
old bookcase of yours.

The book fell open in Dantu's hands and he saw that it was
the *Life of Pasteur*. Biting his lip, he squeezed Balaram's
shoulder. Don't worry, he said. I'll look after it. He raised the
book in a brief salute, and hurried away.

Don't lose it, Balaram called out after him. You'll need it
someday; someday it'll help you remember Reason.

It's all my fault, Gopal said afterwards, wringing his hands.
I'm responsible, no one else. I shouldn't have let it happen.

What could you have done? said Balaram.

I don't know, but I shouldn't have let it happen. I knew it
would happen, I knew it. I should never have let you become
president of the Rationalists. I foresaw it: I knew you would
bring disaster on yourself and the society if you ever became
president.

Balaram laughed and winced a moment later, as a spasm of
pain shot out of his legs. Do you really think, he groaned, that
there was anything you could do about it? You're wrong if you
do. Nothing you or I could have done would have made any
difference. This happened because it had to happen. There's a
meaning in it – for me.

Oh God, thought Gopal, he's going to start lecturing again,
in this state. Aloud he said: Balaram, don't start making up one

of your theories again. There's no meaning in this. It was just an accident. You shouldn't have run and you shouldn't have jumped. They wouldn't have done anything at all. It was just a moment's foolishness – an accident. Now you should rest.

Balaram pounced on the inconsistency: If it was just an accident, why did you say you shouldn't have let it happen? Nobody can prevent accidents.

Gopal, confused, said huffily: Don't be silly, Balaram, and you shouldn't argue in this state. It *was* an accident. Everybody says so. And accidents happen by chance. Chance doesn't have a meaning – that's why it's chance.

Balaram chuckled with delight and winced again. An event, he said, is what you make of it. You don't really believe it was an accident, either. It had a meaning, and you know what the meaning was. You just said so. I shouldn't have run. I should have stood my ground. I know that now, and next time I *shall* stand my ground, for Reason has nothing to fear.

Balaram, Gopal said wearily, it was just an accident.

It wasn't any ordinary accident, Balaram said. And the proof of it is that it fell into the lap of the man who could make the best use of it. All right, you tell me, when that plane had a whole country, a whole state, a whole district, a whole village to choose from, why did it crash on Bhudeb Roy's school, a few yards away from his wife? Why?

Why? echoed Gopal.

Because that plane was a gift from the sky.

And from the very first hour Bhudeb Roy showed that he was not the man to throw away a gift.

After he had led Parboti-debi back to the safety of their house, he went back to the school and took charge at once of the villagers' haphazard fire-fighting efforts. Under his coolly efficient direction they soon reduced the flaming wreck to a sizzling, steaming heap of metal. But they could not prevent more than half the school from burning down. When the last embers were finally stamped out, only a few rooms, including Bhudeb Roy's office, were left standing.

Bhudeb Roy did not pause for an instant. He called for the tough young men who collected his rents from the shanties. At the same time he sent his sons out to recruit a few more. Within half an hour he had twenty willing and hungry young recruits. He armed them with stout wooden sticks and ordered them to herd the villagers out of the school grounds. When that was done he deployed them around the school and left them to guard it through the night.

Next morning, after breakfasting, he went to the school and conducted a careful inspection to make sure that the wreck of the aeroplane had not been tampered with at night. Then he had his office desk carried out. He placed it carefully in the shade of a remnant of the school's veranda. He wedged himself behind it, spread a cash register open and sent his sons out to let it be known that he was ready to take bids.

Soon a crowd thronged into the school, and Bhudeb Roy was glad that he had had the foresight to organize a private army to keep things under control. Under the watchful eyes of his lean young men, the bids poured in, in a well-organized, disciplined kind of way.

Bolai-da decided that the metal sheets of the fuselage would make a good roof for his expanding cycle and hardware shop. It would be a kind of advertisement as well: people would go out of their way to visit a shop which had an aeroplane for a roof. And, besides, at the time business was so good that he had money to waste. So he made an opening bid of five hundred rupees. But other people had the same idea. In the long run good steel or aluminium or whatever it was, polished and factory-made anyway, would be cheaper than corrugated iron. In the end Bolai-da outlasted the others – he was a little carried away by the sight of all that shining silvery metal and its cabalistic decorations of figures and numbers – but he had to pay almost a thousand rupees.

Parts of the wings sold well, too: people bought them to put across ditches and canals as tidy little bridges. Bhudeb Roy managed to coax a total of five bridges out of those two wings. He sold them for four hundred rupees each. There were good bits of glass to dispose of after that, and rubber, and a whole heap of nuts and bolts.

Bhudeb Roy did well that day. In the evening, after every little scrap had been sold, he plodded back to his house, happily rubbing the folds of flesh on the back of his neck. He called his sons into a room and passed around wads of notes. He smiled as he watched them sensuously running their fingers over the rustling paper. That's right, he said, his tiny eyes bulging. You can't ever know what money means unless you feel it.

Later, he assembled his twenty or so young men outside his house and handed out bonuses. They had hardly dared expect so much money so soon. They burst into cheers – jug-jug-jiyo, Bhudeb-dada, jug-jug-jiyo – and ran off to their shacks and shanties to buy food for their families. That was perhaps the only false note in the whole day. They were gone by the time Bhudeb Roy had heaved himself up the stairs to his balcony so that he would be able to acknowledge their cheers properly. He found himself waving and bowing at an empty courtyard. But he didn't let it spoil his mood; later he could teach them to do things properly. At that moment he had nothing but goodwill for the world. In his elation, he even told one of his sons to take a sackful of coconuts over to Balaram's house.

You see, Toru-debi told Balaram in the kitchen that night while they were eating their dinner, in his own way Bhudeb-babu really likes you. He respects you; he wants your friendship. He's a nice man in his own way just like everybody else. If only you read a little less and knew the world a little more.

Balaram frowned and would not look at her. She turned to Alu, who had finished and was sitting quietly on his piri licking his fingers. You tell him, she appealed. You tell him, because he won't listen to me. Why can't he just live and let live? Why can't we just live in peace like everyone else?

Balaram bit grimly into a fried fish-head. Toru-debi looked helplessly at him.

After he had washed his hands Alu went back into the kitchen. Balaram had gone back to his study. Don't worry, Alu said to Toru-debi. Nothing will happen. She bit her lip and shook her head, trying to keep her tears back. Something *will* happen, she said. I know it will; I've seen it in my dreams. But still I'll do what I can to stop it. I'll keep on trying as long as I can.

So the next evening Toru-debi decided to go and meet Parboti-debi. It was a long time since she had left the house, and years since she had been to visit anyone.

Sari chosen, face powdered, she picked her way down the path mumbling: First I'll say, Parboti, where have you been?

haven't seen you, haven't seen you for months. And all that.
Then: Such nice coconuts. . . . Then: What about some
blouses? I'll make you some blouses. Six.

One of Bhudeb Roy's sons, swinging on the gate, spotted her
coming down the path in a white sari and peacock-green
blouse, swinging a brown shopping-bag, her hair hanging
down in knots, her face like a streaky white mask. He called out
to his brothers and they all ran out to the gate and watched her,
sniggering.

They led her into a room that was crowded with cloth-
covered sofas and pictures of Bhudeb Roy. She sat down,
clutching her empty bag, and said: Parboti . . .?

She's sick, said the oldest boy, fingering his moustache. She
can't come out.

Toru-debi waited for ten minutes, surrounded by the boys,
while a cup of tea and biscuits were fetched for her. What
should I do? she thought, pulling at the knots in her hair. Go
away? Stay? How'll I tell Parboti? She drank her tea so fast it
scalded her tongue, and rushed out. She stood under the
balcony and shouted up: Parboti, I'll make you six blouses. Tell
Bhudeb-babu. It's all right: six blouses.

Walking worriedly down the path, swinging her bag, she
thought: I've done what I can; it's in Ma Kali's hands now. Soon
she was back listening to the reassuring drone of her sewing
machine and the blouses were forgotten.

A few days later the whole village learnt that Bhudeb Roy
had been given several thousand rupees by an insurance
company as compensation for the burnt parts of the school.
Everybody was taken by surprise. Very few people had heard
of insurance, and almost no one knew that buildings could be
insured. Certainly nobody had known that the school buildings
were insured. The question which flew around the banyan tree
and the tea-shop and Bolai-da's shop was *when* had Bhudeb
Roy insured the building.

Soon a curious crowd was paying daily court to Bhudeb Roy.
He enjoyed it immensely but made sure his hired men were
never too far away to prevent indiscipline. People brought him
disputes to settle, questions to answer, and they heard many of
his views on the world, but nobody had the courage to put the
real question to him.

In the end, by common consent it fell to Bolai-da, because ever since Bolai-da had accompanied Bhudeb Roy on his visit to his patch of toddy palms people had assumed that he had a special claim on Bhudeb Roy. They pushed Bolai-da forward and urged him on, but it took him a while to pick up the courage. Finally, one evening, with fingers prodding him in the small of his back, Bolai-da cleared his throat. By that time, the years had twisted Bolai-da's face incurably sideways and curved it outwards, like a crescent moon. His lower jaw had moved an inch or so away from the upper, so that he had to speak out of a gap at the corner of his mouth. Bhudeb-babu, he said, squinting with concentration, tell me, *when* exactly did you insure the school?

Bhudeb Roy, chewing slowly on a plug of tobacco, said: Exactly fifteen days before the crash.

His electrified audience gasped. All those years to do it in, or not to do it in, and he had done it fifteen days before the crash.

Bolai-da swallowed and sucked his teeth. Bhudeb-babu, he said, tell us, did you *know*?

Bhudeb Roy did not answer. He looked away, into the far distance, and his bulging jaw chewed steadily sideways, while a smile slowly worked its way across it.

That night they went back to Bolai-da's shop in awestruck silence. Was it possible? No, it couldn't be. Even Bhudeb Roy couldn't have shot down a plane all by himself. But, then, said Bolai-da wagging his head, it was certainly more than mere coincidence.

The very next day, with his insurance money in his pocket, Bhudeb Roy hired a truck and took his sons and his twenty young men to Naboganj. He bought them T-shirts and a few knuckledusters and handed out another bonus. On its way back the truck scattered a triumphant cloud of dust over the village, while Bhudeb Roy sat massively enthroned on it, surrounded by his sons and the young men, acknowledging their cheers: jug-jug-jiyo, Bhudeb-dada, jug-jug-jiyo.

All the other hungry young men, sitting under the banyan tree thinking of ways to finance cycle-rickshaws, were lashed by envy when they saw the bright T-shirts flash by. They cursed the fate which had singled out their onetime friends while leaving them stranded under the banyan tree, as hungry as ever. That night they begged Bolai-da: You talk to Bhudeb-babu. He listens to you. Tell him he needs some more people. Bolai-da blew through the corner of his mouth and shook his head: No, no, how can I? And, besides, why me? But of course he was flattered that they had chosen him to be their spokesman, and it did not take them very much longer to persuade him to lead them to Bhudeb Roy's house.

So, in a procession, with flaming torches, they marched down the lanes, shouting: jug-jug-jiyo, Bhudeb-dada, jug-jug-jiyo. The twenty young men, who were lounging on Bhudeb Roy's veranda, heard them when they turned into the red-dust path which led to the house. They were not slow to recognize a threat. Snatching up their sticks and their knuckledusters, they rushed out of the house, like wolves swarming to defend a kill. Bhudeb Roy's sons, who lacked their fine streamlining, floundered after them, panting.

Shatup goddam fool-fuckers, waking Master, shut your traps and all this hungama-business, stinky-smelly goondas and chhokra-boys.

But razor blades and sticks and cycle chains appeared magically in Bolai-da's followers' hands, too. So, in a barrage of shouts and insults, the two groups held off for a moment and each managed to push their leaders in front, while somehow conveying the impression that they were actually trying to hold them back.

Bolai-da stepped into the breach. He twisted his face haughtily sideways and out of the corner of his mouth he whistled: We want nothing to do with the likes of you. We want to meet Bhudeb-babu.

Bhudeb Roy heard him, for the commotion had drawn him out into the garden. Let them come in, he roared. I'll hear them.

The twenty young men drew back, with extreme misgiving. They couldn't help doling out a few pinches to the stragglers and pulling a bit of hair. Bhudeb Roy rolled his little eyes when he saw the crowd and growled: What is it now, Bolai? Bolai-da smiled his most ingratiating smile and said: Bhudeb-babu, these young fellows want some work, too. They're as good as the others. Why not hire them, too?

Bhudeb Roy rolled his eyes over the ragged young men and smiled. He put his arm across Bolai-da's shoulders and led him aside. You see, Bolai, he whispered in a whisper which resounded around the garden, what this village needs is a kick in the arse, something to get it moving. I've tried kindness and persuasion but it doesn't work. There's something wrong with the basic character of the people. They're illiterate like you, not educated like me. They need a kick in the arse. But, then, someone has to do the kicking and someone has to provide the arse. If everyone was kicking, do you see what I mean, what would become of the arse? You understand me?

Bolai-da nodded, thinking hard. But then he said: Bhudeb-babu, can't you give them something to do? How will they live? They need work, too.

Bhudeb Roy thought for a moment and rubbed his huge flat forehead. His fingers touched on a bump and suddenly a smile of dawning revelation spread itself across his jaw. Why, he said, let them make straight lines. Straight lines are the best way of moving ahead, the shortest distance between two points. You tell them that: the need of the hour is straight lines.

The twenty young men, smiling with sly satisfaction, ushered Bolai-da and the others out of the garden.

It was sometime that week that Balaram first noticed the organ of Order sprouting obscenely on Bhudeb Roy's eyebrows.

About ten days later two jeeps full of uniformed men were spotted turning into the dust track which led off the main road to the village. The village had emptied long before they reached the banyan tree. The blue-uniforms didn't seem to notice. The jeeps drove straight to the school and the uniformed men fanned out over the yard, inspecting the pit the crash had made and picking up stray nuts and bolts and shavings of metal. Then the jeeps roared and wheeled, and drove straight to Bhudeb Roy's house.

Nobody ever really learnt what happened there, but over the next two days the blue-uniforms went unerringly to the shops with sheet-metal roofs, the canals bridged by reinforced steel, the rickshaws decorated with shiny bolts, and recovered every last bit of scrap the plane had deposited in the village. All

that anyone knew was that when the jeeps drove out ranks of
blue-uniformed arms appeared in the windows waving cordi-
ally to Bhudeb Roy, and he waved back, smiling happily.

Naturally Bolai-da was chosen to lead the delegation of
villagers who marched to Bhudeb Roy's house to ask for their
money back. They were stopped at the gates by the twenty
young men and Bolai-da was singled out and led into the house.
Bhudeb Roy met him in a dark empty room. His little eyes in
their bulging sockets were suddenly very menacing. What do
you want? he spat at Bolai-da.

Well, that is to say, Bhudeb-babu, Bolai-da managed to
stutter, we were just wondering, since we paid you all that
money for those bits of the plane, and since they've been taken
back now, shouldn't we – er – perhaps, get our money back? No
one richer, no one poorer, all quits.

Bhudeb Roy's eyebrows shot forward. His jaws opened as
though they would have liked to fasten on Bolai-da's scrawny
neck. Be grateful, he roared, that you're not in gaol for being
found in possession of government property. Do you know who
you owe it to? Me. Me. Me. Should I charge you lawyer's fees?
You'll end up even poorer. If you know what's good for you,
you and all your bad-element friends will start working on
straight lines instead of hanging around the banyan tree, doing
nothing but rearing your heads and thinking anti-social
thoughts.

Bolai-da was led out in a hurry by one of the young men. The
other young men began to rattle their sticks and shine their
knuckledusters, and the whole delegation was soon hurrying
down the lane jaldi-toot-sweet.

Nobody ever talked of getting their money back again. After
that, people said, not a bird chirruped in Lalpukur but with
Bhudeb Roy's permission, and under the supervision of his
twenty young men.

And then, a couple of months later, someone spotted
Parboti-debi, who had disappeared for a while, on the veranda
of their house. She was unmistakably pregnant.

Calendars of every sort and variety, sweetshop and govern-
ment-issue, Bikrami, Hegiraic and Gregorian, rustled under
the banyan tree that night. The conclusions of the Bikrami
were supported by the Hegiraic and were not contradicted by

the Gregorian. But still people couldn't believe it. They woke the oldest midwife in the village and put the problem to her. She had no doubts, either.

The plane had conceived the child. There could be no other conclusion. Nobody could believe Bhudeb Roy capable of fathering another child (though gossip had it that hardly a night passed without his trying). It had to be the plane. Or at any rate it had happened on the night of the crash, which was the same thing. The heavens had intervened. The plane was a gigantic chrome-plated penis thrown down by the skies to Bhudeb Roy's wife; a sort of metallic, heavenly starch, sent to stiffen Bhudeb Roy's ageing member.

Bolai-da led another awestruck delegation to Bhudeb Roy. Be generous, Bhudeb-babu, he pleaded. Allow her to come out of her seclusion. After all, if she has the gift, shouldn't she share it with the rest of the village? The barren women of the village would worship her, and you, if she would only agree just to touch them. Perhaps you could even charge a fee.

Bhudeb Roy was so gratified by the speech that he actually giggled. Nothing would have pleased him more than the buttressing of his mundane powers with an element of the supernatural. Bolai-da swore later that Bhudeb Roy went into the house right then, and for a full half-hour argued with Parboti-debi and scolded her, urging her to go into the village with the delegation. But for once Parboti-debi, usually so compliant, was adamant. She would not go. The delegation returned, disappointed, and nobody saw Parboti-debi again during her confinement.

When the child was born, the whole village was invited to the house to see the baby and feast on sweetmeats, and nobody had any doubts about its divine instigation left.

The child was a girl, and it was well known that Bhudeb Roy had long wished for a daughter. And she was beautiful, far more beautiful than any child Bhudeb Roy could have fathered unaided. She was obviously sickly, but still the most beautiful child anybody had ever seen – eyes like liquid jet, skin like honeyed milk, hair like curled ebony.

Like everybody else, Bhudeb Roy interpreted the birth of the child as a sign. It was probably at that time that he first began to think of closing the school down. He had kept it going somehow, in the two or three rooms that were left standing. But it had long been clear that the school was only a diversion which took away time from politics, from his children, from money, from the village.

But the day he finally decided – when the child was less than a year old and still sickly – it was only after an immense effort. After all, he had devoted a large part of his life to the school; it was a testament to a youth he was still loath to part with. There was some vanity in it, too: he liked to walk down those corridors looking at pictures of himself and he liked to hear visitors' compliments.

The tears which rolled down his cheeks on the day he invited the villagers into the school to hear his last speech as headmaster were therefore very real and painful tears. When his twenty young men led in the villagers, the tears were pouring down in a stream. Through his own he saw answering tears in the crowd. Don't worry, he wept, waving a consoling hand at the garlanded pictures of himself which had been arrayed behind him on the podium. These aren't going away. They're going to be closer to you than ever. They'll be right among you, everywhere, in the banyan tree, in your houses, in your shops. You'll never be far from me.

The tears flowed faster as he read accusations into the crowd's silent, fixed gaze. I couldn't help it, he cried. It had to come to an end. It was a good school in its time, but that time is past. A new time beckons. The time to teach is over. The time has come to serve the people.

The time has come, he said, his tears drying on his cheeks, for straight lines. The trouble with this village is that there aren't enough straight lines. Look at Europe, look at America, look at Tokyo: straight lines, that's the secret. Everything is in straight lines. The roads are straight, the houses are straight, the cars are straight (except for the wheels). They even walk straight. That's what we need: straight lines. There's a time and an age for everything, and this is the age of the straight line.

He stopped and his eyes scanned the crowd. Unerringly, with an inevitable certainty, they found Balaram, his *alter ego*, his *doppelgänger*, the twin who had journeyed with him so long through the same school, and there was not a soul in that schoolyard who would not have sworn that he was asking Balaram for his approval.

But Balaram was looking away, his face strained with concentration, his head cocked, for all the world as though he were listening to a voice. But that voice was not Bhudeb Roy's.

Do you think that was when he thought of it? Alu asked Gopal one day when he was in hiding in Calcutta after it was all over.

Yes, said Gopal sadly, he told me so. In a way it was only natural – he had to think of something. After all, the closing of the school meant the end of his livelihood. But Balaram being what he was, of course, that was the last thing on his mind. By that time he was certain that Bhudeb Roy was lying about his reasons for closing the school down. He was quite convinced that it was really the carbolic or antiseptic or whatever it was. He told me so. He said: Bhudeb Roy lives in mortal fear; there is nothing in the world that he fears as much as carbolic acid. His whole life is haunted by his fear of antiseptic. He'd do anything, go to any lengths to destroy my carbolic acid. He fears it as he fears everything that is true and clean and a child of Reason. He's closing the school down because he thinks it'll put an end to my work with disinfectants.

Of course, it all seemed very strange to me, so I said: But, Balaram, be reasonable. Surely he could find other ways of putting an end to your work with carbolic acid? Maybe he really *is* busy and wants more time for his work or politics or something like that. . . .

Balaram was very angry. He said: Don't be a fool, Gopal. I know that man. I've grown old with him. I've watched Ideality and Wonder and Hope disappear into depressions in his skull, and I've watched his squamous suture bloat like a dead dog in a ditch. There's nothing I don't know about that man. I know him better than I know myself. And I know this: he lives in terror of carbolic acid, and he'll do anything he can to destroy my supplies. But I've learnt my lessons, too, and he won't find it easy. I'll fight him to the end. I know how. I knew it when he started talking about straight lines.

So that was when the idea came to him. That was when the battle lines were finally drawn.

(Gopal had always had the romantic spectator's tendency to dramatize.)

That was when the Pasteur School of Reason was conceived in Balaram's mind.

Chapter Five

The School of Reason

People were always surprised to discover that Balaram had a
genuine flair for organization.

The Rationalists, for instance, even Dantu, were no less than
amazed at the energy, determination and capacity for attention
to detail he showed once he set to work in earnest after being
elected president. Many of them were frankly admiring. That
alone was a considerable achievement, for it was quite a
different matter when Balaram first put his idea to them soon
after his election. They were quite horrified then.

After the first shocked silence someone had managed to
croak hoarsely: A campaign against dirty underwear? Balaram
nodded cheerfully while dubious glances perforated the silence. The gloom deepened, for no one knew what to say. It had
come as a shock: dirty underwear was tough meat after a diet of
salutations to the Cosmic Boson and exposés of mythologized
fireworks.

But, Balaram, do we know, is there any concrete evidence to
suggest, that Pasteur felt as strongly about dirty underwear as
you seem to think?

Balaram had an answer ready: No, there's no direct evidence, really; but, as you know, biographers often skip over
great men's opinions on these somewhat . . . unconven-
tional . . . subjects. But I don't think there can be much doubt
that he felt strongly on the subject. We know, for example, that
whenever Pasteur sat down to eat he would first pick up his
plate and his glasses and examine them minutely, and then
he'd carefully wipe them clean of germs with his handkerchief.
He'd do that wherever he happened to be, no matter whether
his host was a king or a dishwasher. Petty social conventions
never worried Pasteur. If he felt so strongly about crockery, we
don't have to think very hard to imagine his views on underwear.

But most of the members of the society were far from convinced. There was a plaintive cry from the back of the room: Why does it have to be a campaign against underwear? Can't we think of something else? Couldn't we start a campaign to teach people the principles of hygiene or something like that instead?

To everyone's surprise that aroused the usually mild-mannered Balaram actually to pound his fist on his palm. Don't you see? he cried in appeal. That's the whole point. The Principles of Hygiene are exactly the same thing as the Cosmic Boson or the last pterodactyl. They're all like interesting books which you can thumb through and put back on your shelf without once feeling a need to change yourself or your own life in any way at all. That is precisely what we *don't* want: we've had enough of that kind of thing. We want something immediate, something none of us can turn our backs on; something which holds a new picture of ourselves in front of our eyes and says: Look! This is what you must become! Maybe we can't do very much, but at least we can make a beginning. All we want to do is make people think. And what better place to begin with than the body and its clothing? No one can turn his back on his body and his own clothes. If only we can sow the germ of a question in their minds, their own clothes and limbs will do the rest for us. They'll become daily reminders, daily pinpricks, to shake them out of their smugness.

But, Balaram – a shame-faced cough from a new member – think of the embarrassment. How can we talk of underwear in public? What will people say?

Balaram smiled at him gently. Our embarrassment will be the first sign of our victory. If we're embarrassed, it will be *because* the matter is so close to us; *because* talking of our underwear in public means thinking about ourselves in a new and different way. None of us was embarrassed to talk about the Cosmic Boson precisely because it meant so little to us. This is different, and for that very reason we must expect, indeed hope, to be embarrassed.

And just then, when the issue was as good as decided, Dantu rose to his feet. Balaram, he said, everyone here knows that we are friends. They know that I've never had any doubt that you are the best person to be president of this society. But today –

and I wish it were not so – today I have to say that on this business I think you're absolutely, totally wrong.

Balaram glanced quickly around the room. He could see from the watchful faces around him that everything hung in the balance now; that his answer would decide the future of his enterprise. He clasped his hands before him and leant back: Why?

Because I can't help remembering what you said to Gopal once in this very room. You said: What good will it do anyone if the people of Hindusthan begin to chant *He Boson* instead of *He Ram*? I think you have to answer the same question today. What good will it do anyone if the students of this college begin to wash their underwear not only every day, but also every hour? Will it make any difference to anyone? Dirt doesn't lie in underwear. It is the world, the world of people, which makes dirt possible. How can you hope to change people's bodies without changing the world?

A painfully slow moment dragged by. Then, very gravely, Balaram said: Why do we always think of changing the world and never of changing people? Surely, surely, if we succeed in making even one person, just one, ask of himself how can *I* be a better, cleaner human being, we *will* have changed the world; changed it in the best of possible ways.

Dantu hesitated, torn between loyalty to Balaram and his own beliefs. He could sense that Balaram had carried the others with him.

It's a mistake, Balaram, he said quickly, a terrible mistake – you'll see. And then he dropped on to the mat and huddled back against the wall.

There were no more objections. A small but enthusiastic group volunteered to help Balaram organize the campaign. Dantu said nothing more about the matter. Once, days later, when Balaram tried to talk to him about it, he murmured sadly: It won't work, Balaram, you'll see. I only hope nothing terrible happens. And he went racing off to a lecture and left Balaram standing in the middle of the corridor.

There were a few other sceptics among the Rationalists who whispered behind their hands that this was just another of Balaram's fancy ideas. He wouldn't be able to do anything about it – how could anyone organize a campaign for clean underwear? It was just a lot of talk; he wouldn't even be able to begin when it came to it.

Balaram proved them wrong.

He began by racking his brains for a catchy name for the campaign. A few days' thought produced: The Campaign for Clean Clouts. The majority of the Rationalists were enthusiastic. Some went so far as to call it a masterpiece of alliteration. But one of the English literature people objected: It's an archaism; no one will know what it means. Balaram swept him aside: All the better; it'll make them curious.

He decided to launch the campaign with a public meeting. The venue was a problem at first. A few of the Rationalists argued that it ought to be held in a lecture room. Balaram considered the proposal quite seriously but eventually decided against it. Lecture rooms, he said, are no better than bookshelves; as soon as you enter one you know that everything inside is dead. Instead he decided to hold the meeting at the top of the great flight of stairs which lead up from the portico in the main building of Presidency College to the wide veranda of the first floor. No one can ignore it there, he said. They'll come in their hundreds, you'll see.

After that Balaram wrote out notices announcing the meeting. He kept the notices deliberately vague. They said only: Meeting to launch the Campaign for Clean Clouts – come, see, listen and begin a new life. Underneath he wrote the date and the time in small but distinct letters.

Over the next two weeks Balaram leaked the notices out a few at a time. He stuck a few up on pillars and in other prominent places, but always took them down a few hours later. Occasionally he slipped one or two into a few chosen rooms in the Eden Hindu Hostel. People will be more intrigued, he explained, if there aren't too many of them.

It worked. Days before the meeting there was a buzz of curiosity in the college and in the hostel. The Rationalists were under strict instructions to say nothing; but a few, as Balaram had calculated, could not help dropping scattered hints. That only served to whet the general curiosity.

When the day came, even the most sceptical of the Rationalists admitted that they had been wrong. The meeting was a triumph for Balaram even before it began. There were no less than a hundred and fifty students crowded on to those stairs. Middle Parting and his friends were conspicuous in the centre of the crowd. They were as boisterous as ever, but they were also curious. When Balaram, shivering with nervousness but immensely elated, climbed on to a chair to begin the meeting, the crowd was still growing. It was the best possible tribute to his talent for organization.

So Balaram was perhaps the only person in Lalpukur who was *not* surprised by the success of the Pasteur School of Reason. He had a shrewd appreciation of his own abilities.

Once the idea of the Pasteur School of Reason had been conceived in his mind, Balaram had no doubt that he would be able to organize the school successfully. But he was also astute enough to know that he would have to work hard to make other people share his optimism. He had learnt that lesson from his experience with the Rationalists.

He was not wrong. Shombhu Debnath burst into frank laughter when Balaram first put the idea to him. You're wrong, Balaram-babu, he said hoarsely, you couldn't be more wrong. I'm no teacher. I certainly wouldn't be able to teach in a school.

Balaram was determined to be patient. Shombhu Debnath was essential to his plans. He thought for a moment, looking around him at Shombhu Debnath's bare courtyard, dappled by the failing evening light. He gripped the edge of the rickety chair that had been carried out for him and leant forward, towards Shombhu Debnath, who was squatting on the earth. You're a very good teacher, he said and he pointed at Alu, who was working in the loom-shed. Look how well you've taught Alu. It's your duty to teach others as well. There are so many people in the village today who have nothing to do, no way of earning a living. You could teach them a way, and you must. It's your duty, not just to them, but to yourself. Teaching is your destined vocation – it's written all over your skull. You *cannot* squander your gifts. You could teach them your craft and together we could teach them more than a craft. We could show them the beginning of a new history.

Shombhu Debnath snorted. You can keep your history, he said, picking at his blackened teeth with a blade of grass. I don't want anything to do with it. Whenever people like you start talking about history you can be sure it means nothing but trouble for people like me.

He rose to his feet and looked away. No, Balaram-babu, he said, you're wasting your time. There's no point in going on with this.

Suddenly he paused and his red eyes narrowed. Does this business have anything to do with Bhudeb Roy? he said sharply.

Certainly not, said Balaram.

But this . . . school *will* be right next to Bhudeb Roy's house? I mean, it *will* be in your house? Will it?

Balaram nodded eagerly. Shombhu Debnath smiled. His red eyes gleamed at Balaram. All right, he said. Maybe I'll teach in your school. It won't do me any harm. Why not?

Balaram jumped to his feet in elation. He had expected days of argument before Shombhu Debnath agreed; it was nothing less than a windfall. He slapped Shombhu Debnath on his bare back. You're doing the right thing, Shombhu-babu, he said, choking with joy. Our school couldn't have a better beginning.

Shombhu Debnath had been the really important uncertainty in Balaram's mind. The rest of his plans were clear. The School of Reason was to be open to everyone in Lalpukur – to men and women, boys and girls, people of any age at all, but the illiterate were to be given preference. The School would have two main departments. After much careful thought Balaram had decided to name one the Department of Pure Reason and the other the Department of Practical Reason: abstract reason and concrete reason, a meeting of the two great forms of human thought. Every student would have to attend classes in both departments. In the Department of Pure Reason they would be taught elementary reading, writing and arithmetic, and they would be given lectures in the history of science and technology. Balaram was to be the head and probably the only teacher in that department. In the Department of Practical Reason, the students would be taught weaving or tailoring (but that again was uncertain, for it depended on Toru-debi's assent). Alu and Maya were to teach Elementary Weaving – the techniques of starching, winding, warping and basic coarse weaving – while Shombhu Debnath would teach Advanced Weaving. Shombhu Debnath would be the head of the Department of Practical Reason, but Toru-debi, if she agreed, would head her own section. Balaram would be headmaster of the school or, as he preferred to put it, the Fount of Reason.

Every student would have to enroll for two years. It would be assumed that the students would carry on working on the land, or doing whatever they usually did for a living, while they were studying at the school, so the classes would be held in the late afternoon and early evening. Night classes were a possibility to be thought of later.

But a question nagged Balaram: ought the school to charge a fee? He disliked the idea. Fees will never cover our costs, he said, and they might keep some people away.

Shombhu Debnath scratched his head. It's not the money that's important, he said. It's something else. If you don't charge fees, no one will come, you'll see, and people will laugh. People never take anything seriously unless they have to pay for it. It's like those missionaries' Bibles, given away by the truckload and only good for firewood.

So they decided to charge a fee of four rupees a month; not enough to deter anyone, nor too little to be considered a serious investment.

But mainly the school would finance itself by selling the cloth produced by students during class and by taking orders for tailoring. And here there was a job for Rakhal, too. If he agreed, he could be the school's Sales Manager, in charge of the business of selling the school's cloth in Naboganj. Balaram was a little worried about a possible charge of nepotism for hiring every member of Shombhu Debnath's family; but, on the other hand, as he explained conscientiously, Rakhal was perfectly suited to the job – there were few people in Lalpukur who had his expert knowledge of Naboganj and its markets, and he had already proved his worth in marketing Alu's cloth.

The money earned by selling cloth and by tailoring would be used to buy yarn and dyes and possibly more looms (more work for Rakhal), and for the teachers' salaries. Balaram was adamant that everyone who taught or worked in the School would be paid a proper wage. This is not charity after all, he said. We want everyone to work hard, and no one works too hard for a charity.

If there was any money left over after paying salaries and buying fresh yarn and so on, it could be distributed equally among the students. But Balaram was willing to recognize, realistically, that that was an unlikely prospect for some time.

As for the site, that was a problem already solved. There was plenty of space outside Balaram's house for a bamboo-and-thatch shed to house the weaving section. A couple of looms could easily be installed there. Toru-debi, if she agreed to teach, would probably prefer to take her classes in a room inside the house. And there were plenty of other rooms, and the courtyard besides, for Balaram to teach in.

They would need some money to start with, of course, but Balaram had solved that problem, too. He had a little money put away in the bank, enough to get the school going. It would be only a loan, of course, and the school could pay him back once it was on its feet.

So it's all very simple, you see, Balaram said, looking straight into Shombhu Debnath's eyes. Simple and beautiful: knowledge coupled with labour – and that, too, labour of a kind which represents the highest achievement of practical reason. Our school will be the perfect embodiment, the essence of Reason. And so, naturally, it can only be named after the greatest of all the soldiers of Reason – Louis Pasteur.

Shombhu Debnath smiled and looked away. But that's not all, he said, is it? There's something else on your mind, too, isn't there, something you haven't told me? I haven't heard you say anything about that carbolic stuff you're so fond of. Where does that fit in?

Balaram started guiltily. This is enough, he said, for the moment. One has to think of a beginning before one can think of an end.

With his first major hurdle crossed Balaram went ahead with redoubled energy. He had always been fairly sure that he could count on Alu and Maya, and he was proved right. They agreed willingly. Even Rakhal jumped at his offer. Balaram did not know it, but Rakhal was passing through a period of bewilderment and anxiety then. His income from his bombs had dried up because the market for home-made bombs in Naboganj had suddenly and unexpectedly collapsed. Some of his regular customers turned him away saying that there had been a shift in the political climate. His friends whispered that the big producers had stepped in to drive the small fry out, and there was a rumour that the stockpiles from the war had suddenly been released on the market. Rakhal neither knew nor cared. His newly acquired skill had given him endless pleasure, and suddenly it was useless. And, as though that were not enough, the kung fu class, so long the centre of his life, had shut its doors on him. He had twice absent-mindedly beaten the teacher (who had advertised a few more skills than he actually possessed) into a dead faint. Nobody else would fight him. He was too forgetful, they said; he could never remember that it was just practice. The only consolation left to Rakhal was an occasional kung fu film at a morning show in Naboganj, and even those he would not have been able to afford if it were not for his percentage of the money he made from selling Alu's cloth (which was not so much after all). Balaram's offer came when Rakhal was steadying himself to face a choice between giving up cigarettes or films – or, worse, asking Alu for a loan. When Balaram told him about the job, he could hardly believe his luck.

Balaram was still left with the problem of persuading Toru-debi to teach in the school. Twice he began to explain to her, but both times his courage failed him and he ended in stammering confusion. To his enormous surprise, when he did finally ask her, she was not merely willing, but enthusiastic. No sooner had she heard him out than she bustled off to her room to find her old cut-out models and plan her first lessons.

The school could not have had a better beginning. After that it was just a question of building a shed outside Balaram's front door and installing Shombhu Debnath's looms there, and of buying a few slates and some lead, possibly a few blackboards as well, and stocking up on a fair quantity of yarn.

Balaram delegated the building of the shed to Shombhu Debnath, Rakhal and Alu. Of course, said Shombhu Debnath. I'll take charge. But once they started work he spent most of his time squatting on his heels and throwing sidelong glances down the red-dust path which ran past Balaram's house while Rakhal and Alu planned and built the shed. It was a very simple structure – long and rectangular with chhanch walls, flimsy squares of plaited bamboo shavings, held up by bamboo posts driven into the earth at two-foot intervals. They cut the posts from the thickets behind Balaram's house. Only the plaited shavings and thatch for the roof had to be bought, and that was a matter of a couple of hundred rupees.

Balaram tried to help Rakhal and Alu build the shed, but they would not let him, for it was almost certain that he would hurt himself. So Balaram had to content himself with sitting on the steps outside his front door and watching them.

Rakhal and Alu worked fast, and the shed shot out of the ground. They were interrupted only once. Bhudeb Roy had been watching the shed go up from his veranda. He was intrigued as well as suspicious. One day, a few days before sending off his monthly report to the police station, he decided to make inquiries. He walked down the red-dust path to Balaram's house, with a few of his sons behind him.

Shombhu Debnath saw him coming down the path and scrambled into the branches of a tree. Bhudeb-babu, he called down, how's it going? Getting it up still or are you going to bring some more planes down on us? Any more on the way?

Bhudeb Roy ignored him, but his sons threw a few pebbles into the tree. Shombhu Debnath cackled with laughter.

Balaram was sitting on the steps outside his front door. Seeing Bhudeb Roy turn into the path which led to the house, he was suddenly very flustered. He rose quickly to his feet and looked around him. Then he hurried across to a drum of carbolic acid which had been left outside the house, against a wall. Planting himself in front of it, he spread his hands protectively across.

Bhudeb Roy saw him, smiled politely, and made his way towards him, skirting round the shed. Don't come any closer, Balaram rapped out when he was a few feet away.

Bhudeb Roy stopped and looked at him in surprise. What's the matter, Balaram-babu? he said. I only wanted to ask you whether you're buying cattle. This shed . . .?

Balaram glared at him: No. It's for a school.

Bhudeb Roy's cordiality drained away. His tiny eyes hardened. Have you bought this land? he said.

Balaram, watching him closely, his face drawn with tension, said: No.

Bhudeb Roy rubbed his huge jaw and bared his teeth in a

smile. Then, I have to tell you, he said, that you can't build here. You're encroaching on government property.

Balaram stood erect and swept a mass of silver hair from his forehead. Bhudeb-babu, he said, Pasteur didn't allow misguided and superstitious people to stop him from building his laboratory at Villeneuve l'Etang. Nor shall we. If the government wants its land, let it file a case in the district court. That's all I have to say to you.

We'll see, Bhudeb Roy said through his teeth. We'll see. He turned and walked back towards his house. Be careful, Shombhu Debnath called after him, from his perch. A man could hurt himself at your age.

Balaram, shaken, went into the house. He came out with an old tattered blanket and threw it over the drum of carbolic acid.

Next evening Alu wandered into Balaram's study. Balaram was making notes by the harsh light of a naked electric bulb. He was pleased to see Alu, for it was a long time since he had stepped into the study. He smile and, prompted by years of half-forgotten habit, patted the arm of his easy chair. Come here, he said. Come and sit. Then it occurred to him that Alu had long since grown too heavy for the arm of the easy chair, and he hastily changed his gesture and waved at a chair. Sit down, he said, get that chair.

Alu did not seem to hear him. He stood over the easy chair, looking at the floor and shifting his feet. What's the matter? Balaram asked, surprised. Are you looking for a book?

No, said Alu, and scratched his head.

Then? *Science Today?*

I want . . ., Alu blurted out, I want to get married.

Oh! said Balaram. He ran his hand through his hair: That's a big business. We must set about it scientifically. We have to think about the right personality types and things like that. We can't set about it in a hurry. . . .

Balaram stopped; he had a sudden glimpse of regions of immense effort and risk. Nervously he said: It takes a lot of work. You'd better talk to your aunt. Maybe she knows a girl. Perhaps she could advertise in the newspapers. I don't think I'll be able to help.

No, no, Alu broke in, I already have a wife. He stopped,

flustered: What I mean is I already know someone. A girl. That's what I mean.

You mean . . .? Balaram looked at him in disbelief. You mean . . . love? A love-marriage?

Alu was almost tearful with embarrassment. Yes, he said, his voice a strangled bleat. I want to marry Maya. Maya Debnath.

Balaram rose from his chair and threw his arms around Alu. Hugging him to his chest, he ran a hand over his knobbly head. I'm very glad, Alu, he said, his voice choked. Very glad, and very happy. She's a good girl. You have . . . you have the blessings of the Cosmic Boson, as Gopal would say.

He stopped and dropped his arms. But I don't know, he said pensively, what Toru will say. Because, you know, Maya works here, and women have their own ideas about these things. But that doesn't matter. Mere prejudice. We can persuade her. . . .

Then a thought struck Balaram and he cut himself short. Frowning, he began to pace the floor. Alu watched him in silence. After a minute or two Balaram stopped opposite Alu and said: Maybe you should wait a bit, Alu. You know what weddings are. People everywhere. There'll be dozens of people running in and out of the house and we can't keep an eye on everyone. It's not safe. Anything could happen to the carbolic.

He leant towards Alu and whispered: Did you see Bhudeb Roy yesterday? Did you see how he looked at the carbolic? He's planning something; I know him. He's thinking of ways to get at it. We have to be careful. Very careful. We have to watch him. There's nothing he won't do to get his hands on that carbolic.

But he wasn't looking at the carbolic acid, Alu said in surprise. He went across to talk to you.

Balaram silenced him with a gesture. You don't know, he whispered angrily. You're too young. That's how he always goes about things. The carbolic is what he really wanted. He fears it like a fox fears light. He fears it because it's clean. He'd do anything. . . . No, it wouldn't be safe to hold a wedding in the house now. He could easily slip his men into the house. No, Alu, you'll have to wait a bit. Wait till the school is properly on its feet, then we'll give you a wedding to remember.

But . . ., Alu began.

No, said Balaram. He squeezed Alu's shoulder. Listen to me
– just this once.

All right, Alu said reluctantly.

Balaram led him to the door of his study. He patted him on
the back and said: Just a few months. That's all. Right now we
have the school to think about.

A week later the shed was ready, and in another two weeks
the looms had been installed, the slates and the yarn bought
and an order placed with a carpenter for two blackboards. A
board painted by Balaram and Alu appeared on top of the shed
declaring the Pasteur School of Reason open for admissions.

The news spread, and over the next few days most people in
Lalpukur found one excuse or another to wander down the
red-dust path and steal a suspicious look at the new school. But
nobody stepped in. There was not so much as one admission.
The shed didn't look like a school. It was not even remotely like
the familiar tiled, yellow, corridored buildings that people
associated with schools. Nor did it look at all like the tin-roofed
garages of the commercial and secretarial colleges in Naboganj.
It was something else altogether; possibly malign, possibly not.
People were curious, but no one was willing to be the first to
find out.

It was Rakhal who stepped in at that critical point in the
school's history when it was teetering on the knife's edge of
oblivion. Rakhal had temporarily lost interest in the school
after helping to build the shed. Then one day he noticed Alu
and Maya sitting dejected by the empty loom-pits in their
courtyard, steaming gloom.

He laughed when he heard of the school's straits. Why didn't
you tell me? he said. A simple thing like that and there you are
sitting all long-faced and weepy. You wait, there'll be a crowd
outside the school tomorrow.

There was; not precisely a crowd perhaps, but quite as good
as far as Balaram was concerned. Rakhal had gone off to the
banyan tree and found a few of his old cronies. He had slapped
a few backs and twisted a few arms. Bolai-da, who was well
disposed towards the school, had added a few encouraging
words, and it was done. Next morning six young men stepped
nervously into the school.

The Pasteur School of Reason was in business at last.

Once a lead had been given the more timid picked up courage. In a few weeks the school had twenty-two students. There were, after all, as Balaram knew, so many people in Lalpukur who had nothing to do; people who spent the long days dreaming of learning a trade. In a few months the school had forty-eight students, many more than it could take comfortably, and Balaram had to close the rolls and turn away new applicants. The School of Reason was full: it had ten-year-old boys, married men with families who did odd jobs during the day, young men saving to marry, wizened old men too bent to work in the fields. There were women, too, young and old. Women had overcome their initial suspicion of the school after they had been given the lead by a determined and desperate young widow of twenty-five who had three children and no means of support apart from a cousin's capricious generosity. Balaram did his best to encourage them to join, and when he closed his rolls the school had eighteen women. All but two of them had opted to join Toru-debi's tailoring section.

Soon the school was producing more cloth than Rakhal could handle alone, and he had to hire the occasional helper (who went down in Balaram's register as Assistant Sales Managers). The Tailoring Section did even better than Weaving; they were taking in orders from all the villages around Lalpukur, for their work had somehow, by word of mouth, acquired a reputation for durability. At the end of six months the school had earned a substantial sum of money. Balaram was frankly envious when he added up the total. I wish, he said wistfully to Alu and Shombhu Debnath, I wish Pure Reason had a product – something one could sell to gauge its worth.

But he was also delighted. After paying off arrears of salaries, buying new stocks of yarn and so on, there was still a fair amount of money left. Part of it was spent on acquiring a new loom and a secondhand sewing machine for the school. The rest was used to start a fund which would help the students acquire their own sewing machines and looms after they graduated. Balaram gave the students a little lecture when he started the fund. You won't be in the school for ever, he said, and you must think of the future. You may think you would rather have the money in your pockets now, but you would

only regret it later. Someday you'll have to start working on
your own and. if you don't have any machines then, your skills
will be wasted. It's then that you will thank me for starting this
fund.

The students clapped. Balaram looked around his courtyard,
crowded with smiling students, and he was filled with pride.
Afterwards, earthen cups of tea were handed out to everyone
(Nonder-ma had been busy making tea for hours, in prepar-
tion). The courtyard was full of laughter and cheerful optimism.

The school is a success, Balaram said to Shombhu Debnath,
waving a hand at the courtyard. It's a greater success than
anything we could have imagined.

Shombhu Debnath grunted. He had wrapped a white cotton
shawl over his bare shoulders for the occasion, but he had not
changed out of his usual red gamcha. He looked slyly at
Balaram. But that's not all, Balaram-babu, he said, is it? A
success of this kind wouldn't be enough for you. You have
something else in mind, don't you?

Abruptly Balaram turned and walked away. Shombhu
Debnath's voice followed him: What is it, Balaram-babu?
When are you going to tell us?

He was not to know till a few more months had passed.

The school was nearing the end of its first year then. Some of
the more promising students in the Weaving Section had
graduated beyond coarse weaving, and had started producing
fairly intricately worked saris. The Tailoring Section had more
orders than it could handle and the list never seemed to stop
growing. All but two of the students passed the small
examination Balaram set them. When Balaram did his accounts, after Rakhal had handed him the money the traders
had paid him in Naboganj for that month's consignment of
cloth, it was apparent that the school had made a handsome
sum of money.

Balaram called another meeting. Classes were cancelled that
evening and everyone in the school crowded into the courtyard, cheerfully expecting a repeat of the earlier meeting. To
begin with, it was. Balaram read out the accounts and
explained how much money had been spent on salaries and
how much exactly had been put away in the students' fund. But

when he read out the total figures at the end of it there were still three thousand rupees left unaccounted for.

There was a curious hush. Balaram was suddenly solemn. Today, he said, I have to say something very difficult; I have to tell you about a dream. The school as you see it today has only two departments. But when I first dreamt of it, when the idea was first born in my mind, there was a third department as well. The time has come to tell you about that third department, because at last we have enough money to realize that dream. Let me put it like this: Practical Reason and Pure Reason are fine and wonderful things, and what we have already achieved in this school, even though I should not be the one to say it, is in its own way fine and wonderful. Practical and Pure Reason are like two halves of a wheel: without one, the other is incomplete and useless. But a wheel, by itself, is useless, too – it cannot roll forward on its own. Left to itself, it only falls on its side. In the same way, our school, too, is in danger now of falling on its side, into a bed of smugness and complacency, like a wheel which has nothing behind it. It is doing well, true; but a school is not a shop or a factory. A school, like Reason itself, must have a purpose. Without a purpose Reason decays into a mere trick, forever reflecting itself like mirrors at a fair. It is that sense of purpose which the third department will restore to our school. It will help us to remember that we cannot limit the benefits of our education and learning to ourselves – that it is our *duty* to use it for the benefit of everybody around us. That is why I have decided to name the new department the Department of the March of Reason. It will remind us that our school has another aspect: Reason Militant.

Most of the students had drifted into apathetic boredom during Balaram's speech. A hum of subdued talk ebbed around the courtyard. Balaram raised his voice. The first task before the Department of the March of Reason, he explained, was to disinfect the village – disinfect it so thoroughly that no trace of a corrupting germ would surface in it again. And to that end the remaining three thousand rupees would be spent on purchasing carbolic acid.

There were a few murmurs of protest: most of the students would much rather have had the money they had helped to earn for themselves. But there were others who were curious, and some of the younger students remembered seeing Balaram busy with buckets of carbolic acid during the war and after; it had looked like fun – licence to douse one's neighbours' houses with pungent liquid. So Balaram had no shortage of volunteers; fourteen students offered to go with him to Naboganj to help bring back the carbolic acid.

Next morning Balaram gathered his volunteers together early and rushed off to Naboganj without eating his breakfast. Toru-debi protested: What's the hurry? Your what's-its-name, marching reason, won't miss the bus if you go an hour late.

There *is* a hurry, Balaram said shortly, and almost ran from the house. He came back in the afternoon, with his volunteers, in a hired truck piled high with sacks of carbolic powder and a small arsenal of squirt-guns, water-pistols and plastic buckets. He set the volunteers to work at once. They rolled a few clean oil-drums into the patch of garden in front of the house next to the shed which housed the Weaving Section. Balaram directed them while they mixed the carbolic powder into a dilute solution. When they had finished, he gave them precise instructions. They were to assemble in the school at four o'clock the next day. That was usually the time he took his classes in reading and writing, but they were to be excused class for once.

Balaram was up early the next day, bright-eyed and feverish with excitement. He spent the day pacing his study in nervous agitation, jerking his thick lock of white hair from his eyes, his fine, slim face drawn with tension. Long before four he was out of the house, peering down the path, waiting impatiently for the volunteers. Alu, who had decided to go with him, went out to join him a little later. At four-thirty only six of the fourteen volunteers had arrived. Balaram was furious. Where are they? he shouted at one of the students, a fifteen-year-old boy with no front teeth.

The boy was taken aback, for Balaram had never shouted at anyone in the school before. Maybe they're at the banyan tree, he said apologetically, sucking his canines. Don't you know, Balaram-babu, Bhudeb-Roy-shaheb is holding a meeting, a proper microphone-and-loudspeaker meeting, under the banyan tree today? He's going to lay the first stone for a road, an absolutely straight so-big-and-black macadam road from the banyan tree to his house. His men are going all over the village taking people to the meeting. We had to hide and come round through the ricefields.

Was it coincidence? Was it part of Balaram's plans? Had he known?

He must have, Alu said to Gopal in Calcutta several months later. He must have wanted it to happen, otherwise why was he in so much of a hurry?

At the time, Balaram gave nothing away. With quiet determination he said: This is only one of the obstacles which will litter the path of Reason. Then he handed out water-pistols, squirt-guns, mugs and buckets of carbolic solution and led them down the path.

Where are we going, sir? one of the students asked.

To the banyan tree, said Balaram. There's no part of the village more littered with filth.

But when they were only a few hundred yards away from the banyan tree and could hear the hum of the crowd and Bhudeb Roy's voice booming through loudspeakers – This road will be an example; an example in straightness and hard work, which are the needs of the hour – Balaram faltered. Alu saw him hesitate and tugged at his elbow. Let's go back, he said. There's still time. There's no need for this.

Balaram stopped and put his bucket down. The volunteers stopped behind him. Balaram's face was drenched in sweat. Alu saw his courage draining away with the blood in his face. Come on, Alu said. Let's turn back. . . .

But before he could finish Shombhu Debnath was at Balaram's elbow. Alu stopped in surprise; Shombhu Debnath had not been with them when they left the school.

Turning back already, Balaram-babu? Shombhu Debnath sang out. He laughed and his red eyes shone into Balaram's: You mean to say the march of reason is being turned back by a single germ? Come on.

With a wink at Balaram, Shombhu Debnath unrolled his ashen hair and knotted it tightly into place. He unwound his strip of red cotton, and tied it on again, like a loincloth. Then he turned to one of the volunteers, snatched a bucket and a squirt-gun out of his hands and led the way to the banyan tree.

Shamefacedly Balaram followed, with Alu behind him. But the volunteers lagged behind.

The crowd under the banyan tree was large by Lalpukur's standards, but not huge. There were perhaps eighty people crowded into the open space around the tree. Some were squatting on the ground and picking their teeth; some stood leaning on each other and against the tree's massive, twisted aerial roots. Bhudeb Roy's sons and the twenty young men stood around the crowd, blocking all the paths out of the clearing. A small wooden platform had been erected near the banyan's huge trunk, between Bolai-da's shop and the tea-shop. A portrait of Bhudeb Roy, inexpertly painted on a sheet of cardboard almost as large as Bhudeb Roy himself, was suspended from the tree, directly above the platform. The painter had obviously tried to reach a compromise between Bhudeb Roy and a famous filmi face. As a result Bhudeb Roy's jaws and tiny eyes, immensely distorted, leered grotesquely at the crowd in an attitude of screen tenderness. Bhudeb Roy, heavily garlanded, stood under the portrait, thundering into a microphone. He was dressed as usual in a spotless white dhoti and kurta, but a white political cap covered his baldness. There were dozens of other pictures of him accompanied by slogans (Straight to Progress) stuck up on the trunk of the ancient banyan and on the shops.

Bhudeb Roy checked for a moment when he saw Balaram entering the clearing with a bucket. Then he recovered and roared into the microphone again, but with a trace of uneasiness in his voice: This is a new beginning, a straight beginning. . . .

Balaram stopped and looked around him in indecision. Now that he was actually there he was not sure what to do. Shombhu Debnath had vanished with his squirt-gun and bucket. Alu was beside him, but there was so sign of the volunteers. Two of Bhudeb Roy's men turned and saw him. Bhudeb Roy roared from his platform: Nothing shall turn us from our straight advance. . . . The young men advanced towards them stroking their wooden clubs. The loudspeakers screamed: The road will be straight, the straight road of progress, straight to my house. . . . The men were barely an arm's length away, and Alu thrust himself in front of Balaram. One of the men raised his club.

And then suddenly with a gurgling whoosh a stream of disinfectant poured out of the tree, right over Bhudeb Roy. The microphone drowned in a cacophony of squeaks and screeches. Bhudeb Roy collapsed on to the platform, spluttering and coughing. A jet of carbolic shot out of the boughs of the tree and slammed into the suspended portrait. The cardboard sagged and swung backwards on its rope. For a moment it hung by a thread and then the rope gave, and it plummeted down in a soggy mass. Bhudeb Roy was floundering wetly on the platform, directly in its path. His head took the cardboard, square in the middle. He was flung backwards. When he struggled up again, the cardboard was hanging damply over his garlands and his head was staring out of a ragged hole in the painted jaw.

Bhudeb Roy's sons and the twenty young men were motionless, their eyes riveted on Bhudeb Roy in dismay, as he struggled blindly, with the portrait hanging around his neck like a soggy octopus. Alu saw his chance and jogged Balaram's elbow. They picked up their buckets and emptied them on the two men in front of them. They were gone before the men could open their eyes again.

When Bhudeb Roy sat up again his sons and his hired men were all around him, spewing apologies; trying to help him up; fastidiously picking bits of cardboard off his garlanded neck. The clearing was empty. There was no sign of Balaram or Alu. The boughs of the banyan were tranquil and uninhabited. But he could hear laughter rippling through the ricefields.

Bhudeb Roy insisted on being driven straight to hospital.

The next day, while Shombhu Debnath and Maya were at the school and Rakhal was away in Naboganj, their huts caught fire. They burnt down to a heap of smouldering ashes and rubble before Maya and Shombhu even knew of it. Later, sifting through the rubble they found two charred kerosene-tins that were not their own.

They lost everything: the grain they had stored away, hanks of yarn, their pots and pans, Rakhal's carefully accumulated shirts and trousers. The ear-rings and the two brass pots which were Maya's only mementoes of her mother had vanished, too.

Balaram took it for granted that Shombhu Debnath, Maya and Rakhal would come to live in his house. Where else could they go? So Alu carried the few odds and ends Maya had recovered from the ashes back to their house. Maya stumbled after him, blinded by her tears.

Later, they went back to fetch Shombhu Debnath and found him squatting beside the rubble staring into the sky. Maya, he said softly, remember – this is what happens when a man ties himself down and builds a house. It burns down. Nobody has to do it: it's only Sri Krishna reminding you what the world's like.

He would not leave the rubble, though Maya did her best to persuade him. Maya's own grief was swept away by another worry: what would Rakhal do when he came back from Naboganj and heard about the fire? She knew he might do anything at all when he heard about the kerosene-tins they had found, and she knew she would be powerless to stop him.

But to her surprise Rakhal did nothing when he was told. He asked Alu innumerable questions about the kerosene-tins, and later he spent a long time scratching about in the ashes, looking for scraps of his clothes. When he found none he went back quietly with Alu and Maya and fell peacefully asleep on a mat in the shed he had helped to build.

Maya trembled with relief. But a few days later Alu saw Rakhal hiding sacks of old soda-bottles, tin cans and rusty nails in the rubble of their huts.

Rakhal was making bombs again.

Chapter Six

Taking Sides

At last we meet Assistant Superintendent of Police Jyoti Das properly. He is a slight man, of medium height, dark, with straight black hair. He has a long, even face with a rounded chin and a short, straight nose. His only irregular features are his eyebrows, which are slightly out of alignment, one being a fraction higher than the other and slightly more sharply curved, and that tends to make him appear a little surprised even when he is not. His eyes, which he has trained over the years to record the minutest details of plumage and colouring, are sharp and meticulously observant. He is clean-shaven and prides himself on it, for it distinguishes him from his col-leagues, who tend generally to be aggressively moustached. He is pleasant- if not good-looking, and he looks younger than his twenty-five years. He is often mistaken for a college student.

He is waiting in a small police station a few miles from Lalpukur. The police station is on the main road that runs from Naboganj, past the outer fringes of Lalpukur towards Calcutta. It is a tumbledown old police station, with cracked tiles and gaping holes in the plaster of its yellow walls. Jyoti Das is sitting beside (but not behind) the Head Constable's desk in a damp gloomy room lined with tattered duty-charts and bunches of keys. The room is acrid with the smell of burnt spices wafting in from the constables' quarters, and he can hear a drunk or a lunatic talking to himself somewhere in the cells inside.

It is eleven in the morning and Jyoti Das is waiting to meet Bhudeb Roy for the first time. Bhudeb Roy is already half an hour late, though it was he who specified ten-thirty in his telegram to Calcutta, and Jyoti Das is more than a little irritated and impatient. But he is not surprised, for, though he has never met Bhudeb Roy before, in a way he knows him well.

After being handed the case he has had to read all the reports Bhudeb Roy has ever filed, and he has not had the impression that Bhudeb Roy is a man who is likely to be unduly flustered about keeping someone waiting. Jyoti Das smiles, remembering the arguments he has often had with his colleagues about their pungent views on filthy little district and mofussil politicians who have suddenly come into so much power that they think nothing of pushing around gazetted officers of the Government of India.

The Head Constable, a big, burly man with an oily face and handlebar moustaches, who has been standing stiffly at the far end of the room looking out of the window, sees Jyoti Das's impatience and begins to worry. ASP-shaheb, he says, will you have some tea? Jyoti Das smiles and nods.

Assistant Superintendent of Police, the constable calls Jyoti Das. He is not wrong, for that is Jyoti Das's rank technically. But actually Jyoti Das has a different designation now. About a year ago he was seconded out of the police to an organization which likes to make itself inconspicuous under the name of Union Secretariat (though it has an arsenal of other names stocked away for various contingencies). Like most of his colleagues in the intelligence services Jyoti Das still holds a rank in the police, his parent organization, but officially he is now called a Deputy Central Research Officer. Still, whatever his official designation, one cannot really call someone Deputy Central Research Officer, or even DCRO. On the other hand, ASP is a name, a rank, a class, a standard of living, a life-insurance premium, a metaphysic, while DCRO means nothing, not even what it says.

Besides, few, even in the Union Secretariat, know precisely what their ranks and designations mean in terms of salaries, benefits and seniority. Its sister organizations have their own rankings, blessed by tradition, and only the oldest of the secretarial staff are able to reckon the fine shades of parity between ranks in the different organizations. More than once have the highest levels of the Ministry resounded with the noisy strife of organizations at war with each other over a misunderstanding between officers on ranking or precedence or Additional Dearness Allowance. Inevitably, in their dealings with other organizations and services, the officers of the

Union Secretariat tend to fall back on the common factor in their rankings – the police. Correspondence and liaison would be impossible otherwise: officers would end up being dragged before protocol committees for writing semi-official letters to seniors or some such thing.

Four years have passed since Jyoti Das sat for the Civil Service examinations and, somewhat to his surprise, was awarded a good enough result to qualify for the police. He was only twenty-one then; one of the youngest people to qualify. But his father, who had carefully supervised his preparations for the examinations, was not at all pleased. He had intended Jyoti's first attempt at the examinations to be a kind of trial run, as it were, a preparation for a really serious attempt the year after. It upset all his plans when Jyoti got a place in the police. He had wanted Jyoti to enter one of the coveted, prestigious services, perhaps the Administrative Service like his mother's uncle, the Secretary, or the Foreign Service, or even at a pinch the Audits and Accounts Service. It appalled him to think of Jyoti spending his life shouting 'Quick march' at constables in funny shorts, and dealing with petty criminals and all kinds of other nastiness. And, anyway, he sneered, what are the police going to do with *him*? Do you think they have time for people who sit around painting *birds*? You mark my words; he'll end up being suspended for immoral behaviour and spend the rest of his life hanging around our necks.

He spent months trying to persuade Jyoti to turn down the police and sit for the examinations again. But for once Jyoti was stubborn; the police was a Class I service like any other, he said; and gazetted, too, a secure job with a good pension and gratuity scheme and a house-rent allowance. What more could they want? He had done enough to please them, and if they didn't like it they would just have to live with it – the examinations had been pure agony and nothing anyone could do would make him sit for them again.

As for his painting, it would be better protected in the police than anywhere else, for it is only when the world you have to make your way in has no real connection with you that your private world is safe.

His father was cold to him for two years afterwards. Jyoti ignored him and tried hard during his training. As a result he

did well enough at the Academy to be taken into the Union
Secretariat. That was a considerable achievement, for usually
getting into the Union Secretariat was a matter of knowing
people and talking to uncles. His father thawed, for he soon
discovered that, far from shouting 'Left, right' at constables,
Jyoti's work consisted in analysing files and writing reports like
any other Class I bureaucrat.

Jyoti was relieved because he liked peace at home, and in his
own way he was happy in the Union Secretariat. The initial
training had been exhausting and the work often seemed
pointless, but that was only to be expected. But on the whole it
wasn't too demanding, and at least he didn't have to wear
uniforms. Actually, though he would never have admitted it to
his father, he had dreaded the prospect of being posted to a
district and having to spend years rushing about catching
dacoits and ordering half-trained constables to shoot at mobs.
But much more important than any of that was that the Union
Secretariat left him time to draw and paint birds. His painting,
with his knowledge of ornithology, had improved vastly. A
well-known illustrator had been impressed by his watercolour
of a green bee-eater – a common bird, but tinted with
gradations of colour that were not at all easy to capture in
watercolours. There was even some talk of a contract to
illustrate a children's book.

Twelve o'clock and still no sign of Bhudeb Roy. In a way
Jyoti Das was not surprised. He had never thought the case
would amount to very much. But for some reason his boss,
the Deputy Inspector-General (actually, the Additional Director of Research), had decided to take the case very seriously. Handing over the files, he had said: This is going to
be an important one. Let's see how you handle it. I want you
to give it all your time; it may make a lot of difference to
your career.

Jyoti Das had read through the files conscientiously, but at
the end of it he was still unable to understand why the case was
so important. To him it seemed a thoroughly trivial affair.
There appeared to be no rational grounds to substantiate the
principal source's belief that a retired schoolmaster in his
village was being used by a foreign-trained agent of some kind,
disguised as a weaver, to run a network of extremists. Of course

it was possible – there were so many refugees in those border areas and they were good clay for anyone's hands. But somehow in this case, Jyoti Das noted on the file, it seemed more likely that some kind of petty village rivalry lay behind the whole thing. At any rate, the local police could easily handle the matter. The Deputy Inspector-General was furious when he saw Jyoti Das's notations on the file. He had summoned Jyoti Das to his room and said: Mr Das, how long have you been in the Secretariat? A few months, if I'm not mistaken. What the hell, man, you are still not knowing a case from a cauliflower? You think this is a joke? You think you're already some kind of James Bond and you can question my judgement? When I say this is an important case, you treat it as an important case, and none of your bloody opinions and chit-chat, shit-shat. Jyoti Das had sprung to attention and snapped off a salute. Stop that, the DIG had said. You're not in the police now. Then he had smiled and given Jyoti a fatherly pat: And never talk of handing the local police a case. The first rule in this bloody garden is that no one hands any cuttings to the police. You'll soon find out. Those buggers are always trying to hog our work anyway. If we go around handing them cases, we'll soon have nothing to show for ourselves and no work to do. Now, get out of here and keep me up on how the case develops.

Now it looked as though the case wasn't going to develop at all: the chief source had disappeared. Tell me, Jyoti Das said to the Head Constable, I suppose you know him – is he always late, or do you think something serious has happened?

The constable shuffled his feet and nervously rubbed the brass buckle on his belt with his thumb. Jyoti Das looked at him and sat up: What's the matter, Constable?

Sir, he may have been held up, the constable said uneasily. People say he's been having trouble.

Trouble?

Trouble at home, sir.

Come on, Constable, Jyoti Das said. Wake up. Haven't you been trained to give reports properly? Now, explain: what trouble?

The constable left the window and shuffled across. He lowered his voice: ASP-shaheb, it's his wife. She had a child

five or six years ago – a girl. The girl's always been very sickly
and recently she fell seriously ill – you know what happens
when people have children at such a late age. Bhudeb Roy-
babu has taken the girl to all the best doctors, but nobody has
been able to do anything. And now, they say, the girl's illness
has driven Parboti-debi, that is, Bhudeb Roy-babu's wife, a
little mad. I heard from a man in the village – he owns a cycle-
shop and knows Bhudeb-babu and his family very well – he said
that twice, late at night, Bhudeb-babu and his sons have caught
Parboti-debi trying to sneak out of the house with the child.
Bhudeb-babu was very angry, sir, naturally. He slapped her –
in front of all his sons – and asked her: Where are you going to at
this time of the night? But she, she didn't cry at all. She looked
straight at him, without lowering her eyes, and said: I'm taking
her home; she's sick because she's not at home. Right in his face
like that. Naturally Bhudeb-babu was even angrier. He
shouted at her: What do you mean, 'her home'? This is her
home. But then she shouted back at him and said: No, this is
not her home; her home is there – and she waved outside,
maybe towards the school. You see, sir, they say that the night
the child was, if you'll excuse me, conceived there was a plane
crash in the village – it was during the war, you see – and
people say the crash warped her brain a bit. She thinks the
plane had something to do with the child, and wants to take her
back to the place where it crashed. It's very sad. She shouts at
Bhudeb-babu all the time: Let me go. Let me take the child
home. You'll kill it. It'll die if it stays here. Poor woman; soon
they'll have to send her to Ranchi or some other asylum. Of
course, he can afford it.

Jyoti Das was incredulous. You mean to say – you mean to
say he's kept me waiting for almost two hours because his wife's
going mad?

The constable looked at his feet. Maybe, sir, he said.

At a quarter to one, they heard a car stop outside the police
station. Greatly relieved the Head Constable announced:
He's here, sir – and sent two constables running out to escort
Bhudeb Roy and three of his sons in. Jyoti Das did not move.
He sat as he was, his legs crossed, leaning back in his chair.
He decided not to stand up when Bhudeb Roy entered the
room.

Bhudeb Roy's huge bulk entered the room by degrees. His three sons helped him into a chair opposite the Head Constable's desk. Jyoti Das nodded at him and frowned. He shot his cuffs back and looked pointedly at his watch. Bhudeb Roy ignored him. He snapped his fingers and with a flick of his wrist sent his sons and the constables hurrying out of the room. He was silent for a moment, breathing hard, and looking Jyoti Das over critically. Then he leant across and smiled. I hope you had a nice rest this morning. I hope the constable made you comfortable. He's not a bad man but a little foolish.

Jyoti Das looked at his tiny, glassy eyes and flat nose; he saw the thin smile splintering the sagging flesh of his face, like a crack cutting through a mound of baking mud, and quickly looked away, out of the open window. He said curtly: Your telegram said your business was very urgent.

Yes, said Bhudeb Roy, it is. I was held up a little at home. My wife and daughter aren't well. I have to go back home in a few minutes. So I'd better tell you quickly.

Yes?

You have to act fast now, fast. You've read all my reports. Now you have to do something. I think the time has come to raid Balaram Bose's house and to arrest him and his associates.

Jyoti Das sketched a smile: Have there been some new developments, then? Something serious enough to justify that kind of action?

New developments? What do you mean, 'new developments'? Aren't the old developments good enough? I wrote to you six months ago about how the extremists attacked me while I was holding a public meeting in the village. They attacked me with all their foreign weapons and everything and tried to kill me, and they disrupted the whole meeting and wrecked the law and order situation in the whole area. I had to go to hospital. You know all that; I wrote to you.

Yes, said Jyoti Das, but I don't think we can do anything on the basis of that one incident. Has there been anything since then?

Of course there has, or why would I send you a telegram? Do you think they're going to stop, now that they've tasted blood? I'll tell you what happened. You know I'm building a road for the people of the village? Naturally, the extremists are doing everything they can to hold it up so that I'll be discredited. Last week, the surveyors and some of my men were plotting the course of the road, and they found that it has to run through an unauthorized construction this man Balaram Bose has erected on government property. I warned him not to do it at the time, but he defied me. Anyway, I sent my men to tell him to have the construction demolished in a week. Do you know what he did? He got one of his hired men – a notorious goonda and Bad Character called Rakhal Debnath (he's the ringleader's son; I've referred to him in some of my reports) – to chase my men out of his house. Then he came with all his people to my house, and stood outside and shouted: You'll never destroy my school (he calls it a school). Never. If you want to try, you'll have to fight me to the end. He's always been a little crazy, and now he's gone completely mad, under the influence of that man Shombhu Debnath. So inconsiderate, too – disturbing my wife, who's not well. I didn't say anything then, but I sent more men to his house the next day. They found that he's turned the whole place into a fort. He's surrounded it with drums of acid and he spends the whole day patrolling the house armed with a squirt-gun. He never goes inside. He even sleeps there at night, in a kind of tent he's put up outside. He shouted at my men and shot at them with acid. Tell your master he'll never destroy me or my acid, never. You see what the situation is? He's gone crazy, he looks it – his hair is like a bird's nest and his eyes are blood red. I can't even walk to the village along the path any longer; I have to go through the ricefields. You see what the situation is? You have to act now, before they become too dangerous to handle. Any day now they may escape across the border.

Jyoti Das picked up a pencil and held it poised between his forefingers. Bhudeb-babu, he said, I'm not convinced this matter is serious enough to warrant action on our part.

Not serious enough? After all I've told you? They're a threat to my life. I'm telling you right now, you must raid that house, or you'll regret it. That's all I'm asking for – a raid. I'm not even asking you to make any arrests. You can decide on that yourself when you see what's inside the house. You'll find bombs and guns and God knows what else. I have definite information that Shombhu Debnath and his son have been getting weapons from across the border. Maybe they're even making them in there. They completely control Balaram Bose now, and they're thoroughly dangerous. You *must* raid that house.

Jyoti Das frowned: To me it seems a matter for the local police.

Bhudeb Roy hammered his fist on the desk. Local police? he said angrily. What use are the local police? The DSP has a heart condition and spends all his time praying in the temples in Naboganj. They're no use to anyone. And anyway this is your job. This is a border area, which is why the case was given to you people in the first place. Haven't I told you they're receiving guns from across the border? *You* have to do something. What does the government pay you for?

Jyoti Das was flustered but he kept his voice under control. Look, Bhudeb-babu, he said, don't lose your temper. I'm answerable only to my superiors. I have to discuss the matter with them before any action is possible.

Bhudeb Roy rose from his chair. Glaring into Jyoti Das's eyes, he said: If you don't do something soon, *I'll* write to your superiors. Maybe you'll learn then. He turned and stormed out of the room.

Three days later, while Jyoti Das was still working on the report of his meeting with Bhudeb Roy, a clerk brought him a telephone message that had come in from a post office near Lalpukur. Jyoti Das read it and decided that he had no alternative but to take it to the DIG at once. He rang the DIG's personal secretary and asked for an immediate appointment.

From Bhudeb Roy? the DIG asked, stroking the thin moustache that bisected his large, square face. Jyoti Das nodded. The DIG read the message and looked triumphantly at Jyoti. Wasn't I telling you? he said. This case is hotting up. You'll have to leave immediately. Take a few men and ask the DSP in Naboganj to give you a few more. I'll send him a telex, too. But don't let him get his toes in. Shut him out.

Yes, sir, said Jyoti.

Then the DIG glanced at the telegram again and looked up, a

little puzzled. Tell me, Das, he said. I can understand the first part, this stuff about . . . bomb attack . . . bring forces immediately, and all that. But tell me, what do you think the bugger means by 'wife abducted'?

Chapter Seven

The Ghost in the Machine

At first Maya heard the knocks faintly, through a muffling fog of
sleep. She was asleep in a small, dark store-room next to the
kitchen, which she had cleared out for herself, on Toru-debi's
instructions, after she and Rakhal had moved into their house.
She could hear Nonder-ma in the kitchen, breathing heavily
through her open mouth. She heard the sound again; three
distinct taps. For a moment she wondered whether it was Alu;
but he never knocked when he came at night and he knew that
her door was not barred. The taps sounded as though they were
farther away, on the back door perhaps. Through the barred
window at the other end of the room she saw the courtyard and
the tiled, sloping roof, daubed with patches of moonlight
filtering through the mango tree. It was very quiet; even the
cicadas were still.

The taps again, and she was almost sure now that they were
on the back door. Quietly, wrapping her sari tight around her,
she went out of her room, down the passage to the door. There
were three clear knocks on the thick wooden door. She stood
undecided for a moment, wondering whether she ought to call
Rakhal or Alu. But then she decided against it and whispered:
Ke? Who's there?

Ami, she heard her father's voice. It's me, open the door,
Maya, he said urgently, in an undertone. Maya sighed with
relief: it was three days since she had seen him last. He had
come to the house, late one night, weak with hunger and asked
for a handful of puffed rice. He would eat nothing more and,
though she had begged him to stay, he had disappeared again
that night.

She pulled the latch open and flung her arms around his
bony, naked waist. Quiet now, he said, laughing and running
his hand over her head. Quiet, quiet. Look who I've brought

with me. And only then did Maya notice that there was a woman standing beside him.

She was tall; Maya noticed that even in that first moment of bewildered surprise, but she could not see her face, for she had her sari hooded over her head. She had a bundle on her waist, or so Maya thought, but then the bundle stirred and whimpered, and she saw that it was a child. Shombhu Debnath ushered them into the house and turned to latch the door. The woman put out a hand and caught Maya's arm. The anchal of her sari slipped off her head, and Maya saw that it was Parboti-debi. Parboti-debi smiled at Maya and pressed her arm. Her thin, lined face was radiant with joy. I've come, Maya, she said. He got me out at last.

Maya stared at her dumbstruck. Parboti-debi held up her daughter, and stroked her pale, delicate cheeks with a finger. Look, she said proudly, she's better already now that she's with her father.

Maya looked at her father, and for the first time that she could remember he would not meet her eyes. He turned away and lowered his long craggy face, like a boy waiting for judgement. And when she was silent he shot her a sheepish glance and whispered: You'll look after her tonight, Maya? Give her a place to sleep? No?

Slowly Maya stretched out her hand and touched him on his arm. Yes, she said, I'll look after her, and now you go and rest, too. He would have liked to draw her to him and kiss her on the top of her head as he used to when she was a child, but Maya was suddenly as old as he was, and stronger – strong enough to embrace every element of his being with love and compassion – so he turned gruffly away, while she led Parboti-debi to the store-room by the kitchen.

In the morning Maya's mind teemed with confused explanations as she waited for Toru-debi in the kitchen. She had already told Alu and Rakhal about Parboti-debi's sudden arrival. Alu had said little; his only interest in the matter was how it would affect her, Maya. But Rakhal's face had mottled with anger and his scar had burst open. The puritanical code of physical strength and purity which ruled him like some deep inviolable instinct was outraged; his mind had recoiled reflexively from the offence. He had stormed away from her. But, still, Maya didn't worry too much about Rakhal – he had hardly spoken to his father for years anyway. Toru-debi was a worry of a different kind, founded on a fear of shame and embarrassment; Maya had no equipment to deal with situations of that kind.

Maya rose as Toru-debi came into the kitchen with her hair hanging loose over her shoulders, on her way to the pond for her morning bath. Parboti-debi was sitting cross-legged in a corner, feeding her daughter out of a bowl. Toru-debi saw her as soon as she stepped in and froze in the doorway. Parboti-debi rose to her feet and covered her head with her sari. Maya darted protectively in front of her and began to blurt out an explanation.

Toru-debi ignored her. She smoothed her hair back with one hand and looked away, smiling crookedly. So that's it, she murmured. I should have known. Maya stopped, for she saw that Toru-debi was talking to herself. So that's it, she said again.

What? Maya said apprehensively. Toru-debi frowned at her significantly, pressing her lips together, and beckoned. It's the blouses, she whispered into Maya's ear. She wants the blouses.

Blouses? Maya said.

Yes, yes, Toru-debi whispered impatiently, she wants the blouses. I know. Toru-debi squared her shoulders, drew her loose hair into a knot, and arranged a strained social smile on her face. Ah, Parboti-didi, she said, I'm glad you could come, but you shouldn't have bothered. Of course, I knew you were coming, I dreamt – I dream a lot, you know – I knew you and Bhudeb-babu would come today. But you shouldn't have gone to so much trouble. I haven't forgotten, really. It's just that . . . so much work. But never mind. I'll finish them, right now. You can show them to Bhudeb-babu and tell him that he doesn't have to come.

Maya tried to break in again, but Toru-debi stopped her with an angry frown. Just wait here, Parboti-didi, she said, assuming her smile again. Have some tea. It won't take long; I'll finish them in a couple of hours.

And, forgetting her bath, Toru-debi hurried back towards her room.

Alu was in the courtyard, watching the kitchen. He ran up to Toru-debi: What happened? In an agitated rush, Toru-debi said: It's the blouses, she wants the blouses. I promised her six embroidered blouses and then I forgot. And now she's told Bhudeb-babu and he's going to come, too, and God knows what'll happen when he finds out that they aren't ready yet.

Involuntarily Alu grinned: It's got nothing to do with blouses.

The blood rushed to Toru-debi's face. She drew her hand back, and for the first time in his life she slapped him. Fool, she cried trembling, half-witted idiot. Can't you see how serious it is? He's coming, and it'll be the end of everything if the blouses aren't ready. Only the sewing machine can save us now. Whatever happens, I'll never let your uncle say that it was because of the blouses.

Alu, rubbing his cheek, watched her run into her room.

Balaram had spent the night in the canvas shelter he had rigged up on the dust path which ran past his house to Bhudeb Roy's. It was surrounded by a circle of heavy oil-drums, with an opening where the circle met the path which ran to the front door of his house. The shelter was only a canvas sheet, stretched over the drums, and held in place by stones. There was a small tarpaulin-covered heap at one end of the circle, across from the shelter. That part of the circle was forbidden to Balaram; Rakhal had told him, at least ten times a day for days on end, never on any account to touch that heap or even go near it.

It was a long time since Balaram had slept through the night. It was at night that he expected Bhudeb Roy to make his move. The night, he told Alu and Rakhal when they tried to persuade him to spend his nights in the house, the night is that man's element; we can never rest at night, not till it's over. And so he spent his nights dozing fitfully and watching Bhudeb Roy's house. He slept when he could during the day; there was plenty of time, for over the last few weeks the number of students in the school had dwindled away until one day none had turned up at all. Sometimes, obscurely, he worried about their absence. There was something watchful and wary about it, as though they were waiting for an outcome, a result: a verdict which they would do nothing to influence. He knew he ought to do something to bring them back, but at the same time their absence was a relief. The students would only be a complication, an extra, nagging worry, when all he wanted was to get the waiting over with; this unbearable waiting to see what Bhudeb Roy would do next.

Early that morning he had an intuition that something was going to happen, and soon. His shelter had been placed so that it commanded a good view of Bhudeb Roy's house. Since dawn he had caught glimpses of Bhudeb Roy and his sons rushing about on their balcony and their roof. The walls blocked his view of the garden but now he could occasionally hear Bhudeb Roy bellowing at his men.

He had a strange feeling that something unusual was happening in his own house as well. No one had come out to him that morning. Even Alu, who always brought him a cup of tea in the morning, had not appeared. He ought to check perhaps but, then, on the other hand, it wouldn't be wise to leave his post when there was so much happening in Bhudeb Roy's house. He thought of shouting for Rakhal and Alu, or even perhaps beating the signal they had agreed upon on the empty kerosene-tin. But he decided against that, too: they probably wouldn't hear him if he shouted, and the signal was only for emergencies. For all he knew, this was a damp squib. And anyway, if something happened, he had only to reach out for the tin, and Rakhal would be there; he had worked out that it would take him no more than five seconds to reach the circle of oil-drums from the house.

Balaram slapped his face twice, for his eyelids were growing heavy again. He shook his head. It seemed to him suddenly that the noise in Bhudeb Roy's garden had grown louder. Then, equally suddenly, it stopped. Balaram leant forward on his battlement of oil-drums, tense as a spring, looking from Bhudeb Roy's empty balcony to the gate which led out of his garden to the path, and back again.

The gate opened and Bhudeb Roy slowly steered his bulk out into the dust path. His sons and his hired men swarmed out behind him. Balaram, breathless, snatched up the empty kerosene-tin and a bunch of hooped wires, and hammered out the signal. The bangs and rattles were deafeningly loud, but

Balaram couldn't help adding his voice: Alu, Rakhal . . .
ashchhe re, ashchhe . . . they're coming. His voice sounded
oddly feeble to him; perhaps it was just the noise of the tin. He
felt his knees trembling, and absent-mindedly he reached
down to steady them with his hands. Then he slapped his
thigh, angry with himself for wasting time, and leant against an
oil-drum and watched Bhudeb Roy advance down the path
with his men, in a cloud of dust.

Bhudeb Roy was no longer in the lead; he and his sons were
surrounded by his hired men. They were walking fast. They
were close. He could see their faces clearly now; he could see
the splinters on the sharpened ends of their wooden poles and
the bicycle chains, looped expertly around their wrists, like
bracelets, with their barbed ends swinging loose; he could
almost feel the oiled links in his palm, snaking out stiffly when
they turned sideways, swinging freely when they hung downwards. He reached down and ran his palm over the two-foot
brass cylinder of his best squirt-gun. He pressed his thumb on
the tiny pointed mouth of the nozzle and drew the handle back.
Once again he rehearsed his plan: all he had to do was reach
Bhudeb Roy with one burst of carbolic, only one, and he would
turn and run as fast as his legs would carry him. That was all.
His stomach churned: but would it work? Would it work? It
had seemed so certain when he planned it, but now, with them
so close, their dust in his nose. . . . He could see the sweat
hanging on their moustaches now, and their pocket combs, and
the folded flick-knives sticking out of their breast pockets. How
could it be? It usually took minutes to walk from Bhudeb Roy's
house to his; how were they so close so soon? He sensed his
front door opening, heard feet flying down the path, and then
Alu and Rakhal were crouching behind the oil-drums on either
side of him.

Bhudeb Roy, less than a hundred yards away, saw them, too.
He shouted, and his men came to a halt, milling around him,
raising a cloud of red dust. Bhudeb Roy cupped his hands
around his mouth and shouted: Balaram-babu, I want to talk to
you. Balaram could see his face, but Bhudeb Roy had been
careful not to expose himself any more than strictly necessary.
Two men stood in front of him, shielding his immense body.

Balaram-babu, Bhudeb Roy shouted again, don't worry; this

has nothing to do with you. It's that swine Shombhu Debnath I want. Do you know what's going on in your house? Do you know that he's kidnapped my wife and daughter and hidden them somewhere in your house? It's true; my men have seen foot-prints. Are you, a respectable man, a teacher, a colleague, going to shelter someone who's kidnapped your neighbour's wife?

Balaram, intent on gauging the distance between them, heard hardly a word, but he shouted back: Bhudeb-babu, the one thing I've learnt from you is that there's only one answer to anything you say.

As he spoke he wondered at the inexplicable note of politeness that had crept into his voice. He pointed the squirt-gun into the air, deciding that a high trajectory would add to his range, and aimed. Then Rakhal, who had been crouching beside him, ducked below the oil-drums and crawled across the circle, to the tarpaulin-covered heap at the other end. He reached under the tarpaulin and brought out a bottle and a rag. Then he dipped the rag in a tin of kerosene and stuffed it into the neck of the bottle. With a wink at Alu, he struck a match. At the same moment, Balaram drew his shaking hand back and took a grip on the wooden bar of the handle. They heard Bhudeb Roy shout: Balaram-babu, don't make trouble, stay out of this. . . . And then Balaram slammed the bar forward.

The carbolic acid shot out in an arc and spattered on to the path, raising little mushrooms of dust, a good twenty yards short of Bhudeb Roy and his men. In a burst of jeers and angry shouts, the men started forward. Rakhal leapt to his feet with a tearing scream – Joi Ma Kali! – and threw the flaming bottle high into the air. It sailed out, where he had aimed it, towards the rice field which bordered the path, and disappeared into the rice. A moment later there was a muffled explosion, and the rice around the spot where the bottle had landed was blown flat against the ground, and shards of glass and scraps of metal shot harmlessly upwards.

For a moment Bhudeb Roy stood rooted to the path. Then he turned and ran, with quick waddling steps, towards his house. His men had already sprinted far ahead of him.

Come back for more later, Rakhal called out after them, laughing. We'll have some more ready for you.

*

Half an hour later, when it was clear that Bhudeb Roy's men were not going to return soon, Alu ran into the house to look for Maya. He shouted her name in the courtyard, and looked in the rooms, but she was not in the house. He found her behind the house with her father. They were sitting on the stone parapet which encircled the well, with their legs dangling over the side. He jumped up beside her and began telling her all about it at once. Yes, she said, I know. I watched it from the room above the front door. But he was too excited to stop, and he carried on, gesticulating and stammering, wishing he had the words to tell her of the indescribable excitement, the sheer gut-wrenching thrill of that moment after Balaram's burst of carbolic fell short, and the men started to run towards them, and Rakhal threw the bottle into the air.

And they'll come again, he ended lamely, when he noticed that they were not really listening to him. Rakhal said they would come back at night – with some more men and maybe even guns.

What did Bhudeb Roy say? Shombhu Debnath asked. Tell me again.

Alu told him, trying to remember the words he had used. Shombhu Debnath became very quiet, and stared thoughtfully down at the flashes of light in the water at the bottom of the well. Soon after, he jumped off the parapet and walked away.

A little later, when Alu was back in the circle of drums, talking to Rakhal about what might happen next, the front door opened and Shombhu Debnath came out with Parboti-debi and the little girl. Shombhu Debnath was bare-chested, as always, but he had changed out of his usual red gamcha into a threadbare but clean dhoti, and a pair of green plastic sandals. His hair, washed and oiled, hung loose below his shoulders, framing his long angular face. He had a small cloth bundle balanced on his waist. Parboti-debi, her face covered, was leading her daughter by the hand. The girl, showing no sign of her illness, hopped up and down on the path, and Parboti-debi had to scold her to be still.

Shombhu Debnath hesitated before the oil-drums and cleared his throat. Balaram-babu, he said tentatively. Rakhal abruptly turned his back on him and began to hum a tune.

Shombhu Debnath had to call out again before Balaram stirred. He turned, distracted and irritated: Ah, yes, who?

Shombhu Debnath smiled crookedly, showing his blackened teeth. Balaram-babu, he said, I've come to tell you that I . . . that is, we are going.

Going? Where?

In the two hours that had passed since he pushed the handle on the squirt-gun, Balaram had experienced a curious sensation, as though every minute that passed were a strop, honing his senses, his memory and his mind together into a ferociously sharp edge of concentration. It was as though that one act, that simple moment of action, had dissolved the past and the present, sensation and memory, mind and body, and distilled them into a blissful wholeness. Nothing mattered, nothing existed now but the ecstasy of waiting for the climax, the discovery which he knew to be at hand. Did Pasteur have an inkling of this terrifying joy when he went to examine Joseph Meister the morning after he had inoculated him with his untested vaccine? Did Einstein, in the last moments before his formula appeared before him on paper? And, still, with him it was different, for with him it was his own life, the past, the present, the future. Nothing else mattered, nothing else mattered now, but the discovery. He could hear a voice, and he even knew it dimly to be Shombhu Debnath's voice, but it was just words strung together, a jumbled noise; it had no more meaning for him than a rumble of thunder does for an ascetic awaiting a vision.

Shombhu Debnath, ill at ease, shifting his feet, went on disjointedly: Yes, it's best that we go. It's me and her and the child that he wants. He has no quarrel with you: you're two halves of an apple if you only knew it, one raw, one rotten, but the same fruit. I'm his real enemy, and I've won as much as I want to win, and now it's time to run. Any healthy animal tricks what it can't beat. He'll never find me, and I'll start again somewhere. This is how I came here – with a woman and a child and a bundle of clothes – and this is how I'll go.

Balaram threw him a quick, anxious glance, and turned back to the red-dust path. Shombhu Debnath, misinterpreting his look, said hurriedly: Don't worry about me, I'll manage; I even have some money saved away (and he patted a lump next to the

knot of his dhoti). The boy and the girl won't grudge it to me;
after all, I've brought them up. It's not much, but enough to
buy a loom somewhere. No need to worry about me. It's *them*
I'm worried about, Rakhal and Maya. Maya won't come; she
cries but she won't come. Anyway, that's God's doing. I've
brought her up, and now she's old enough and she has her own
life here. And the boy, why, he won't even look at his father
now.

Shombhu Debnath stopped, but there was no sign that
Balaram had noticed. Shombhu Debnath stepped into the
circle and shook his shoulder. Balaram started and sprang
upright. A thick silvery lock of hair fell across his eyes, and
brushing it away he noticed Parboti-debi for the first time. In
embarrassment, he straightened his collar and tried to brush
the dust and grime off his shirt. With an immense effort, he
smiled politely and folded his hands. *Nomoshkar*, he said, and
stopped, for he could think of nothing else to say. Going out?
he started again, in desperation. You're waiting for Bhudeb-
babu, I suppose. He was here a moment ago; he'll probably be
back soon. . . . He swallowed his words in confusion, and
threw up his hands in a small, barely perceptible gesture,
defeated by her presence. Instead he turned angrily on
Shombhu Debnath: What is it? What do you want now? Can't
you see we're busy? Let me get back to my work.

Shombhu Debnath tried to summon a laugh. Balaram-babu,
he said, I don't want anything for myself. I only want you to go
back into the house and go away to Calcutta for a holiday. You
must stop this: this is madness. There's no reason to go on like
this. No reason. Stop; I beg you, stop, and go away somewhere
for a few days.

Balaram ran his eyes coldly over him. Certainly not, he
snapped, and turned back to look at Bhudeb Roy's house.

As the knowledge of his helplessness slowly dawned on
Shombhu Debnath, his face crumpled. He groaned: *He
Shibo-Shombhu*. Balaram-babu, you'll destroy everyone without even stopping to think about it. You're the best sadhu I've
ever known, Balaram-babu, but no mortal man can cope with
the fierceness of your gods.

Shombhu Debnath fell to his knees and clutched at Balaram's feet. Tears streamed out of his red eyes. Balaram-babu,

stop, he said, catching his breath in sobs. For the last time, I beg you, stop.

Balaram did not take his eyes off the house down the path, his enemy's lair, so familiar that it was almost friendly, but now he saw in front of him a crowd of students, their clothes and features blurred and indistinct like an old photograph. They are crowding in all around him, on the floor, on the great flight of stairs opposite him, in the corridors. They are looking up at him – for he is standing on a chair – listening to him, listening intently. He can see that they are with him, that he has carried them past their initial embarrassment, accustomed them, in fifteen short minutes, to hearing someone talk rationally about underwear. He sees them stir; a little more and they'll be cheering, just a little more. And then he hears a suppressed giggle somewhere in the stir and he raises his voice to meet this most dangerous of threats, laughter: a clean body is a new body, a new body a new life. . . . For a moment it hangs in the balance, but then the laugh breaks through, and behind it is Middle Parting's Calcutta-sharp face, split by an immense grin. Staring, disbelieving, he hears him shout: And what're your little knickers like? He sees thin, shy Dantu throwing himself against Middle Parting, trying to stop him, and then he sees him going down as Middle Parting and his friends push forward. He hears them roar: Let's see his clean little *knick*-ers for ourselves. We should have finished the job the first time. Come on. And the crowd breaks and surges towards him. He totters on his chair in unspeakable, bowel-loosening terror.

But this time he is not pushing his way out, not racing down the corridor with Middle Parting's whoops behind him, his legs are not over the balustrade of the balcony, the ground is not rushing up to meet him. No, not this time.

Balaram stood erect and tall and looked straight into Shombhu Debnath's streaming eyes. No, I cannot go, he said, rejoicing in the strength of his voice. Nobody shall move me from here. Here I stand, and here I shall stay.

Despite his tears, Shombhu Debnath could not stifle a chuckle. Stand on what, Balaram-babu?

Once Shombhu Debnath was on his way, Maya, painfully dry-eyed, ran out of the house, and together she and Alu watched

him leading Parboti-debi and the little girl into the rice fields
on the far side of the bamboo forest. Soon they were lost in a
clump of coconut palms. Rakhal was looking angrily in the
other direction and Balaram was crouched over an oil-drum,
staring down the path.

Soon after, the gates opened and a car drove out, turned
right and speeded away, sending up two plumes of dust. They
could not be sure whether Bhudeb Roy was in the car: Rakhal
said he was, but Alu had not seen him. After that the house was
quiet. Rakhal grew restive. They'll be back soon, he said,
rubbing his hands restlessly, and then the real fight will start.
But the sun climbed higher in the sky, the oil-drums began to
radiate waves of heat, and the house was still quiet. Once
Rakhal skirted through the rice fields, crouching low, until he
could look through the wrought-iron gates. He saw four men
sitting under the mango tree in the garden and smoking, but
nothing else. Back in the circle of drums, he spat: *Dush-shala*; I
should have got them with the bomb the first time.

Why didn't you? said Alu. Rakhal looked at him in surprise:
What? Get them with a bomb and spoil it all for myself? No, I
want to get them when they're really close; when I can pick out
the motherfuckers who're wearing the clothes they stole from
me. I'll break their bones individually, with my own hands,
and then I'll wrap them up in those very shirts, those very
trousers, and throw them back over the garden wall. Here,
look: this'll break more bones than they've got. He pulled a
bicycle chain, dotted with rust, out of his pocket and handed it
to Alu.

Maya snatched it away, crying: For God's sake, *dada*. . . .
But Rakhal looked at her so fiercely that she handed it back to
him. Yes, kill us all, she said, we're all weapons – and went back
to the house.

At midday, with the sun overhead, the oil-drums began to
blast heat, like a furnace. Even Balaram, though he never took
his eyes off Bhudeb Roy's house, drew back from the drums.
Rakhal and Alu decided that they had to move into the house at
least until the sun grew a little less fierce. Balaram protested
feebly, but Rakhal was not in a mood for argument, and he
threatened to carry him if he wouldn't go of his own accord. So
they all went, carrying Balaram's squirt-guns and two buckets

of carbolic. They went straight up to the room above the front
door, so that they would be able to keep a watch on the path
outside and Bhudeb Roy's house.

The day wore on and there was still no sign of any activity in
Bhudeb Roy's house. Alu sensed that the village was unnatur-
ally quiet: all day long he had not seen a single person out in the
fields. It's as though they're waiting, he said to Rakhal; but
Rakhal only laughed. In the afternoon, soon after Alu, Maya
and Rakhal had eaten a quick meal of rice and fried potatoes,
Nonder-ma disappeared. Where'd she go? Rakhal asked Maya.
She said she was going out for a minute to Bolai-da's to buy
something, Maya said, and then . . . Rakhal shrugged, and
Maya busied herself cooking their dinner.

At sunset Rakhal came to a decision. They're going to come
at night, he told Alu. That's why they're doing nothing now.
That circle of drums isn't going to be of any use now; if they
come at night, they'll get at the house first, perhaps from the
back. We've got to move everything into the house. We'll roll
the drums here and stand them up before the front door. You
can do that. But, first, we'll have to get Maya and Toru-mashi
out of the house.

How? said Alu doubtfully.

I'll talk to Maya, said Rakhal, but his face was eloquent of
uncertainty. They both climbed down to the courtyard, and
Rakhal went to the kitchen. They both came out again soon,
Rakhal crestfallen, Maya calmly wiping her hands on her sari.
Alu looked from one to the other: So? If I leave, Maya said,
where will I go? All right, all right, said Rakhal, but now go and
talk to Toru-mashi. Maya nodded, and they watched her go to
Toru-debi's room, and hesitantly push the door open.

She came hurtling out a moment later. She threw the
scissors at me, Maya gasped. She says the machine is about to
save us: she's finished four and she's halfway through the
fifth.

Didn't you tell her, Alu said, that Parboti-debi . . .?

If you want to tell her anything, you can go and talk to her
yourself, said Maya, and turning her back on them she went
straight to the kitchen. Rakhal shrugged.

They went out to the circle of oil-drums, and Rakhal put Alu
to work at moving the drums. It was a pointless and exhausting

job, for the drums were all half-full of carbolic solution, and
very heavy. Alu could only move them by levering them over,
and rolling them along the ground, and that meant spilling
most of the carbolic solution. But Rakhal insisted that it had to
be done. In the meanwhile, with minute, painstaking care,
Rakhal wrapped the contents of the tarpaulin-covered heap in
jute sacks and carried them into the courtyard. He would not
let Alu touch them. When he had finished, the stack of sacks
seemed even larger to him than it had outside. But Rakhal was
worried. It won't be enough, he said, examining it. I'll have to
go and get some more. You stay here and don't go out of the
house. I'll be back in ten minutes.

He ran out of the house, in the direction of their huts. He
was back again soon, with a plastic sack over his shoulder.
When he had added the sack to the others, the stack seemed
huge to Alu. But Rakhal shook his head, dissatisfied. I don't
know if it'll be enough, he said, but it's too late now. . . .

Soon after the last glow of twilight had faded away, they
heard the whine of engines in the distance. A minute later
Balaram shouted down: They've come, they've come. Alu
raced up the ladder with Rakhal. Balaram was rigid in front of
the window, pointing out, and for a moment his look of blissful,
rapturous relief stopped Alu dead.

Looking out, they could see three jeeps at Bhudeb Roy's
gate, and they counted more than a dozen shadowy figures as
they climbed out. Then three powerful searchlight beams
simultaneously flared out of the jeeps' hoods, blinding them.
Rakhal caught Alu's shoulder and led him to the ladder. He was
perfectly calm and unhurried but the scar was shining brilliantly on his cheek.

There are more of them than I thought, he said as they
climbed down the ladder. I'm not sure we have enough to deal
with them in the sacks. And now it'll be impossible to meet
them hand-to-hand.

Alu caught a glimpse of Toru-debi, squatting in a corner of
the courtyard with her head in her hands. But Rakhal had his
back to her, and he went on urgently: You'll have to do
something. I can't leave the house now. You remember the old
loom-shed in our courtyard? The pits are covered with palm
leaves and earth now, but you just have to pull and the palm

leaves will come away. You'll find a sack in the pit; it's a sort of plastic, the kind you get fertilizers and insecticides in. Pick it up, but very, very carefully – do you understand? very very carefully – and bring it here. Don't open it, don't look into it, don't shake it, don't drop it. Just bring it here. And run as fast as you can. They'll surround the house soon, and you won't be able to get back after that.

It's no use.

They both spun around. Toru-debi, watching them from her corner, let slip a bitter, mocking little laugh. It's no use, she said again. Her hair hung around her face in damp, tangled knots; her sari had slipped off her shoulders, and her blouse had come undone. Her right hand was resting on her sewing machine beside her.

Nothing's any use now, she muttered. It's the end. Just one blouse left to go and he's died. She ran her hand over the machine's shining wheel and pulled, with all her strength. The wheel was absolutely rigid. She smiled at them: You see; he's haunted. There's something in him.

Suddenly her face lit up, as though something had occurred to her. She tore her blouse away, and her heavy breasts spilled out. She lifted the black, sinuously curved machine off its wooden base and settled it on her lap, clucking to herself.

Maya darted forward and caught her hands. Toru-debi looked up shamefacedly, straight at Alu. I thought it was you, she said confusedly. Aren't you going to do something? Then all at once her naked breasts and shoulders collapsed as though an immense weight had been lowered on to them. What's the use? she said. It's the end.

Alu felt his throat go dry as he looked at the terrible incandescent desolation in her eyes. Then Rakhal was shaking him, whispering: Run, there's no time to lose. And Maya was beside him, holding his hand: Yes, go. I'll look after her; don't worry.

In a daze, Alu found his slippers and went to the back door. But before he could slip out Toru-debi shouted again: Alu, come here. For one minute; only one.

Slowly Alu went back to her. She stood up and put the sewing machine in his arms. Throw it into the pond, she said. It's dead. She leant forward and searched his eyes. But you'll get me another, Alu my bit of gold, won't you? she said, her voice full of trust. A better one?

Alu turned and ran blindly out of the door. Listen! he heard Maya shouting after him. He turned and saw her, framed in the doorway, smoothing back her thick black hair, biting her lip in worry. Come back soon, he heard her shout, and then he was running again, blindly, hardly noticing the weight of the sewing machine in his arms.

Before he could reach the forest, he heard footsteps and stopped, alert again. Then he recognized a familiar bandy-legged figure racing towards him. *Kahan?* Where are you going? Bolai-da shouted, panting. He spoke in Hindi, as he always had to Alu, ever since he taught him the language. Where? What's happening? Nonder-ma said. . . .

Then he noticed the sewing machine and his eyes widened. Alu put the sewing machine into his arms. There, he said, look after that. I'll take it back from you some day. And don't go to the house.

And then he was running again, flying down the path, grateful that he knew it so well, that the darkness made no difference. One of his slippers tore and he kicked it off in mid-step, without checking. He was almost there, no further than a few yards, when a microphone boomed behind him: This is a warning to you; this is a warning. Come out peacefully.

Alu stopped and turned towards the house. The bamboo thickets where the house lay were silhouetted against a curtain of metallic light. He forgot all about the loom, all about Rakhal's instructions, and began to run towards the house. The microphone boomed again: This is a warning, this is the last warning to you. Then, with a high whistle, a brilliant sunburst of light arced into the sky and the whole forest shimmered in the eerie silver glow. He saw it reach its zenith and curve downwards, and fall out of his sight, behind the bamboo. There was a moment of absolute stillness when it struck him that the light must have fallen very near the house. And then the earth shook and the air seemed to come alive and hit him with walls of force, and when he opened his eyes again exactly where the house ought to have been there were orange flames shooting into the sky.

Alu began to run again. His whole mind went blank, except

for the rhythm of his pounding feet. He saw a figure standing on the path ahead of him, but the familiar bandy legs meant no more than an obstacle blocking his way, and instinctively he turned his shoulder and threw himself at it. But Bolai-da sidestepped deftly and next moment he had Alu pinned to his chest in a wrestler's lock. What d'you want to go back to the house for? he said as Alu struggled against his arms. There's nobody there any more but the police buggers. There's nothing for you to do there. God's cremated them all.

Alu twisted and clawed at his arm, trying to break the lock. Exasperated, Bolai-da pulled one of his hands loose and hit him hard across the cheek, and Alu slumped over. Bolai-da put a shoulder under one of his arms and half-carried, half-dragged him into the forest. God, he mumbled, you should have seen that flare . . . right over, straight into the courtyard, and the whole place – up like a bomb. They'll be all around it now, looking for you. But they're not going to get you. I named you and I'll see you safe somewhere. . . .

Alu, stumbling along beside him, inert and uncomprehending, could only see the flames of the known world licking the skies.

Chapter Eight

Going West

Until very recently it used to take three days to travel to Mahé
from Calcutta by train (it takes a little less now because of the
New Bongaigaon Express). It takes so long because Mahé is at
the other end of the subcontinent – on the west coast, only a
few hundred miles north of the southernmost tip of the
Peninsula.

The older part of Mahé town is on a knoll, overlooking the
sluggish green Mahé river which flows down from the thickly
forested Idikki hills to the east. The town and its tiny
hinterland are surrounded by Kerala, and at first sight it looks
like any other coastal Malabar town. But actually Mahé is not a
part of Kerala. It owes this, like the church with its slate-
topped steeple which juts above the town, to the fact that it was
once a French colony – a tiny island of Gallic domination in a
sea of British-occupied territory.

The sea which breaks on Mahé's beaches is the Arabian Sea
and it washes in wealth. Mahé has the air of a boom town, but
on a modest, muted scale, for it is actually a very small and
inconspicuous place. Those who have heard the name usually
remember it only indistinctly or for an examination, and very
few know where to find it on a map.

On the morning of the third day of his journey, when he was
only a few hours away from Mahé, Jyoti Das was very bored
and very restless. He knew he ought not to be, for the
landscape he had woken up to that morning was strikingly
beautiful, especially after – to give things their proper names –
the desert he had shut his eyes on in Tamil Nadu the night
before. It was like waking up in an extravagant garden.
Everything was green; there were greens of so many shades
whirling past his window – the new-leaf green of banana trees,
the deep emerald of rice, the feathery darkness of coconut

palms. There seemed to be no exposed surface, no bit of rock, no sand, nothing that was not draped in green. The soil seemed to be writhing in labour, in its effort to push greenery out at every angle. Even the air smelt rich – of loam, cardamom and cloves, salted with a tang of the sea. The coconut palms jostled with each other on both sides of the tracks, crowding out the horizon and shrinking the sky to a little blue patch, directly above. Sometimes, through the mass of slender trunks, he could catch the scimitar flash of a lagoon in the distance. And in the east, hanging in the air, above the palms, he could see pale, silvery mountains.

But three days of sitting still, even if in a first-class compartment. would bore anyone. All that Jyoti Das could feel now was the stiffness in his joints and the grime on his skin. He could see veins of dirt in the creases of his shirt and trousers, but there was nothing he could do about it, for he had used up all the changes of clothing he had brought with him on the train. That worried him, for it meant that he would have to meet Dubey, the ASP in Mahé, in grimy clothes. Dubey was a real ASP, posted in a district, and ASPs in districts live like minor potentates, with platoons of orderlies to wash and iron their uniforms. Jyoti Das knew Dubey a little; they had been contemporaries at the Academy, though not friends, for Dubey had been known there chiefly by his reputation for stupidity (which, thought Jyoti, was saying quite a lot in *that* crowd). Dubey, very likely, never wore the same uniform twice in a month. He had lived well, even at the Academy. Especially after his marriage, when he was given, or so people said, a television set, a refrigerator, a car *and* several lakhs of rupees along with a wife. But, then, those were the going rates for a police officer in Bihar and eastern Uttar Pradesh.

At least there was the possibility of seeing a paradise flycatcher. He had brought his watercolours with him, just in case. He had seen one the last time he was in Kerala, on a compulsory tour of India during his training, but his colleagues were with him then, and he would not have dreamt of pulling out his sketchpad with them watching. This time, perhaps. As for the case, it was almost certainly going to be a waste of time, despite Dubey's urgent telex. Five months had passed since the raid, and the case was more or less closed as far as he was concerned. But he shut his eyes, and turned away from the window, for even now he could not help shutting his eyes whenever he thought of the raid and saw that flare – fired only as a warning – sending up the whole house. God, there was no point in going on with the business. But Dubey's telex had arrived, and the DIG had sent him on his way. What was the use? Dubey could have handled whatever there was to handle himself, instead of dragging him all the way from Calcutta.

Of course there was the paradise flycatcher, but hardly worth being dragged all the way from Calcutta for, especially in winter with the zoo full of birds. There was something else, too, but about that he didn't know whether to be relieved or angry. His mother had wanted him to take a look at a girl. He had more or less ritually refused to go. But his mother had gone ahead and fixed a day, and in the end he had agreed to go with her. He didn't particularly wish to be married, but he didn't particularly wish not to be married. And if it brought peace at home – well, then. But now it would have to wait. Of course, there was the flycatcher.

As the train draws in at Mahé, Jyoti Das is irritated and thoroughly resentful – at being made to sit in a train for three days, at the unnecessary exertion, at the waste of time. . . . A waste of time, he thinks. He is wrong, but he does not know it. He is about to be launched on the greatest adventure of his life.

Dubey was Jyoti's first surprise: looking for the lean gangling figure he remembered, he saw instead a plump, sleek man spilling over with an unexpectedly warm welcome. Dubey disposed of his luggage by snapping his fingers at a constable, and led him out of the little station to a jeep.

Jyoti found himself squeezed between Dubey and the driver, trying to think of something to say. Surreptitiously he glanced at Dubey's uniform. It was perfectly creased and ironed, the material much finer than any a mere uniforms allowance can buy. That's the life, he thought. Be a small-town cop and prosper. Aloud he said: You're looking healthy. How's your asthma?

Oh, all right, Dubey answered. How're your paintings?

Taken aback, Jyoti Das said: Not bad, not bad. And how's Mrs Dubey?

Fine, fine. Went back to Delhi last year. Doesn't like it here. And you? Still a happy bachelor?

Yes, Das said quickly. Now tell me what all this hurry was about. Have you got him?

No. Not yet. But we know he's in this area, and we'll definitely be able to trace some of his associates, so we'll probably get him soon. That's why I thought it would be best if you came personally. After all, it's your case and I don't want to take any undue credit for it (No, thought Das, I'm sure you don't). It's a good thing you've come actually, because just this morning some of my chaps in one of the villages around here brought in someone promising. If we get anything out of him, we should be able to pick up your bugger in a day or two, maybe even today. You've come just in time.

That's very quick work, said Das. How'd you do it?

Well, we got the report you people sent – that the Suspect was believed to be somewhere in this area. There are a number of extremist groups around here, so I thought at once that he'd probably try to contact them. Then we got the sketch from your artists and I called in my station-house officers from the villages and showed it to them and told them about the case. After that, information began trickling in. It was easy. But this man we've picked up today is the real key.

Have you talked to him yet?

No, he's still in a station outside the town, Dubey said. We'll go and talk to him a little later.

The car stopped outside a yellow, tiled bungalow over-looking the sea. This is where you'll stay, said Dubey, leading Das to a veranda. He gestured at a cane chair and ordered tea. Now, he said, what can you tell me about this business? In answer Das took a thick file from his briefcase and handed it to him. Dubey grimaced: Hell *yar*, can't you just tell me? Why all this reading-sheading?

There's not much to tell, Das said abruptly. You've seen the report we sent out already. I suppose you know there was an encounter with an extremist group in a village about five months ago? There was an accident, sort of, and most of them died. But one got away – there was a corpse missing. We managed to trace him to Calcutta. He was hiding with one of his uncle's associates. I put some chaps on the job, and that was a mistake, for the bird had flown by the time they got there. Anyway the old man told them that the Suspect had ganged up with some Keralites in a textile factory in Calcutta. We got hold of one of the gang but we couldn't get much out of him. Only that the Suspect was heading south, probably towards Kerala. I talked to the old man myself later. He had nothing much to say, that is, nothing important to say – he had a lot to say otherwise. After that we just followed the routine and sent you people a circular and a sketch. Frankly, we didn't expect anything to come of it. Actually, to tell you the truth, I'd be quite happy to put an end to this business – I can't see that it's important in any way. But the DIG. . . .

Das stopped to look at Dubey. The DIG, he continued, thinks it's very important. He shrugged: Anyway, that's more or less all that's in the files.

Jyoti Das was right – that was all the files said. What else could they say? They knew nothing of the days Alu spent after Bolai-da smuggled him into a truck and sent him to Gopal's flat in Calcutta. They knew nothing of the time he spent wandering blindly through the city, without stopping to eat, without even wondering how it came to be that he had lost the sensation of hunger. Or of the bench in the Maidan where his straying feet led him every night, to sit and wonder whether a match would still burn his skin, whether that at least was still left to him.

And when he returned to the flat on Hazra Road, Gopal, waiting for him, every night, would ask gently: Where did you go today? Every night the same question and every night Gopal would watch the same bewilderment play across the potato face, for really he did not know. For nights without end Gopal would sit in his easy chair and weep for Balaram, friend of his youth, his tears splashing heavily into the open book on his lap; and, weeping, he would watch Alu and wait for the first hint of an answering tear – for a sign at least – of grief, anything but that dumb, blank bewilderment. But there was nothing.

Only once did Alu have anything to tell him, and then for hours: he talked of a machine, a sewing machine in a display window. He talked of its sinuous curves, its bulging, powerful chest and tapering underbelly, of its shining blackness and dull gold lettering, of its poised needle and the inexhaustible miracle which can join together two separate pieces of cloth. He talked on until dawn, while Gopal wept unheeded, not only for Balaram this time, but for Alu, too, and his ebbing reason. Gopal did not know that that day Alu had won a battle for his spirit.

But soon Gopal stopped worrying for him, for one night Alu showed him two boils, the size of duck's eggs, one on his leg and the other under his armpit – not ordinary boils, but suppurating craters of pus, as though his flesh had gathered itself together and tried to burst from his body. Gopal embraced Alu that night and laughed. Let them be, he said. They have nothing to do with you; it's only Balaram trying to come back to the world.

But Alu covered his leg and glowered at him. Not just Balaram, he growled.

Gopal nodded wisely and turned away.

There were more and more, all over Alu's body, and the pain drove him to walk farther and farther afield – to the crowds fighting their way out of Sealdah Station, to Howrah Bridge, across, and still farther, until sirens were shrieking all around him and he was swept away by crowds pouring out of factory gates. It was then that by some inexplicable turn of fortune Alu did something he had not done before – he stopped at a tea-stall and asked for a cup of tea.

It was there that he met Rajan.

That day, dark, brooding Rajan told him about the great factories all around them. He talked of Jacquard looms and streams of punched paper which could draw patterns with warp strings faster than the eye could see; of looms blessed with the sense of touch, automatic looms, which could send out feelers to sense whether their shuttles were empty or not; of looms without any real shuttles at all, in which hurtling projectiles flew through the empty space of the shed, between the two parted streams of the warp yarn, to bite into a waiting bobbin and carry it back; of looms in which curled iron rapiers served for shuttles, snapping through the shed to carry the weft in a pierced eye; of shuttles of which he had only read, which fly on jets, like aeroplanes. . . . That night Gopal was awake again till dawn, listening to Alu talk of the factory and Rajan and, of course, machines.

After that Alu went back to the tea-shop every day, before Rajan's shift. Sometimes he talked of his own loom and the cloth he had woven, and to his astonishment he found that his language was no mystery to Rajan. For Rajan was of Kerala's great caste of Chalias who for centuries have woven and traded in simple white cloth. There was no loom anywhere that was a mystery to Rajan.

One day he smuggled Alu into the mill he worked in: a huge bustling vault, the machines new, awesome in their potency and their size; the men minuscule, compressed, struggling under the weight of the giants. It was a miracle which had no end – webs of yarn shooting into the maws of the automatic looms from whirling bobbins, cloth pouring out in waterfalls, folding itself into ordered bales. . . .

But where are the peanuts? Eyes riveted to the stage, craning over the hundreds of shoulders in front of him. Alu sends his hands wandering through his pockets, looking for that just-bought jet of twisted paper, filled with nuts, whole coarse-veined nuts waiting to be broken, waiting for the red kernels inside to be worried out and rubbed in minty green salt, for the shells to drop to the floor to be stamped into the earth by those thousands of feet, all shifting nervously now, as the whole great tent watches, awestruck, while the demons dance, encircling the heroes in rings of fire, beating them to the ground with their uncountable arms, dancing on their chests with their clawed feet, reaching for the victory that is almost theirs. And just then, suddenly, all too accidentally, a spanner drops into the shooting rapids of cloth, into the heart of the grinding machine, and, screaming, the demons freeze. A sigh of relief rises from the men on the floor, and they lean back for a few stolen minutes to finish conversations and light cigarettes. But Alu is on his feet, cheering and throwing peanuts, until he has to be led outside, still noisily celebrating the tiny victories of the men who live with demons.

Outside they found Gopal, standing at the tea-shop, his face crumpled with anxiety, holding a cloth bundle. When he saw Alu he ran across the road and hugged him, stammering with relief.

Such news! An elderly brother-in-law in the High Court (mainly revenue and taxation, but also a few criminal sometimes to make a bit of money) was visiting a prospective client in Lalbazar Police Station when he heard search orders being given out for an address in Hazra Road – Gopal's address. Gopal's house was to be searched; there could be no doubt for whom.

The bundle was thrust into Alu's hands. Alu opened it and found the few clothes Gopal had bought him, Gopal's own copy of the *Life of Pasteur* and 8000 rupees. Gopal smiled in embarrassment. Your uncle had left it with me, to invest. It's yours now. Alu looked at him and Gopal looked away. But Alu didn't argue. He bent down and touched Gopal's feet. Gopal hugged him once, blindly, and then he was gone, back to the flat in Hazra Road, to send his wife away and wait for the police alone.

Rajan knew, as soon as he saw Alu standing in the road with a bundle in his hands. Alu tried to mumble an explanation, but Rajan stopped him. What was the use of talking and ex-planations? Everyone saw these things every day. It was not the time for talk. Within minutes Alu had a list of addresses and a letter. With those, and boils erupting all over him, he passed down a chain of Rajan's Chalia kinsmen, scattered over every factory along the South-Eastern Railway, paying out parts of his 8000 rupees where Rajan had told him to, down, down, steadily southwards, stopping to catch his breath in the great mills of Madurai and Coimbatore, till whispers came that the police had orders and a sketch, Rajan had been taken in. . . . Then it was time to leave the railways behind, time to slip into the forests of the Nilgiris, led by Rajan's great-grandfather's cousin's great-grandson, along elephant trails and deer tracks through clouds in blue mountains, then over the watershed, into Kerala, a step into a magical prawn malai curry, redolent of cardamom and cinnamon, sharp with cloves, sweet with the milk of coconuts enough to float the world. He spent the nights secreted away in the Chalia quarters of scattered villages, lulled to sleep by the cheerful knocking of hundreds of fly-shuttles in familiar looms; but then again, suddenly, rumours of informers, of reports to the police, so faster still, westwards, down through the mountains, faster and faster. . . .

Where were the files then?

*

A little before sunset Das and Dubey set out for the village in which the prisoner was being held. The car took them into the little town and towards the river, through narrow roads lined with brightly lit shops. Their windows were crammed with bottles and their signs read: IMFL – Indian-Made Foreign Liquor.

Dubey pointed out of the window. Do you booze? This is the place for it. Dirt cheap and good stuff, too.

Das's eyes slid down to Dubey's wrist, to a heavy gold watch. He stared at it enviously. Of course, he could have got it from his father-in-law. Could have. A town which lives on the liquor trade – gold watches were probably thrown at everyone from the revenue clerk upwards. What else could one ask for? No DIG sitting on you, forget about promotions and life insurance and provident funds and house-rent allowances. Money no problem – a peaceful, simple life.

Dubey was pointing at a large pink and green house with round portholes for windows. It bristled with air-conditioners. Some of the houses around it were larger, some newer, some even more strikingly opulent.

That man went to al-Ghazira for five years, Dubey said. He was just a mechanic and look at him now. Look at all the rest of them. He's almost illiterate, you know, but I'm still ashamed to ask him to my house.

Don't worry, Das murmured. You'll catch up; it's just a matter of time.

Of course, Dubey went on, ignoring him, a lot of them are smugglers. You won't believe how much smuggling goes on here. Mainly it's gold coming in, from all over the world – Kenya, Tanzania, Iran, the Gulf. But there are other things, too – electronic things, watches. . . .

Look! he jogged Das's elbow. A paper-thin slice of metal lay in his palm, barely filling it. He poised a finger over a button. There was a soft electronic chime and the display panel lit up. He ran his fingers over it and numbers flashed on to the panel and disappeared, accompanied by a tattoo of chimes. Nice thing, no? Dubey said. Lots of these things lying around here.

He jabbed Das in the ribs, grinning: Maybe your DIG likes these little things? I'm sure he has a son or two who have exams? No?

Das shook his head and looked out of the window. They were passing a lagoon. The water flamed with the crimson of the setting sun. Palms leant languidly across the water and they could see boatmen in conical hats rowing their catamarans out to sea.

It's very beautiful here, Das said.

Yeah, yeah, Dubey said. It's beautiful for five days, a week. After that. . . .

Das spotted a Malabar kingfisher on a telegraph pole and turned in his seat as they drove past it. What's the matter? Dubey said curiously. It's a . . ., Das began and stopped himself just in time. He remembered an occasion at the Academy when, interrupting one of Dubey's monologues on their colleagues, he had pointed out a pheasant-tailed jaçana.

Which year did he join? Dubey had said worriedly, searching his mind. Is he in the police? I don't think I've heard the name. . . .

It had made a good story, but on the whole it had told against him rather than against Dubey. People had thought he was showing off. Dubey had been furious. Still, Malabar king-fishers were probably all right, but if Dubey ever heard him talking about some less familiar species, like Siberian cranes or something like that, he was more than likely to send off a telegram to their superiors reporting him for consorting with undesirable foreigners. He was said to be very competitive, Dubey, for all his thick-headedness. Wouldn't stop at anything.

What? said Dubey again, waiting for an answer.

I was wondering, Das said quickly. You explained what they smuggle in, but what do they smuggle out? Coconuts?

Coconuts! Dubey laughed. Those people don't want coconuts over there. No, what they smuggle out is people.

He stopped and stroked his moustache. Sometimes I wish, he said, that someone would smuggle *me* out – to another posting, I mean. I'm sick of this place. It would help if I got a promotion or an especially good annual report. If we get your chap today or within the next couple of days, maybe your DIG. . . . They say he knows a lot of people.

He looked anxiously across. Das nodded. The car turned off the main road and turned into a narrow lane flanked by banks of earth and laterite walls. A little later it stopped outside a flat-roofed yellow building, unmistakably a police station. The squat, ugly building contrasted sharply with the houses around it, which were white with ornately carved wooden posts, and tiled roofs that stopped just a few feet short of the ground.

A constable in starched khaki shorts came running out of the station. He stood at attention and saluted, his stiff shorts swinging like bells. Dubey acknowledged the salute with a brief gesture. Das saw a crowd of children gathering across the street. As he walked past one of them called out shyly: Hul-lo hul-lo, jol-ly fel-low.

Embarrassed, Das looked quickly ahead, fervently hoping the constable would not make a scene. The constable had not noticed. As he stepped into a large neon-lit room, he heard the boy chant again, somewhere behind hin: Hul-lo hul-lo, jol-ly fel-low.

A table at the far end of the room was covered with plates of food and bottles of soft drinks. Dubey rounded on the constable. How many times have I told you not to waste money like this? he shouted in Hindi.

The constable looked down at his sandalled feet, smiling shyly and wriggling. Automatically, drawn by the force of years of habit, his hand reached under his shorts to pull his shirt straight. Stop that! Dubey snapped. Stand at attention when I'm talking to you.

The constable jumped to attention. Dubey shrugged and turned to Das: Come on, we may as well eat, now that it's here. They sat behind the table on straight-backed chairs and filled their plates with banana chips and crisp muruka.

Have you talked to the man? Dubey asked the constable.

Yes, *saar-ey*, the constable answered.

What did he say?

The constable scratched his head. This man is a Chalia, *saar-ey*, he said, and he has a relative in Calcutta. A man came to him with a letter from his relative, so he led him to Mahé. After that he won't say anything.

What do you mean, he won't say anything? Dubey said and stopped abruptly. There was a low but distinct rumbling sound outside the police station. He listened for a moment, his head cocked. He decided to ignore it: Why won't he say anything?

We tried, *saar-ey*, the constable said, but he won't talk. Perhaps you could talk to him.

Does he speak Hindi or English?

Yes, a little bit of Hindi.

All right, Dubey said, bring him in.

The constable gestured to another, who disappeared into a corridor. Again they heard the rumbling sound outside. Dubey picked up a cane and pointed out of the window: What's that noise?

The constable screwed up his eyes and peered out of the window into the darkness. Just some local people, *saar-ey*, he said dismissively, gathered outside the arrack-shop across the road.

The other constable came back, leading a bare-chested man in a green lungi. He was a powerfully built man, with a broad muscular chest, but now his eyes were bloodshot and he hung his head. Dubey looked him over and told a constable to switch the neon lights off and train a light on the prisoner's face. Das smiled wrily: Copy-book technique.

Dubey gave him a twitch of his lips in acknowledgement. Then, patting his open palm with the cane, he walked up to the prisoner and said softly: I just want to know one thing, that's all. Where is that man now?

The prisoner hung his head in silence. Dubey looked at him for a moment, then he spun on his booted heel and smiled thinly at Das: Why don't we see what the Union Secretariat can do?

Das hesitated, taken by surprise, but Dubey was watching him, smiling. He got up and went up to the man in the lungi, trying hard not to advertise his nervousness by swallowing. He took Dubey's cane from him and prodded the man in the chest. Listen, you, he said. He raised his voice, for he could sense a hint of a tremor at the back of his throat: Don't make trouble for yourself. Just tell us: where is that man now?

The prisoner stared silently at Das's shoes. Das rubbed his right hand. Then he pulled his hand back and smashed the back of his palm across the prisoner's face, swivelling with the blow, throwing all his weight behind it. The man howled and clutched his cheek. Slowly he crumpled to his knees.

Das stuffed his smarting hand into his pocket before the

temptation to rub it could become irresistible. He felt his bile churn and rise, searing the back of his throat. He glanced across the room hoping Dubey would not notice his hand shaking. Dubey raised a congratulatory eyebrow. Tough cop, he said.

Suddenly Das was startled. He seemed to hear a chant somewhere: Hul-lo hul-lo, jol-ly fel-low. The noise outside had grown; now scattered shouts pierced the rumbling. He heard the chant again, close by. Looking around him he spotted a pair of eyes peeping through a crack in a shuttered window. He said quickly: Dubey, we should move to some other room. This isn't at all suitable.

Dubey rapped out an order and the prisoner was led out of the room holding his bleeding cheek. Dubey made a remark as they followed the prisoner out, but the noise had grown so loud that Das could not hear him. What? he shouted.

I said, we've got to get him to talk now or. . . . Das strained forward to hear him, but Dubey's words were lost, for suddenly the noise outside gathered itself together and erupted into a full-throated roar. In the moment's silence that followed Das heard a thin voice piping: Hul-lo hul-lo, jol-ly fel-low. Then another roar, even louder. They could hear the glass rattling in the windows. Quickly they moved into a small windowless room inside.

What are they shouting? Das asked, trying to speak calmly. Dubey did not answer.

Han? Dubey?

I don't know, Dubey said shortly.

Das thought for a moment. You mean to say, he began. A stone flew through the outer room and rolled down the corridor towards them. Preoccupied, Das picked it up and rubbed it between his hands. You mean to say, he said, that you haven't passed your departmental language examinations?

There were more shouts outside, and stones clattered on the shuttered windows. Frowning, Das went on: Doesn't it hold up your salary increments?

It's much worse, Dubey confided in a rush. Not only are they holding up my increments, now there's talk of withholding payment into my gratuity and provident funds. It's terrible – you don't know. You chaps in your home states are lucky; you don't know what it's like for us. (Das flinched as a roar shook the walls.) I've got myself a teacher and I've tried to learn the bloody lingo, but it's impossible. You'd never believe the kinds of words these buggers think up.

A constable stood before them, nervously shifting his weight from leg to leg. He looked scared. *Saar-ey . . .*, he said.

Dubey went to the prisoner and prodded his chin up with the point of the cane. Look, he said, tell us the truth and you'll be out of here in ten minutes. We don't want to keep you – just tell us the truth. Don't talk, and I'll see to it that you're here for ten years. Now, just tell us: where is that man right now? Don't make me lose my temper.

The man swallowed and brushed a trickle of blood from his cheek. There was a heavy thud on the outer door of the station, and they heard it creak. Dubey ignored it. Looking straight into the prisoner's eyes, he laid the tip of his cane on the bridge of his nose. Come on, where is he now?

He's on a boat for al-Ghazira, the prisoner said in halting Hindi. *Mariamma*. It left two days ago.

In his disappointment Dubey smashed his cane on the floor, so hard that it splintered and broke. Das patted him on the back: Never mind, you'll get your report anyway. I'll talk to the DIG.

Dubey ignored him. Glaring, he shouted at the prisoner: Why al-Ghazira?

The prisoner was no longer hanging his head. He was looking straight at Dubey, and there was a faint hint of triumph in the angle of his head. He said nothing.

Dubey shouted again: Why al-Ghazira? Does he have connections there? People who work with him?

The outer door was groaning and creaking ominously now, and the constables were cowering in a corner. The prisoner was still silent. Das tapped Dubey on the shoulder, but his hand was brushed away. Doubling his splintered cane, Dubey held it to the prisoner's stomach. He drew his arm back: Come on quickly. Does he have connections there?

Silently the prisoner nodded. Turning to Das, Dubey said sharply: Any more questions? Das shook his head.

Good, said Dubey. He waved to a constable. Let him go after we've gone, but keep an eye on him.

In the outer room shards of glass from a broken window-pane crackled under their shoes. Das noticed an orange glow filtering in under the door. He put his eye to a crack in the shutters and looked out. He caught a glimpse of flaming palm-leaf torches and a dense mass of people thronged into the narrow road outside the police station. Then suddenly there was another eye opposite his and a voice was singing: Hul-lo hul-lo, jol-ly fel-low.

Das jumped back. Dubey, he said, maybe you should issue arms to the constables. Dubey nodded and spoke to the Head Constable. They watched the constables filling registers, unlocking the arms cabinet and fingering the rifles inside.

Dubey said: Let's hope they don't join the crowd – they haven't got their dearness allowance for three months.

The Head Constable prised the heavy outer door open and prodded the tip of his ancient rifle through. A hush fell on the crowd. The other constables fanned out behind him and the two officers stepped out.

Their driver had prudently taken their car to a lane a little way off when the crowd had begun to collect. The constables cleared a path for them with jabs of their rifles. Das walked quickly, trying not to notice the angry silence rustling around them and the shuffles and the lunges that were arrested by indecision. He could see no faces, only shadows flickering in the torchlight. He forced his head up and slowed his pace. He sensed running feet behind him, and he felt his muscles stiffen with tension. He looked down without turning his head. It was the same little boy.

They were at the edges of the crowd now. He could feel the tension snapping in the air; he saw feet thrust out, arms drawn back, hesitating, waiting for a lead. Then they were through, climbing into the car, trying not to look back.

Das sank into his seat and breathed deeply. Then he saw the boy's face again, at the window: Hul-lo hul-lo, jol-ly fel-low. The boy drew his head back, opened his mouth and spat. But Jyoti Das had already managed to wind the window up, and the spit dribbled harmlessly down the glass.

Next moment the car jumped forward and the boy was thrown aside. The crowd roared and surged into the lane, but the car was already picking up speed. They heard two stones strike the roof and roll off clanging loudly. And then they turned a corner and left the crowd far behind them. The gob of spittle was soon blown off the window.

Really, Das said, looking at Dubey, it's incredible. Something should be done about it – stopping your increments *and* your gratuity and provident fund instalments! Can't the Officers' Association do anything?

Dubey shook his head. He was huddled morosely in a corner. How's a man to live? he said. At least you people get city-compensatory allowance; in this place we don't even get that. And it's not bad enough for a hardship allowance, either.

For a while Dubey stared silently out of the window. Then he clenched his fists and muttered: Someday I'll clean the place up, really clean it up. Chaos, nothing but bloody chaos. Give me one battalion of the Central Reserve Police, just one, and I'll clean them up like they've never been cleaned up before. They won't know what hit them. These local constables are no good. They're paid by those buggers – same lingo, same bloody people. . . . Just *one* battalion.

He saw Das looking at him and stopped. He drew a deep breath. So, Das! Congratulations!

Congratulations? Das said, bewildered. Why?

On your foreign trip, you fool. Don't you see? If you give your DIG or whoever the line that the Suspect has joined up with some Middle Eastern terrorist groups or something, they'll have to send you there to follow up. That's why I wanted to get that man to confess that the Suspect has connections there – all for your sake. Now you can safely put it in your report. It's very simple: there are hundreds of terrorist groups and things there and he's bound to get involved with them. You *must* follow up that angle and even use a bit of pressure perhaps. And you watch; if you're sensible, you'll get a foreign trip. To al-Ghazira. Don't let them take you off the case now.

Really, Das thought, he's not at all as stupid as people say. In fact, he's quite shrewd. He felt a little dizzy; he had never been abroad before. A pleasant thrill of apprehension coursed through him and he shivered.

I wonder what daily allowances and travel allowances the Ministry will give you, Dubey said enviously. Lucky bastard. God, the things you'll be able to buy! Everything imported.

Jyoti Das did not answer. He was thinking of al-Ghazira. A new sky, a whole new world of birds. Wasn't al-Ghazira on one of the major migration routes? He would have to do a bit of reading at the National Library. What would the colours be like? he wondered.

That night Dubey took him to dine with the Chief Administrator of Mahé. When they arrived, Jyoti spent a long time marvelling at the house: a great blue mansion, set in a luxuriance of magnolia, hibiscus and frangipani, with a façade draped in tiers of jalousies and wooden shutters. The Administrator, a tall, smiling man, answered Jyoti's questions with a casual wave – the French built it, their administrator lived here before – he was clearly bored with an explanation too frequently asked for. He led them to a paved terrace behind the house that looked out over the Mahé river and the sea beyond. They drank cold beer and listened to the shouts of fishermen in butterfly-sailed boats wafting in on the sea breeze.

Soon Dubey was very drunk and the Administrator was frowning worriedly. He went into the house, and when he came back he said: Come up, we'll have dinner now. He tried to hurry them up a wooden staircase to his apartments above, but halfway up Dubey caught Jyoti by the elbow and ran down the stairs, while the Administrator called after them, annoyed. Still holding Jyoti's arm Dubey led him to a glass-panelled door at the far end of the terrace. Like boys, they cupped their hands and peered through the glass. Jyoti could see nothing, for it was very dark inside. Dubey tried the handle on the door, and it opened, creaking on rusty hinges. Light streamed in from the terrace, and Jyoti saw that they were in a large, high-ceilinged room, divided by fluted columns. Chandeliers covered with grimy sheets of tarpaulin hung from the ceiling. A wall of dust-encrusted mirrors shone dully at the far end of the room. The room hummed with the roaring of the sea outside.

This was the ballroom, said Dubey. He looked about him open-mouthed, his eyes shining with wonder. Jyoti was surprised; he had not thought Dubey capable of wonder.

This is where all those French lords and ladies used to dance, Dubey said. He slid a foot along the wooden floor, leaving a trail in the dust. Then he raised himself on his toes and swung his plump, sleek body around in a drunken pirouette.

Not bad, no? he said. He stopped and stared wistfully out to sea.

Chapter Nine

Becalmed

At dawn on their second day at sea, while two boils quivered ripely on Alu's left leg, *Mariamma*'s engine spluttered, broke into a whine, and then coughed sullenly into silence. Sajjan was at the wheel then: a lean, sunken-cheeked boy, not yet sixteen though already stamped with that dour arrogance which sometimes marks the mechanically skilled. Hajji Musa Koya, who usually took the wheel at dawn, was still dozing, propped against the wheelhouse with a sun-bleached blanket draped over his chest. An almost-empty arrack-bottle had been tucked with drunken parsimony into the waist of his lungi.

Sajjan went to the rails, leant over and spat into the sea. For a moment he stood looking down at Hajji Musa's skullcap and wispy white beard. Then, shaking him by the shoulder, he shouted: Get up, Hajji, get up, up.

Hajji Musa, hovering near wakefulness, snorted into his beard: All right, boy, stop shouting. You know what to do – go and do something.

Sajjan stepped over him and bent down to run his hands over the steel hoop of a hatch. Then, spreading his legs, he took a firm grip on the hoop and pulled. The hatch creaked but would not open. He pulled off his oil-soaked vest and wound it around his hands. Then he spat on the hinges and pulled again, grunting, and now the hatch squeaked open, leaking whiffs of acrid diesel fumes.

Mariamma was not a big boat, and at first glance her unusually broad waist made her seem smaller than her twenty-eight-odd feet. Her hull sat high in the water, squat and ungainly, but strong. She had a low cabin, deep in the waist, and a tiny wheelhouse with barely enough space for two men to squeeze into, set well forward, close to her bows. Fence-like wooden rails, warped by the sea air, ringed her splintering decks. A rusty tube-well, which was sometimes used to pump water out of the bilges, perched on the stern like a heron, with its spout angled sharply over the rails.

In the many long and peaceful years she had spent in Calicut harbour and the backwaters around Alleppey, *Mariamma*'s prow and the sides of her cabin and wheelhouse had acquired a dense coating of murals – out of the cabin grew emerald palms and houses with banks of crimson tiles; ochre tigers leapt on the wheelhouse; and fiery-eyed silvery fish stared out of the prow into the horizon. When Hajji Musa had decided to turn *Mariamma* to the lucrative al-Ghazira trade he had had her painted a nondescript bluish grey in the hope that it would make her less visible to coastguards and harbour police. But the contractor had mixed water in the paint and every year splashes of blue-grey flaked off till only a few patches, floating like clouds on the colours beneath, remained.

Hajji Musa had also installed a 400-horsepower diesel engine and he had strengthened *Mariamma*'s bulkheads so that jerrycans of diesel fuel could be stored below deck. Over very short distances, when, for example, prudence required her to drop quickly below a horizon, *Mariamma* could do 35 miles per hour and sometimes even 40, but at the cost of a shuddering that threatened to dismember her. At her usual cruising speed of 20 to 25 knots she took the heaviest seas with the placid confidence of a tug in a harbour.

When he first took to the business Hajji Musa had listened carefully to the stories people told up and down the Malabar coast of boats setting off for al-Ghazira with twenty, forty and even (so they said) a hundred eager emigrants, but only to run out of fuel halfway, or else to be swallowed into the sea with the first mild gale, borne down by sheer weight. Unlike many other boat-owners, the Hajji's cupidity was easy-going, and he had that love of life peculiar to the morose. So he took note of the stories and made a few rules which he never broke – he sailed only in winter, after the retreat of the north-east monsoon when the sea was like a lagoon and he could be sure of a gentle breeze behind him. And he never took more than eight passengers, but he charged them almost three times the going rate. Yet, despite his high rates, he never had any trouble finding passengers, for he had a considerable reputation and people were willing to pay extra to make sure that they were not left stranded on a sandbank at low tide somewhere in the Arabian Sea. His overheads he covered by a little discreet trafficking in the highly priced hashish of the Idikki hills. And he always carried enormous quantities of diesel fuel: apart from the mounds of jerrycans below deck, there were a few drums in the cabin and a couple in the stern which also served to curtain off a plastic slop-bucket.

Alu and the two other male passengers, Rakesh and Professor Samuel, had found themselves a place to sleep not far from the bucket, in the narrow space that was shielded from the wind by the cabin. There they had erected a rain-shelter, a sheet of tarpaulin which was harnessed to the cabin at one end and to the deck-rails at the other. Hajji Musa often looked at the flapping sheet with melancholy misgiving: It'll overturn the whole boat if it catches a gust. But Rakesh, who was very thin and a little sickly, insisted that they keep it; they had to have something to keep the deadly morning dew from their chests, especially in winter and at sea; there was no telling. . . .

The men were not alarmed when they heard the engine die out: twice before the engine had coughed and spluttered, only to drum back into its regular rhythm moments later. After a while, yawning and stretching, they drifted to the wheelhouse. Hajji Musa was squatting near the open hatch, silently smoking a biri. Sajjan was idly shining a torch down at the engine. It was still dark, though the eastern sky behind them had turned scarlet. The sea, tinged with violet, was lapping gently at *Mariamma*'s sides.

Alu squatted beside Hajji Musa: What's happened? Hajji Musa, in his perfunctory Hindi, scratching his skeletal ribs, answered: Don't know. Let's see. We'll have to let it cool before we do anything.

For a while they all looked silently down the hatch. Then, Rakesh, leaning his thin, lanky frame over the rails, began to clean his teeth with a twig of neem. Soon Professor Samuel wandered away towards the cabin. He was a short, stocky man, bespectacled and balding. He folded his lungi up to his waist and climbed down the three steps which led to the cabin. When he reached the curtain which hung across the cabin's entrance he turned, averting his eyes from the interior with painstaking modesty, and reached inside. He drew out a large pot of tapioca, a bottle of coconut oil and a tin of salt. Then he leapt back up the steps and, squatting in the passageway, began to knead the tapioca with coconut oil and salt.

Suddenly he stopped, cocked his head and beckoned at Alu: It's her again. A moment later a long, pain-racked groan rasped out of the cabin, shaking the whole boat. The Professor wagged his head: Yes, it's her again – Karthamma.

They had only had a glimpse of her once, when she clambered on at Mahé: tall and luminously black, heavy with child, her belly straining before her like a full sail. God, said the Professor with his ear to the cabin wall, it's a strong woman who can groan like that.

At midday when the sea shone like a white light *Mariamma* was still sitting on the glassy water, rocking in the occasional gusts of wind that gently corrugated the surface. Rakesh, Professor Samuel and Alu soon bored of keeping a look-out for coastguards as Hajji Musa had told them to. Gradually they drifted towards a patch of shade near the cabin. Alu propped himself up against the cabin wall and stretched his legs stiffly ahead of him to dull the pain of his boils. Rakesh and Professor Samuel squeezed in beside him. They could hear Sajjan tinkering with the engine: in that shimmering silence it seemed as though the sound was echoing back at them from the horizon.

Presently Professor Samuel began to talk about queues.

If you want to understand queues – understand them seriously, that is – you have to begin by admitting that you know nothing about them. They aren't simple things, queues. Whole books have been written about them – in America, in Poland, Japan, Czechoslovakia. . . . People see queues and they think, Why, here's a simple thing, I'll just go and join it. But it's not simple, not at all. They're there before you see them; they have nothing to do with you. They were there before you came along and they'll be there after you leave. A queue's not just one man or two men or ten men standing in a line. Even if those two men or ten men weren't there you'd still have a queue, stretching away in principle. It's a thing of the mind, with its own humours and properties.

Squinting short-sightedly at the cabin wall, the Professor chipped away a flake of blue-grey paint to reveal a minute but very detailed elephant standing under a coconut palm: it wasn't as though he'd sprung from his mother's womb with all that he knew of queues hanging on him ready-made like a polyester shirt. For that matter, nobody in Tellicherry Science College where he had taught these last eight long years had known anything about queues: nobody had time for anything but government quarters, convents for their children, the price of fish, quarrels in the Municipal Council, who the Sub-Collector was, where he was being transferred, who's in, who's out. . . .

It was just pure chance, if there was such a thing. One day, passing through Cochin on his way to the station, he had stopped at a library in a small college; not a big library, but quiet, a nice place to spend an hour. And there it was on an almost-empty statistics shelf, its blue hardboard cover plastered with dust and perforated by weevils. He'd picked it up idly – it hadn't looked very interesting – *The Theory of Markov Processes*. And it wasn't very interesting for the most part; he'd almost put it back on the shelf. But then somehow his thumb had caught on the last chapter – ten sparse pages on the Theory of Queues. That was how it began. . . .

The Professor stiffened and swallowed his sentence. Look! he dug Alu urgently in the ribs. It's her. It's her again: Zindi at-Tiffaha.

They saw the back of her head first, wrapped in a yellow scarf. It rose slowly, like a winter sun, above the roof of the cabin. Then, swaying gently, she turned into the passageway. Her head and hands seemed incongruously small now, almost misshapen beside the immense rolling bulk of her body: she looked as though her body had somehow outgrown her extremities. She saw her path blocked by the three men and stopped, arms akimbo, eyes narrowed against the sun. Her face was very dark, but only in patches, as though it had been scorched unevenly by the sun, and it glistened under a sheen of sweat. Her cheeks hung down in heavy, muscular jowls, every fold of them quivering with vitality. In Mahé she had been inexpertly swathed in a sari; now she wore a black dress which enveloped her in a cocoon of cloth, billowing outwards where great quivering breasts rested on her stomach and then ballooning over her massive hips to fall to the ground like a tent, over her feet.

In one hand she held a red folding umbrella printed with flowers. She pointed the umbrella at the men and pressed a knob. It flew open, almost leaping out of her grip, and the men flinched and shrank back. She raised the umbrella and swept past them towards the screen of oil-drums which hid the slop-bucket. They could see the umbrella even after she had disappeared behind the oil-drums; it hung poised above the rim, like a small flowered dome.

Squinting at the umbrella, the Professor leant towards Alu and whispered: Yes, no doubt about it. No doubt about it at all. What they say is true – she's a madam. It's stamped on her – you can see it in everything she does. And anyway, if she wasn't, why would she be herding these poor women across the sea? Why would she be keeping them shut away like prisoners in the cabin? I tell you, she's going to sell them into slavery in al-Ghazira. Something like that. Or worse.

But they don't look like prisoners, Rakesh said timidly, smoothing his oil-sleek hair. They seemed quite happy to come on to the boat. Of course we couldn't see Karthamma properly, but that woman she calls Kulfi – the pale *gori* one in the white widow's sari – she sits up front in the evenings and laughs and chats with Hajji Musa. Chunni, too, the other one. They seem quite as happy to be going as us.

Rakesh stopped as a low rumbling groan shook the cabin walls. The Professor cocked his head and nodded in quiet triumph: Yes, you'll soon see how happy they are. We'll be hearing more of that soon, much more. I'll tell you one thing – we're going to go through hell, stuck here in the middle of the sea with this woman starting her labour.

In the engine compartment below deck Sajjan jerked hard on a cord and twice the engine whirred. Once it beat momentarily into life and then spluttered out again. They heard Hajji Musa quietly urging him to try again.

There was a splash of water behind the oil-drums and then the umbrella rose as Zindi stood to shake her skirts out. She turned and lurched purposefully towards the Professor. Squatting beside him, she stared hard into his face.

You're good at this, *han*? she rapped out in fluent guttural

Hindi. Good at talking? Talk for hours, talk, talk, no thought
for other people's headaches and worries, just talk, talk, any
shit, any filth that comes into your mind? You think we can't
hear you down there?

The Professor edged away. Zindi thrust her face within an
inch of his; a black mole with a single hair, twitching like an
insect's antenna, sat on a deep line at the corner of her mouth.
All right, she said, we all want to hear some more talk from you
now, some real talk. What are you going to do about this boat?
Are you going to fiddle with your balls while we die in the
middle of the sea or are you going to do something?

Professor Samuel swallowed and shut his eyes.

What can we do? Rakesh appealed to her. You tell us – what
can we do? We don't know anything about engines.

His voiced trailed off. Of course, he said, peering at the
horizon, we could row. . . .

Yes, row, said Zindi. That's the answer. Hang your cocks
over the side and twitch hard. That'll get us to al-Ghazira by
sunset.

There was a sudden pounding on the cabin wall. An instant
later a half-strangled shriek shook the deck. The pounding
grew till *Mariamma* began to rock, sending circles rippling
outwards towards the horizon. Zindi whirled around and
rushed down to the cabin. Soon after, the hammering
weakened into feeble knocks. I told you, the Professor said
with mournful satisfaction. I told you.

Later, when the sun had dipped low in the sky and a cool
evening breeze was gently rocking *Mariamma*, Alu found
himself suddenly shaken out of a doze. Professor Samuel was
crouching over him. I'm not going to die like this, he said, his
voice shaking. I'm not going to die floating on a boat in the
middle of the sea. We have to do something. It's our duty
towards those poor women. Get up. How can you sleep now?
Get up. We have to do something.

Alu heaved himself up and limped over to the wheelhouse
with the Professor following close behind. Hajji Musa was
sitting in the shade of the wheelhouse, holding up a filter while
Sajjan polished it with a rag. They were surrounded by grimy
bits of machinery.

How much longer, Hajji? Alu said.

The Hajji shrugged and thrust an open palm at the heavens: Who knows?

Criminals, villains, the Professor muttered into Alu's ear in English. Bringing helpless men and women out to die like animals on the sea. Why is the government not doing something?

Alu picked up a bit of wire and a file and hobbled back to his place in the waist of the boat. He wound the wire around his fingers and began to file one end.

What are you doing? the Professor said, watching him, his eyes wide behind his round spectacles.

Making a hook to fish with, said Alu.

But why?

Why? Alu looked at him in surprise. What else is there to do?

You're going to make a hook while we die slowly of—

He was cut short by a great ringing crash. What's the matter? he cried, clutching at the rails. What's happened?

It rang out again: a harsh, metallic sound as though one of the oil-drums in the cabin had been hit, gong-like. They heard a torrent of hoarse, choking speech, and a moment later Zindi's voice, shouting confused, breathless orders: Hold her legs. Don't let her kick. Why're you holding her like that? Do you think she's a horse or what? Then the cabin erupted again; there was another crash and another burst of hoarse, strangled speech. The men had all gathered around the steps now. They heard Zindi's voice again, pleading.

In the lull that followed a woman in a white sari pushed the curtain aside and stumbled out. What's happening, Kulfi-didi? Rakesh cried. Is she in labour?

Kulfi-didi wiped her face with the end of her sari. She was a slight, fragile woman with long, slender arms and a thin, hollowed-out face. Her cheeks looked as though they had collapsed, like the skin of a punctured drum. Grey smudges surrounded her eyes, spilling out, mask-like, towards her temples. She had taken her name from her complexion, which was pale, slightly yellow and grainily coarse. Her age seemed oddly indeterminate, for with her worn face and haggard cheeks she combined an incongruously girlish manner. Now, red-eyed and sweating, she stood panting at the entrance to the cabin. Her hair hung around her head in damp, stringy knots

and her white sari was streaked with blood. She thrust a mug at
Rakesh: Water, quickly.

Rakesh ran to the side, threw himself flat on the deck and
reached down to fill the mug. Has it started? he asked, handing
it back to her. Is she delivering now?

Rolling her eyes, Kulfi said: Yes. No, it's her time but she
won't. . . . She won't let the labour start. She's sitting on the
floor and kicking and fighting. She's stuffed her hands into her
womb, right in, up to her wrists. Maybe she's trying to kill it.
She keeps saying things in her language. . . .

Like lead grating on a slate, hysteria shrilled through her
voice. Then Zindi stepped out and pushed her back into the
cabin. Her scarf had slipped off and her coarse greying hair lay
matted on her forehead. She spotted Professor Samuel. Hey,
you, she said, beckoning with a finger. You know Malayalam,
han? Come into the cabin and tell us what she's trying to say.

There was a silence. Then Professor Samuel said with quiet
dignity: You know that is not possible. I cannot go into the
cabin with her in a state like that. It won't be right, it won't
be—

He stopped, mouth open, searching for the Hindi word he
wanted.

The blood rushed into Zindi's eyes. Arsehole, *sala*, she
shouted. You come here quick right now, or I'll break your
legs.

All right, all right – the Professor held up his hands – but I
won't go in. I'll stand with my back to the curtain.

He climbed carefully down the steps to the cabin. When he
reached the last step he turned to face the wheelhouse and
edged backwards towards the cabin. Catching the curtain with
both hands, he held it to his cheek so that his ears were inside
the cabin but his face outside.

There was another outburst behind the curtain. The Professor stiffened, frowning in concentration. His lips moved
silently as the hoarse voice muttered on. At length he said: She
says she won't deliver without signing the right forms. That's
what she says. She says she'll keep it in for as long as she has to.

Are you mad? Zindi shouted at the Professor. Are you lying,
you bastard? What form? Where form? Do you think this is a
passport office?

The Professor silenced Zindi with a gesture. Cocking his head, he listened intently to the whimpering inside until it had sunk into exhausted gasps. He looked up then, and shifted his eyes uneasily from Zindi to Alu. She's delirious, I think, he said. It was madness to bring her on to a boat in this state. She's just babbling, on and on. She says that she knows that the child won't be given a house or a car or anything at all if she doesn't sign the forms. It'll be sent back to India, she says, and she would rather kill it than allow that to happen; kill it right now with a bottle while it's still in her womb.

Zindi pushed him aside and vanished into the cabin. They heard her growling in a soothing whisper and soon Kartham-ma's murmurs faltered and died.

After nightfall, sitting around the deck, they ate a silent meal of rice, fish-paste and pickle off tin plates – all of them except Hajji Musa and Sajjan, who were still cleaning bits of machinery. Zindi sat cross-legged, enveloped in a black, cloak-like tarha. Beside her was Chunni Devi, a dark, taciturn, square-faced woman, dressed in a yellow kurta and green bell-bottomed trousers.

Presently Kulfi-didi broke the silence. What I can't under-stand, she said thoughtfully, licking a grain of rice off her fingers, what I can't understand is how she got these ideas. *Kahan se?* She's so uneducated she doesn't even know when a baby's been stuck inside her, but she still wants to sign forms. It's not like she's from Bangalore or some big city or something. You can tell as soon as you see her that she does eight-anna jobs in ricefields and things like that. And here she is, convinced that if she signs a form her baby will get cars and houses and all that. Where do these villagers get these ideas?

Maybe, Rakesh said, looking at his plate, maybe she wants a birth certificate. You really need a birth certificate nowadays: can't get into school without one; can't get a job, can't get a bus-pass, nothing. . . .

You're wrong, the Professor said sharply. What she wanted is quite clear. Someone's brought her on to the boat by making all kinds of promises – your child will be this, it'll be that, it'll have houses and cars and multi-storeyed buildings if only you can get across to al-Ghazira. Sign a few forms and the child will be a Ghaziri. In her state the poor woman believed what she was told. Now her time has come and she wants those forms.

The Professor stared hard at Zindi: Someone here has done something sinful to that woman; someone with no conscience.

Zindi pushed herself slowly upright and emptied the remains of her rice into the sea. Quietly, speaking to no one in particular, she said: Karthamma came to me herself in Mahé. She had heard of me from someone or the other. I didn't have to tell her anything – she had already heard more stories about al-Ghazira than I could make up in a year. She begged me, she even offered me money, to take her away from your India.

She glanced around the deck. Nobody met her eyes. She clasped her flapping tarha tightly around her and vanished into the cabin.

An hour later there was a rattle below deck as Sajjan cranked the engine. It pattered irregularly for a moment and then the beat caught and held. The engine roared and *Mariamma* surged ponderously forward. There was a burst of cheers; Zindi and Kulfi-didi rushed out of the cabin, and Professor Samuel ran into the wheelhouse and thumped Hajji Musa on his back.

In answer, Hajji Musa merely smiled, baring his grey gums, and looked ahead at the moonlit sea.

Late on the fourth day Alu finished filing his bit of wire to a point. He had worked on it for hours every day, to distract himself from the racking pain of his boils. Next morning he set about making a line. First he gathered together all the rags he could find and unravelled them. Then he twisted the bits of string together, into three separate lengths of yarn to begin with, and then into a three-stranded cord.

Rakesh and Professor Samuel sat beside him and watched. There was nothing else to do. The sea was glassily empty. Sajjan and Hajji Musa ran *Mariamma* in uncommunicative silence, brusquely refusing all offers of help. The cabin had fallen eerily silent ever since the second day. One evening Kulfi-didi had confided that she could hardly tell any longer whether Karthamma was dead or alive – she just lay there, barely breathing, and yet, incredibly, the child still seemed to be growing within her.

Early on the sixth day Alu's line was finally ready. He bent his bit of wire to form an eye at one end and a serviceable hook at the other, threaded the line through the eye and baited it with a lump of tapioca. Rakesh and Professor Samuel gathered around to watch as he prepared to make his first cast.

Just then Zindi emerged from the cabin, umbrella in hand, on her way to the bucket in the stern. She shot her umbrella open as soon as she stepped on to the deck and looked around, her eyes narrowed against the glare of the midday sun. She saw the men gathered in a knot near the bows, chattering excitedly. For a moment she thought of ignoring them, but then curiosity got the better of her and she shuffled forward, rolling her immense bulk with the pitching of the boat.

What's happening? she said, leaning over the rails to look. Before they could answer, a gust of wind snatched at her umbrella, bending the ribs backwards. She tried to snap it shut, but another gust caught it, tore it from her grip and carried it over the side.

Do something! she appealed to Rakesh and Professor Samuel.

They shrugged in silent amusement and shook their heads: What can we do?

Then she saw that Alu had already jerked his line out of the water and cast it after the upturned umbrella. That's right, she cried, thumping him on the back. Catch it like a fish.

The umbrella spun as the hook slid over its rim and then swirled away on *Mariamma*'s bow wave. Alu pulled himself upright and limped quickly to the stern. Throwing himself flat on the deck, he waited for the bobbing umbrella with the line ready in his hands. As the spinning patch of red nylon floated alongside he cast the line. The hook caught in one of the umbrella's ribs and it checked for an instant. Alu's hand flashed out and he caught the crook and fished it out of the water.

Shaking the water off it, Alu handed the umbrella back to Zindi. She took it and nodded, scratching her mole. I'll remember this, she said, and plodded off towards the stern.

Late that night Alu was sitting alone in the waist, trying to hold his throbbing leg still against the boat's pitching, when he felt the deck creak. He turned and saw Zindi lumbering down the passageway. For a while she stood braced against the rails and watched his huge, lumpy potato head in silence. Then, lowering herself to the deck, she whispered hoarsely: Hey, you, boy. What are you going to do in al-Ghazira?

Alu didn't answer. She raised her voice: You're a babu-type, no? You can read and write and everything?

Alu nodded.

That won't help you, she said. Not if you haven't got any friends there. What are you going there for?

I'm going to buy a sewing machine, Alu said.

Oh! Zindi scratched her mole. A sewing machine? That's odd. But you'll need a job first. It's not easy to find a job there if you're on your own. Don't think you'll find people pissing money there. There are hundreds, thousands of chhokren like you, begging; begging for jobs.

She prodded his shoulder: Why don't you talk? Why do you limp like that, with your leg stuck out like a telephone pole?

Alu said: I have boils, here, look. Zindi pushed his pajamas up to his knees and examined his legs. She pressed one of the boils with her thumbs and he recoiled in pain. Zindi rose. Wait, she said, I've got something.

She fetched a small glass bottle from the cabin. Just hot coconut oil, she said. It might help and it won't do any harm. She rubbed the oil on the boils while Alu bit his lip and gripped the rails. How does it feel? she asked, and when he didn't answer she shouted suddenly, her mouth inches from his ear: Why don't you talk? Has anyone stuffed your mouth? What's that man Samuel been telling you?

She caught his elbow: You shut your ears to all the shit and filth these people tell you, do you understand me? All that dirt is in their own minds. You listen to me and I'll tell you the truth. What I have in al-Ghazira is a kind of boarding house. Also a little tea-shop. Everybody knows it; in those parts Zindi the Apple's house is famous. You'll find out; everywhere you go you'll hear people saying: *Beyt* Zindi, *beyt* Zindi. People crowd to my house; boys like you offer money to be taken in. They know I know people and there's no end to the jobs you can get in al-Ghazira if you know people – in construction, sewage and drainage (though that's bad work even if it pays well), sweeping, gardening, even shop work. Oil work's difficult, for they usually find their own people. Still, I can find any man a good job. And, as for women, why, when I go to India I don't have to do anything. These women find me and come running:

Take me, Zindi – no, me, Zindi-didi – don't take her, she's got lice. They go on like that. But I don't take them all. I take only the good girls – clean, polite, hard-working. That's why I have to go to India myself to look. I find them jobs and they pay me a little, not much, something reasonable. The whole of al-Ghazira knows Zindi's girls are reliable and hard-working; everyone comes to me and I say, *Ya Shaikha*, you know my girls, they have to get a little extra, and they say, Yes, yes, Zindi, they'll get whatever you ask for. And so I get a little extra, too, not much. It's not a business; it's my family, my aila, my own house, and I look after them, all the boys and girls, and no one's unhappy and they all love me.

That's enough of all that. Now, listen: I'll give you a chance because you're a helpful kind of turd and one look at your face and I can see that on your own you'll be crushed like dung at a crossroads within one week in al-Ghazira. And *wallahi* I don't want your death on my soul. So listen: I'll give you a place and I'll find you work – something good in construction, maybe even in a shop since you're lettered, but only maybe, for shop jobs aren't easy to get. You'll see, you won't have to pay much, just a little. You'll have plenty to send back home. You're so lucky you won't believe it when you get to al-Ghazira. What do you say, then, *han*?

Alu rubbed his leg in silence. Zindi said again, sharply: So what do you say?

*Kya pata?*Alu said. I don't know. . . .

Zindi looked hard into his face. Then she pushed herself up, spat into her hands and rubbed them together. You don't know, she said, turning towards the cabin. You don't know. But you'll find out. Just wait till you get there.

Later that night Alu's boils burst. The pain oozed away with the bloody pus and he slept soundly for the first time in their six days at sea.

With his first cast next morning Alu felt a jerk on his line. It snapped taut and sang through the water for a second. Then suddenly it was limp again. He pulled the line in and found that the tapioca had been taken neatly off the hook.

Rakesh, watching him, nodded slowly. That's what it's like, he said. The fish get away if you wait for them. You have to go out and get them.

Alu baited his hook and tossed it out again. He and Professor Samuel leant drowsily on the rails and watched the line cutting through the water. It was warm and very bright and the spindrift prickled coolly on their faces. Then Rakesh began to talk. That was unusual, for Rakesh rarely talked; he found so much occupation in his own appearance that speech was usually unnecessary to him as either expression or diversion.

Till about a month before he found himself in *Mariamma* Rakesh was a travelling salesman for a small Ayurvedic pharmacy in Bhopal which specialized in a patented herbal laxative. It was the only job he had been able to find – despite his bachelor's degree in commerce – and that, too, only after a year's efforts. So he worked at it hard, though it was tedious and very frustrating.

The trouble really lay in the product. It was soon clear that people no longer wanted Ayurvedic laxatives. There was no market for black viscous liquids in old rum-bottles; they wanted sparkling, bubbling salts which dissolved in water, or milky syrups in bottles with bright labels. They wanted advertisements and slogans which promised more than mere movement – promotions and success at work, marital triumphs, and refrigerators in their dowries. Regularity, balance and inner peace no longer sold.

After he had been working there for close on six months there came a particularly heart-breaking day in a small town south of Bhopal: not one of the town's four pharmacies agreed to stock so much as half a bottle of his wares. He had nothing else to do, so he wandered down the narrow bazaar, kicking at the grimy dust, towards the ghats on the river. And then, passing the opening of a narrow lane, he heard the unmistakable throbbing of *Mere Sapnon ki Rani* spilling out.

For a while he stood there transfixed, overwhelmed by reminiscence. The song was from the first film he had ever seen – he and a cousin had stolen out of his aunt's house in Indore, where his mother had taken him to visit her sister. Despite the thrashing afterwards, the magic of that burning July afternoon had stayed mirror-clear in his memory; even years later when he was seeing three or four films a week.

There was nothing he could do about it: the song led him in as though it were a rope around his wrists.

He found himself in a sweetshop, a large hive of a room, all brightly tiled and calendared. A young man in a striped shirt sat, legs folded, behind a steel box, taking in money. Rakesh could tell at once that the shirt was of the finest terry cotton; he noted the gold chain that hung around his neck; envied the easy-going stylishness of his curling, oiled sidelocks. On the wall behind the young man, just beneath a small earthen figure of the Devi Lakshmi, hung a gigantic, pulsating cassette recorder.

Rakesh ate two gulab-jamuns and three samosas. When he went up to the counter to pay, the young man expertly shot back his cuffs and pressed a series of minuscule knobs on his watch with the tip of a pencil. An answer flashed on to the dial. One rupee forty-five, he said.

It took Rakesh an age to pay. Then he could no longer contain himself. Boss, he burst out, how? How did you do it? How did you get all this, Boss?

In al-Ghazira, boss, said the young man. Two years and the grace of Lakshmi Devi. . . . He pressed another knob and the watch shrilled out a tune.

Later, after an hour of questions, Rakesh walked down to the ghats and, unmindful of fish and pilgrims alike, threw his bottles of laxative into the Narmada. Within a month, his share of his father's land sold to a brother, savings collected, Rakesh was in Mahé. . . .

The Professor yawned and blew his nose into the sea. What Rakesh had to say bored him – he had so many untold stories of his own left to tell – but he would never have said so. It was the first time he had heard Rakesh say anything more than a few words and he had said it with so much earnestness that it had seemed as though an interruption would wound him into ages of silence. So he nodded politely and said: And then . . .?

Rakesh shook his head and shrugged: That's all. The Professor's eyes lit up: he saw his chance and quickly cleared his throat. But before he could begin the sea had robbed him of his moment. A sleek black hump curled through the water right in front of them and was lost again before they could be sure they had seen anything at all. And then five, ten, twenty finned backs appeared all at once, weaving through the water with such fluency that they could hardly be told apart from the

waves. One leapt out of the water, a grinning bottle-nosed
dolphin, and with a single blow of its flukes sent a wave
splashing over *Mariamma*'s deck. Then the huge smiling
creatures were all around them, riding *Mariamma*'s bow wave,
nudging each other out in turn while the others leapt and rolled
nearby, flashing their white undersides. They all rushed to the
side and laughed and shouted till *Mariamma* yawed and rolled
and Hajji Musa had to call out to them not to crowd to one side.
Then suddenly, as if to a signal, the sea emptied again and
Professor Samuel was left brimful of untold stories and no
audience.

But later that night he had his chance again.

An hour or so after their evening meal the Professor heard
the quick patter of footsteps near the cabin. He was just in time
to see Chunni lean out over the side and empty her stomach
into the sea. After a minute-long bout of retching she leant back
against the cabin and covered her face with her hands. Slowly,
with growing dismay, he realized that she was sobbing.

Yes, Miss Chunni? he said, standing well back from her. Is
there anything I can do? Any help . . . ?

How much longer, she whispered, her face still covered with
her hands, how much longer will this go on? Are we ever going
to get there? Where is he taking us?

Then her chest heaved spasmodically and she had to rush to
the rails and lean out again.

Water, water, Professor Samuel muttered to himself. I'll get
some water.

By the time he was back she had collapsed on to the deck
with her head on her knees. Here, he said, thrusting the
jerrycan at her. Here's some nice, clean, fresh water.

She made no move. He tapped her uncertainly on the
shoulder. Miss Chunni. . . .

He heard her choke back a sob. You need water, Miss
Chunni, he said softly. That's all. He poured a little into his
hand and splashed it gently on her face.

She took the jerrycan from him then and washed her face and
sat down again beside him, shivering and hiccuping. *Koi baat
nahin*, he said. It's all right now. And soon he was talking to her
in a gentle, quiet monotone, soothing her with the theory of
queues.

Much later, long after he had told her about his researches and his tabulations and all his newly minted formulae – the formulae that were to solve the queuing problems of every busy bus-stand and ration-shop and sari-bazaar and obstetrician's clinic (especially the last; for, make no mistake, there's no queue longer than that which winds theoretically away from every obstetrician's door – an unending line stretching into dim infinity, of Teeming Millions waiting to be born) in all of Tellicherry and Cannanore – he looked down at Chunni and saw that she was asleep.

Miss Chunni, he whispered sadly, you've been . . .?

No, she whispered back, I'm listening. Go on.

And do you know, Miss Chunni, he said, none of them would have anything to do with me? I took them plans which would have revolutionized their entire selling strategy, and they wouldn't even listen to me long enough to laugh. When I took my brand-new counter design to the Dreamland Saree Centre they threw me and the blueprint. . . .

He looked down at her again and this time there could be no doubt that she was soundly asleep. For a long minute he looked into her dark, pitted face and then with the languor of a sleepwalker he raised a finger and touched her on the lips. The sensation went through him like a shock. He snatched his hand back, leapt to his feet and wandered confusedly back to the tarpaulin shelter near the stern.

When they awoke next morning an oil-tanker lay before them. It was so vast it seemed to straddle half the horizon. *Mariamma* passed so close to it they could see clearly the cross-hatching of pipes and turrets on its deck. It seemed to take an age before they had sailed its length. Its wake was like a gorge swinging through the sea, and when it struck *Mariamma* the boat almost stood on its stern. They saw a couple of other tankers that day and a few smaller ships, too, mainly freighters and ancient tramps wheezing columns of smoke. In the evening Chunni, sitting with Professor Samuel in the stern, saw birds and pointed them out. When the Professor told Hajji Musa about them the Hajji nodded. Yes, he said, it's the ninth day. We'll be in al-Ghazira soon. To celebrate they cooked the one fish that had somehow entangled its gills in Alu's line.

Late that night Karthamma's groans started again. By

sunrise the cabin was shivering to her screams. The men sat on the steps and stared at the curtain; they could only guess at what was happening inside. They heard a fist pounding on the cabin wall, and Zindi shouting curses. At times the oil-drums rang out as though someone had been thrown against them; at others, eerily, the noise stopped and torrents of words came pouring out of the cabin. In those pauses the Professor would lean forward and listen intently. Once he nodded at the others and said: It's those forms again. She wants them right now, God help her.

At that Rakesh, who was combing his hair distractedly, rose and fetched a bucket of water. We have to do something, he said helplessly.

A moment later Zindi's huge bulk stumbled backwards through the curtains and collapsed on to the steps. She sat huddled forward, bent almost double, trying to catch her breath. She saw the others watching her and threw up her hands. What can I do? she said, her voice cracking with exhaustion. The mad bitch is going to kill it and herself, too. It's all we can do to keep her hands from her womb, and how long can we go on?

She looked hopelessly at the Professor: Can't you do something?

Professor Samuel took off his spectacles and polished them on his vest, lips pursed. Then, squinting thoughtfully at the cabin, he said: Yes, I think there *is* something we can do.

She jumped to her feet: What? What will you do?

Wait, he said, fitting his spectacles on again. You'll see. He turned to Alu: Have you got any paper? Printed paper – paper with fine, close print on it?

Alu nodded. The Professor slapped him on the back. Come on, then. They hurried back to the stern, and Professor Samuel threw aside the tarpaulin sheet that covered their bundles and pulled out his tin suitcase. With deft, controlled haste he unlocked his tin suitcase and took out a pair of trousers, a tie and a black cotton jacket. Dropping his lungi he stepped into his trousers, pulled the jacket on over his vest and wound the tie quickly around his neck. Alu, he shouted, get me the paper, quick.

Untying his bundle of clothes Alu took out the copy of the

Life of Pasteur that Gopal had given him and very carefully tore off a page. Despite its age the paper was stiff and crisp. The Professor snatched it from him and, taking a pen out of his jacket, drew a straight line at the bottom of the page. Beside it he wrote in English: 'Signed.'

You think it'll work? Alu asked. Oh, yes, said the Professor, she's in no state to tell the difference between a form given to her by a government babu and a sheet of paper held under her nose by a suited-booted stranger. . . .

He broke off in dismay, looking down at his bare feet. No shoes, he muttered. No shoes.

She won't look at your feet, Alu said.

Let us hope so, the Professor said, and straightening his jacket he hurried forward to the cabin. At the curtain he stopped and looked back at Alu and Rakesh. Alu waved him on. Looking studiedly downwards, Professor Samuel stepped into the cabin.

They heard him talking rapidly to Zindi. Then his voice changed, rose into a high official monotone and they couldn't understand him any longer. They heard gasps and a long rattling sigh and after that silence, and then a scream, but of a kind very different from that to which they had grown accustomed: the full, disbelieving cry of a woman in labour.

The Professor stumbled out of the cabin and sat on the steps looking blankly at his feet. Alu prised the sheet of paper out of his fingers. Three shaky Malayalam characters were sprawled across the paper. He rolled the page into a ball and tossed it over the side.

Later, after the bustle and the cries in the cabin had ceased, Zindi came smiling up to the deck. She had a baby cradled in her arms. They all crowded around her to look. It was a boy, very small and wrinkled, dark like his mother and still slimy with her blood. His umbilical cord lay curled on his stomach.

Karthamma still hasn't seen him, Zindi said. She's fast asleep. Her face creased into a smile as she looked at Professor Samuel: Maybe she'll beat you up once she knows what you did.

Kulfi-didi brought warm water and they washed the child and laughed at his shrill, resentful screams. Zindi swaddled it in her tarha and hugged the bundle to her breast and kissed it.

My eyes, she said, he will be like my own two eyes to me.

Hajji Musa, standing beside her, tickled the child's chin and said: It's a fine boy and where could it grow up better than in the house of Zindi the Apple?

Then it was Rakesh's turn. He raised his hand to tickle it but his courage ebbed away at the last moment and he dropped his hand and stood staring, shaking his head. Boss, he said in wonder, boss. . . .

And so the child was given his name.

That night, while the others were crowding into the bows in their eagerness to get their first glimpse of al-Ghazira, Alu was sitting alone in the stern, trailing his line, savouring the silence, when he saw Zindi weaving her way down the passage towards him. With a long sigh she settled herself beside him. I'm tired, she said. God give me strength. She had changed into a fresh black fustan and tied a new scarf around her head.

She sighed again and patted his hand. Do you know now? she asked. Are you going to come to my house in al-Ghazira?

I can't tell yet. Alu's reply was barely audible. I'll have to wait and see.

Bring the others if you like – Rakesh and Samuel. They're all right, and it so happens that for once I have room now.

She peered closely at him: Well?

Alu shrugged: I don't know. . . .

Zindi sat absolutely still for a moment looking at his lumpy, swollen potato face. Then she hammered her fist on the deck. Idon'knowyet Idon'knowyet, she mimicked him. What *do* you know? Do you know anything at all?

Alu rose quickly to his feet but she shot out a hand and pulled him down again. He jerked his leg back but her fist had closed on it like a clamp. Pulling himself up again he braced himself against the rails and tried to kick his leg free.

Zindi smiled at him, immense and immovable. Why so shy? she said. Where can you run to?

Then in one quick movement she pulled him down and planted a hand in his crotch. She laughed, and he could feel her breath hot on his cheek. Now, she said, let's see if you know about anything at all.

She tore open the knot in his pajamas and pushed them

down to his knees. Good, she whispered in his ear, so there *is* something you know. With a flick of her wrists she flung her skirts back over her waist, baring a dark, surging pile of a belly and trunk-like thighs. She took hold of the small of his back and with one powerful heave of her shoulders, pulled him astride her.

So that was how Alu first saw the lights of al-Ghazira peering over Zindi's shoulder, half-smothered by her breasts, her gasps loud in his ears. He gazed at the distant pinpricks of light and his dazzled sight meshed with every other sense in his body till the lights grew and clamoured and burnt like suns, swallowing the voices suddenly risen around him: Professor Samuel in some distant part of the boat, voice high with excitement – You see, Chunni, I only realized too late that it was I who was wrong, not the shopkeepers, not the obstetricians, but I; and then Zindi spent and fighting for her wind – Never again, don't dare, don't dare try this again, don't even dare look at me again; and somewhere else – Do you understand that, Chunni? I was wrong because there aren't any queues there, it's near those lights that the queues are, because there aren't any queues without money; and Zindi's hot breath again – And don't ever talk about this in al-Ghazira, not if you want to live, for if Abu Fahl even imagines this, even dreams of it, you'll be holding bricks together till the Judgement for he'll cut you into pieces and feed you into a cement-grinder; and still the lights grew, and it did not matter whether they burnt in al-Ghazira or the moon, any more than it matters to an insect whether a fire burns in a lamp or a furnace, for through a century and a half the same lights have shone in one part of the globe or another, wherever money and its attendant arms have chosen to descend on peoples unprepared for its onslaughts, and for all of those hundred and fifty years *Mariamma's* avatars have left that coast for those lights carrying with them an immense cargo of wanderers seeking their own destruction in giving flesh to the whims of capital.

Part Two

RAJAS: PASSION

Chapter Ten

Falling Star

Six months after *Mariamma* arrived in al-Ghazira, Alu was buried in the collapse of an immense new building. The building was at one end of the Corniche which swept around al-Ghazira's little bay in a blaze of tarmac. Though it was not quite finished, it had a name: it was called an-Najma, the Star, because of the five pointed arms that angled out from its domed centre. People said later that the fall shook the whole of al-Ghazira, like an emptying wave shakes a boat. A tornado of dust swirled out of the debris while the rubble was still shuddering and heaving like a labouring beast, and for a few moments the whole city was wrapped in darkness, despite the full mid-afternoon brilliance of the desert sun. It was, after all, the Star, one of the largest buildings ever built in al-Ghazira; not as long as the concrete tents of the airport, nor half as high as the tallest bulb on the desalination towers, but larger than both of them put together. When it fell it was in an avalanche of thousands and thousands of tons of bricks and concrete and cement, and Alu was almost exactly in its centre.

When the first rumbles of the collapse started Zindi was standing transfixed in the murky twilight of one of the Souq ash-Sharji's tunnel-like lanes, her eyes flickering between a shop and the flaking signboard above it. 'Durban Tailoring House,' the sign read, in Hindi, Arabic and English, and Zindi spelt the letters to herself over and over again as though she had never seen them before.

The momentary darkening of al-Ghazira's skies after the collapse passed unnoticed in the Souq ash-Sharji, for even during the day the gloom in the old bazaar's honeycomb of passageways was a live thing, coiling through the tunnels, obscuring every trace of the world outside. The bright lights of the rows of shops in the passageways merely chipped at its flanks. Inside the Souq the passing of the day was marked only by the innumerable clocks and watches in shop windows, and the computerized system of loudspeakers that ran through the whole complex of passages and corridors and punctually relayed the call to prayer five times a day (even at dawn, when the only people in the Souq were a few soundly sleeping vagrants).

Nor did any but the most alert in the Souq feel the soil of al-Ghazira tremble when the Star fell, for its thick mud walls reached deep into the earth, and they reduced the shock to a barely perceptible tremor. In any case the Souq was a long way from the Star. Its squat main gateway, the Bab al-Asli, with its two horn-like towers, looked out into a crowded, dusty square known as the Maidan al-Jami'i, cuckolded of pre-eminence by the newly painted façade of the Old Mosque opposite. The square was the heart of the old town. The Star was almost another country. It stood at the farthest end of the bay, where the Corniche turned inland towards the straight roads of the new city. It was minutes away from the border, within shouting distance of the rival airport in the neighbouring kingdom.

Zindi noticed nothing, not even when the news of the collapse was broadcast over the radio after the midday prayers, for the Durban Tailoring House still absorbed her wholly. The muted swell of celebration which rose soon afterwards in the shops around her welled out and trickled down the corridors, leaving her untouched.

In the many years she had spent in al-Ghazira Zindi had passed that shop at least twice a week, often more, but that afternoon she stood in the passage forgetful of time and everything around her, as though she were seeing it for the first time. She stared at the dusty panes of the display window, at the long-collared shirts on their hangers, folded blouses, pajamas, and shimmering satin petticoats; she gazed at the few grimy lengths of cloth on the tottering shelves, at flapping calendars on the walls and pictures of men in suits, cut out of Italian magazines and pasted on the window. When at last Forid Mian, the old tailor, whom she had known since her first days in al-Ghazira, saw her standing outside and came out of the shop squinting, she looked blandly into his shrivelled, pock-marked face with its sinister trails of moustache and beard, and let herself be led in as though she were in a trance. Inside, she stood marooned among the snippets of cloth that carpeted the shop and swivelled about, sniffing the pungent sharpness of terylenes and rayons and the mustiness of cottons with their blue factory marks still fresh on them. She fingered through the piles of clothes Forid Mian had finished. He had always drawn his custom mainly from the women in the old Indian merchants' quarter of the city so there were petticoats, and blouses, and frocks for girls not old enough for saris. She nodded and grunted as Forid Mian told her stories about his customers. But she heard very little. She had to hold on to the counter to steady herself, for the shop was dancing around her as he spoke, spinning, dissolving, transfiguring itself.

It was a long time before she heard Forid Mian asking her whether she was feeling quite well, and when she did she laughed and wandered out of the shop leaving her glass of tea untouched. Forid Mian followed her out and stood staring after her as she swayed slowly down the passageway and disappeared into the brilliant pool of sunlight at the foot of the Bab al-Asli.

Zindi crossed the road into the dusty square and found a bench. She sat prodding at a struggling tuft of grass with her toes, absently gazing at the digital figures on the tiled clock-tower in the centre of the square. A boy in buttonless trousers, with key-rings and nail-clippers on chains draped over his arms, came up to her. He laid his chains out on the bench and tugged at her elbow: *Libnak*, for your son, and this one for your daughter, or another for your daughter-in-law. . . .

He turned around and shouted across the square. Another boy came running up, shaking yellow packets of dehydrated soup: Just try one; see how you'll like it. . . . Zindi sat unmoved, staring ahead of her. One of the boys leant over and tweaked her plastic bag open. Zindi, suddenly alert, snatched her bag away. She rose with a howl and sent the boy staggering with a blow of her open hand: Get away from me, you son of a bitch, *ibn kelb*.

She walked across the square flailing her bag and rolling her eyes: *Yalla, yalla*, out of my way, sons of bitches, can't sit a minute anywhere any longer, crowd around your feet like shit on a beach.

Crossing the road, she stood on the pavement, panting and wiping her forehead. Then something in one of the cavernous shops that ringed the square caught her eye and she went inside. She pointed it out to the shopkeeper, nestling between piles of aluminium pots and plastic buckets. It was a baby's comforter. Holding it like a talisman before her, she went across the square to her bus-stop, deaf to the suppressed excitement that was now rippling through the whole square.

She had a long way to walk after she got off her bus. By the time she was struggling up the side of a long, high embankment, every layer of her black dress was soaked in sweat. Once she had scrambled up to the road which ran along the embankment she stopped to catch her breath, shielding her face from the sun with her bag. On the far side, a finger of land, invisible from the other side of the embankment, jutted out into the sea, bordered on one flank by a narrow inlet. Far away, at the end of the inlet, was the old harbour, crowded with sambuqs and motor-boats. That narrow spit was known as the Ras al-Maqtu', the Severed Head, a sandbar garotted by the road on the embankment.

The Ras shimmered and blurred in the heat of the afternoon as Zindi looked confusedly about—at a group of neat whitewashed houses in a corner by the sea, at the jostling, crowded walls of wooden planks and broken crates which covered the rest of the spit, all but a narrow strip of beach. She looked over the roofs of corrugated iron and halved oil-drums, with their crazily angled wooden platforms and tracery of pumpkin vines, and at last, led by a strip where the dense patchwork was cut through by charred, blackened frames of shacks, her eyes found her own house, solid and thick-walled, its brick-and-cement permanence setting it apart from the others, a reef in a shifting tide.

She stopped when she reached the house, for she sensed something amiss. She looked down the narrow lane, at the blackened stubs of wooden planks and collapsed, soot-covered sheets of corrugated iron which lay all around the house. Then she pushed against the heavy wooden door of her house and almost fell in, for, to her surprise, the door was open. The door opened into a short, dark corridor, which ended in an open courtyard. There was a room on either side of the corridor and more around the courtyard.

Zindi stood in the corridor and shouted: Karthamma . . . Abu Fahl. . . . The only sound that answered her was the cooing of pigeons in the courtyard. Frowning, she went into the room to her right and hung her plastic bag on a nail in the wall. The room's complement of mats stood rolled in a corner as she had left them. A kerosene-stove lay beside them. She picked it up, held it to her ear and shook it. She knew by the sound that it had not been used since she left. She looked into a biscuit-tin and saw that none of the tea inside it had been used, either.

She hurried out into the courtyard and shouted again: Professor . . . Kulfi . . . Alu. . . . Once again there was no answer. Turning, she threw open the door of the room opposite her own. It was the door to the room in which the men of the house lived. Mattresses were spread neatly on the floor. Trousers, lungis and jallabeyyas hung from pegs on the wall and wet clothes dripped on a line which ran from one barred window to another. The windows were shut as they always were during the day: that was one of Zindi's rules.

Suddenly uneasy, she dug into her petticoats, pulled out a bunch of keys and hurriedly opened a steel cupboard which stood in one corner of the room. The cupboard was tidy, as it always was; Rakesh's pile of shirts and printed T-shirts lay stacked in a neat pile, beside Professor Samuel's bulging wallet; cassette recorders and transistors stood in a row on the bottom shelf, undisturbed. Sighing with relief, Zindi locked the cupboard.

Back in her own room Zindi unlocked her wooden provisions chest and went through it carefully. The sacks of wheat, rice and sugar and the packets of tea lay untouched. Breathing hard, she went down the corridor, into the courtyard, shading her eyes from the sudden brightness of the sun.

A storm of cackles greeted her. Several plump chickens flapped out of her way, and in a wired pen in a corner a long-necked gander hissed and spread its wings protectively across its flock of geese. The sides of the roof above were lined with grey pigeons looking down into the courtyard, their heads cocked. Zindi saw that the birds had not been fed and she fetched corn and wheat and half a cabbage for two rabbits in a wire-covered wooden crate.

Then she crossed the courtyard and unlocked the door to the women's room. The room was divided into cubicles by lengths of cloth nailed into the walls and ceiling. She went around the room, pulling the makeshift curtains apart. The room was undisturbed and empty. Experimentally, she tried the heavy brass lock on the door of the next room. It was firmly locked, and that was the one lock in the house to which she had no key.

Zindi went back to her room, the heavy folds of her face knotted into a scowl, her jowls dripping sweat. She spread a mat on the floor and sat down to wait.

It was sundown when she heard the knocks she had been waiting for. She switched on the naked bulb in the corridor and stood there for a moment, her hands on her hips, shaking with anger. The rapping grew louder, and she flung the door open. Karthamma, Professor Samuel and Rakesh stood outside. Rakesh held Boss, the baby, cradled in his arms. Behind them, dimly outlined in the darkness was a man in a jallabeyya, stocky, dark and powerfully built, the texture of his face that of supple leather. He had only one eye; the other was an even grey, glowing dully beneath a half-closed lid.

Zindi's eyes fastened on him. When the first wave of her roar broke it sent them all staggering backwards into the shadows: So it's you, Abu Fahl, you bastard, you son of a bitch. It's you who's been behind everything all along? So this is your plan, is it? Lure the others out of the house like cattle, in the middle of the day, and leave it open for half the world to come in and take what it likes? You know what we've been through and now you plan this? This is the way you're setting about it? *Wallahi, wallahi*, you don't have to wait any longer. As God is my witness, you can have all your things and wander off for ever to eat out of a ditch. That's where you were born, that's where you'll end. Wait.

Zindi ran into her room. An instant later a tin case flew out of the door and crashed on the wall opposite with such force that its hinges fell apart, spilling clothes, money, cassettes. Then she heaved one of the two mattresses in her room to the door and threw it out. There, she shouted, that comes to an end now, and I'm happy at last.

Abu Fahl pushed Professor Samuel aside, jumped over the mattress and leapt at Zindi. Wrenching her arms behind her, he pushed her down on to the mattress. He knelt beside her and put a hand, as large and horny as a goat's head, on her heaving shoulder. Zindi, he said softly. Zindi, calm yourself. Calm yourself. Haven't you heard?

Zindi rolled her eyes at Karthamma and Rakesh. I've heard enough, she growled deep in her throat. I'll give you something to hear about.

Abu Fahl looked up at the others and rubbed his wrist on his blind eye. She doesn't know, he said. God the Living, she doesn't know.

Zindi was suddenly still. She looked at Karthamma and saw the tear-clotted smudges of dirt on her face. She saw the rents in Rakesh's clothes and the gash of dried blood on his shirt. *Ya satir!* she whispered, looking from one to the other. What? Tell me.

The Star collapsed today, said Professor Samuel. Abu Fahl and the others were meant to be painting the basement. But when it happened only Alu was inside. He was trapped in the basement, right in the middle of the building. Abu Fahl saw the whole thing. And all the others. There wasn't a wall left standing. Tons and tons of concrete. All of it right on him. But we have to be grateful. It was only him, just one man, while it could have been everyone.

The lines and ridges on Zindi's cheeks seemed to sink deeper. Her jowls trembled and then the whole of her face collapsed inwards. She struck her forehead with the heel of her palm. Him, too! she cried, and her voice rasped like sandpaper on lead. All the others and now him!

Zindi rose and went to Karthamma. Putting her arms around her, she pulled her head on to her shoulders and for a long while the two women held each other in a firm, consoling embrace, until Zindi took her hand away and stroked Karthamma's head in recognition of the especial poignancy of her grief. Then Zindi took her by the arm and led her towards the women's room. At the end of the corridor Zindi turned to the men and said, in a voice taut with determination: All the others

and now him. But he'll be the last. No more weeping! The time
has come to do something.

It was a long time before Zindi came out of the room. She
went straight to Rakesh, took Boss from him and carried him
into her own room. The men straggled aimlessly in behind her.
She found the comforter she had bought for Boss, washed it
and put it in his mouth. Then she seated herself on a mat at one
end of the room with the baby on her crossed legs. She sat
stiffly upright, her face grimly set. When Zindi sat like that the
massive stillness of her presence reached into every corner of
the room and patterned everything, every object, every
person around her like iron filings around a magnet. She
gestured to the men to unroll mats and seat themselves. Then
she pulled a brass kerosene-stove before her, pumped it till it
hissed and lit it. Carefully placing half a cob of corn, scraped
clean of its seeds, on the flame, she asked: Where are the
others?

Still there, said Professor Samuel. I went as soon as I heard,
and so did everyone else. We came to take you.

No, said Zindi. I'm not going. There's nothing to be done
there, God knows. It was here that the whole business started
and it's here that we'll fight it. God give me strength, he will be
the last.

What are you talking about? A note of pleading had crept
into the Professor's voice. What do you mean, 'it started here'?

Zindi's eyes narrowed into sharp, brilliant points and bore
into the Professor's. You know very well what I mean, she said.
You've heard it before. You're not a child. Frowning Abusa was
the first. Then Mast Ram. Then the others, and now this. Are
they accidents?

Professor Samuel dropped his head. In the silence Karthamma slipped into the room. At length Abu Fahl gripped his
knees and leant forward: So what is it, then, Zindi? Tell us. We
want to hear it again.

Zindi pressed damp tobacco into an earthen cup with her
thumb. The cup was part of a narjila made from a glass bottle, a
length of rubber tubing and two bits of hollow bamboo. She
stuck the cup on one of the bamboo tubes and gingerly flicked
the glowing corncob on to the tobacco. Abu Fahl took the
narjila from her and pulled hard on the rubber tube. The

corncob glowed and smoke bubbled through the water in the bottle.

In the fog of silence hanging in the room, the gurgling of the narjila echoed eerily, like waves on a distant cliff. Karthamma shivered and shifted closer to Zindi. The hairs prickled on their necks and stood in runnels on their arms as they waited for Zindi to begin, yet again, on her terrible litany of calamities.

Perhaps Abusa the Frown was the beginning, even though he wasn't the first. In a way, it was his goodness, his good fortune, his gentleness and the love everyone had for him that lay behind it all: Frowning Abusa, cousin to Abu Fahl's mother, Zaghloul the Pigeon's brother-in-law (and cousin as well), raised to manhood with them in the same village in the Nile Delta; named by the whole village the moment he was born, for he was taken from his mother with his face bent and a frown carved for ever into his forehead because his mother had dreamt of barbed wire the night before. He could have had no better name, for he was always apart, frowning and silent – at home, when he walked to the fields, even when the cousins and uncles who grew like grass in his village played and sang all around him – and strangely everyone loved him for it.

He came to the house as soon as he arrived in al-Ghazira, and he lived in it for a year and a half, frowning silently in a corner, seldom speaking. Every last dirham he earned he sent back to the village; his only clothes were his one good jallabeyya and the grey fellah's cap his grandfather had made him for his first frowning visit to Alexandria to get his passport. He rarely spoke, but no one ever forgot him. It was to him that everyone turned when there was trouble. *Mariamma*'s last voyage brought a good time. There had never been so much money in the house. Everyone had a good regular job, everyone was bringing in good money. And then, as though that weren't enough, Jeevanbhai Patel appeared. That was soon after his wife died. He was too old to look after his tottering house near the Souq, so he begged to rent a room – it was all he could ask for: food on time, people around him to help him forget his loneliness and all that had happened to him. So he was given the corner room, next to the women. And since he paid double no one minded his sad, wizened monkey's face, nor the red

pan-stained teeth sticking out of his mouth like mudguards,
nor the huge lock he put on his door. Soon there were
television sets in the house, transistors, washing machines
even – the best you could find in the shops in Hurreyya – the
courtyard was bursting with poultry, and there was a goose or
chicken for dinner every night. That was sign enough, though
nobody saw it then, for the whole of the Ras and everybody in
al-Ghazira looked at Zindi's house and saw it prospering and
too much good fortune invites its own end.

Late one night – it was a Thursday night and everybody had
been paid for the week – when everyone was sitting on the roof,
drinking tea and talking, there were knocks on the door, soft
but unmistakable. Zaghloul the Pigeon, always eager, ran
down and opened the door.

A boy lay on the path outside squirming like a wounded rat,
with blood pouring from his head. That was how Mast Ram
came into the house.

Somehow, from some remote part of the north Indian hills,
Mast Ram had trickled into the plains, where a relative put him
into the hands of a labour contractor. Once they were in al-
Ghazira, Mast Ram found himself with only a third part of the
wage that he had been promised in his pocket, for the
contractor took all the rest. Mast Ram was young enough to
burn at the injustice of it. One night he found something to
drink, and his rage grew too large for him to hold. In front of all
the others he flew at the contractor's throat.

That was how he found himself with his skull split half-open,
without a job, without a place to stay, and blood all over his
clothes.

All he could think of then was a certain house his relative had
told him about. So somehow he wrapped a pajama around his
head and dragged himself across al-Ghazira to the Severed
Head, trailing blood, and crawled into the house, blood,
wounds, injustices and all.

He couldn't be turned away – his relative had stayed in the
house once, and he was a good enough man. Besides,
somehow, despite the state he was in, Mast Ram had managed
to bring his papers with him. Still, the moment he came under
the light in the corridor everybody shivered and nobody knew
why. He was ugly, there could be no doubt about that – his face

was so closely covered with pock-marks and holes it looked as though it had been dug up to lay the foundations for something better. But it wasn't just his ugliness – Abusa was uglier, with his barbed-wire face, and Abu Fahl, and Alu with his potato head. Of the lot only Rakesh wasn't ugly; and Zaghloul, of course, is any girl's dream. But with Mast Ram it was something more than just ugliness: it was the way his eyes darted about, like a snake's, always open, never missing the slightest movement.

But, still, Professor Samuel tied a bandage around his head and a mattress was put out for him in the corridor (for the house had never been so full). He lay on his mattress all through the next day. The day after that everybody could see there was nothing wrong with him any more, so Abu Fahl told him to go out to work with the others. Mast Ram didn't move. They left him alone that day, and the next day everybody forgot about him because that was the day Kulfi came home crying.

At the time Kulfi used to cook in a rich Ghaziri's house. The pay was good, the work simple, and the whole house was air-conditioned. It was a small family and they liked Kulfi, so she was happy there and everybody envied her. But there was a daughter in the family and that was where the trouble started, for she was fat and very ugly. She couldn't keep her hands away from ghee and butter, and so on some days her face was covered with so many bursting pimples it could have been taken for a pot of boiling water. Her parents had done everything they could to marry her off, but nothing worked. Then one day they heard of a boy. His family was poor, but he'd worked hard, got a scholarship, gone to America and come back with a suitcase-ful of degrees. Now he wanted to go into business and he needed capital. Of that the girl's father had plenty. So they came to an understanding, and it was decided that the boy would come to their house to meet the girl.

There was turmoil in the house: great preparations. The girl's mother, half-crazy with worry, ran about roasting chickens, boiling legs of lamb, pouring buckets of saffron into every pot of rice. The father went to the Swiss shop in Hurreyya and bought so many sweets and cakes they had to close down for the whole day. All Kulfi had to do was cook a couple of vegetables and heat the food.

It looked very simple. The car arrived. The boy got out, his mother got out, and there were little cries of joy in the house for they couldn't have wished for nicer people. Then they saw his grandmother, and suddenly everyone was nervous, for despite her burqa they could see that she was as thin as a whip, with fangs and a moustache.

All went well for an hour or so: though the grandmother's voice shrilled through the house, the boy and the girl talked prettily to each other through her mother. When it was evening the men said their prayers and afterwards they asked for dinner.

All this while the grandmother had been peering suspiciously at all the signs of wealth around her. When the talk of dinner came up, she said: So you have someone to cook for you?

The girl's mother, wanting to impress her, said: Oh, yes. An Indian woman.

At that the grandmother rose and said to the boy: Come on, let's go. (Later they found out that she'd been against the marriage from the start – didn't want another woman in the house.)

His mother was furious. Why? she said. Why now? Before dinner and everything? Think of your indigestion.

No, we're going, said the grandmother. I'm not going to eat food cooked by an Indian. Don't you remember how your uncle told us that these Indian women spit into the food because they like the flavour?

Commotion. The girl's mother pleaded with her, told her it wasn't true, Kulfi was a good clean girl who never spat into the food or anything like that, but the grandmother wouldn't budge. Not a bit.

Almost in tears now, the girl's mother pleaded with them and said: Come into the kitchen and right in front of you I'll ask Kulfi whether she spits into the food.

The boy frowned at his grandmother (he was very eager to get his capital), so she had to agree. They all went to the kitchen – the grandmother, the boy, the girl, almost everyone in the house – and crowded around to watch.

At that time Kulfi knew very little Arabic. She knew simple things like 'too hot' and 'more salt', but little else. The girl's mother remembered this with foreboding once she was in the kitchen but it was already too late.

She gestured to Kulfi to watch and leant over a pot and made little spitting noises. Then she screwed up her face and gestured as though to say: Do you do this?

Kulfi was already very nervous. She saw the woman bending over the pot, spitting and gesturing, so she thought to herself, Why, here's something new – and as helpfully as she could she made a sign to the woman to wait. For a moment she blew and puffed, and when at last she had worked up a good mouthful of spit she bent over the pot and spat right into it. Then she looked up and smiled at the woman. There, she thought, you can't do better than that and *I'm* not going to eat it anyway.

Pandemonium. Kulfi was out on the street in a minute. It was a pity, for the family was a nice one. But in the end the girl's mother had to promise that she would never again have an Indian in the house, before the marriage could go ahead.

But Kulfi was without a job, and what with hearing the story over and over again nobody noticed Mast Ram. Then one day Abu Fahl remembered him and took him out with the others to teach him how to paint houses. It was the simplest job in the world, even for someone who was just a boy like Mast Ram. But he wouldn't work. He'd sit by himself, smoke cigarettes and do nothing, nothing at all. Far from doing any painting, he wouldn't even scrape the floor afterwards to take off the stains.

One day Abu Fahl said: Enough. If he won't work, he'll have to leave. So they tied his things together and threw them out of the house. But Mast Ram wouldn't go. He sat in a corner and held on to the bars in the window, while his eyes ran around the room like spiders. He made Abu Fahl mad with anger. He got his crowbar, stood with his legs apart, towering over Mast Ram, and raised it above his head to break his skull again, where the crack still showed.

When Mast Ram saw Abu Fahl, with his bull's shoulders, standing over him, holding the crowbar with both hands and glaring with his one, red eye, fear began to steam off his skin. For once his eyes were still. He cowered against the wall and began to weep.

It was Frowning Abusa who stopped Abu Fahl. Wait, he said. Maybe he'll be able to do some other kind of job.

At that time Abusa was working in a rich sheikh's house as a gardener. The sheikh was one of the brave ones who had bought land on the outskirts of the town. He had built himself a palace there but he could do nothing about the land, which stayed desert, despite all his efforts.

Now, Abusa had one great gift: all living things grew under his fingers as though to please him alone. In his village ever since he started working on his father's land, their cotton grew longer and heavier than anybody else's. In years when the whole village's fields lay devastated by worms their crops threw off insects at will as though they found strength in Abusa's very presence. Within a month of taking the job with the sheikh he made grass push through the sand. The sheikh, in his gratitude, doubled Abusa's wage within the year and soon Abusa was earning a lot of money. Abusa knew the sheikh would listen to whatever he said, so no one doubted he would find Mast Ram a job there.

Abusa never talked about his work (or much else), so no one knew how Mast Ram was faring in his new job. No one gave it much thought, either, then suddenly some odd things began to happen. First, four men from one of the construction gangs in the Ras died, when a high-tension cable fell right on them. They died in agony, thrashing about on the ground. That was the first time such a thing had happened. Then one of Hajj Fahmy's sons drove his truck right off the embankment at a hundred kilometres an hour. It was impossible to explain, for he had driven along that road for years. By the time they found him they couldn't pick his body out of the wreckage. Soon after, fever hit the first few shacks on the outskirts of the Ras.

In the middle of all that stories about Mast Ram began to reach the Ras: how a live flowering bush had withered and died moments after Mast Ram touched it; how Abusa's famous pumpkins, each one the size of a fattened sheep, were opened and found to be as hollow as footballs after Mast Ram had watered them.

None of it was Mast Ram's fault. He was as bewildered as everyone else by the death which surrounded him. In the end Abusa, fearing for his job, had to put him to laying paving stones so that the garden would be safe from his hands.

Then people began to notice a change in Mast Ram. He saw how every living thing flourished and grew under Abusa's hands and he was filled with admiration, even love. He took to following Abusa wherever he went, inside the house and outside, staring up at him with dog's eyes. Abusa for his part was always kind to him, like a stern brother.

Mast Ram began to do everything he could to earn Abusa's respect. Abusa had a few rabbits which he kept in a cage in the courtyard. He looked after them well and they bred faster than they could be eaten. One day Mast Ram decided to feed the rabbits. Next morning there was a dead rabbit in the cage. Everybody in the house saw it, but nobody said a word, not even Abusa. The next day Mast Ram fed the rabbits again. Again, the morning after, they found a dead rabbit. That evening, when Mast Ram went to feed the rabbits yet again, Abusa stopped him and quietly, in their own language, half signs, half words, he told him not to feed the rabbits again.

Mast Ram said nothing, but there were tears in his eyes.

After that Mast Ram's behaviour became even stranger. At that time Abusa had taken a great liking to Kulfi. He spent a lot of time looking at her and sometimes he even bought her presents. Kulfi used to toss her head and pretend not to care, but of course she was pleased, for like everyone else she liked Abusa.

Then one morning Chunni said: Mast Ram has fallen in love with Kulfi. And soon it was clear that she was right. He was just a boy after all. His eyes never left Kulfi. He took to sitting in the courtyard, waiting for her to pass by. He even tried to talk to her, but Kulfi, like most people, shuddered whenever she saw him and ran into her room.

And then one morning Mast Ram rose very early and hid himself in the courtyard. He knew Kulfi was the first to get up in the morning. He lay flat behind the rabbits' cage and when she came out of the room he leapt out. In his hands he held half of all the money he had saved in his time in al-Ghazira. That was how desperate he was.

Think of Kulfi: on her way to her morning shit, half-awake, when this man with snake's eyes jumps out from behind the rabbits and flings money at her feet. She screamed and flung her tin of water right into his face and, while he was still hopping around spitting out water, she locked herself safely into the shithouse.

After that there was no sleep for Mast Ram. He spent his nights squatting in a corner, brooding. Abu Fahl said he should be watched, so for a while he was never left alone; but then people forgot him again, for that was when the Professor was arrested.

The day we heard everyone was stunned. How? How did it happen? Had he talked about queues again, at his new job, even after everyone had sat around him at night and told him not to, at least a hundred times?

No. It was something else altogether.

The Professor had a fine job in those days: the best in the house, and one of the best anyone in the Ras could hope for. He was a manager's assistant in a huge supermarket in Hurreyya Avenue. He spent his days wrapped in air-conditioning and the smells of freshly frozen Australian lamb and Danish mutton, French cauliflowers and Egyptian cabbages, Thai rice and Canadian wheat, English cod and Japanese sardines, prawns and shrimps and lobster from the world over. . . . All that and nothing to do but sit at a desk and add up numbers. It was just luck, getting that job. Of course, it made good sense for them, for they paid him less than they should have because he had no work permit.

The morning he was arrested the Professor left the house in a great hurry. He had been told to get to the shop early, but when he woke up he found that he had no clean trousers to wear. So, neat as ever, he tied on a starched white lungi and went off. Nobody noticed on the bus and, since he was early that day, no one saw him go into the shop. Once he was behind his desk all they could see of him was his spotless white shirt.

At about eleven o'clock, when most of the other people in the shop were drinking tea in a back room, a rich and beautiful Ghaziri woman came into the shop. Seeing no one, she wandered about until she spotted Professor Samuel at his desk at the far end and she went up to him and asked in Arabic: Please, can you tell me where the prawns are kept?

Now, the Professor had been working hard since morning, staring at figures, adding them, dividing them, and he was just a little confused. The moment he saw her he stood up. She was very beautiful: no burqa for her; she was dressed in the most expensive of European clothes and her hair was piled high on her head.

She asked him again, and this time he was even more confused. He heard the word *gambari* and knew that he had heard it before but couldn't remember what it meant. Scratching his head, blinking distractedly, he stared straight into her face and tried to speak.

The woman had been just a little alarmed when the Professor first stood up. Now, with him staring at her, mouth open, a tiny chill of fright crept up her spine. She looked quickly over her shoulder, wondering whether to call out. As it happened, the Professor's desk was at one end of a long, deserted corridor of shelves. It was the darkest and gloomiest part of the shop. When she saw that she was really scared.

The Professor was still thinking, half about *gambari* and half about his accounts and figures, so absent-mindedly he did something he would never otherwise have done in public: he reached down, pulled his lungi up over his knees and tied it up at his waist, as people do when they're at home.

The rich woman saw this blinking, staring man suddenly pulling his clothes up. She saw him baring his stout, hairy legs, and in terror she cowered back into the shelves.

Just then the Professor remembered. *Gambari!* Oh, *gambari!* he cried, flinging his arms open and rushing towards her. Come, Madam, come, I will show you gambaris like you've never seen. . . .

The woman leapt backwards with the strength of the terror-stricken, right into the shelves. The Professor shrieked – No, Madam, that's the tomato sauce! – and lunged forward to save her. She swooned into the shelves, the Professor fell upon her and five hundred bottles of American tomato sauce fell upon them.

When the other attendants arrived after the crash they saw the Professor sprawled on an unconscious rich lady, lying in a small blood-red lake. When the Professor stood up and tried to explain they fled, too, right into the street, where they screamed and screamed till the police arrived.

Abu Fahl and Alu had to spend a lot of money to get him out of gaol, and there's at least one shop in Hurreyya now which

will never hire an Indian again. After that the Professor had to
be content with the job Jeevanbhai gave him, so that was
another person in the house who'd lost a good job.

Again, in the telling of that story Mast Ram was forgotten.
But he had forgotten nothing: not his broken skull, or the
contractor, or Kulfi, or the shrivelled flowers and the dead
rabbits. He crouched in a corner and brooded and brooded on
the whole of his life and fate until jealousy and hate were
pouring from his body like sweat in the midday sun and he was
no longer a man but an animal, beyond reason and sanity. One
night he roused himself from his corner and prowled around
the house until he found Abu Fahl's crowbar. In the dead of
night, while the whole house slept, he fell upon the locked
door to the women's room with the crowbar. He attacked it as
though it were a wild animal, and while he beat upon it he
screamed, in his nasal, mountain Hindi: Why not me, you
cunt? You'd fuck a dog if it had money, why not me?

By the time Abu Fahl got to him he had almost battered the
door down and the women inside were cold with fear. And
then for the first time in his life Mast Ram fought. Even Abu
Fahl couldn't hold him down, and Alu and Zaghloul had to
help.

And still we couldn't rid ourselves of him, for by then he had
grown into us like a curse. The others would have been willing
to forget the past, but it was no use; Mast Ram's half-crazy head
was a storm of love and hate and envy, and Abusa the Frown
was at the centre of it.

Soon after that the fever hit the house, and one day while
Rakesh, Zaghloul and Chunni were lying in bed, half-delirious,
Mast Ram slipped out with his passport and his papers and
went straight to the police and told them how Abusa's work
permit had lapsed a year ago. They caught Abusa next
morning, on his way to the sheikh's garden. They lay in wait for
him in a car and Mast Ram pointed him out.

When they caught him Abusa lost his head. He fought, and
he fought so well he cracked a policeman's jaw. If it weren't for
that, perhaps it would have been all right; a little money in a
few places would have got him out in a matter of days. But after
that nothing could save him.

Abu Fahl and the others did everything they could, but it all came to nothing. Nobody could tell them when they would see Abusa again.

At first Abu Fahl wept. Abusa was dearer to him than any of his own brothers. Then he put his revolver in his pocket and set out to scour the town for Mast Ram.

In the house everyone waited, aching with fear. It was certain that if Mast Ram were found the courtyard would become an abattoir that night. Abu Fahl would smash his teeth first, then dig his eyes out with the crowbar and break the bones in his body on the paving stones till they were like links in a chain. And only then would he leave the body on the beach for the tides to wash away. Mast Ram would not be the first man Abu Fahl had killed, and previously Abu Fahl had not killed in anger.

But none of it came to pass, for there was no trace of Mast Ram; he had vanished like a ghost in a graveyard. That night Abu Fahl came back to the house alone and sat drinking tea with everyone else in silence, while Zaghloul wept like a baby. Everyone's mind was full of Abusa's goodness and Mast Ram's treachery.

It was then, while they were sitting there, empty-eyed and silent, that the first barks sounded, far away, at the edges of the Ras, somewhere near the embankment. Suddenly, like the beginning of a storm, the noise grew until every stray dog in the Ras seemed to be howling together. It was all over and around us, like waves, crashing and breaking on the house. Then Boss began to cry in terrible strangled sobs and a moment later the whole courtyard seemed to explode; every animal in it went into a frenzy, geese honking, chickens screeching. . . . Inside, nobody moved. Everyone was absolutely still, staring at the windows. You could feel your bowels growing cold. There are few things more frightening than the midnight frenzy of animals.

Then there were voices, shouts, far away, pricking through that curtain of sound like needles. The noise seemed to gather itself together in the distance, near the embankment, and suddenly it was moving, moving straight towards the house. Faintly you could hear the drumbeat of feet echoing in the lanes; running towards the house, panic-stricken screams and pounding feet, dogs howling after them.

And then a hammering on the window and screams tearing through the house: *Ya khalg gum* – rise, you created! – *gum ya khalg*.

Abu Fahl and Zaghloul sprang up like deer, for since their childhood they had seen those dreaded words send their parents and relatives pouring into the village lanes. And no sooner were they on their feet than we saw the first wisps of smoke curling down, through the courtyard and the corridor, into the room.

Abu Fahl was the first one up on the roof – by some miracle the ladder still stood, though the fire was all around it. When he saw what he did he tried to push the others back, but there were too many of them and they shouldered past him.

There were flames everywhere. But Mast Ram's head and his face were untouched and unblackened. His eyes were closed and at peace, while the rest of his body was burning so hard it couldn't be told apart from the straw and wood of his pyre. Lying beside him, away from the flames, were the matches and the tin of kerosene he must have stolen from the courtyard, whenever it was that he slipped back into the house and up to the roof to put an end to his love and his remorse, his treachery and his hate, in the only honourable way he knew.

By that time the fire had leapt to the neighbouring shacks and barastis. They were like matchsticks – gone in minutes. Though every man and woman in the Ras helped to carry water, at least fifty shacks were burnt to the ground. It was a miracle the whole of the Ras didn't go up in flames. The house was saved by its cement and bricks, but only after a battle which lasted through the night.

The others had trickled back: Zaghloul the Pigeon, barely twenty, his handsome, friendly face, with its cleft chin and sharp, straight nose, tired after the day; Chunni and Kulfi, exhausted by their long vigil at the ruins of the Star. They crouched on mats around Zindi, listening intently to every word. They had lived through everything Zindi spoke of and had heard her talk of it time and time again; yet it was only in her telling that it took shape; changed from mere incidents to a palpable thing, a block of time which was not hours or minutes or days, but something corporeal, with its own malevolent wilfulness. That was Zindi's power: she could bring together empty air and give it a body just by talking of it. They could never tire of listening to her speak, in her welter of languages, though they knew every word, just as well as they knew lines of songs. And when sometimes she chose a different word or a new phrase it was like the pressure of a potter's thumb on clay – changing the thing itself and their knowledge of it.

Zindi looked around the room at the circle of frowning, intent faces. All that, she said, and now this. The house already empty and without work, and then still another accident. Is it going to end or is it going to take everyone?

Abu Fahl leant forward. He pulled his grey taqeyya off his head and ran his fingers through his short, wiry hair. So what are we to do, Zindi? he said, looking straight at her.

Zindi rose briskly to her feet. I'm thinking of something, she said. Maybe I'll even tell you about it some day. But not today, not now after all that's happened, with Alu lying dead under tons of rubble.

Professor Samuel rose to go and the others shuffled out after him. Only Rakesh hung back, nervously flipping through the leaves of a calendar on the wall. Twice he turned, bit his lip, and turned back again. Then he could no longer contain himself. Listen, Zindi, he burst out. Alu isn't dead. At least I don't think so. He's alive. I heard his voice under the rubble.

Zindi stared at him, speechless.

Yes, he said, it's true. I'm almost sure I heard him.

Go to sleep now, Zindi said. The collapse has been too much for you.

Chapter Eleven

A *Voice in the Ruins*

Next morning Professor Samuel came back from his morning visit to the beach (he preferred sand and the clean sea breeze, he said, to the evil-smelling darkness of the lavatory in the house) looking very bemused. Chunni, who had made him a glass of tea, found him sitting on his mattress staring blankly at a wall.

What's the matter, Samuel? she asked him. Are you unwell?

The Professor shook his head. So, then? she snapped. Why're you sitting here like a wet cat? Do you know what the time is? Do you want to lose this job, too?

The Professor hesitated and threw a glance around the room. Except for Zaghloul snoring in a corner, it was empty. He patted the floor beside him. Sit down, he said. I'll tell you. It's nothing really. Just a foolish story Bhaskaran told me on the beach.

Outside, in the courtyard, Kulfi and Karthamma were cooking their usual morning meal of rice and fried potatoes on a mud oven. When the rice was done they carried the pots into Zindi's room and called out to the others. The women ate at one end of the room and the men at the other. While they were eating, Chunni said loudly: Samuel heard a strange story on the beach this morning.

Professor Samuel frowned at her across the room. He shook his head as the others looked at him curiously. It was nothing, he said dismissively. Just a foolish story.

Abu Fahl banged his tin plate on the mat and shook the Professor's knee. Tell us what you heard, Samuel, he said. I don't like secrets. What did you hear?

All right, said the Professor, irritated. If you want to waste your time. You know Bhaskaran from Kerala, who lives down by the beach with all the others? In their house they're saying

Alu was seen in the ruins of the Star last night. The story is that he's not dead at all, but just hiding in the ruins. I asked Bhaskaran: why should he hide in the ruins in all that dirt when he has a bed to come back to? It would be irrational. He had no answer, of course. All he could say is that everyone in the Ras knows that Alu survived by some miraculous chance, and now he's hiding in the ruins.

Karthamma rose eagerly to her feet: What else did you hear?

Allah il-'Azim! Zindi exclaimed. Sit down, Karthamma; you're not a child. You know whenever anything happens people think of a thousand stories. This is just the beginning. Alu's alive, Alu's hiding – there'll be no end to the tales people will think up now.

Zindi's sentence died away as Jeevanbhai Patel came into the room. Karthamma settled reluctantly back on the mat.

Jeevanbhai smiled vaguely around the room. His eyes were heavy with sleep; he had come back to the house very late the night before. He was a short, slight man, neatly dressed in a white shirt and grey trousers. A few grey strands of hair were combed carefully across his head. He would have had a gift for inconspicuousness if it were not for his teeth. They protruded like fingers from his thin, deeply lined face: great, chipped, triangular teeth, stained blood red by the pan he incessantly chewed.

'*Aish Halak?* How are you? he said politely to Zindi in Ghaziri-accented Arabic.

How are you? she answered, looking away. She frowned at Professor Samuel, biting her lip.

Jeevanbhai lowered himself on to a mat. His tongue flickered delicately over his teeth. Were you saying something about Alu? he asked softly. I thought he died in the collapse of that big building on the Corniche.

Yes, yes, said Zindi. That's what I was trying to explain to Karthamma here. We would give anything to save his life, but he's beyond that now.

Does someone say he's alive? said Jeevanbhai.

No. How could they? Zindi began to collect the plates, banging them together till their ringing filled the room.

Later, she managed to find Professor Samuel before he left with Jeevanbhai for his office near the harbour. Don't tell him anything, she whispered urgently, taking him aside. Not a word of all the nonsense you heard this morning. You don't know him. He spreads even the most foolish stories all over al-Ghazira, and God knows who they get to.

Jeevanbhai appeared at the end of the corridor, and Zindi hurried into her room. Leave me alone this morning, she shouted into the courtyard. I've got things to do. The door closed upon her with solemn finality.

But soon she had to open it again. Kulfi, sent out with an empty bottle on a string to buy two days' supply of cooking oil, came running back to the house. She stood in the courtyard and shouted, her pale cheeks pink with excitement, her voice girlishly high: Alu was seen getting into the plane for America this morning; he didn't die in the collapse, though he was pale and ghost-like and covered in dust. He discovered a huge store of gold in the wreckage of one of the Star's jewellery-shops.

They crowded around her – all but Zindi, who stood apart, only half-listening. At least, Kulfi said breathlessly, he's alive. Maybe he'll be back someday, with all his money.

Who told you all this? Abu Fahl demanded.

Kulfi had gone to a shop near the embankment that was owned by an Egyptian from the Fayyum called Romy. There she had met a woman who had heard from someone else. . . .

Abu Fahl caught Kulfi by the shoulder and shook her. You can't believe these stories, he said. Someone heard from someone who heard from someone. They're just wild fancies. I was there. I saw it all. I know what the truth is.

Karthamma pushed past Abu Fahl and Kulfi. She was halfway down the corridor when Zindi said sharply: Karthamma, where are you going?

I'm going to look for him, Karthamma said.

Karthamma, don't forget yourself, Zindi said. We know what there was between you and Alu, but don't display it before the whole world like this. Where's your shame that you're running about like a bitch on heat, and you with a son? Do you think, if there was a chance of his being alive, Abu Fahl wouldn't have gone himself? Get back into the courtyard.

The blood rushed into Karthamma's eyes. She lunged at Zindi, but Abu Fahl caught her around the waist. Zindi stalked into her room, and the slam of her door set the geese hissing in the courtyard.

By midday the house was awash with stories. Zaghloul went out to buy a cigarette and came back with a story he had heard on the way: the policemen who had surrounded the Star soon after the collapse had seen a hazy figure in the wreckage at night. Two of them went into the ruins to investigate. They spotted the figure a number of times, always a little way ahead of them. After stumbling about for hours on piles of steel and broken glass, their hands torn and bleeding, their expensive new uniforms in shreds, they were about to turn back when they saw the figure waving in the distance. They hurried after it, but when they got there it had disappeared. Instead they found a body – Alu's body – since there were no others there. They pulled and tugged at the corpse, but try as they might they couldn't shift it, not by so much as a hair's breadth. They ran screaming out of the ruins.

Rakesh had spent the morning tossing restlessly on his mattress. The men had no work for the day, for Abu Fahl had decided that the collapse had cancelled his agreement with the contractor. Rakesh heard Zaghloul through, lying on his mattress. When he had finished, he jumped to his feet and began to pull on his trousers. We have to go, Abu Fahl, he said. We have to look for ourselves. I'm almost sure I heard Alu in the ruins yesterday, even though Zindi thinks it was all just imagined. But now there are all these stories, too. Anything might have happened; he may still be there.

Still be there? Abu Fahl snorted contemptuously. Are you mad or dreaming? I saw the whole thing with my own eyes, and I've had years of experience of these things. Do you know, I saw the collapse of the huge cinema hall near Sadiq Square? There were six men working in the building then and not one survived. And that was a much smaller building than the Star. Yesterday I saw five storeys of concrete fall on the basement, and then I saw the basement's ceiling collapse. I don't want to say it, but Alu's as dead as a skeleton in a graveyard, God have mercy on him. It would be madness to go to that place now and be taken for thieves by the police.

All right, said Rakesh quietly, buttoning his shirt. If you won't go, I'll go myself.

Zaghloul stood up: I'll come with you.

Abu Fahl was thrown into a quandary. A police cordon had been thrown around the Star soon after the collapse to guard what could be salvaged of the stocks in the wrecked shops. If Rakesh and Zaghloul went, they would be caught and arrested; there could be few doubts about that. They would be no more able to slip through a police cordon than they would be able to break into a bank.

Abu Fahl stopped them at the door. He would go, he told them, but he had a few conditions: only he and Rakesh would go – the police were more likely to notice three men than two – and they would leave only after he had had time to make a few inquiries.

Elated, Rakesh pushed open the door to Zindi's room and shouted: Zindi, we're going to the Star after all.

Zindi was abstractedly rocking Boss to sleep. What? she said.

We're going to the Star to see if Alu's alive.

Yes, said Zindi, without interest. Maybe you should go, since everyone says. . . . Her voice trailed off.

She looked up suddenly as Rakesh, offended by her lack of enthusiasm, turned to go. Wait, she called after him. Come here. I want you to do something.

When Rakesh was squatting beside her on the mat she whispered: Go to Romy Abu Tolba's shop. Tolba, Romy's boy, goes to the Souq at this time to buy things for the shop. Tell him to give a message to Forid Mian, who works in the Durban Tailoring House in the second lane. Tell him to say this: Forid Mian, Zindi wonders why you haven't been to her house for so long. Is there something wrong with the tea? This evening she's going to make some very good tea.

Zindi broke off and scratched her mole. And then, she added, tell him to say: Jeevanbhai is usually away in the evenings.

She met Rakesh's curious glance with a finger on her lips. Now, listen, she said, don't tell anyone about this. No one – not Abu Fahl, not Zaghloul, no one. Just go.

When he returned Rakesh went straight to her room. She was pacing the floor, with Boss cradled in her arms. Did you tell him? she asked eagerly.

Yes, said Rakesh, seating himself on a mat. He looked expectantly at her.

You want to know about the message? Zindi asked. Rakesh said nothing. Zindi shut the door and seated herself beside him. She leant towards him until her black scarf was almost touching his face, and only then did Rakesh notice how anxiety had changed the pattern of lines on her massive jowls.

A shop! she whistled into his ear. That's my plan: a shop!

Rakesh, in surprise, belched in a huge, rumbling gurgle. Zindi, looking straight at his averted eyes, ignored it. Don't you understand? she appealed, and Rakesh sensed a wall within her beginning to crumble. I know where I've gone wrong now. Here I am with this house full of people. I make a good enough living from them most of the time – they give me a bit of money, it's hardly enough, but still. . . . I can look after them while they're in the house. But where does the money come from? It doesn't come from the house; it comes from the outside. It's not like having land. It's taken me all these years really to understand that. I knew it, but I didn't understand it. While everything is all right outside, things seem fine in the house – money keeps coming in and I can manage. But let something happen outside, and that's the end – there's nothing I can do. Why? Because I can give them food, I can give them a roof, but I can't give them work. When it comes to work, this house is like an empty crate – people can kick it here, kick it there, and I'm helpless. That's why all this has happened – Mast Ram and Abusa; Professor Samuel and Kulfi losing their jobs. Everything else. The house is almost empty now and the work's gone. It doesn't matter to you; you can always go back home. Where can I go? Do you think Abu Fahl would stay if there was no money in the house? He's my cousin and he's not a bad man, but he has to live. I have to stay here, and if the house stops bringing in money one day I'll be found floating on the beach with all that shit. I'm not young. I have to do something now. It's my last chance. And now I know what the answer is: a shop. We have the people; we could run it. It'll give work to everyone, if it goes well, and we'll be safe.

What kind of shop? asked Rakesh.

At that, Zindi's vision of the Durban Tailoring House came pouring out of her. It was only an ordinary tailor's shop really –

one which hadn't kept up too well with al-Ghazira – familiar,
unsurprising. And yet she hadn't known it at all, never really
seen it or understood its promise and its possibilities, till that
morning when the Star fell; while she was wandering through
the Souq, her head aching with fear and worry for her
crumbling house. Suddenly that morning it wasn't a shop at all,
not a simple room of bricks and cement, not a thing which
could be touched and felt, but a promise, a future: its dusty,
be-calendared walls had grown heavy with shelves and bright
with cloth, the cobwebbed ceiling was glowing with neon
lights, and the empty echoing interior was suddenly full of
people – people flowing in and out, their hands digging into
bags full of money, looking, choosing, buying, asking her,
enthroned behind the cash-desk, what's the best? what's the
cheapest? what's the newest? what's from America? from
Singapore? – and she, gracious, benign, inclining her head and
passing them on to Abu Fahl, sleek in his new suit, or Kulfi or
Karthamma or Chunni floating by in nylons and chiffons; and
advertisements, too, everywhere, coloured lights winking all
over al-Ghazira on the Corniche, in Hurreyya; queues stretching out of the shop and through the Souq, crowds rioting to get
in. . . .

Isn't it possible? she asked Rakesh. Does it seem too much?

Rakesh shook his head in doubt, but his eyes were shining
with excitement: all the clothes, think of all the clothes!

He hesitated. But how will you *get* the shop, Zindi? he
asked.

Ah! Zindi's eyes narrowed. That's what the plan is
about. . . .

The Durban Tailoring House belonged to Jeevanbhai Patel.
It was his beginning in al-Ghazira. He had acquired it when he
first arrived, years and years ago, after his parents, in distant
Durban in South Africa, discovered his secret marriage to a
Bohra Muslim girl (and he a Gujarati Hindu!) and expelled him
from their home and family. Jeevanbhai knew then that he
must leave the town his family had lived in for a generation, the
only home he had ever known. And he knew, too, that he had
to act fast, before the wind carried the news along the coast. So
his wife hid her few bits of jewellery in her bodice and they tied
everything they had into a bundle and waited for the chain of

Indian merchants along the coast to pull them northwards like a bucket from a well. First they went to Mozambique, then Dar es Salaam, then Zanzibar, Djibouti, Perim and Aden. Everywhere he met with all the hospitality due to a son of his father, and he for his part took care to keep his bride hidden and stay at least two days ahead of the news. In Aden he looked up and down the coast, sniffed the breeze and tasted the currents and decided, decided with an absolute certainty, that al-Ghazira was where he would go. He bought himself a ticket on a rusty British-blessed steamer run by an enterprising Parsi in Bombay, and soon Jeevanbhai, with his spade teeth and bundled-up wife, was standing in al-Ghazira's harbour, looking past the booms and sambuqs anchored in the little muddy inlet, at the steaming, dusty township beyond. Al-Ghazira was small then, an intimate little place, half market-town perched on the edge of the great hungry desert beyond, half pearling-port fattening on the lustrous jeevan pearls in its bay. It was a merchant's paradise, right in the centre of the world, conceived and nourished by the flow of centuries of trade. Persians, Iraqis, Zanzibari Arabs, Omanis and Indians fattened upon it and grew rich, and the Malik, fast in his mud-walled fort on the Great Hill behind the town, smiled upon them, took his dues and disbursed a part of them in turn when British gunboats paid their visits to the little harbour.

The Indian merchants of al-Ghazira, some of whom had been settled there for generations, never quite knew what to make of Jeevanbhai. Soon after his arrival, for some reason, they had decided not to drive him out. But they had never accepted him and never let him into their houses. All his life Jeevanbhai circled just beyond the thresholds of respectability. So, when his wife died and his businesses began to fail and his money disappear, he had turned instinctively towards the Severed Head, and not to the Indians of the city.

In those early days, with the last bit of his wife's gold, Jeevanbhai had bought himself a shop in the Souq ash-Sharji. The shop was to pass through a progression of avatars; it started as a cloth-shop, switched to dates and general groceries, then changed to hardware and later to carpets – in its first decade it changed almost every year. It didn't matter; none of the shop's incarnations ever made much money. That was not the intention. All through those years, it was in a little room behind the shop that Jeevanbhai's real business lay.

One day, in his first year in al-Ghazira, Jeevanbhai was sitting in his empty cloth-shop wondering how he was going to buy the day's food, when a rich Sindhi pearl merchant dropped by for a cup of tea. Within moments he was pouring his heart out, laying bare his shame as he never would have to anyone but an outcast: he had a daughter, still unmarried at twenty-five, and he was at his wits' end.

Jeevanbhai had not been idle on his journey from Durban; his instinct had driven him to ferret out names all along the coast, and his memory had clung on to them more successfully than his wallet had held on to money. That morning, providentially, his mind disgorged a suitable name in distant Zanzibar. The marriage came about and spread happiness in waves across the ocean. He was asked for a few more names, and his memory proved its worth every time. His reputation was soon established; families which would not have let him cross their courtyards flocked to his back room from all the kingdoms around al-Ghazira and from places as distant as Socotra and Khartoum, and none of them was ashamed to ask help from Jeevanbhai, for there was nothing to be feared from such a shadowy, harmless creature.

In his little back room Jeevanbhai spun out his web, spanning oceans and continents, and such are the ironies of fortune that he, whose marriage had cast him out of his family, found fame as the most successful marriage-broker in the Indian Ocean. As his 'marriages' blossomed and grew rich in progeny, Jeevanbhai grew rich with his bridal pairs, for he had another talent – he had learnt the secret of spinning gold from love.

He went into the 'gold trade' between India, al-Ghazira and Africa. Within months he had almost eliminated the competition, for in all the ports around the Indian Ocean grateful husbands and eager grooms stood by to receive his consignments and hurry them across borders (and of course they were none the poorer for it). Soon he began to diversify, first into silver, then a few guns. That was when, they said, he first began making his trips to the Old Fort. . . .

Jeevanbhai grew rich. In gratitude he founded the New Life

Marriage Bureau, for he never forgot that his money had come from marriages. And, besides, there were the commissions, and nothing is as good as the account-books of a marriage bureau for throwing a pleasing fog of confusion over inexplicable flows of money. Soon his business had grown so large that he had to move out of the Souq ash-Sharji into an office near the harbour. Looking around for someone to run his shop in the Souq he came across Forid Mian, then a sailor on a British line. In his childhood Forid Mian had learnt tailoring in his native Chittagong (in what was then East Bengal), but circumstances had forced him to go to sea. Jeevanbhai learnt of his trade somehow and persuaded him to leave his ship. Ever since, Forid Mian had worked for a monthly wage in the newly named Durban Tailoring House. Usually the shop lost money, and in the best of years it just about managed to balance its books with a few tricks, but Jeevanbhai wouldn't part with it, despite his steadily lightening purse. He clung to it; it was his talisman, the only thing left to him of his best years.

But, then, said Rakesh, perplexed, why that shop? Why not some other shop?

Zindi smiled: Do you know of any other shop? Do you know of anybody in the Souq who'd sell, especially now with so much money coming in? That's the important thing – Jeevanbhai doesn't make money from that shop; it's just sentiment. He's a practical man. If something went wrong, if it became too much trouble to keep that shop. . . . Suppose Forid Mian decides to leave. I'm not saying he will, but just suppose. Then what would that shop be worth to Jeevanbhai? He has enough to worry about at the moment – would he still want that shop? It's just a question, no one can answer it yet, but maybe then he might want to sell. Who knows? And, besides, it's a lucky shop. It brought Jeevanbhai luck once, only he didn't know how to hold on to it – he meddles too much. It ought to go to someone who knows how to use it. Maybe. . . .

Why not just ask him to sell it, Zindi?

That's the trouble, Zindi said angrily. People like you have no experience of practical things. Do you think one can just ask a man like Jeevanbhai something like that? There has to be a situation, some possibilities, something that might help him make up his mind. You see, you have to be practical, like me, and not spend your time brooding uselessly about the Star. It's only when you learn to accept that what's happened has happened that you can use your knowledge of the past to cheat the future. That is what practical life is.

Abu Fahl's inquiries yielded the information that the guard around the ruins was changed three times a day: in the morning, at dusk and at midnight. He found out that at dusk, because the change coincided with the evening prayers, the relieving detachment sometimes arrived ə little late. So, for about half an hour after dusk, the Star was usually unguarded. He decided that he and Rakesh would leave the house a little before dusk.

Before leaving, they told Zindi of their plans. She listened absent-mindedly. Yes, go, she said. *Allah yigawwikum*, and God give you strength.

Her mind was elsewhere. Rakesh could see that her anxiety was not caused by their enterprise. Before they left, she took him aside and whispered: Rakesh, do you think he'll come?

Who?

Forid Mian, of course, she said impatiently. Rakesh shrugged and combed his hair. As they walked out of the house towards the embankment, they saw her looking worriedly up and down the lane.

Soon after they had left there was a knock on the door. Zindi leapt to open it. An elderly man in a blue jallabeyya and skullcap stood outside, a wan smile wrinkling his square, good-humoured face. How are you, Zindi? he said.

Zindi covered her disappointment with a shower of greetings: Come in, come in, Hajj Fahmy, welcome, *ya marhaban*, you have brought blessings, welcome *ya*, Hajj Fahmy, you have brought light, how are you? Come in, have some tea.

Hajj Fahmy seated himself ceremoniously on a mat and placed his hands on his folded knees. Zindi, he said, as she pumped her stove, where's my son Isma'in?

Isma'il? said Zindi, surprised. He hasn't been here.

But I sent him here. We heard the rumours, you see, and I wanted to find out. He didn't come so I was worried.

Zindi clicked her tongue in sympathy. How you've aged, she said, since Mohammad's accident, God have mercy on him.

She threw an extra handful of tea and mint into the pot. Hajj Fahmy was the house's oldest friend and he had a right to its best tea.

Hajj Fahmy's family was said to have been founded, several generations ago, by a weaver called Musa, who had fled his village in the far south of Egypt after a blood feud. He escaped to Sudan and the Red Sea coast with his child bride, and there, penniless and starving, he had entered himself and his bride into servitude.

After innumerable adventures in Ethiopia, Somalia and the Yemeni coast, Musa had found his way somehow to al-Ghazira with his no-longer-young wife and many children. The Malik of the time took them into his service, and Musa and his still growing family lived in the Old Fort and wove their cloth in peace. Eventually Musa and his family came to be known as the Malik's dependants, his Mawali. His descendants were known forever afterwards by that name, even when they depended on no one but themselves.

Then the old Malik died and Musa died, and one day the Mawali found themselves not quite as welcome in the Fort as they had been in the past. So they moved, not into the town, because the townspeople still looked on them with suspicion as strangers of uncertain provenance, but into an empty sandflat which people called the Severed Head. They built themselves barasti huts, spacious airy dwellings, built with palm fronds and wooden stakes, and they installed their looms and lived and worked in proud penury.

It was Hajj Fahmy who changed all that. He saw the first oilmen coming into al-Ghazira, and he knew at once that the Mawali could profit from the future. Against all his instincts, he stopped teaching his craft to his sons and his kinsmen, and told them to be ready to learn other trades. When the oil began to gush, Hajj Fahmy was the only man in al-Ghazira who was ready for it. Within a few years one of his sons was in the construction business and making more money than he could count; another had three Datsun trucks which were never short of work (it was he who died when he drove one of his trucks off the embankment); a third had filled every Mawali with pride by going to Alexandria to study medicine.

But Isma'il, Hajj Fahmy's fourth son, did nothing at all. He had no skill at weaving, and though he talked occasionally of learning plumbing no one took him seriously. He was known to be unusually dim-witted, more or less an idiot. He spent his days wandering about the Ras, talking to people and wandering into whichever shack took his fancy for his meals. Yet, of all his sons, Isma'il was the dearest to Hajj Fahmy. He wouldn't hear of his wife's plans to push him into a trade. We have enough, he said. Isma'il helps us live with it in peace.

Soon after Hajj Fahmy and the other Mawali families began to make money, they tore down their barasti huts and built themselves large, strong houses of brick and cement. At the time, some of the Mawali had said to Hajj Fahmy: Why don't we leave the Ras and its stinking beaches, and go into the city?

Never, Hajj Fahmy had answered. In al-Ghazira the Ras is where we belong. Still, some of the Mawali left. But most of them stayed, for they knew instinctively that Hajj Fahmy was right – the Mawali had always kept to themselves in al-Ghazira. Old Musa had fetched wives for his sons from his own village in Egypt. After that the Mawali had always married amongst themselves. They spoke the Arabic of Musa's village with each other. They even wore its dress – jallabeyyas and woollen caps. Often, the men wore shirts and trousers, but never the flowing robes of the Ghaziris. Why this should be, no one knew. It was just so.

When the Ras began to fill up with shacks and people from all the corners of the world, the Mawali were alarmed. They went to Hajj Fahmy and said: What shall we do now? Soon our houses will be pushed into the sea.

Hajj Fahmy had laughed: How will they push our houses into the sea, when ours are the only solid houses in the Ras? Let them come to the Ras if they keep out of our way. The Ras gave us shelter; let it give them shelter. Besides, think of the business they'll bring.

One of his cousins opened a grocery-shop at one end of the Ras and within months he was rich. After that the Mawali never again worried about the crowds in the Ras. And the others in the Ras, for their part, left the Mawali alone and never encroached on their houses.

It was only natural that there should be a close link between the Mawali and the inhabitants of the only other permanent house in the Ras – Zindi's. No one knew how long back the connection stretched, but it was said that when Zindi first came to al-Ghazira from Egypt, as a young and buxom beauty, it was Hajj Fahmy who first found her a place and cared for her, almost as he did for his own wife. Zindi's house grew and she found other friends, but nothing ever interfered in her friendship with Hajj Fahmy. Zindi and her house kept his interest in the world alive, Hajj Fahmy would say, and he was always one of the first to visit her house when she returned from one of her trips to Egypt or India. It was inevitable that he would meet Alu sooner or later. But, as it happened, when *Mariamma* arrived the Hajj did not hear of it for a few days. Instead, one evening a young, lumpy-headed man whom he had never seen before was led into the room in which he received guests.

He had heard, Hajj Fahmy said, that we have a loom in the house. Of course no one uses it now but me, and that rarely. When I do I think myself a fool, because in the past I wove because I needed the money, and now I weave because I have nothing else to do. Anyway I showed it to him. He walked around it, looking at it carefully, but he didn't touch it. He was thinking. Who knows what he was thinking? We couldn't ask him because then he didn't know any Arabic, and all we had to talk in was signs. Next day he was back, with yarn. He set about warping the loom and a week later he was weaving. He was a little clumsy in the beginning. He said the loom wasn't like those he knew. But after a few days his hands were flying over it, and everyone in the house used to gather around to marvel at his skill. After that he used to come in the evenings, when he had finished the day's work with Abu Fahl and the others. He said it made him feel well again after a day of painting walls. He wove cloth for the whole house – soft, fine cloth (of course, we gave him a little money) – cloth of that kind is beyond my skill, Zindi, really. To tell you the truth, I often thought to myself: Why, I could start a business with the cloth this boy makes. If he could work on that loom all day long, instead of painting houses, *Allahu yia'alam*, God knows how much money he could make. I tell you, I often thought of setting up a business with that boy, often. . . . Anyway, my heart was glad to see that loom being used at last, and my father would have been glad, too. And once Alu began to talk Arabic like any of us everyone in the house came to love him, though he wasn't a Muslim. I myself, I loved him like a grandson. Yesterday, when we heard about the collapse, my house wept. I wept. Then today we heard rumour after rumour. Of course, the women in the house started talking about the Sheikh. . . .

What sheikh? Zindi broke in.

Oh, no one – an odd idea some of the Mawali women have. Anyway, as soon as I heard the rumours I sent Isma'il to your house to find out. He didn't come back, and only our Lord knows where he is. So then I set out myself. I said: I must find out from Zindi herself what's become of Alu.

Zindi stiffened suddenly, alerted by a noise in the lane outside. She was at the door before the first knock. She flung the door open, throwing her tarha askew in her haste. There were half a dozen men outside, some of them Mawali, some Indian and some Egyptian. Forid Mian was not among them.

Zindi, tell us the truth, one of them said. What's happened to Alu?

I don't know, Zindi said abruptly. Abu Fahl has gone to find out.

What about some tea, then, Zindi? someone else called out.

Reluctantly Zindi let them in. For many years the men of the Ras had gathered at Zindi's house in the evenings to talk and drink tea. There were no cafés or tea-shops in the Ras or even near it, so Zindi's house had become a surrogate. Zindi usually made a fair profit, for she charged much more for tobacco and tea than any café would have dared. People complained, but not much. They knew no café could match the stories and the tea that were to be had at Zindi's. It was said that a man learnt more about the Ras and al-Ghazira and even the world in one evening at Zindi's than from a month's television.

As the evening wore on, the knocks on the door grew increasingly frequent. Every time she heard a knock Zindi jumped, with the surprising agility she could sometimes command, to open the door. Each time she was disappointed. As the news of Abu Fahl and Rakesh's expedition spread around the Ras, the curious crowd in Zindi's house grew. But of Forid Mian there was no sign.

Slowly, as the rooms filled, the heat and tension grew. Zindi

had to open the windows, much as she disliked it, for the room
had become a steaming oven, and everybody was drenched in
sweat. The whole of Zindi's attention was concentrated on the
door and Forid Mian. Her hands began to shake and she could
no longer bring herself to make tea, so Zaghloul had to do it,
while she stared out into the lane.

Soon conversation in the room faltered and died away. Two
men began to argue about a narjila. The argument grew into a
quarrel, and suddenly the room was divided. Zaghloul nudged
Zindi. She took one look and she was worried – usually Abu
Fahl handled these situations. One of the men reached for the
neck of the other man's jallabeyya, and at that moment Isma'il
burst into the room, his jallabeyya torn, his plump, pink cheeks
and light brown hair smudged with dust.

Where have you been, Isma'in? his father said gravely.

Isma'il smiled happily and his blue-grey eyes shone as he
went around the room shaking hands. I was with Abu Fahl and
Rakesh, he said. We went to the Star.

Then Rakesh and Abu Fahl came into the room, their clothes
ragged and dishevelled, their faces ghostly, pale with dust.
They sank into a corner, and Abu Fahl ran his glazed eyes over
the room. Everyone was leaning forward, staring intently at
the two men.

What happened? Hajj Fahmy asked.

Abu Fahl mumbled: Wait. Some tea first. His head dropped
and he ran his hands over his face. Suddenly he hugged himself
and shuddered. As though in response, an involuntary shiver
rippled around the room. Abu Fahl smiled.

Soon after we left the house, Abu Fahl said, we met Isma'il.
He followed us, asking question after question – What's
happened to Alu? Where are you going? We answered him,
but at the embankment I waved him away and told him to go
home or his mother would worry. Yet when we were halfway
down the Corniche he was still behind us. I shouted and
showed him my fist. He stopped then, and we went on.

We must have been walking faster than we knew, for we
turned a bend and there was the Star, before us. It was only an
outline, black against the purple sky. I stopped Rakesh and
went ahead alone, trying to keep to the shadows of the rocks
beside the road. There were no policemen, not one.

When Rakesh came up beside me he stopped and stared, as I was staring. It looks bigger than it did, he said to me, and I saw him shiver a little. So I said loudly: Things change when you see them from different places. And sometimes the light plays tricks.

It was twilight, the last red light before darkness, and even your own face looks different then. But still it was a strange thing, for the Star *did* look bigger, much bigger. Those concrete pillars and steel girders reached above us like eucalyptus trees; we could hardly see where they ended. There seemed to be no end to the rubble and the wreckage. It towered above us. It was like the pyramids at Giza; small mountains with jagged edges and dust blowing into spirals off the sides. We heard the muezzins calling, somewhere far away in the city, but then the crashing of the waves killed the cry and we were as alone as two men on a rock in the sea.

I said to myself as we walked closer: Why, we were working here only yesterday, and when we're closer it'll seem all right. But even when we were standing at the foot of the first slope of rubble it seemed no smaller. And then we heard it whining, eerily, in a strange whistle. It rose and died away and rose again, blowing straight out of the centre of the ruins.

I caught Rakesh by the hand, for I know what he is. And if I'd left it a moment later, for all that it was he who took me there, I know he'd have turned and bolted like a rabbit, for the hairs were standing all along his arm. So to give him strength I shouted: It's only the wind whistling. Come on, be a man. At that he took heart, and even tried to smile.

But that smile never stretched very far, for the very next moment there was a flash of white beside him as someone pushed past him and sprang on to the rubble. Rakesh had turned to stone, his mouth open, as he gazed at that figure, waving at us. I shook him hard and shouted into his ear until he heard: It's only Isma'il. He must have followed us. Nothing to worry about.

So we went on again, following Isma'il. Right before us was a gentle slope of rubble, about ten feet high. We climbed it, but very slowly, for there was broken glass and bits of torn steel, like razor blades, lying everywhere.

At the top it was I who lost heart, for everywhere, all around us, as far as we could see, there were hills of shattered concrete. The slopes and tips were just visible in the last light, and the black darkness was climbing fast. Isma'il had disappeared.

I could see no sign of him, so I gave up looking and hit my head with my hands. There was a lavatory bowl behind me, protruding through the rubble; a very beautiful thing, gleaming new, painted all over with flowers. I sat down on it, for I saw no hope in going on. Rakesh sat down, too, leaning against a slab of wall. I said to him: Let's go back. We'll never find him. There could be a fleet of trucks in here and we wouldn't see it for days.

Then it was Rakesh who gave me courage. A little before the Star collapsed Rakesh and some of the others were working with Alu in the basement, directly in the centre of the building. That part of the building was, in a way, hollow, for above it there was only an empty space topped by a glass dome. That space was a five-storey greenhouse, for inside it thousands of plants grew in pots hanging on chains. The contractor said that people would flock to the Star simply to marvel at the hanging plants. Because that part was hollow, when the Star fell and its five pointed arms became towering mounds of rubble, its centre settled into a low valley. Rakesh had been there soon after the collapse. So at that moment, when I had lost hope and wanted to turn back, he pointed to a distant dip in the rubble and said: That's where we have to go, I think, though it's difficult to tell in the darkness.

Like the eager boy that he is, he jumped to his feet and, clear as the light of day, he saw and I saw a dark shape springing up with him, inches from his face. Rakesh would have screamed or shouted if he could, but all he could do was fall sideways, gasping for breath, his eyes starting from his head.

Even before he was down, a chunk of rubble was in my hand, and I threw it with all my strength.

It was just a mirror, but Rakesh was still holding his throat, sobbing and gasping, when it shattered and the glass fell at his feet.

Maybe when the Star still stood that place was a great gilded bathroom, hanging high in the sky, looking out to sea.

When Rakesh had stopped trembling I took my torch from

my pocket and we went on. What a journey it was; Sitt Zeynab
grant that I never have to do anything like that again. Every
yard seemed to take hours. We had to slide our feet forward,
picking our way through the glass and steel. Sometimes the
rubble would slide away from under our feet. Our legs and feet
were cut open so often there must be a trail of blood across
those ruins. And again at times the wind would whine within
the ruins and rise to a howl, and we would have to stand and
wait for it to die away again. All around us shadows leapt
behind the light of my torch, flickering this way and that. But of
Isma'il there was not the slightest trace.

At last we reached the edges of the mound and the valley was
before us. It was like the handiwork of a madman – immense
steel girders leaning crazily, whole sections of the glass dome
scattered about like eggshells, and all over, everywhere,
thousands of decaying plants.

Still, we sighed with relief when we saw that valley at last.

I turned sideways and began edging down the slope, towards
the valley. Rakesh was close behind me. Halfway down, my
foot caught on something in the rubble. I heard glass cracking,
and a moment before it rolled away I saw a television set. As it
fell, the rubble began to slide with it, more and more of it, until
it was a landslide. We would have been at the bottom of it if
Rakesh had not managed to hold on to a girder that was still
upright. I caught his leg and somehow we managed to keep
ourselves safe as the rubble fell past us.

When the dust and the wreckage settled we heard a noise. It
was a voice of some kind – of that there could be no doubt –
muffled but steady, somewhere under the rubble. He's there,
Rakesh shouted. He slithered and stumbled down the slope to
the spot and began to dig with his hands. Wait, we're coming!
he shouted, but the voice underneath carried on without a
break.

We cleared away the rubble until we reached an opening. At
once I reached down, for I knew what it was. I found it, groping
about, and gave it to Rakesh. It was a transistor. The falling
rubble must have switched it on somehow.

Rakesh would not take it at first. He just stood there and
glared. But there were three more, and eventually we tucked
them into our trousers and went on.

What wonders there were in that valley! For a long time we stood and marvelled. We found the head of a coconut palm which had snapped off the trunk. It was heavy with fresh, tender coconuts. Right there we broke open six of them with a bit of steel and drank their water. There were roses still blooming, and clouds of wilting magnolias.

But it was when we reached the basement that we stood gaping with astonishment – even Rakesh, who had seen it before. The basement's ceiling had collapsed as I thought, but miraculously a massive slab of concrete had fallen across the opening, sheltering it from the storm of wreckage that must have come after the collapse. Even more amazing, it had not sealed the basement completely. It lay at a steep angle, held up on one side by a bent girder, so all the wreckage had slid off it, and no rubble blocked the hole in the basement's ceiling.

Still, it was tricky there, for we were standing on a part of the basement's ceiling that might collapse at any moment. We lay flat on our stomachs and crawled forward. I looked up, but I had to look quickly away again for there were immense girders and huge slabs of concrete poised over us, hanging, as though they were waiting to fall. Once my elbow broke something, and at once there was a smell, so strong and so sweet, it sent us reeling. I shone my torch down and we saw hundreds of tiny bottles of perfume, strewn all around us. Near the edge of the basement we were hardly breathing, for the slightest slip could have sent us straight into that hole. At the lip we stopped and looked into the still blackness beneath.

As soon as I shone my torch down we both exclaimed, for we could hardly believe the depth of that room. We talked about it for a while, but in the end there could be no doubt that it was the same room we had been working in that day. I shone my torch all around it, but it was like using a pin to cut a bale of cloth. We could only see a thing at a time – overturned sewing machines, ovens with their doors thrown open, like huge laughing mouths, all kinds of things. We worked the torch all over that room, but all we could see was machinery strewn about the place, and rubble. There was no sign of Alu.

We should go down, Rakesh whispered, maybe he's unconscious. And I said: How? We'd need ropes and many more men. We have to come back tomorrow.

Then Rakesh said: We should call the police or the contractor and tell them to get him out. And I said to him: What would happen then? Maybe they'd get him or his corpse out, but the first thing they'd discover after that is that he has no work permit and no passport. He'd go straight into gaol. Then they'd find out who he was working with. And then we'd follow him into gaol. We have to leave that to the last – only if we can't get him out ourselves.

Suddenly, behind us: Phow! Like a revolver. I turned around as quick as a thought, my hands ready.

Phow! again. It was Isma'il, standing on a girder, pointing an electric hair-dryer at us and pretending to shoot. He called out to us, happily, as though we were at a wedding: He's there. Haven't you found him yet?

Then Isma'il went to the edge of that black hole and shouted down: Alu? His shout grew inside that huge pit, echoing and booming until the rubble behind us started to slide. I clapped a hand on his mouth and pulled him back before he could do it again. Then the echoes died away, and quite distinctly we heard Alu's voice.

All right, all right, Hajj Fahmy smiled across the steaming, smoke-filled room at Abu Fahl. Was he there or not? What did he say? Just tell us.

Yes, said Abu Fahl. He was there, but we couldn't see him. He was under a heap of rubble, broken machinery and pots of paint. There were two massive concrete beams projecting out of the heap. We couldn't believe that anyone could be alive under all that. It seemed impossible. Then he said he was trapped under the heap, but there was a steel girder across him holding up the beams.

Was he hurt? Hajj Fahmy asked.

No, he said he wasn't hurt at all. He was perfectly all right.

Did you see him?

No, we couldn't. I told you. But that's what he said. We asked him if he needed food or water and he said: No.

That was a strange thing. He said: No, I'm all right, I don't need anything. We told him we would be back tomorrow and he laughed. Yes, he laughed. He said: It's all right. Come when you can. And while he was speaking your son Isma'il shouted down to him: Alu, have you seen the Sheikh of the Mawali?

Abu Fahl broke off and looked curiously across at Hajj Fahmy: Who is this sheikh?

Hajj Fahmy looked away, embarrassed, and twisted the hem of his jallabeyya around his fingers. Before he could say anything, Isma'il broke in: He's Sheikh Musa the Mawali. He was buried there and he protects everyone who passes by.

Hajj Fahmy clapped a hand on his shoulder. Be quiet, Isma'in, he said sharply. He turned to the others: It's just a bit of harmless nonsense the Mawali women believe. It's blasphemous, and I've argued with them a thousand times, but they believe it. Never mind. Carry on. Did he say anything else?

Yes, said Abu Fahl hesitantly. He took off his cap and ran his hands through his hair. He turned and called out: Zindi, are you listening?

Zindi was staring out of the door, biting her lip, her face screwed small with worry. She started and turned to Abu Fahl: Yes, yes, of course I'm listening. Go on.

Abu Fahl said: For a while he was quiet. Then he told us that he was thinking. We said: What are you thinking about? And he answered: I'm thinking about dirt and cleanliness. I'm thinking and I'm making plans.

Dirt and cleanliness? Hajj Fahmy's voice rose in incredulity.

Yes, that's what he said. He said: I'm thinking about cleanliness and dirt and the Infinitely Small.

Chapter Twelve

From an Egg-Seller's End

Abu Fahl woke early next morning, worrying. It was taken for granted that, if there was to be another expedition to the Star, Abu Fahl would be its leader. So, as if by right, it fell to Abu Fahl to worry.

First, there was the problem of finding men to go with them to the Star. And where were they to find the men? They would probably have to hire them from one of the construction gangs in the Ras. But they would almost certainly expect to be paid (for they would be losing the day's wages). In all likelihood they would have to be paid extra because of the risks. Where was the money to come from? And tools: they'd need shovels for the rubble; ropes; maybe ladders as well, to lower themselves to the basement; perhaps even blowtorches for the steel girders. Where was he to get the tools? And, even if he found some, how were they to carry them through a cordon of policemen?

Abu Fahl shook Zindi, asleep beside him: What are we to do, Zindi? Can you think of a plan? Zindi grunted, pushed a leg between his and shut her eyes again. Abu Fahl taxed her later: You don't care whether that boy you brought into this house – you, yourself – you don't care whether he lives or dies.

Zindi gave him a drowsy answer: I know he's alive and I know you'll get him out somehow. What more is there to say? In the meanwhile someone has to think of the future and other things, too. We still have to go on living.

Abu Fahl fell silent: the beginnings of a plan were already stirring in his mind. He and Rakesh would visit the two construction gangs in the Ras before they left for work, and explain the situation. Some of the men might agree to work free. After all, it could happen to anyone – that was the point to press home.

So planned Abu Fahl, the organizer, at dawn, complaining

but with secret relish, for in his instincts Abu Fahl was a storyteller and plans are the fantasies of the practical life.

Before Abu Fahl's plans were ready there was a sharp, insistent hammering on the door to the lane. Abu Fahl opened it. Isma'il stood outside, a hacksaw in his hands. Behind him, in the lane, there was a large group of men. Some of them were brandishing axes, some crowbars, and others shovels.

Once or twice Abu Fahl, too, had visited a house or a shack with a crowbar in his hands. He smelt a threat the moment he saw the men crowding into the lane. Without flinching, betraying nothing, he parted his legs and planted them squarely in the doorway. Folding his arms across his chest, he clamped his one, red eye on Isma'il: What is this?

This? said Isma'il, surprised. This is a kind of saw. In demonstration he sawed a groove into the wooden doorpost.

Abu Fahl caught his wrist. No! Not that, this. He waved a hand at the crowded lane.

Ya salaam! Isma'il exclaimed, turning. Are there so many now? You see, I was coming to help you get Alu out of the Star. I brought this saw with me, for I thought you might need it. On the way I met some people, and they said: Where are you going, *ya* Isma'il? And I said: I'm going to get Alu out of the Star; he's been buried three days and he's still alive, and they say he has something to tell us. But there was no need for all that; they already knew about Alu and they all said: Wait, Isma'il, we'll come with you. Everyone wants to know what a man can have to say after being buried alive for three days.

Isma'il scratched his head and smiled at Abu Fahl. The next moment Abu Fahl found himself overwhelmed with shouted offers of help.

There were too many men, far too many. Abu Fahl soon realized that he could only take a small group safely into the Star. But then there was a new problem – the men would not leave. Some even tried to force their way into the house, and Abu Fahl barely kept his temper.

Abu Fahl's problems grew through the morning. People began to arrive from every part of the Ras, virtually from every shack. A whole construction gang arrived, determined to get Alu out of the Star before going to work. They wanted to set out

at once, and Abu Fahl had to quarrel with them to keep them
from doing so.

Soon the house was in turmoil: Abu Fahl shouting, astonished, gratitude turned to exasperation; Professor Samuel,
loudly complaining until Jeevanbhai Patel led him away to his
office; Karthamma and Chunni racing from the courtyard to
Zindi's room with glasses of tea; Isma'il fighting the geese with
Kulfi-didi's newly washed sari.

Only Zindi sat through it all unmoved. She greeted the men
who flooded in and out of her room politely enough, but when
they began to talk she turned silently away. Soon she was
forgotten, left to herself, in her corner. She was grateful, for
later, when she caught Rakesh's arm and whispered into his
ear, nobody noticed her. Go one last time, she said, just one
more time. Go to Romy Abu Tolba's shop and tell Tolba to give
Forid Mian another message – Zindi will be waiting for you this
evening. Just that.

Rakesh did not see at first that she was begging. When he
did, he put his arm around her and squeezed her shoulder.
Much later, he slipped out of the house and was back again
before anyone missed him.

Abu Fahl was still under siege. He decided finally that he
would go to the Star with perhaps five men, and only a few
tools: some crowbars, ropes and torches, nothing else. The
others resisted at first, but Abu Fahl cajoled, argued and
shouted, and in the end he had his way. Only Isma'il, who
appeared to know the way to the basement in the dark, Rakesh,
and three other men, all of them experienced construction
hands, were to go with him.

At dusk, when the six men were to set off, the crowd, swollen
by people on their way back from work, had spilled out of
Zindi's house into the lane and beyond. The six men were
pushed along the lanes of the Ras with cheers and shouts of
encouragement. At the embankment Abu Fahl stopped and
shouted into the crowd. If there was a crowd on the road the
police would notice, and that would be the end of it all; they
would just have to go back to their houses and wait till Alu was
brought back.

The crowd watched the six men till they disappeared. Then
some people wandered back to their shacks and some trickled

back to Zindi's house. As the evening wore on the trickle grew, and before long Zindi's house was crammed with people again.

Zindi, frustrated and angry, her nerves worn by two days of waiting, doubled the rates for her tea, but still people called for more, faster than she and Karthamma could make it. They ran out of tea altogether, and Kulfi had to be sent to Romy Abu Tolba's shop to buy more. She came back frightened. She had never seen the Ras so empty before; everyone who could walk was waiting at Zindi's house, for Alu's return. Once, Zindi left her room to go to the lavatory. She found her courtyard packed coffee-pot full and boiling over. Karthamma had prudently moved the geese, the rabbits and the chickens to the roof. Amazed, Zindi picked her way through a group of squatting Mawali women: the Mawali women rarely left their quarter and they had never been in her house before.

Then suddenly the excitement mounted. They heard a boy running and a shout: They're coming, they're coming. The younger men ran out of the house, pushing their way through the lane. After that word came in relays: Only Isma'il's back. No, they're all back, Isma'il's running ahead. What about Alu? Have they got Alu?

Uncertain murmurs ran around the room and the courtyard: They're leading someone; there's a seventh person with them. And then voices somewhere in the lane: No, that's a shadow – it's just the five of them and Isma'il.

What about Alu? Is he dead? Has the Star killed him at last?

Abu Fahl stepped into a crackling silence. The crowd in the courtyard stirred and rose; people shoved and elbowed each other, straining for a glimpse of the men. And then it was certain – the only men with Abu Fahl were those who had gone with him. No Alu.

At once Abu Fahl was struck by a thunderclap of questions. The crowd surged towards him, jostling and pushing. He stumbled, fell, picked himself up again and shouted. He shouted again, and again, but even his bull's bellow was lost in the commotion. Then Rakesh began beating an empty kerosene-tin, and slowly the metallic clanging prevailed and the shouts died away. Rakesh upturned the kerosene-tin on the floor and pushed Abu Fahl on to it.

Abu Fahl stood precariously still on the tin for a moment,

rubbing his blind eye and looking at the faces that were raised towards him. He saw Hajj Fahmy's wife, a lean string of a woman, and he heard her rumble: So tell us, Abu Fahl, is he dead at last?

No, said Abu Fahl. He isn't dead. He's as alive as you or me.

A long sigh blew through the courtyard, stirring up a volley of angry questions: Then, why isn't he here? Why didn't you get him out?

Abu Fahl held up his hand: There was nothing we could do; there were too few of us. He's lying under a pile of rubble, and do you know how large that pile is? It's a mountain. Even after we managed to get down to the basement, it was a long time before we could so much as see him. He's right at the bottom of that mountain.

But just above him was a concrete slab, almost flat on the ground. At first we thought there couldn't possibly be any living thing under that slab.

Then we saw that the slab was inclined very slightly. At one end it was about a foot or two off the floor. In the beginning we couldn't see what lay under it there, for there's a tangle of webbed steel blocking it at that end. And then, when we managed to look through, we saw him there, right in front of us, lying flat on his back, with that huge slab of concrete so close to his nose he could have touched it with his eyelashes. Another hair's breadth and he would have been a dead man.

How did it happen? Why did that block of concrete stop there, just a hair away from his nose? Do you know why? Because beside him, on either side, were two sewing machines, of the old kind, of black solid steel. They must be the only ones of their kind in al-Ghazira now, real antiques, probably kept for display. But, if it weren't for them, our friend Alu would have been flattened days ago.

He was lying right in front of us, but there was nothing we could do. We'd have had to cut through the steel mesh, move the rubble and shift the concrete slab to get him out. That slab's two feet thick, two feet of ground rock and sand held together by steel. It's so strong it could hold up a shopful of cars. And the girders fallen around it are as thick as tree-trunks and a thousand times stronger. On girders like that you could hang the whole of the Ras. It would have taken dozens of men with a truckload of equipment to move them, and we were just six.

We didn't dare move a thing: the slightest slip, and who was to know? Perhaps the whole mountain of rubble would come down on him. We had to stand there and stare at this man, hardly more than a boy, buried alive under a hill of rubble, with death barely an inch from his chest, and miraculously still alive. All we could do was marvel; all of us, we marvelled, for there was not a man amongst us who had seen a thing like that before.

I could hardly speak. I remember at last I laughed, to make the whole business seem ordinary, and though we had taken nothing with us I said to Alu, Do you need food or water? – and he said simply, No, I'm all right.

I tried to think of something else, but nothing would come to me, so I asked him, Alu, how are your boils? – and he answered, They're gone. So then, trying to laugh again, I said: Alu, do you want to come out now, or do you still want to lie there and think about dirt and cleanliness and your Infinitely Small?

He said: Take me out of here, Abu Fahl. I have been here long enough, I have thought enough, and now I know what we must do. . . .

Abu Fahl stopped and glanced over the courtyard. The whole crowd was staring intently up at him. He drew a deep breath.

I asked him: Alu, what must we do?

And he said: We must have a war.

Abu Fahl beat down the stifled gasps and murmurs that rose all around him: I said to him, What kind of war?

And Alu said: We shall war on money, where it all begins.

After that Abu Fahl would say no more: he waved the crowd out, telling them to go home and think about what he had said. Then he went into Zindi's room and demanded tea from Karthamma.

Zindi set about the business of clearing the house with energetic enthusiasm. Her insults soon emptied the courtyard and the lane outside. But there was nothing she could do about her own room, which was so crowded there was barely room for the smoke. She saw from the way Hajj Fahmy was sitting, with his hands planted firmly on his crossed legs, that it was likely to remain so, for it was always he who gave the lead to the others.

In despair, she tucked Boss under her arm and went to sit on the doorstep. And there she found Forid Mian, waiting timidly in the shadows of the lane, inconspicuous in his usual starched shirt and checked green lungi. For an instant she gaped at his long parched face and his ragged beard. Then her surprise was swept away by waves of relief and hope, and all at once she was babbling strings of phrases of welcome, squeezing his twig fingers, and pushing him through the door.

Forid Mian drew back when he saw the crowd in her room, but she tightened her grip on his arm and led him in. Once he was inside, he straightened his shoulders with an effort and worked his way slowly around the room, shaking hands and whispering Salaams. Everybody was listening to Abu Fahl telling the story of his journey to the Star again, and only Hajj Fahmy held Forid Mian's hand long enough to talk to him. You're here after a long time, Forid, he said curiously. But, before he could answer, Zindi appeared at his elbow and led him away.

Zindi cleared a space in a corner near the stove by pushing two men aside and sat Forid Mian down. She settled Boss on her lap and lit the stove. So how are you, Forid Mian? she said softly in Hindi. It's a long time since you drank tea with us. Hajj Fahmy is right.

Forid Mian combed his beard with his fingers. Not so long, he said. You know there's a lot of work in the shop. And now you have Jeevanbhai staying here. I'd feel strange sitting with him in the evenings.

Zindi smelt a promising spoor and leapt: Why? Then she checked herself. No, she said gently, I only meant. . . . There hasn't been trouble, I hope?

No, said Forid Mian. No trouble. Not really trouble. But you know how prices are going up and what rice costs. What can a poor man do? So when I see Jeevanbhai I ask him for some more money. And he says, where will the money come from? and he looks at my accounts and he doesn't seem happy. That happens every other day. It would be too much if it were to happen in the evenings as well.

Zindi nodded: Yes, but we've been missing you. We all

wonder where Forid Mian is. Tell me, Forid Mian, how many years is it since you've been working in al-Ghazira?

Forid Mian sighed and counted on his fingers. Must be fifteen, he said. Fifteen years!

Fifteen years! Zindi clicked her tongue. That's a long time. Chittagong in Bangladesh, wasn't it?

Forid Mian stared into space. Yes, he said, Chittagong, Chatgan, where the Karnophuli pours into the sea, almost Burma. . . .

Hah! Zindi squeezed his bony thigh. So, Forid Mian, tell me, how many wives and how many children have you got hidden away in your Chatgan by the Karnophuli?

Forid Mian brushed her hand away. You're laughing at me, Zindi, he said sharply. You know quite well I don't have a family or a wife or children. I was too young when I left, and there was no money in the house anyway. Then I was at sea, and there was no time. And then here in al-Ghazira. . . .

Zindi raised a hand to cover her mouth: No wife, no children! Nothing? What are you going to do? Are you going to stay here for ever, in the Souq? Until your fingers are too stiff to hold a needle?

What can I do? Forid Mian's head fell until he was staring at his crossed feet. I have some money saved, I could afford to get married now, even start a small shop of my own. But I have no family left there now. Who would find me a wife? I'm afraid, Zindi: going back to a place alone, starting again, a man can't do that at my age.

How old are you, Forid Mian? Zindi asked.

Fifty? Sixty? Something like that.

Forid Mian shrugged.

Zindi gurgled with laughter: Just the right age to get married. Something will have to be done for you, Forid Mian.

She tweaked his bottom, and Forid Mian broke into laughter: Zindi, you don't know, you can't imagine, how I long for a wife. I've spent too many nights thrashing about on dry sheets. You don't know how it hurts. You wake up in the morning and you're bleeding, but you can't stop. . . .

Zindi laughed with him, her huge shoulders rolling like round-bottomed pots. But Forid Mian noticed people turning to look at them, and he frowned in embarrassment. Zindi tapped him on the knee and said: Forid Mian. But he shook his head and pointed across the room, at Hajj Fahmy. The Hajj was holding his hand up and waiting for silence. Zindi decided to say no more; she had said enough for one day.

Hajj Fahmy, eyes shining, smiled across the room at Abu Fahl. I have a question for Abu Fahl, he said to the room. Let us see if Abu Fahl can answer it. I've understood what Abu Fahl has said – why he couldn't get Alu out today, and so on and *fulan* – I've understood it all, but for one thing, and this thing troubles me. Abu Fahl talks of how strong the concrete and the steel in the Star was, and how that concrete can hold up a mountain of rubble and a shopful of cars, and how you could hang the whole of the Ras on one of those girders. But here is my question: if that concrete and steel was so strong, why did the Star fall?

Abu Fahl slid a finger under his cap and scratched his head. It wasn't strong all over, he said, only in parts. He stopped, flustered.

If it was strong only in parts, why did the whole of it fall?

Abu Fahl recovered himself. It's quite simple, he said confidently. Everyone knows that the contractors and architects put too much sand in the cement. They've been doing it for years. A cement shortage, they say. But actually they're busy putting up palaces with the money they make from that cement – for themselves at home in England, or India or Egypt, America, Korea, Pakistan, who knows where? The cement they were using for the Star was nothing but sand. Not all of it, of course. For those parts of the building which were going to bear really heavy weights they cast very strong concrete. It's one of those parts that Alu is lying under. The rest of that building was like straw. Anybody who had any experience of construction at all knew that it wouldn't last. I wasn't surprised when it fell; I'd been expecting it. That day I actually saw the whole thing begin, and I knew at once what was going to happen. Rakesh, Alu and some of the others were the only people working at the time. It was lunchtime, just before the afternoon prayers, and everybody else had stopped work. Our people had something to finish, so they were still inside. I was sitting outside talking to some people and suddenly a piece of plaster fell right beside me. I looked up and

I distinctly saw the whole building beginning to shake, and somewhere, deep inside the Star, I heard rumbles. I knew at once what was going to happen, so I raced in and called out to Rakesh and the others to run, for the Star was going to fall. Ask them. If it weren't for me, they wouldn't be alive today. They all ran, except Alu, and that was because Alu has no experience; he knows nothing of buildings and construction. But let that be. The Hajj asks why did the Star fall. The answer is this: because, though parts of it were strong, the whole of it was weak because of bad cement and sandy concrete.

Abu Fahl sat back, assured and commanding, accepting the thoughtful silence that had fallen on the room as a tribute to his good sense. Hajj Fahmy was the first to speak, smiling, teasing him: You're wrong, Abu Fahl.

Abu Fahl frowned: What do you mean, I'm wrong?

Just that. I know you're wrong.

How?

Because I know the real story; the true story.

If it's true, how's it a story?

All right, then, it's a story.

Abu Fahl challenged the old man: If you're so sure, *ya* Hajj, why don't you tell us?

Hajj Fahmy looked around him: Are you sure everyone wants to hear it?

Voices rose: Yes, there's tea, there's tobacco and what else have we got to do?

Hajj Fahmy inclined his head, smiling.

It's just a story.

Once many, many years ago, so long ago that the time is of no significance, an odd-looking man, a very odd-looking man, appeared suddenly one day in al-Ghazira. Thin and small he was, of course, as people often were in those days, though his wasn't the thinness of hunger so much as that of the mangled rag: he looked as though he had been twisted and pulled inside out, for his colour was a strange yellowish brown, as though he were carrying his bile on his skin. At first people would have nothing to do with him; he upset everyone he met, because when one of his eyes looked this way the other looked that. He was so painfully cross-eyed it was said of him that when other people only saw Cairo he could see Bombay as well. And, in addition, one of his eyes was always half-shut, as though his eyelid had been torn off its hinges. That was the deceptive one; it roamed about, taking everything in, while the other acted as a decoy.

No one knew anything about him. He didn't even have a name for a long time. But then someone discovered that he was from northern Egypt, from the town of Damanhour, and so of course he was named Nury – Nury the Damanhouri. Soon he was found to be a quiet man, always willing to laugh, and never any trouble to anyone, so people grew to like him.

It's true; he *was* a quiet man, but in his quiet way he changed things while nobody noticed. Take his trade, for example – he brought something altogether new to al-Ghazira. But that's a story in itself.

Now, no one ever really knew why Nury had left Daman-hour and come to al-Ghazira; in those days Damanhour was probably a better place to make a living than al-Ghazira. But a few months after he arrived a rumour went around al-Ghazira. People whispered that Nury had tried to divorce his wife because she had borne him no children. But when the council of elders was called they said everything was turned upside down – it was she who accused him of being as impotent as a wet rag, and challenged him to prove otherwise. They said he had fled Egypt in shame.

People were curious, of course, but it wasn't known for certain whether the story was true. Here, Nury married a widowed Mawali woman decades older than himself and they were happy together, for she never once talked of how they spent their nights. It didn't matter. Nury was a philosopher; he knew that people always believe the worst. Though nobody knew for certain, there wasn't a man in al-Ghazira who didn't, at heart, believe the rumour to be true. No one ever stopped to ask where the story came from; no one ever imagined that perhaps it came from Nury himself. Once it began to be whispered, people believed it absolutely, indisputably.

In his own small way Nury was a great man; he had the wisdom to see the world clearly. And like a logician he drew clear conclusions from what he saw.

Here is a lesson: all trade is founded on reputation.

Nury's trade was selling eggs.

Nobody had ever sold eggs in al-Ghazira before. Not in a properly organized way, at least. In those days, everyone in the town had a few chickens in their houses, and when they laid they ate eggs, when they didn't they didn't. No one would have thought of buying or selling eggs, except perhaps from a neighbour.

Nury changed all that. He found out who had chickens and whose chickens laid when. Every morning he would set out with his basket beside him and go from house to house, buying eggs from some and persuading others to buy a few on the days their chickens weren't laying. He was successful, but none of it would have been possible but for one thing, and Nury had thought of it. That was the sign of his genius.

Selling eggs is a trade like no other. Who looks after the chickens in a house? Who sells their eggs? Everyone knows the answer: the women of the house. Nury's trade was founded on dealing with women. There was not another man in al-Ghazira who could have gone from house to house talking to the women and been left alive for a week. But no one so much as asked a question about Nury the cross-eyed Damanhouri, for everyone had heard his story. Nury was safe and his trade prospered. Nury, harmless and ageless, went from house to house buying and selling, talking of God knows what.

Nury built a trade on a story. Soon people were used to eating eggs every day, or whenever they wanted to, and people began to count on the extra money they made from selling eggs. Nury did quite well out of it all; soon he even built himself a little house. Nury's trade was a work of craftsmanship; a masterpiece in the art of staying alive. Nury's crossed eyes had the gift of looking, not just ahead, but up and down, right into the heart of things.

But here is another lesson: Blindness comes first to the clear-sighted.

Never mind. Most people in Nury's place would have been happy merely to carry on with their trade. Not Nury. Nury the Damanhouri was an artist. For him every egg was an epic, a thousand-page song of love, death and betrayal. By looking at an egg Nury could tell what the chicken had been fed; from that he knew whether the house he had bought it from was close to starvation or had finally found a pot of gold. If one day a house had no eggs to sell, Nury would wonder why and ask a few questions and discover that they'd killed their chickens to feed a man who had a son who was the right age for their daughter. If a poor man's house suddenly began to buy eggs, Nury would be the only man in al-Ghazira to know that they'd found a pearl the size of a football. Nury had imagination. But, more important, Nury was the only man in al-Ghazira who went from house to house every day, talking to people, even going into courtyards, taking in, in one glance, as much as other people take in in ten. Not a leaf fell, not a sheep shat in al-Ghazira without Nury's knowing of it. But all this he did quietly, for silence was in his nature.

There is a moral in this: an eye in a courtyard is worth a hundred guns.

Inevitably, Jeevanbhai Patel was the first man to see what Nury was worth. Patel was already a well-to-do man then, and he gave Nury some pointless job to do in the evenings, when he wasn't doing anything else. The job was unimportant. What Patel wanted was his knowledge, for he saw power in knowledge, and for him power meant money. In barely a month Patel's investment paid off.

At that time the Malik – this very same Malik who lives shut away in the Old Fort now – was a young man, recently returned from a school for princes in India, where the British had sent him. He had become Malik after his father's death, only a year before, but already people knew that here was a man very different from the senile and foolish old Malik, his father. This new Malik was a storm of energy. No one met him who did not come away reeling. People said that it was impossible even to look at the Malik for more than a minute at a time – his whole face was blood red like the setting sun. They said he had secret ways of making the blood rush to his face to terrify people. He never laughed, never smiled, and such was his temper that much of the time people were grateful to leave the Fort alive.

At that time something happened which made his temper worse than ever. A few years ago the British had found oil in some of the kingdoms around al-Ghazira, and already there were rumours that al-Ghazira was just a speck of sand floating on a sea of oil. So the British, for the first time, sent a resident to al-Ghazira, to make the Malik sign a treaty which would let the British dig for oil.

With great fanfare the Resident arrived, in a battleship. People liked him: he was a fat, round little man who laughed a lot and slept a lot. He liked fancy clothes and pomp and ceremony and parading soldiers. Everywhere he went in al-Ghazira hundreds of people followed him, because whenever he spoke he made his lips into a circle of such perfection that everyone who saw him held their breath waiting for a black, wonderfully rounded goat's turd to fall out. And so it was that he came to be known as Goat's Arse.

Once every week Goat's Arse would go to the Old Fort and plead and argue, trying to persuade the Malik to sign the treaty, but the Malik wouldn't hear of it. He had seen what had happened to the princes of India and he had sworn he would never let himself be reduced to their state. So, inevitably, the day came when – much against his will, for he was a peaceable man – Goat's Arse began to talk of calling for battleships and the Malik began to despair.

The Malik used to read a lot, and at that time, in his worry, he began to spend whole days reading until it became a kind of madness – histories of the great Baghdadi and Cairene dynasties, lives of the caliphs and the kings and so on. From one of these he got an idea. In his madness he decided he would teach the British a lesson.

He decided to fry Goat's Arse.

Carefully the Malik made his plans. He invited Goat's Arse to a private dinner to celebrate, he said, his birthday. Goat's Arse was delighted; he thought the Malik had finally decided to sign the treaty. It was a special occasion, he thought, and ought to be treated with proper ceremony. When the day came he dressed himself in his best uniform, all scarlet and black, and mounted his great white charger. Before him, with their lances and flags and raised pennants, rode his small squadron of Indian cavalry, and ahead of them marched four Sikhs, immense men in turbans, playing bagpipes and kettledrums. It was something to see: plump little Goat's Arse on his white horse, with all those troops, turbaned and bearded, sashed and sabred, parading through the town, past the harbour, into the Maidan al-Jami'i, straight through towards the Fort on the hill.

The whole town came running out of their houses to follow them. At the foot of the hill the crowd was stopped by the Malik's Bedouin guards, for the Malik had given them strict orders that nobody was to be allowed near the Fort but Goat's Arse and his entourage. So the crowd stopped at the foot of the hill and watched Goat's Arse and his troops till they disappeared.

Outside the Fort, Goat's Arse's troops presented arms and blew their bugles and did many other things of that kind, until the great old gates swung slowly open. Then Goat's Arse rode majestically to the head of his squadron, stately and erect on his white charger, and led them towards the gate. . . .

How was Goat's Arse to know that right above that gate the Malik had stationed the man he most trusted – a eunuch, ebony-black and so enormously fat he had come to be known universally as Jabal the Mountainous Eunuch – with a vat of boiling oil, or that in seven kingdoms Jabal was renowned for his cowardice, and at that very moment, waiting for the Malik to fire the flare which was to be his signal to tip the oil over, he was a quaking heap of flesh almost ready to jump into the oil himself?

Goat's Arse rode serenely on, the plumes in his helmet nodding in the wind, his squadron trotting behind him, on and on; and at the right moment, just when the charger's head entered the shadow of the gate, the Malik fired his flare and Jabal the Eunuch, in one shivering rush, heaved at the vat of boiling oil.

The trouble was, something went wrong with the flare-gun. The flare looped into the courtyard and burst into light about a foot from the horse's nose. The horse reared, whinnying, throwing Goat's Arse wide of the gate, and charged straight into the Fort. There was a waterfall of oil, but all that was fried was the end of the horse's tail, only a few hairs, which were of no use to anyone.

In a flash Goat's Arse's soldiers had him off the ground – bruised but very alive – and galloping through the city. What they were going to do was no mystery: they were going to radio their warships to bombard al-Ghazira. The streets emptied behind them until in moments the city was midnight-still, every door locked and every last grain of gold hidden away under secret bricks. At the Fort the Bedouin were trying to hurry the Malik into the desert. Even there they could hear the wails of the women rising above the town, already lamenting the sack of al-Ghazira.

But there was one thing no one knew; only one townsman had been in the Fort at the time of the Bloody Fry-day as it came to be called – only one who had seen precisely what had happened – and naturally that was Nury the sharp-eyed Damanhouri, who had heard of the feast and raced to the Fort with a donkey-load of eggs. He was coming out of the kitchen when the flare exploded, and no sooner had the first drop of oil sizzled on to the horse's tail than Nury was on his donkey, heading straight for the Souq, for he knew that here at last was something Jeevanbhai would value.

Till then Jeevanbhai had had a few dealings with the Malik. The Malik spoke to him in Urdu, which he had learnt in India, and they dealt well together, but not as well as Jeevanbhai would have wished. On the Fry-day, Jeevanbhai saw his chance. He raced to the Fort on Nury's donkey and set about persuading the Malik that to escape would be to admit guilt. No, he argued, the only wise thing to do was to counter Goat's Arse's moves before he made them.

At once Jeevanbhai drew up a message for the British Viceroy in India, Goat's Arse's boss, a man famous for his enthusiasm for local customs and suchlike (so Jeevanbhai said). Goat's Arse, the message said, had broken into and disrupted the most ancient of Ghaziri ceremonies, one that took place only once every seven years, on the reigning Malik's birthday. This was the ceremony of the Ant-Frying, when the Ants under the Fort's south gate, a most ancient line of ants, were cooked in a shower of boiling oil. The desecration of the Ant-Frying had placed the timeless traditions of the Ghaziri monarchy, and thus the prestige of the whole British Empire, in, yes, in jeopardy. If Goat's Arse were taxed with this, the message warned, he would probably deny everything. In all likelihood he didn't even know of the ceremony; such was his contempt for the customs of al-Ghazira, he had not made even the smallest effort to acquaint himself with them. . . . And so on and so on.

It worked. They sent the message on the Malik's new radio

set; two warships stopped on the horizon and turned back; and within a week Goat's Arse was recalled.

Two warships, or a good eye and a quick mind?

But still the Malik had to pay a price. Back in his own country Goat's Arse made a tremendous noise and wrote a book about how close he had come to being a deep-fried fritter in his king's service. Eventually they sent out a new resident known for his toughness; a thin-lipped fish of a man who arrived with a whole regiment of Indian soldiers. He left the Malik in the Fort, but posted a guard outside and exiled his Bedouin tribesmen. After a few months the Malik was forced to sign the oil treaty. Even at that stage, he tried to keep a hold on things by insisting that only Ghaziris would work in the Oiltown. But Thin Lips wouldn't hear of it; he wanted only his own men, men he could control. Finally, the Malik signed when warships appeared again, but on one condition: that the Oilmen never leave the Oiltown and never enter al-Ghazira.

For many years things went on, uneasily but peacefully: the Oilmen stayed inside the Oiltown with their hirelings; the Malik was more or less a prisoner in the Old Fort, allowed out only on state occasions; Thin Lips virtually ran the town; and every seven years the Ant-Frying was ritually performed. One man did well out of it all, and that was Jeevanbhai Patel. He posed as the Malik's accountant, and Thin Lips could think of no reason to keep a harmless old man like him out of the Fort, so he became one of the Malik's few contacts with the outside world. Jeevanbhai went in and out of the Fort running the Malik's errands, and the Malik used the influence he still had to get Jeevanbhai the contract for the customs. So Jeevanbhai turned his links with the Fort to good use and made money. The Malik had use for him, too: he was making his own plans for the future, and Jeevanbhai's dhows, which at that time were sailing all over the Indian Ocean, often came back lying deep in the water. They were weighed down, people said, with guns and ammunition which somehow found their way into the Old Fort.

So things went on.

The Oiltown prospered and grew, and the time came when they wanted more space. They took permission and went around al-Ghazira looking for some more land, and eventually they decided on a few acres at the far end of al-Ghazira, almost on the border with the next kingdom. It was a marshy, sandy bit of land by the sea. To them it looked unused, and they assumed that they would have no trouble buying it – for more than it was worth, if need be.

But actually that was a very special piece of land. It was special for the Mawali because old Sheikh Musa was said to be buried there; it was special for the shopkeepers of the Souq because they held fairs there on all the great feast-days, and in those times, before borders had guards, thousands of people flocked to them from all the neighbouring kingdoms and the shopkeepers grew richer every year; the Malik loved that bit of land, too, for twice every year thousands of birds flew over it, and on those days the Malik was allowed out of the Fort, for there was no better place in the world for falconry.

So, when the Oilmen went blithely up to the Fort to buy that piece of land, the blood almost burst from the Malik's face. Something terrible might have happened again if Nury the Damanhouri hadn't seen them going in and told Patel. Patel ran to the Fort and calmed the Malik down. Of course, he had a plan. He went around the Souq, got the shopkeepers together, and they met Thin Lips and told him that if that bit of land were sold they would all shut down the Souq and emigrate to Zanzibar.

The Oilmen had one last try. They went to the Malik with a new treaty, and offered to double his share of the oil money if he sold them that land.

Later, people said that the Malik spat on the treaty and drove them out of the Fort with a whip.

No more was heard of buying land for a while: the Oilmen went back to the Oiltown; the Malik stayed in his fort; and Jeevanbhai continued to prosper. But that was when the world first heard rumours about the Mad Malik of al-Ghazira, and soon after Thin Lips took the Malik's half-brother, the Amir, whom the Malik hated more than anyone else in the world, even more than his father, out of the Fort and sent him to England or America or somewhere, to study. By then Thin Lips had his own friends in the town, none of them very fond of the Malik, and he sent their sons with the Amir as well. The families who were loyal to the Malik – and there were many –

complained, but there was nothing anyone could do, and soon things were quiet again.

Years passed: the Malik stayed in his fort, the Amir and his friends stayed abroad, and all was quiet in al-Ghazira. We heard of wars, then the British left, and Thin Lips with them. The Malik was free again, but by that time he had lost his old fire, and already a new embassy with a new Thin Lips was on the ascendant, so all was still quiet in al-Ghazira.

Then one day the oil company changed, and at once the whole of al-Ghazira was agog. New men arrived. They looked over the Oiltown, and it was as clear as daylight they weren't happy with it. They surveyed al-Ghazira for a few weeks and eventually they found a new, better site for an Oiltown. You don't have to wonder where that site was.

Soon after the Oilmen were seen going into the Old Fort, with a carload of money to buy the land, people said – but after barely ten minutes shots were heard in the Fort and the cars came hurtling out. No one was hurt, but the Malik had made a mistake. These men weren't lightly to be shot at. For them life was a war. Nothing was going to stop them getting what they wanted; certainly not the Mad Malik of al-Ghazira. The battle for the site was no longer a game. It had become a feud, like the old desert feuds: a battle of honour.

The first move came soon after. One night a helicopter landed in the desert, far outside the city, and Nury the Damanhouri, who happened to be chasing a chicken, saw the Amir, the Malik's almost-forgotten half-brother, and his friends step out. The Oilmen's cars were waiting for them, and they were whisked away to a huge glittering new palace which had sprung up overnight on the far side of the city.

Who can describe the excitement, the near-frenzy of curiosity which gripped al-Ghazira then? People crowded into mosques and cafés, talking feverishly through the night; rumours blew like hurricanes through the Souq and you had to pay to stand under the Bab al-Asli. We heard stories of strings of pearls being given away for one little driblet of news. But there was no news to be had. The ornate silver doors of the New Palace stayed firmly shut, the Malik stayed in the Old Fort and the Oilmen in the Oiltown.

That was when Nury made his fortune. Inevitably, he was

the only man in al-Ghazira to go freely in and out of the New Palace – it turned out that in his years away our Amir had developed a terrible weakness for boiled eggs.

In a matter of days Nury was a celebrated man: the café he went to had to build an extension over the road; the mosque he prayed at was always full to bursting; and soon we saw a new floor rising on Nury's little house. Nury's name became a byword, for he was always truthful and always right. When he said the Amir had been appointed Oil Minister, people laughed at him, for no one had heard of an Oil Minister before. But in a week there was a proclamation and Nury was proved right. It was Nury who first said that one of the Amir's friends was going to become Defence Minister, and he was right. He was right about the Education Minister, the Culture Minister and the Foreign Minister as well. But, still, when Nury said the Amir would soon become Public Works Minister, doubt was born again. Why would the Amir want to be Public Works Minister as well as Oil Minister? It seemed meaningless, so we assumed it to be untrue, and suddenly Nury found himself alone in his café again.

Meanings are never apparent.

Late one night, when the whole town was asleep, Nury galloped out of the road to the New Palace on his donkey, hoofs flying, eggs scattering, dogs barking, through the harbour, straight towards the Maidan al-Jami'i, past the Souq, heading directly for Jeevanbhai's house. There, without so much as tethering his donkey, he flung himself on the door and hammered with all his feeble strength.

But no one can reckon for chance. Unusually for a man so quick and alert Jeevanbhai sleeps like a dead man, and it so happened that just a few days earlier his wife had gone to India on a visit. She was a rather suspicious woman, so before leaving she had gone around al-Ghazira looking for a woman of suitable age and decrepitude to work in the house while she was away. She found Saneyya, grandmother of Ali the taxi-driver and Nasser of the blue café, then a woman of seventy-five, famed in all the kingdoms for her astonishing ugliness, much loved of the pearl divers and boatmen because she could scare sharks into tearing out their own entrails simply by grinning into the water; widowed at sixteen, on the dawn after her wedding,

when, after the darkness of a night in which she conceived her
son, her bridegroom rose eagerly to lift the veils from her face
and died at once, of shock (blinded, some say). For Jeevanbhai's wife, Saneyya seemed God's gift. Poor woman: little did
she know what fires smouldered in Saneyya.

On that night when Nury hammered on the door, with fate
hanging in the balance, the only person in the house apart from
Jeevanbhai was Saneyya, and it was she who awoke and came to
the door, creaking and complaining, it was she who whispered,
hoarse and suspicious: Who's there?

It's me, Saneyya, Nury answered, I have something terribly
important to say, can't wait another moment. Open the door a
crack, *ya* Saneyya, and as God is Great let me in.

There was something in those words, some hint of a memory,
which played havoc in Saneyya's heart. Trembling with disbelief, her voice shaking with eagerness, Saneyya whispered: At
last, at last, Nury, you dilatory Damanhouri. At last after all
these years. Say it again, *ya* Nury, let me hear you again.

And Nury, as though he were reciting a poem, whispered:
Quick, Saneyya, quick, I can't wait any longer. Open up, open,
let me in.

At that Saneyya could not keep herself from giggling, and
giggling she said: Wait, *ya* Nury, there's no hurry. We have the
whole night.

Outside, Nury was beside himself: Saneyya, there's no time
to waste. Open up. I tell you, you'll be well rewarded.

Talk of rewards already, *ya* Nury? Do you think I need a
reward? Your heart's enough, no less than the other things.
Hold tight and wait a little. What can I do with my petticoats all
tied up?

Nury was desperate; his eyes had gone wild and sweat was
streaming from his face. He started to explain what he had
overheard at the New Palace, but then he stopped himself, for
there was no telling who might overhear him. Instead he spoke
in riddles: Listen carefully, Saneyya, and use your mind. What
happens when you have a pot of rice about to boil over and
somebody calls you to the door? Do you stand there chattering? No, you run back because you have to stir your pot. It's
like that, Saneyya. Now, stop talking, open this door and let me
in.

Like a whip Saneyya's hand flashed through the door, slapped him and shut the door again. For shame, Nury, she cackled. Why all this dirt? Boiling or not, you'll have to wait.

Then Nury understood, and he understood, too, that if Saneyya were denied she would drive him from the house and make sure he didn't meet Jeevanbhai for as long as she could. There was no escape for Nury. When Saneyya opened the door at last, he screwed his courage together and resigned himself to his fate.

What had to happen happened: Nury the Cross-Eyed Damanhouri and Saneyya, Terror of the Deep, coupled. It was no ordinary coupling: after a little awkwardness in the beginning, during which Saneyya learnt not to look into his eyes, and he got used to the gaps in her teeth, they so lost themselves in ecstasy that people say they shook the whole of the Souq, and Nury almost forgot his errand.

Some things happen for the best even though it doesn't seem so at the time. Even if things had taken a different turn later, Nury was a ruined man, a beggar, egg-less for life, because Saneyya was not the woman to be silent about a conquest so long in the coming.

When Nury recovered from his raptures he woke Patel and told him what he had overheard at the New Palace. Years after, people often spent whole days talking about what he said that night, but still nobody knows exactly what it was; most of it is just guesses and conjecture. Some say it was this: that night the Oilmen were planning to fly in two aeroplanes full of specially grown date palms; unique palms, which could thrive on any soil, however inhospitable. The Amir's part was to rush the palms to that empty bit of land by the sea and plant them there, all in one night. Then in the morning he was to make proclamations in all the squares of the city inviting the townspeople to witness the near-miracle; to have a glimpse of the things the world could do for the forgotten land of al-Ghazira. Then, as the Public Works Minister, he was to lay claim to that empty bit of land and fence it off. The Malik was bound to resist, they calculated, perhaps by force. But by then the townspeople, so long loyal to the Malik, would hesitate, dazzled by their glimpse of the Amir's power to turn the desert green, and in the end would rally to his side. And then together, with a little help from the Amir's bodyguards and the Oilmen, they would storm the Old Fort, banish the Malik and the past, and install the Amir and the future.

That was the plan, some say, but nobody knows for sure. What is sure is that, within minutes of hearing what Nury had to say, Jeevanbhai was on his donkey flying towards the Old Fort. What happened there nobody knows. Some say that Jeevanbhai had to lock the Malik into a room to keep him from attacking the New Palace at that very moment with all his hidden arms. What is sure is that Jeevanbhai found some way to stop him, for of course he had his own plan. Within an hour he was back in the town, with Jabal the Eunuch and a wad of letters from the Malik.

Feverishly Jeevanbhai, Jabal and Nury raced around the old city, waking up certain shopkeepers known for their loyalty to the Malik and showing them the Malik's letters. They worked like madmen, for they knew, each one of them, that they were fighting for their survival (though already, unknown to the others, in one of those heads, ripples of doubt about the future were spreading).

Then a large group of shopkeepers led by Jeevanbhai, Jabal and Nury vanished into the Souq. When they came out again they were carrying and pushing barrels and tins of oil – mainly kerosene, but all kinds of other oils as well, mustard oil, cottonseed oil, linseed oil, corn oil, sunflower oil, even ghee. The oil was taken down to the harbour in carts and loaded on to a flat-bottomed boat. When that was done Patel, Jabal, Nury and a couple of boatmen climbed into the boat and rowed down the inlet towards the sea until they disappeared into the blackness of the night.

The next anyone saw of them, Jeevanbhai, naked except for his long white shirt, and Nury were clinging to an enormous horse, white-eyed with fear, galloping crazily up the dirt track which later became the Corniche, towards the harbour. A whole platoon of the Amir's guards, huge bandoliered Pathans from the Khyber, were chasing them on foot, almost as fast as the horse could run, whooping and pot-shotting.

As it was reconstructed in the cafés, Jeevanbhai's plan was to row silently along the coast to the site. The Amir's men, he reasoned, would probably guard the dirt tracks along the road, and turn their backs to the sea. Once there, he planned to soak the whole place in oil, step back into the boat and toss a lighted rag behind him, sending the Amir's dreams up in flames.

Jeevanbhai was too subtle a man to think of acts as important in themselves; that was why he stopped the Malik from attacking the New Palace, even though, with the townspeople behind him, he may well have won the day. But for Jeevanbhai it is not acts, but warnings, meanings, those delicate shades which remove an act from mere adventure and place it in history, which are important. Jeevanbhai didn't simply want to burn the date palms. What would be the use of that? For him the date palms were to be words, to tell the Amir that dreams collapse from the inside, of themselves.

That was the irony of it.

The first part of Jeevanbhai's plan went off perfectly: the palms had already been planted, and the Amir's guards, posted to guard the track to the city, were snoring behind a sand-dune, a long way from the site, while their horses were tethered under the palms. The three of them soaked the place in oil without so much as a sound. In less than an hour they were ready, and not one of the guards had noticed.

Already smiling in triumph, Jeevanbhai reached out for the rag which he had handed to Jabal beside him, but his hands clutched empty air. Jabal was gone.

It was not the Amir's dreams which collapsed from within.

Spinning around, Jeevanbhai saw a mountainous shadow creeping towards the guards, already too far away to stop. Next moment Nury caught his arm and pointed to the beach – the boatmen, never slow to smell defeat, were far out to sea.

But even then the old fox had a trick or two left. He tore off his dhoti, tied one end of it to a kerosene-sodden date palm, and took the other in his hand. Just as Jabal was shaking the guards awake, Jeevanbhai handed the reins of one of the guards' horses to Nury, cut the rest loose and drove them off. With shot spraying into the sand around them, he leapt on to the horse, pulled Nury up behind him, and lit his dhoti. They were lying flat on the galloping horse, holding on for their lives, when the palms burst into flames.

In the harbour the shots were heard from a long way off, and since it was already dawn a crowd soon gathered. When they saw a galloping horse beating up a cloud of dust on the far side of the inlet, there was a tremendous commotion. Some thought it was a Bedouin raid like those their grandfathers had told them about; others thought the sheikhs of the neighbouring kingdoms were attacking at last as people had so often said they would. All was confusion: al-Ghazira had been quiet so long nobody knew how to deal with a crisis. People – men, children, women – ran into the streets, screaming and crying. Then the horse was upon them, rearing, hoofs scything the air, and Nury and poor, half-naked Jeevanbhai were picking themselves from the dust and shouting, Run, run – but before they could turn the earth shook beneath their feet, for the Malik, no longer able to hold himself, was firing his ill-directed bazookas into the sea, raising volcanoes of water where it didn't matter. And then that whole early-morning crowd, half-dressed and un-washed, underweared and unshat, turned as one man and fled down the road with Nury in the lead.

For some reason, nobody has ever understood why, instead of turning into the city, after the harbour, Nury ran straight on, past the sandspits and further, with the crowd flocking behind him in a dust-clouded mass, and shots and bazookas shaking the whole city; on, down past the Ras, along the old road, while behind them, far away in the New Palace, the Amir and his mounted guards were trotting out, towards the Maidan al-Jami'i; and in the Oiltown the Oilmen's uniformed hirelings from every corner of the world were polishing their guns and their batons. . . .

But Nury knew nothing of that, and Jeevanbhai was already lost far behind; he had fallen and rolled into the Ras where he lay hidden for days, in which other house but Zindi's? Nury just ran, on and on, until in front of him, out of the sand, there suddenly arose the barbed-wire fence of the Oiltown. From the other side of the fence, faces stared silently out – Filipino faces, Indian faces, Egyptian faces, Pakistani faces, even a few Ghaziri faces, a whole world of faces. In despair Nury threw himself on the fence begging them to open the gates. But the faces stayed where they were, already masks, staring at his sad, desperate, crossed eyes.

You must remember this was long ago, so long ago that even

oil didn't bring much money and not one Ghaziri in a hundred or even a thousand had cars and houses and palaces in Switzerland. It was before the great strikes and the riots; before the Oilmen's planes bombed the Ghaziris in the Oiltown; before the unions were driven into secrecy; before the women and the schoolchildren poured into the streets to fight, and were murdered with the newest and best guns and helicopters and computers money can buy. It was before all of that.

In those days many Ghaziris wanted work. But there was no work for them in the Oiltown, for the Oilmen knew that a man working on his own land has at least a crop to fight for. Instead they brought their own men. They were welcome: since the beginning of time al-Ghazira has been home to anyone who chooses to call it such – if he comes as a man. But those ghosts behind the fence were not men, they were tools – helpless, picked for their poverty. In those days when al-Ghazira was still a real country they were brought here to slip between its men and their work, like the first whiffs of an opium dream; they were brought as weapons, to divide the Ghaziris from themselves and the world of sanity; to turn them into buffoons for the world to laugh at. And with time on their side they succeeded. So, when Nury threw himself on the fence and clawed his hands to ribbons, begging them to let him in, nothing happened, for there were no men inside to open the gates for Nury the desperate Damanhouri.

When the gates did open, it was to let out the Oiltown's uniformed guards with their batons and shields and water-hoses. There was nothing Nury could do but turn again, and run, with the crowd milling behind him.

By this time the crowd was an avalanche of people and confusion, and they were driven straight on, past the Ras again, straight towards the Maidan al-Jami'i, like fish into a net. The Amir's men had long since ringed the square, and blocked all the lanes and roads leading out of it. Once the crowd was inside, coolly and efficiently the guards let fly.

It was not the End or the Day of Judgement – nothing of the kind. The guards hurled not bullets but tear gas. In a few minutes the excitement died away and the crowd was as docile and drugged as a school of stunned fish. The Amir's men let them out and herded them back to their houses. Some people's eyes watered for days afterwards, a couple of old men were stricken with palsy because of the excitement, and there were a few broken legs and a miscarriage or two. All that was lost was a little breath.

We were wrong. This was no feud: no tyrants died; there was no fratricide, no regicide, no love, no hate. It was just practice for the princes of the future and their computers – an exercise in good husbandry.

Only Nury died. He was running across the Maidan towards the Bab al-Asli when the tear gas burst. Temporarily robbed of his sharp eyes Nury shambled helplessly around until he blundered into a Bedu boy, come to the Souq on his camel to sell wool. The animal, frenzied by the noise and the gas, bit poor Nury's head cleanly off his shoulders.

That was the end of Nury the Sharp-Eyed Damanhouri.

It happened for the best: even if Saneyya had not already blown away the foundations of his trade, Nury would have been homeless in the new Ghazira. There was no place in it for sharp-eyed egg-sellers. All the eggs now came from the poultry farms of Europe, and Nury could never have afforded a plane.

The Malik was rarely seen after that, though he was, and still is, said to be the ruler. He was left in the Old Fort, but more as a prisoner than a king. They say the Amir found and seized a vast trove of arms in the Fort. The Oilmen offered to pension the old Malik off in their own country, but they could only have carried his dead body out of the Fort, so the Amir had to be content with leaving him there, with his own guards posted outside. But, still, he'll never have a day's rest as long as the Malik still lives, for no one can tell what the old man is plotting.

And Jeevanbhai: all his businesses and ships, his warehouses and customs contracts were seized. Only his shop in the Souq and his office near the harbour were left to him. For years he was a broken man. But his happy couples didn't forget him, and with a little bit of help he started again. What little he has today he had to build up anew. Then, just when he thought he still had his gods' blessings, his wife died, and today he is the walking corpse you see. A man can try only so many times and no more. That's why Jeevanbhai has taken to drinking in the secrecy of his shop.

Jabal the Eunuch moved to the New Palace and soon became one of the Amir's closest advisers. The Amir never forgot that he may have lost the Battle of the Date Palms if it were not for Jabal, and he slipped a dozen or so of the most lucrative British and American agencies into his lap, and today they say Jabal the Mountainous Eunuch has grown into a whole cordillera, with enough money to buy a continent to spread himself out on.

The Amir found out which shopkeepers had supplied Jeevanbhai with kerosene that night, and their shops were seized, every single one, and distributed among the Amir's friends. Soon after, the fairs on the empty site were stopped as well.

The New City appeared overnight, like a mushroom. The Oilmen forgot all about a new Oiltown, for the whole country was their Oiltown now.

For years that bit of land on the edges of the New City was left as it was, covered with charred date palms. Then, long afterwards, when the Amir judged the Battle of the Date Palms forgotten, he had the plot cleared, and later the Corniche was laid around it. Then, last year, people said that a group of Ghaziri companies were putting up money to build a market greater than any in the continent; an immense shopping arcade, with five pointed arms, in celebration of the starry future. It would be called an-Najma, the Star, and it was to be built on a marshy, useless bit of land at the far end of al-Ghazira near the border. Nobody knew at first where the money was going to come from; the newspapers gave the names of unknown companies.

Truth lies in silences.

That money was put up by Jabal, King of the Eunuchs, and his friends.

Hajj Fahmy retreated into a long silence. No one in the room spoke, for they knew there were many twists and turns to the Hajj's storytelling. At length, the Hajj put up his hand again.

Let me tell you now, he said, why the Star fell. It fell because no one wanted it. The Malik didn't want it: he hasn't forgotten one moment of the Battle of the Date Palms and never will. Nobody in the Souq wanted it: they haven't forgotten the

Battle, either, nor the confiscations. Besides, none of them had been allotted a shop in the Star. If the Star had actually opened, how long would the Souq have lasted? The Mawali didn't want the Star because of their sheikh's grave. The contractors who built it didn't care whether it stood or fell – they had made their money anyway. The lovers who went there at night didn't want it; the smugglers who landed there didn't want it; Jabal and his friends didn't want it – they'll be happier with the insurance money. Did even the Amir want it? His money's far away in some safe country, and nothing that happens in al-Ghazira matters to him much.

No one wanted the Star. That was why the Star fell: a house which nobody wants cannot stand.

Hajj Fahmy leant back against the wall, sighing with exhaustion. After a long while Abu Fahl broke the silence with a laugh. For an old man, he said, a grain of sand can become the Dome of the Rock. Nothing is simple. Anybody can see why the Star fell: it fell because too much sand was mixed with the cement. Anyone with any experience of building can see that. There is no mystery to it. Alu had no experience of building, so he reacted too slowly and got himself caught in the wreckage while everyone else managed to get away. Finished. Some things *are* simple.

Abu Fahl threw a dismissive glance across the room at Hajj Fahmy. The Hajj did not see it, for his eyes were shut. It was Rakesh who spoke: You really think it's so simple, Abu Fahl? The words were forced out of his throat with a visible effort: Rakesh was not a man who relished being conspicuous in a crowd.

Abu Fahl, artlessly skilled in carrying an audience, looked around the room smiling, encouraging laughter. Yes, he said to Rakesh, it's really that simple.

Then, maybe, said Rakesh, there's something you don't know. You say Alu didn't run out with us because he didn't realize that the building was going to collapse? The truth is that Alu was the first among us to hear the rumbles and the noise of the falling bricks and plaster. At the time he had just discovered two sewing machines, meant for display, under a tarpaulin sheet. When he heard the noise, he left the machines uncovered and pushed us out of the basement. That was *before* you shouted to us. I was already running when I heard you. I stopped once on the stairs – the walls were already buckling all around – and I saw that Alu wasn't behind me. I ran back and looked into the showroom. I couldn't see much because there was dust everywhere but, still, I'm certain I saw him carefully covering those two machines. I shouted to him: Run, Alu. He turned and waved me on, and if it were not for the dust I would swear I saw him smile. Then the rumbles grew louder, and I ran up the stairs, while Alu stayed behind, perhaps still smiling.

Chapter Thirteen

The Call to Reason

As soon as the plane took off from Bombay, Jyoti Das knew that the light-headedness he was feeling had nothing to do with the altitude. He had been in planes before; planes didn't make you feel quite like that. It was a mystery; he could think of no explanation.

It became a little clearer when he talked to the man who was sitting next to him. He was a motor mechanic from Gujarat and he was going to al-Ghazira because he had been offered a job which would pay him, in a month, more or less as much as an ASP earned in a year, allowances included. But, still, there were problems, the mechanic complained: no medical benefits, no accommodation, no security at all. It was all a big worry. Would he fall ill? Would he be able to find a place to live? Would his boss be reasonable or not? Would he save enough money to get married at the end of it? No escape – worries everywhere, no matter what you were paid. Listening to him, Jyoti suddenly felt his light-headedness throwing him into somersaults; blowing the weights off his feet.

He knew then that it didn't matter, at least for a while. Things like that matter only at home, and foreign places are all alike in that they are not home. Nothing binds you there.

And it became clearer still when he looked through his window and saw an indentation on the horizon, barely visible, no more really than a speck of dust on the glass, but enough to snap something tight in his stomach and send surges of excitement coursing through him. The hairs rose all along his arm, and he had to grip the sides of the seat to hold himself steady. He knew that his swimming head had no connection with that hint of sand in the distance. It would have made no difference whether that bit of land was al-Ghazira or Antarctica. The journey was within and it was already over, for the most important part was leaving.

And then, in his exhilaration, he knew also that he was grateful. Even six months of hellish confusion were worth a journey which helped you through time even before it had ended.

He had returned from his journey to Mahé, over six months ago, ripe with enthusiasm. The DIG, he thought, could be no less enthusiastic. After all, it was he who had taken up the case and followed it through, even when he, Jyoti Das, had thought it a dead end. The DIG had trusted his own judgement and gone ahead, and in Mahé he had been proved right, after a fashion. So Das worked hard on his report of his visit to Mahé, ignoring his mother's recommendations of prospective brides. He assumed that once the DIG was shown the hard facts he would leap to push the case through. In fact Das reckoned that he would have to fight hard to play a part in the follow-up.

But when he sent the file up it disappeared and the DIG said not so much as one word about it. A week later Das put up an application for travel allowances and foreign allowances and so on, hoping to prod the DIG into doing something. But nothing happened. When he went to meet the DIG in his room he was leaning back in his chair, mournfully toying with half a cabbage. He refused to discuss the case and instead brought the conversation menacingly around to Das's stationery indents. Exorbitant, he said, and unaccountable – enough to stock a new shop.

Das left the room bewildered. Nothing happened for a couple of months, though Das put up regular memos and reminders. He even cultivated a humiliating familiarity with the DIG's personal secretary. Nothing came of it: a veil had fallen.

After another couple of months, during which he slipped from anger into sleepless, nail-biting frustration, and then finally into frustrated resignation, the DIG summoned him to his office. The problem, he said, absent-mindedly snapping a carrot into bits, was that if he, Das, were to go there had to be a replacement. It would be impossible for the office to manage without so valuable an officer. The answer was, obviously, a replacement. He had already looked at the service lists and decided upon a suitable replacement: a young police officer.

Unfortunately, the application he had sent to the higher-ups in the Secretariat had been turned down. Therefore the delay. Of course, the case was important, but the office couldn't do without a replacement.

He looked at Das meaningfully.

Again Das went away bewildered. It seemed to him that the DIG was trying to tell him something, but he couldn't understand what.

He was still scratching his head a week later when he was called to the DIG's office again. The key to the problem, the DIG said, crumbling a piece of fried potato, was the replacement. He told Das the name; it meant nothing to him. Anyway, the DIG said carefully, stressing certain words, solve the replacement problem and we'll see about your foreign trip. Go away and think about it. Go to Delhi if you like. You have an uncle there in the Ministry, no?

Grand-uncle, sir, Jyoti Das said automatically.

Still confused, he took a week's leave and went to Delhi to meet his mother's uncle, the Secretary. It was embarrassing, for Jyoti hadn't met him in years, and he was afraid he wouldn't be acknowledged. But in the event it turned out well: his grand-uncle was keen to buy a house in Calcutta, and wanted Jyoti's father to look around for something suitable. On the assurance that it would be done, he set to work, and within a week the DIG's application was cleared.

After that, the DIG's office burst into a storm of activity: files hurtled about, the DIG spent hours on the telephone, and suddenly one day Jyoti heard that everything had been worked out. The rest took less than a week.

The day before he was to leave, the DIG came to his office, patted him on the shoulder and said: Don't worry about the delay. Time gives a case a chance to develop properly. And don't hurry when you get there. Take your time. Let the case mature. Then, as a token of his good wishes, he presented Jyoti with a crate of Golden Delicious apples.

And, like one of those golden apples, al-Ghazira rotated slowly below him, as the plane banked. He squinted down, through the glare of the midday sun on white gypsum-laden sand. Black roads cut through the expanses of whiteness; he picked out the radial patterns of planned roads at one end of the town, and a large square far away, with huddled, twisting lanes dribbling out of it. As the plane came in to land, blinded by the glare of the sun, he forgot the Barbary falcon and the Saker falcon and the other birds he hoped to see, for he knew suddenly that al-Ghazira wasn't a real place at all, but a question: are foreign countries merely not-home, or are they all that home is not?

He was already older.

In the crowded, luggage-cluttered, airsick chaos of the airport Das spotted Jai Lal with relief. He was a short, dapper man, with the last traces of adolescent acne still lingering incongruously on his thin, aquiline face. He had met – rather, bumped into – him once, at the head offices of the Secretariat in Delhi. Jai Lal had not paid him much attention then, for he was a few years his senior. But Das knew him by reputation: everyone who had met him talked of his clipped urbanity and his powerful connections with awe.

Hullo, Das said, sticking out his hand, I'm—

Yes, Jai Lal said, tapping his hand perfunctorily, we've met, haven't we?

Jal Lal waved a few cards with careless arrogance and they were soon out of the airport. The air outside was like hot steam, and the sweat leapt from Das's pores. He followed Jai Lal to his car, suppressing an urge to linger in the airport and watch the extraordinary assortment of people. But Jai Lal was already at his car, arguing with the porter in Hindi.

As soon as Das had shut his door, Jai Lal said: What happened, Das? Why did you take so long? I must have sent you over a dozen telexes. Couldn't you have come a little earlier?

With an effort Das wrenched his eyes away from the billowing concrete folds of the airport's tent-like roof. He sighed: You don't know what trouble I've been having. My DIG wanted a replacement, one particular replacement, for my post, and it took months and months to arrange the transfer. I'll tell you about it sometime. Let me just say I'm lucky to be here at all. But forget all that. Have there been any developments in the case?

Lal laughed acidly. He reached out and pressed a button. He

waited until the metallic twanging of an electric guitar had filled the car. Yes, he said, you could say there've been developments in the case. In fact you could call your case overdeveloped. Your man's dead.

Oh? After the plane and the airport, Das could find no stronger reaction in himself. I suppose, he said, I'd better telex back to stop them sending next week's foreign allowance.

Lal thought for a moment. No, he said, there's no hurry. But maybe we'd better telex them to approve your return ticket. You know, to tell you the truth, frankly, I don't think there was any need to send you all the way here. I could easily have handled it myself. After all, it's my job. I even wrote to HQ. But your boss was very keen to keep his fingers in the case, and the higher-ups insisted. But, if they were going to send you, at least they could have sent you earlier.

With an aching sense of loss, Das watched the shining metallic bulbs of al-Ghazira's desalination plant diminishing in his window. Anyway, he said, tell me what happened. I might as well know.

Nothing much, said Lal, as far as I can tell. I only heard about it yesterday, from one of our sources – someone really reliable, who's been living in the same house as your suspect. You see, that's the thing: we chaps in the field do all the work, build up our sources and our networks, and then they send you people out, with no experience of local conditions. And that, too, when it's too late. There really wasn't any need.

Lal frowned at the road, his mouth a thin white line. Yes, thought Das, there wasn't any need at all. You could have sent in a few reports; your uncles in the Ministry would have made sure everyone saw them; you'd have got a couple of quick promotions and an 'A'-class posting – Bonn or Brussels or something. No need at all for anyone else to come along.

Aloud he said: What happened?

Oh, just an accident really, said Lal. The chap was working with some kind of construction gang. They used to do distempering and whitewashing and things like that. They were working in a building when it collapsed. It happened about four days ago. The collapse was in all the newspapers, because the building was meant to be a real showpiece. They called it the Star. These collapses happen all the time here. The contractors save money on material and so the buildings fall down. There was nothing in the newspapers about a death. Apparently your man was the only one, and even the authorities probably don't know. My source says the gang he was working with wants to keep it quiet, because he was here illegally, and they could all have got into trouble. Anyway, you can hear all about it yourself; we'll go and see my source this evening and find out if there's anything to clear up.

Lal looked at Das, and saw him staring out of the window in silent disappointment. He gave him a consoling slap on the shoulder. Never mind, *yar*, he said. You've had a good ride on a plane, you'll get to see al-Ghazira and buy a few nice things and, besides, you've got your travel allowance and foreign allowance for a week, so you'll get something out of it. Don't feel too bad about the whole thing.

Certainly not, thought Das. A week's travel allowance and foreign allowance for me and an Italian car for you. Clearing his throat, he said: Yes, that's true. When do we go to meet your source?

This evening, said Lal. I'll pick you up from your hotel. You must have dinner with us afterwards.

They drove in silence for a while, past fountained round-abouts, and vast pitted construction sites and jungles of steel scaffolding. Soon they were caught in snarling traffic and Lal's little car was lost among sports cars, and limousines with heavily curtained windows, and dust-spattered articulated trucks as long as trains, come all the way from Europe. Then, frowning thoughtfully, Lal asked: Who did you say your DIG is?

Das told him.

And what's your replacement's name?

Das told him, a little puzzled by his curiosity. Lal smiled when he heard the name: Let me see . . . I think they're related; uncle and nephew in fact. Yes, I seem to remember hearing that. I suppose he couldn't think of any way of getting him into the Secretariat without shifting you from your post for a bit.

Das felt as though he had been hit in the stomach. He propped himself upright with an outstretched arm, resisting the temptation to double up.

He had known but he had not noticed.

Oh, he said, I didn't know. What else was there to say?

No, Lal said kindly, I suppose you didn't. I remember hearing that you're always very busy with birds and painting and things.

Jyoti sat out the rest of the drive in silence. He could not bring himself to ask Lal about the Barbary falcon, as he had meant to.

His name's Jeevanbhai Patel, Lal said, hurrying Das through the Bab al-Asli, past the evening crowds strolling through the Souq's main passageway. Das looked around him at the robes and headcloths of the Ghaziri men, at the black masks of the women, at gold watches and silver calculators, jewelled belts and silk shirts. He wanted to stop and look at everything properly, but Lal was ushering him rapidly along.

My predecessor passed him on to me, Lal said. He came here years ago – God knows when – long before the oil anyway. They say that once upon a time nothing happened in al-Ghazira that he didn't know about. He's a businessman. I believe he was quite successful once, but he got involved in something and lost all his money. That's the odd thing about him. Your usual Indian bania's first instinct is to stick to his shop or his trade and not get involved in anything, whichever part of the world he may be in. He knows he can make more money that way. But this man's different: he jumps into things. That was his undoing. He's an old man now of course, and his life's behind him, but he still keeps his ears open. He drinks too much nowadays but, still, I must say we've had some very useful material from him.

They stopped at a shop – the Durban Tailoring House, Das read, on a board hanging askew over the door. It was a very dilapidated shop, in sharp contrast with its glittering neighbours. A figure materialized somewhere in the murky interior and advanced towards them: a man well past middle age, thin and slightly stooped, his face delicately lined, like a walnut, but nondescript except for large, decaying teeth that stuck almost horizontally out of his mouth.

Jeevanbhai led them through the shop to a room at the back. As Das entered the room, he faltered, for the reek of whisky clouded the room like a fog. It was a small room made even smaller by two large steel cabinets. There was a desk in the middle of the room, marooned among scattered files and stacks of paper weighed down by cracked saucers and chipped cups. Bits of paper blew around the room chased by half-hearted gusts from an ancient table-fan. It was very dim; the only light came from a single, dusty table-lamp that had been placed on the floor.

Jeevanbhai cleared piles of paper off two steel folding chairs, wiped them with a duster and hesitantly pushed them forward.

Patel sahb, Lal said, I hope we haven't come too early?

No, no, said Jeevanbhai, not at all, never. No formalities. The man who works here leaves early nowadays. I let him go; he's growing old. This is the best place and time to meet.

Lowering himself into a chair behind the desk, he pulled a drawer open and took out three glasses, one of them half-full, and a bottle of cheap Scotch whisky. A little bit? he said, turning a raised eyebrow from Jai Lal to Das.

Jai Lal glanced at Das and nodded. Jeevanbhai drained his glass and poured whisky into the glasses. Splashing a little water into them, he handed them out. Cheers! he said, knocking his glass against theirs.

So, *Patel sahb*, Lal said, sipping his warm whisky fastidiously, how are you?

Not bad; growing older.

Lal laughed: We're all growing older.

Yes, said Jeevanbhai. We're all growing older. He drained his glass and poured himself another drink.

Lal cleared his throat: *Patel sahb*, this is a friend of mine, Mr Das, who is also interested in what we were talking about yesterday. Could you tell him what you told me – about how this young man died?

Died? Jeevanbhai ran his tongue over his teeth. Who said he died?

Lal raised a quick eyebrow at Das. Didn't you say he died? he said smoothly.

No, said Jeevanbhai, I just said the building fell on him, and that nobody could have survived it. That is not the same thing as saying nobody *did* survive it. No, no.

I see, I see, said Lal. What happened?

What happened? Who knows what happened?

What do you think happened?

Who am I to think anything happened, Mr Lal? Who are you?

Lal half-rose from his chair. Perhaps, *Patel sahb*, we could come back later, when you feel like talking? Or when your head is clearer?

Later, earlier, how does it matter? Jeevanbhai said softly. Whatever it is, whether it's happened or not, it's a little difficult – to use simple words – a little difficult to understand.

Lal shot a glance at Das and motioned to him to keep quiet and sit back. But Das could not keep himself from straining forward to look into Jeevanbhai's face. Abruptly the bulb went out. Jeevanbhai rummaged among some papers on the floor, pulled out a bent candle and struck a match. When the flame spluttered Das noticed that Jeevanbhai's hands were shaking, but he could not tell whether it was drunkenness or only an old man's tremor. Jeevanbhai's eyes glowed momentarily in the candlelight. Then he put the candle on the floor, beside his chair, to shield it from the fan, and at once his face disappeared into pools of shadow, and all Das could see were the enigmatic red teeth.

Late last night, Jeevanbhai said, with an almost imperceptible slur, they brought him back. *Bhagwan jane*, God knows how they did it. They must have taken thirty or forty men into the ruins of that building, and tools and things as well. There's a police cordon around the ruins, all day and all night. How did they get through it? God knows. Perhaps, but of course this is just speculation, Abu Fahl – you don't know him, a very wily man; knows every corner and every turn in al-Ghazira – found a way to pay those policemen to stay away from the building for a while. Perhaps.

Anyway they brought him back. And it wasn't as though he was barely alive, like a survivor from a disaster of that kind ought to be. He was well, hearty, smiling, as healthy as any of us. I know: I saw him later. How does one account for that? A whole building had collapsed on him. No ordinary building, but millions and millions of dirhams in effect. It wasn't good money, but any money on that scale has a certain weight. You can't disregard it. And still he lived through the fall of that whole building. Apparently – this is just hearsay – he lay flat on the floor with a huge block of concrete just inches from his chest. And that, too, for four days. It is no exaggeration to say that many people in that situation would have died of shock. And, far from being dead, he seemed to have come out a new man altogether, if such a thing is possible.

People say, I don't know with what truth, that he had no food or water for those four days. And when they were offered to him, they say, he refused. And when they asked him whether he wanted to leave that place, right till the very end, they say, he said no, he wanted to be left alone to think.

One could say: people think of these things when something unusual happens. But the truth remains, and it is that when he was brought out at last he was unscathed. It came as no surprise to anyone when some of the women there started saying that it was the doing of a dead sheikh whose grave lies under those ruins; one of his many miracles. People say these things.

I believe a crowd had gathered there long before he was brought back. When they saw him in the distance, they ran on to the road and carried him back to a house which belongs to one Hajj Fahmy – you don't know him – an elderly man, greatly respected in that area. They carried him into the courtyard and put him on a platform where Hajj Fahmy keeps his loom – he was once a weaver – and they all crowded into the courtyard to listen to him.

And all evening the crowds grew and grew.

I heard all this, for I wasn't there at the time. I was at my office near the harbour. I went there after I left the Souq, for there were a few things I had to do. Even in my office things weren't as they usually are. My assistant, one Professor Samuel – no longer my assistant, I should add, but that comes later – had left the office even though I had told him to wait. And, very unusually for him, he had left it in great disorder.

But I had my work to do and it was only much, much later that I went back to the Ras, where we all live. Anybody could see that something unusual was happening there. Usually the Ras sleeps early, all except Zindi's house, because people have to work. But last night I had a feeling – if one may talk of such a thing – that no one was sleeping. And yet the whole place was in darkness. Not a light in any of the shacks, not a person to be seen on the lanes, nobody sleeping out on the roofs. The whole place was, to use a simple word, deserted.

But at the other end of the Ras, where Hajj Fahmy lives, there were bright lights, and a faint hum, like a slow-running machine – the noise a crowd makes merely by breathing.

I thought they had organized a film on the beach as they do sometimes, though the place is never so deserted then. But I was tired, and I wanted to sleep, so I went straight back towards my room.

There again, when I pushed the door of the house open, things were not as they usually are. It was empty, or so I thought, and that house is never empty. I called out once or twice, but there were only echoes and the sound of geese hissing. I looked into the room on my left, where the men sleep, and it was empty. I looked to my right, into the room opposite, and – to tell you the truth – I was so startled I almost bit my tongue off.

Zindi at-Tiffaha – you don't know her – a woman large enough to fill a room, was sitting on a mat in the corner, staring at me, but sightlessly, and without a sound, like a corpse. And in her lap was a baby no less silent, staring at me, too, with huge black eyes.

Zindi at-Tiffaha is the key to your mysteries, though you don't know her. She's the solution. It was she who brought your man here; it was she who fed him and found him work; and it was her house that he was living in when the Star fell. She rules over that house like a seth over a shop: nothing happens in it that she doesn't plan. But last night there she was, sitting alone, like a statue, while her whole house was elsewhere.

Something's wrong, I said to myself. This is not how Zindi is. There's something on her mind. To tell the truth, actually, I knew quite well that there's been something on her mind for some time. She's been arranging secret meetings with the man who works in this shop and he's been telling me a few things. But with me at least she's always been able to keep up a brave face. Last night that face had melted away.

I said to her: Zindi, where's everyone else? And when she answered I was, to admit nothing shameful, quite relieved, for even though she looked alive I couldn't be sure.

She said: They've gone to bring Alu back.

Very quietly, I said: And what about you, Zindi? Why didn't you go?

To my surprise – for Zindi is not a woman who tells people any more than they need to know – she answered. She said: If we all spent our time chasing every new madness that sweeps the Ras, what would happen? Some of us have to think of staying alive and keeping the house together as well. And what would I do there anyway? I'm just an old woman trying to cope with the world on my own.

Of course, you don't know her, so you don't know what her words meant. Neither I nor anyone else has ever before seen the slightest crack in Zindi's strength. Even yesterday I would have sworn to you that not even a pile-driver could squeeze anything like hopelessness out of her. When she said what she did, I knew something had driven Zindi at-Tiffaha to the edge of her wits; that she was ripe and waiting for a guiding hand.

But at that very moment a woman called Kulfi, who lives in the house, ran into the room and shouted: Zindi, Karthamma's stolen your money-tin. She's throwing all your money away. Come on, quickly.

Then the old Zindi was back again. Faster than we could see, she counted from the corner, along the wall to the fourteenth brick. She pulled it out and found the hollow behind it empty. And the next moment she was out of the house, rolling like a wave, with the baby still in her arms, and we were running behind her.

The lane behind Hajj Fahmy's house was thick with people, even though you can't see into the courtyard of his house from the lane. But, still, there must have been more than a hundred people there, in a lane where two men usually have to fight to pass abreast. The crowd was like a wall. But Zindi was running fast, and with her weight she had worked up the power of a steam-roller. Holding the baby above her head, she crashed through the crowd, and we were carried along in her wake. She stopped at the door to the courtyard, not because she could not have gone any farther, but because – I think you could say – she was frozen with surprise.

The courtyard was even more crowded than the lane; you could see nothing but people. But, at the same time, it was absolutely silent, and the only sound you could hear was Alu's

voice, clear as water. He was sitting behind the loom on the
platform, weaving very fast, but without so much as looking at
the loom, and talking all the while.

And in a way that was the strangest thing of all; that he was
talking. For Alu was a very silent man. I've seen him in the
house every day for six months now, so in a way I know him
well, for you can know a lot about a man by watching him daily.
Whenever he was in the house he was quiet; most of the time
he was in pain, too, for he always had boils bursting out all over
him. And the rest of the time, when he wasn't at work, he was
at Hajj Fahmy's – weaving, they say. In all those months I
wonder if I've exchanged more than ten words with him. It
wasn't just me. As far as I could tell, all the others were friendly
with him, but none of them was his particular friend. There
were rumours about him and Karthamma, but no one could tell
what to make of those. She's a tall woman, very dark, with the
temper of an animal, but also an animal's courage, for she was
the one person in the house who was never afraid to defy Zindi.
Anyone else who did that, Zindi would have thrown out long
ago, but not Karthamma. For Karthamma has a baby – the
child Zindi was holding in her arms that night – and poor,
childless Zindi treasured her for that alone; because she was a
mother and because she had given her a son. If pure will could
change flesh and blood, that baby would be more hers now
than his mother's.

Maybe the rumours about Karthamma and Alu were true,
maybe not. But Zindi believed them anyway; perhaps because
she wanted to, because she hoped that Alu would take
Karthamma's mind off the baby. But I, who have seen the
world a bit, used to wonder: what could silent Alu and
Karthamma have in common? Sometimes you saw them in the
courtyard, she rubbing oil on the boils on his back. She was
fond of him, maybe she even loved him, but to me it seemed
the love of a sister, not of a lover. Did he talk to her? Perhaps;
for, after all, she had stolen the money anticipating something.
But if she recognized the Mr Alu she saw that night she must
have been the only one in the Ras. To everyone else he was a
quiet morose man, tormented by boils. A mild man, you would
have said, who didn't care much about anything.

But last night nobody else seemed to remember the man as

he was. I was the only one who saw him and recognized a mystery. I saw a man I knew, but I heard a voice I had not heard before. I hate mystery: unless mystery is the tool of business it is its enemy. But, hate it or not, there he was in front of me, as great a mystery as any I've seen, and I could find no explanation.

He was talking softly, but there was a force in his voice which carried it over the clicking of the shuttle, so that nobody missed a word; an extraordinary force, perhaps you could call it passion. It was like a question, though he was not asking anything, bearing down on you from every side. And in that whole huge crowd nobody stirred or spoke. You could see that silently they were answering him, matching him with something of their own.

That was another mystery, for the people who were there are rarely quiet – at work, at night, in the cinema. But last night, peering into the courtyard under Zindi's arm – which as fastidious men you may well appreciate wasn't easy, or greatly facile, if one may put it as such, for as you may know, when Virat Singh, the famous wrestler, the great marble-biceped pehlwan of Bareilly, was living here, he once attempted to press his suit a little forcefully with her, but since he was not greatly to her taste she overpowered him, merely by baring an armpit and blowing gently upon it – but anyway, as I was saying, last night, peering under Zindi's arm in not altogether salubrious conditions, I saw that very crowd absolutely silent, listening to a man, hardly more than a boy, talk, and that, too, not in one language but in three, four, God knows how many, a khichri of words; couscous, rice, dal and onions, all stirred together, stamped and boiled, Arabic with Hindi, Hindi swallowing Bengali, English doing a dance; tongues unravelled and woven together – nonsense, you say, tongues unravelled are nothing but nonsense – but there again you have a mystery, for everyone understood him, perfectly, like their mother's lullabies. They understood him, for his voice was only the question; the answers were their own.

And what of me, looking out of Zindi's dear, half-forgotten arms, in those few moments while her eyes were busy and Abu Fahl elsewhere? I will tell you: I saw mysteries, all around me, one growing out of another, and I could find no grasp on them, not the slightest hold. I was afraid. I was so afraid, I breathed and sniffed until my nose ran, grateful for Zindi's generosity.

He talked about Louis Pasteur. They listened without a sound as he told them in detail about Louis Pasteur's life, his experiments and his discoveries, how he went out into the villages of his country, leaving behind the security of his laboratory, and found cures for incurable diseases, restored the vanishing livelihood of thousands of weavers by saving the silkworm, made milk pure for the world, destroyed the venom in dogs' teeth, and so many other things.

But yet, he said, Pasteur had died a defeated man.

Why? he asked, and you could feel – if such a thing is possible – the silence beginning to stir.

He, and others before him, he said, had thought over the matter for a long, long time, and at last, in the Star, it had fallen to him to discover the answer. There, in the ruins, he had discovered what it was that Pasteur had really wanted all his life – an intangible thing, something he had not understood himself, yet a thing the whole world had conspired to deny him.

Purity. Purity was what he had wanted, purity and cleanliness – not just in his home, or in a laboratory or a university, but in the whole world of living men. It was that which spurred him on his greatest hunt, the chase in which he drove the enemy of purity, the quintessence of dirt, the demon which keeps the world from cleanliness, out of its lairs of darkness and gave it a name – the Infinitely Small, the Germ.

And when Alu came to that all his old mildness vanished. He let the loom be and sat with his hands folded on his lap, absolutely still, but his voice grew in strength and power until it reached beyond the courtyard and into the lanes and gullies outside.

He told them about germs: how they are everywhere and nowhere; how they flow freely from hand to hand, how they sweep through a thousand people in a day, in a minute, faster than a man can count, throwing their coils around people wherever they may hide.

Pasteur had discovered the enemy, the Germ, but he had never been able to find him. All his life he had tried to launch war but, like a shadow, the enemy had eluded him, and in the end Pasteur had died defeated and bewildered.

Why? Because for all his genius Pasteur had never asked himself the real question: where is the germ's battleground? What is it that travels from man to man carrying contagion and filth, sucking people out and destroying them even in the safety of their own houses, even when every door and window is shut? Which is the battleground which travels on every man and every woman, silently preparing them for their defeat, turning one against the other, helping them destroy themselves?

That was the real question, and Pasteur had never known it.

Then he leapt to his feet and with a sigh the whole crowd rose with him. He shouted in Arabic: *Wa ana warisu*, and I am his heir, for in the ruins of the Star I found the answer.

Money. The answer is money.

The crowd gasped, and while they were still reeling he shouted again: We will wage war on money. Are you with me?

And the whole crowd shouted back: Yes. Yes. Yes.

No money, no dirt will ever again flow freely in the Ras. Are you with me?

And again the crowd roared: Yes.

We will drive money from the Ras, and without it we shall be happier, richer, more prosperous than ever before.

But this time only a few people shouted with him. There were other voices which said: How?

I think it can safely be said that there was a note of uncertainty in Alu's voice then, as though he had only just understood what he was saying. Alu hesitated; I think he knew what he wanted to do, but not how to do it. The crowd sensed him falter. Another moment and the first bursts of laughter would have pealed out, sanity would have returned and that would have been the last anyone ever heard of Mr Alu.

But at that moment he was rescued. By whom?

By Professor Samuel, ex-accountant and clerk. He's not really a professor of course. He was a teacher in some small-town college and, as you know, at home every teacher, whether he teaches pundits or pehlwans, is called a professor. This Samuel is an odd man, with peculiar ideas, but in his own way he is also a very clever man, a fine accountant. He had no sooner heard what Alu had to say than he delivered himself of a plan, full-grown and breathing.

First, he said, he would open files, with a page for every earning person in the Ras. Everyone would take their pay to him as soon as they received it, and the sum would be entered in the files against that man or woman's name. The money would go into a common pool. Once a week the Professor and whoever wished to go with him would go into the Souq and buy everything that was needed in the Ras with that money. Then people could come and take whatever they needed, and the cost would be taken out of their accounts. In that way, he said, they would be able to do away with shops, and no longer would the shopkeepers drain away their savings, their sweat, and their labour in profits.

When he said that, the whole crowd rose and shouted and cheered, but the Professor stopped them. The shopkeepers of the Ras, he said, could be given a wage if they were willing to work with the others and help in buying and dividing food. They could be freed from their greed and they would be assured a livelihood. Otherwise, he said, there would be no place for them in the Ras.

Every person, he said, was to leave their address, their country, their town or village, wherever it was that they wished to send their money, and it would be entered into their pages on the files. At the end of every week, punctually, their savings would be sent back. And when the time came everybody there would see for themselves that the money they saved thus greatly exceeded anything they'd saved before.

There were many other things. I forget. Everyone was to be left a little money, whatever they needed to spend outside the Ras. But once they were in the Ras the money would have to be put away in an envelope and not touched again, until it was far outside the embankment. There would be no need for it in the Ras: they would get doctors, food, everything that was necessary, even films. No one would lack for something he needed, if he had no money today. The money would be found for him and taken out of his account later when he earned it.

Then Alu spoke again. He said that the Professor had read what was in his mind and put it in words. He asked the crowd: Are you willing to ask the Professor to work for us? To pay him a wage for his work? And in unison the crowd shouted: Yes.

That was how I lost my assistant.

Alu quietened them again. There was one other thing, he said. Every person in the Ras who wished to fight this war would also have to tie a piece of cloth above his right elbow. And whenever they left or entered a dwelling in the Ras they were to use that bit of cloth to dust the threshold, so that they left no dirt behind nor carried any with them. In this way, he said, they could know who was with them, and who against, and they could carry their fight to every doorstep.

After that there was so much noise, so much cheering, so much laughter that even Zindi flinched. Then I saw Abu Fahl rise and go up to Alu with his hands in his pockets. He pulled his hands out and emptied his pockets on to the platform. Alu tried to stop him, but the money was already there, beside him, and Abu Fahl wouldn't touch it again. Professor Samuel was irritated, as well he might be, by this kind of impulsive foolishness. But he shouted for pencil and paper and counted the money and wrote it all down. There were others after that. First, the people from Zindi's house: Zaghloul, a saner boy, you would have thought, had never lived; Chunni, the woman who swallows most of Professor Samuel's earnings in exchange for I will not speculate what; thin Rakesh, and after him the whole crowd, hundreds of people, until the money on the platform had grown into a mound, and Samuel had run out of paper. By then it was all chaos, and I was grateful for the sheltered certainty of Zindi's arm: women singing, people dancing and shouting. And in the middle of all that Hajj Fahmy's family were busy sending out tray after tray of tea (they kept an account of course, for Professor's Samuel's files).

Then Zindi screamed, and for a moment I thought my head had rolled off my shoulders, for her arm snapped tight around my neck, which as you can see is no tree-trunk.

Far away from us, near the platform, Karthamma had risen to her feet, and in her hands was an old blue biscuit-tin.

Zindi threw herself into the crowd, shielding the baby with one arm and flailing about with the other. And while she fought she shouted, Give me back my money, you thief, you whore, and other things of that nature.

But Karthamma didn't hesitate for a moment. She laughed, showing her brilliant white teeth, and said in her broken

Hindi: It's not your money, it has nothing to do with you. It's the price of *our* sweat, *our* work. And, saying that, she took the lid off the tin and emptied the money on to the mound on the platform.

Zindi howled and her free arm thrashed about like a buzz-saw, but she was powerless – the crowd had imprisoned her.

Karthamma sneered at her as she struggled helplessly in the grip of a dozen men, and said: Give me back my child.

At that Zindi stopped fighting, and clutched the boy to her chest. There was laughter all around her then, though some people were quite angry. You could hear shouts: Send her out, send her out, what's she doing here?

The fight had gone out of Zindi. Silently, hugging the boy, she let herself be pushed and elbowed out of the door. When she was beside me I saw that she was weeping. She muttered, tears streaming from her eyes: What are we going to do? He's going to get us killed. We're ruined, all our years of struggle wasted because of a few days of madness.

I took her arm then, and led her out, through the jeers of the crowd in the lane. And all the way back to her house she said not a single word.

Jeevanbhai stopped abruptly. His eyes rose to the ceiling and he seemed to go into a trance, swaying on his chair. Das, who had been straining forward, drinking in every word, felt himself fall, like a dropped puppet. He looked around him, startled. Jai Lal's eyes were shut, as though he had been lulled into a doze by Jeevanbhai's monotone. Das leant over and shook him. Without missing a breath Lal said loudly: Very interesting, Jeevanbhai, very interesting. And where is this man staying now?

Jeevanbhai fumbled around the desk for the bottle of whisky and poured himself another drink. He was clearly very tired. Propping up his head with his arm, he looked at them in turn.

He's staying in Hajj Fahmy's house now, he said wearily. I believe he's weaving a lot. I'm sure Hajj Fahmy won't lose by his hospitality. This man's a good weaver, they say, and there's a good market in hand-woven cloth among foreigners.

What will happen next, *Patel sahb*?

Who can tell? Jeevanbhai sighed. I know as little as you do.

I can't understand it, Das broke in. I can't understand it at all.

Lal snorted derisively: What don't you understand? He's worked out some kind of new money-making racket. That's all you need to understand. It's something to do with money.

He looked at Jeevanbhai for confirmation. Jeevanbhai inclined his head politely.

But what should we do now, Jai? said Das. What are our options? What can we do?

Nothing, Lal said drily. There's nothing we can do. It's a very tricky situation. We can't alert the Ghaziri authorities. It would be a disaster if they found out that Indians are involved in this business. They'd probably stop giving new visas to Indian workers. They've done that kind of thing before. They might even expel the workers who're already here. That would mean a drop in remittances, and therefore in the foreign-exchange reserves back home and so on and so forth. If anything like that happened, half the embassy here would be recalled in disgrace, with all their increments docked. We can't risk anything like that. We'll just have to try to keep the whole thing quiet, and see what we can do. Maybe, if we're lucky, we'll find some way of getting your man out of here and back to India.

Lal looked despondently at Jeevanbhai: Isn't that true, *Patel sahb*?

Yes, said Jeevanbhai. His eyes searched the floor till they found the heavy leather attaché case Lal had brought with him. He looked at Lal expectantly.

Lal lifted the attaché case on to his knees and opened it. But, he said, you'll keep us informed, *Patel sahb*, no?

Yes, of course, of course.

Lal took two bottles of Scotch whisky out of his case. Jeevanbhai stretched out his hand, but at that moment Das reached across and tapped Lal's arm.

Listen, Jai, he said, I want to go to this place – the Ras – and look it over a bit. If possible, I'd like to see this man; see where he's living and so on. It would give me a more realistic picture, and at least I'd have something for the reports I'll have to send back home. What do you think?

Lal leant back, with the bottles in his hands, and looked

inquiringly at Jeevanbhai: I'm sure you can arrange it, no, *Patel sahb*?

Jeevanbhai clicked his tongue in irritation: No. I don't see how it can be done. How can anyone take an absolute stranger into that place? People would be suspicious at once. I couldn't guarantee his safety, especially if people found out what his connections are.

Das put the bottles on the floor, beside his chair. Try to think, *Patel sahb*, he said sharply. I'm sure you can manage something.

Jeevanbhai wiped his forehead with his sleeve. There's one possibility, he said reluctantly. I can't take him of course, because the people there are suspicious of me anyway. But there's a chance that I might be able to persuade Zindi at- Tiffaha to take him. But it'll take some time, and he'll have to wait.

Lal nodded: That's fine; get in touch when it's arranged. He held the bottles out to Jeevanbhai and smiled: That's good whisky, *Patel sahb*. It would cost hundreds of dirhams for a bottle of that here.

Jeevanbhai almost snatched the bottles out of his hands, and locked them away in a drawer. Lal stood up. *Patel sahb*, he said gravely, we'll need all your help over the next few weeks.

Jeevanbhai nodded. Then, softly, almost timidly, he said: What about the other thing, Mr Lal?

Other thing? said Lal surprised. What thing?

Don't you remember? said Jeevanbhai. I was asking you the other day. . . .

Oh, *that*, said Lal. Oh, yes. We'll work out something.

Jeevanbhai dropped his eyes and led them through the shop. Lal stopped at the door. Tell me, *Patel sahb*, he said. You know these people, and this man. What do you think his game is?

Is it a game?

Isn't it?

You must explain it to me, then. Jeevanbhai smiled at them, very sweetly, and ushered them out with a stoop of his shoulder.

Afterwards, at Lal's large fifth-floor flat in a newly built residential suburb, they sat on a balcony, surrounded by potted palms and ferns, drinking beer and watching the strung-out lights of tankers at sea. Das was very tired but strangely elated: it was as though in the course of one day he had been forcibly stretched into the calm strength and insights of middle age.

He talked desultorily to Lal about their colleagues in India, while Lal's slim, pretty wife offered them bowls of cashew nuts and dalmoth. Then a servant called her away to the kitchen, and Lal yawned and shut his eyes. My God, he said, he talked on and on. I thought he'd never stop.

Das nodded and they fell into a tired silence. After a while, Lal said languidly: Tell me, what did you think of our friend Jeevanbhai?

Das sat upright and thought for a moment. I don't think, he said carefully, that I've ever heard anyone talk as marvellously as he did tonight.

Really?

Yes, Das said softly, embarrassed. But tell me, do you think he's reliable?

Oh, yes. I think so. Besides, he has to be, because otherwise his stock of whisky would dry up. Why?

Nothing really. It's just that . . . though he tries to be businesslike and all that, when he actually talks, he's like a sleepwalker – like a man living in a dream. I wouldn't trust him – not because he's dishonest, though he might be – but because he doesn't seem to be living in this world at all.

Lal laughed: Next you'll be telling me he's a bird of paradise.

Das grimaced in embarrassment. Never mind, he said. But what was that business at the end, about the 'other thing'?

Oh, that. He's got some idea into his head that he wants to go to India and settle there in a small town and start a shop. He wants citizenship and he wants help getting out of the country. He thinks they may not let him out. The trouble is we need him here; he's much more useful here.

Lal stretched and stood up. Let's forget business for a while, he said. Come, I'll show you an interesting game.

He led Das into their drawing-room. At one end stood a streamlined, steel-blue television set. Beside it, on a stool, was a squat, gleaming, chrome-plated machine, bedecked with knobs and buttons.

Lal switched it on. Geometrical images and the word 'play'

appeared on the television screen. He watched Das's surprise with evident delight.

It's a video game, he said. Cost me two months' savings. Even the Ambassador hasn't got one like it.

Of course, he added quickly, it's for children really. I bought it for my son, Sunil. But it's fun sometimes, even for us.

He handed Jyoti Das a set of controls. You have to shoot me down, he said, and pressed a button. The images on the screen began to circle confusingly about. Jyoti tried to make sense of it and couldn't.

Sorry, he said, handing his controls back. I don't think I'll be any good at this.

Lal laughed: You're a washout, *yar*. Wait, I'll show you how it's played.

He went to the door and called out: Sunil. Sunil *beta*, come and play videos. He had to call out three more times before a wide-eyed, knee-high boy in shorts was pushed into the room by a servant. He stood in the doorway, sucking his thumb.

Come on, *beta*, Lal cajoled him. Come and show this nice uncle how to play videos. He hasn't seen one before.

The boy stayed where he was, sucking his thumb. Lal said apologetically to Jyoti: He doesn't like it much. But he has to learn.

He went up to the boy and said sharply: Come on, *beta*. Come and play with your video. It cost money.

He pulled the boy's hand out of his mouth and put a set of controls in it. The boy pressed the wrong button and the image on the screen faded away.

What're you doing, *beta*? Lal exclaimed in irritation.

Jyoti, watching the boy, saw that his hands had begun to shake and drops of sweat had appeared on his forehead. Suddenly a heavy, putrid smell filled the room.

Jyoti glanced quickly around the room in surprise. Then he looked at the boy. A stain was spreading across the back of his shorts, and a yellow mess was dribbling down his thighs. He was sucking his thumb again.

Beta! Lal exploded. He stopped and drew in his breath. Then he caught Jyoti's arm and pulled him out of the room. Slamming the door on the boy, he shouted towards the kitchen: Babs, go and look. He's done it again.

He hurried Jyoti to the balcony. His forelock had fallen across his face and his hands shook as he splashed whisky into their glasses. Jyoti stood frozen in a corner.

Everything's going wrong, Lal said. Nothing's right any longer; it's all chaos. It worries me. I'm very worried.

Chapter Fourteen

Besieged

Zindi counted through the hours for ten days before she allowed herself to go looking for Forid Mian again. On the morning of the tenth day, at ten o'clock – not too early to make her journey seem like anything but an ordinary shopping trip – she put Boss on her hip and set out for the Souq. When she reached the front door she stopped, suddenly remembering the plastic bag Professor Samuel had left for her that morning. She went back to her room to fetch it. It was a large bulging bag, with colourful advertisements for cigarettes printed on both sides. It was very heavy, for it contained forty-two aluminium lemon-squeezers.

Zindi hurried through the Ras to the embankment, ignoring the faces that were pointedly turned away from her on the way. As she scrambled up the slope of the embankment, the plastic bag seemed to grow heavier and heavier, until she was struggling to pull it along, like a ship fighting a dragging anchor. She cursed the lemon-squeezers, cursed Professor Samuel, cursed Alu and the whole of the Ras. When she reached the road at the top, she knew she would not be able to walk all the way to the Souq, as she had planned, so she squatted on the gravel at the side of the road and waited for a share-taxi. There was very little traffic on the road, nothing more than an occasional speeding truck. The road began to shimmer in the heat of the climbing sun, and soon the heavy cloth of her black fustan was drenched to the ankles in sweat. She began to worry about Boss, who was squirming quietly in the sun. After a while, she took off her scarf, baring the thin hair on her head to the sun, and draped it over him. A yellow and black taxi materialized like a mirage somewhere in the shimmering haze on the road, and she ran out to stop it. It swerved neatly past her and disappeared, blaring a tune on its

musical horn. Zindi went back to the side of the road, cursing:
Sons of bitches, shit. . . . Now she was too impatient to sit
down again, and she squinted down the road standing, shifting
Boss from one hip to the other. Ten days was not such a long
time, but some ten days were worse than others. These had
been as bad as any she could have imagined; worse, because
she could not have imagined these. She had had to lock herself
into the house every day to keep herself from rushing off to the
Souq and Forid Mian. The Souq was hope. That was why she
had denied it to herself for so many days – so that the taste of it
would be the sweeter when it came. Not just that, of course.
Every time temptation threatened to overwhelm her, she had
reminded herself of all the reasons why she had decided on ten
days, no more, no less. Ten days was just right: long enough to
make her, Zindi, seem disinterested; enough to let Forid Mian
think a bit, worry a bit; but not so long that their conversation
would slip from his mind. Ten days was just right.

Here was another taxi, a large one this time, an old
Mercedes-Benz. She stood in the middle of the road with her
arms stretched out, like a traffic policeman, and it stopped. It
took her some time, and a little help, to climb out again, when
the taxi drew up at the Maidan al-Jami'i. *Kam?* she asked the
young, curly-haired driver, reaching into the neck of her dress
for her purse.

One dirham, he said.

What? she shouted. You son of a. . . .

He laughed: Yes, Mother?

She had to forgive him: that was clever enough to make him
an Egyptian, even though his accent didn't sound it. Laughing
to herself, she turned and saw the Bab al-Asli across the square,
guarding hope, and everything left her mind but the main
intention. She forgot that she had meant to dispose of the
lemon-squeezers first. She hurried across the square, through
the Bab, and turned into the first lane. There it was, the
Durban Tailoring House, conspicuous by its dimness in that
row of shining shops.

Forid Mian was there after all: that was one ten-day-long
worry she'd forgotten this morning. She stood in the passageway for a minute, and looked the shop over again, critically
judging its length, its breadth, weighing its possibilities. It

didn't disappoint her, as she had feared it might.

She bustled in, trying to look busy. Ah, Forid Mian! she said, putting her plastic bag down on the floor. How are you?

He was working at his sewing machine. How are you? he answered politely.

She lifted Boss with both her hands and put him down on his back on a pile of cloth on the counter.

Don't do that, Zindi, Forid Mian cried in alarm. He'll wet the. . . .

No, don't worry, she said. He never pisses on strange clothes. He's not like other children.

Forid Mian looked at her sceptically and went back to his sewing machine. Zindi seated herself on a stool and leant back against the counter. For a long while she said nothing. The approaches and openings she had so carefully prepared slipped out of her mind while she looked around the shop, taking in small details, like the exposed wiring near the switches. Somewhere at the back of her mind she tried to work out what it would cost to make the place respectable again. Then, with a start, she remembered Forid Mian and turned. She caught him darting her a sidelong glance.

So, Zindi, he said quickly, what brings you to the Souq?

Oh, just some shopping, Zindi said. I was passing by and I thought I'd come around and see how Forid Mian is.

Forid Mian leant back against the wall and looked at her, his dull eyes opaque. You're thinking about me a lot nowadays, Zindi, he said.

Of course, Zindi said blandly, I always think about old friends.

What were you thinking? said Forid Mian.

Oh, many things. I was thinking about that funny thing you said that night. How are the nights going now? Still rubbing hard on dry sheets, hoping to set them on fire?

Zindi threw her head back and laughed.

Forid Mian lowered his eyes and looked at the bulging plastic bag on the floor. What's in that? he said, pointing with a bent, pencil-thin finger.

Oh, that, said Zindi, still shaking with laughter. That's lemon-squeezers. Forty-two lemon-squeezers.

Forid Mian gasped: Forty-two lemon-squeezers! What are

you going to do with forty-two lemon-squeezers? Start a fruit-juice stall?

No, no. Zindi shook her head, wondering why they were talking about lemon-squeezers. They're not for me, she said quickly. I needed some money this morning, and there was no money in the Ras, so Professor Samuel sent these – someone who works in some shop or factory had got hold of them and left them with him. If I want money for the shopping, I have to sell these.

Sell these? For money? Forid Mian looked at her in bewilderment.

Yes, she said exasperated. That's what happened. Yesterday was Thursday, the end of the week. The people in the house usually give me the week's money on Thursday. But now there's no money in the Ras; it's all in accounts and account-books. In banks, and Professor Samuel's files. Anyway, they didn't give me any money. Samuel said he's put it all in my account and entered it against my name and all that. But I wanted money. Money. What's the use of numbers? So I said: You sister-fucking arsehole, I want money. Cash. But then he called all the others, and even Abu Fahl turned against me. I said: I want money. What's the use of an account-book? Can you pay for a bus with an account-book? I haven't been out of the Ras for more than a week and I'm going to the Souq tomorrow. I need money. So she said, that bitch Karthamma: Why'd you want to go out of the Ras? You don't do any work. *We* do the work; you should stay here and clean the house. As if. So I said: I'll tear your eyes out if you try to keep me here for one more day, you ungrateful bitch. Then she shouted, and I shouted. And I said to Samuel: Why don't you give me one of those envelopes with money inside, like you give the others when they go out of the Ras? And he said that all the envelopes had already been given out for the next day. Then later he said he had these . . . these lemon-squeezers, so I took them. Luckily I had a bit of cash in my purse, and Kulfi gave me a bit.

Zindi stopped, her chest heaving, her eyes bloodshot. Why're you asking all this? she said. You'd know all about it anyway, if you didn't live like a snail, hidden away in the Souq.

Then a thought struck her, and she looked at him anxiously: Do you want to buy some? She took a lemon-squeezer from the bag and handed it to him. He played with the handles, opening and shutting it like a pair of scissors.

How much? he said.

Two dirhams? she answered tentatively.

No. He shook his head.

One-fifty?

I don't really want it, he said and handed it back to her.

No, Zindi laughed. I'd forgotten. It's something else you want to squeeze now. No?

What do you mean, Zindi?

Well . . . something like a wife?

Forid Mian didn't answer. Zindi leant towards him: Don't you remember? We were talking about your marriage that night?

Forid Mian rose abruptly from his stool. It seems to me, Zindi, he said, that you're thinking about my marriage much more than I am.

Zindi laughed, attempting unconcern. Of course I think about your marriage, she said. If I didn't, who would? Don't you remember how you said that night that you'd like to get married and settle down in your Chatgan and leave all this behind? Don't you remember? I think there's a chance, just a chance, that it might be arranged.

Forid Mian began to tidy one of the shelves behind the counter. I don't know what I was talking about that night, he said. I must have gone crazy. Why should I want to go back to Chatgan when everyone in Chatgan is trying to get here?

Zindi stared at him in uncomprehending disbelief. But, she began, you said. . . .

Oh, I was just talking.

Zindi looked wildly, tearfully around the shop. Instinctively her hand rose to scratch her mole. But, listen, she said, there must be something. . . .

Why, Zindi, Forid Mian said loudly, are you so interested in my marriage?

Zindi impatiently waved the question away. Listen, she said, what about, what if we get you married *here*?

Here? Forid Mian turned from the shelf and stared at her. To whom?

To someone. Zindi compressed her lips and squeezed out a smile. But you tell me first, what do you think of the idea?

How can I tell you, until you tell me?

To Kulfi-didi, Zindi said, and watched the narrowing of his eyes with triumph. Do you know her? She lives in my house.

Let me see, said Forid Mian, stroking his stringy white beard. Tell me what she's like.

She's fair; very fair. And she has a nice figure – not full exactly, but not thin, either. She's a widow. She's nice. You'll like her.

Forid Mian nodded. Yes, he said, I think I've seen her in the Souq.

What do you think?

Forid Mian shrugged in an attempt at nonchalance, but Zindi was quick to spot the suddenly lustful twist of his mouth. But do you think she'll be willing? he said. She must be Hindu.

Let's see, said Zindi, let's see. She stopped and looked at him hard. But there's one thing, Forid Mian, she went on softly. And that is this. If it's arranged, you'll have to come and live in my house, and you'll have to leave Jeevanbhai and start working for me.

Forid Mian was suddenly very frightened. No, Zindi, he said, biting his knuckles. No, I can't do that. How could I tell Jeevanbhai? What would Jeevanbhai do? No, no, Zindi, I can't.

Zindi rose and patted his shoulder. Don't worry, Forid, she said. I know you're scared of him, but I'm not. You leave him to me; I'll deal with him. And *khud balak*, remember, don't be so scared. There's not a thing he can do to you.

Forid Mian had begun to sweat. No, Zindi, he said wiping his face, I can't. I can't. But when he looked at her there was a spark of hope in his panic-stricken eyes.

Zindi patted him again. You leave Jeevanbhai to me, she said. I'll deal with him. Today if possible.

She smiled, struggling to hold herself in check. She could have shouted with joy. The answers were always so easy and so elusive.

The loudspeakers in the Souq sang out the muezzin's midday izan. Forid Mian looked distractedly around for his prayer-rug and stone.

I'll go now, Zindi said to him. But I'll be back tomorrow or the day after. And don't worry.

*

It took Zindi a long time to sell the lemon-squeezers, and they
fetched less than half the money she had bargained for. It was
as good as throwing them away. But she had no choice – she
had to hurry, for she could see that Boss was hungry, even
though he wasn't crying (he never cried).

Back in the house, with Boss fed and put to sleep, she had
nothing to do but wait for Kulfi or Jeevanbhai. The house was
empty except for her and Boss. It usually was now, because
Abu Fahl and Chunni and Rakesh and all the rest of them
spent all their time after work with Alu, at Hajj Fahmy's
house. What did they do there? Zindi almost didn't want to
know. Often they didn't come back till late at night. They
even ate their dinner there sometimes – Professor Samuel
had made arrangements to transfer the expenses to Hajj
Fahmy's accounts. Only Kulfi came back to the house early,
sometimes. She was a good girl, Kulfi. It's all a lot of nothing,
she told Zindi. Nothing happens there. They just sit there and
laugh and talk and drink tea and listen to Hajj Fahmy and
watch Alu weaving. Late into the night – talk, talk, talk and
weave, weave, weave. So boring: what to do? I wouldn't go at
all except for the films. Now they say they're going to get a
video and have a new film every day.

Maybe Kulfi would be back early today. But early for Kulfi
nowadays was usually quite late at night. She had found work as
a cook for another Ghaziri family, and they ate late in the
evenings, sitting on their terrace because of the heat. Perhaps
Jeevanbhai would be back early. But if he'd bought a new
bottle and gone to his room behind the Durban Tailoring
House who could tell? Nothing to do but wait.

Wait. Zaghloul and Rakesh came to the house to bathe and
change after work, but they went out again half an hour later.
The house was very quiet. She went up to the roof, and she
could see the lights in Hajj Fahmy's house. She could almost
hear the talk and the laughter. She wandered into the
courtyard to feed the ducks and the geese. Her eyes fell on the
door to Jeevanbhai's room. She looked at the lock. It was made
of brass and it looked very strong. She weighed it in her hand.
It wasn't as big or as heavy as it looked. Perhaps it wasn't as
strong, either. She gave it a small tug and something in it
seemed to yield. She dropped the tray of corn she had been

holding, and caught the lock in both hands. She pulled, but the lock held firm. She was suddenly very angry. It was not that she wanted anything from the room – she didn't know what she would do if the lock opened – but why should a door be locked against her in her own house? She spread her legs, took a good grip on the lock and pulled with all her strength. The door creaked on its hinges, but the lock held.

There was a gentle cough behind her. She didn't hear it, for the blood was pounding noisily in her head. She pulled again. There was a sound of wood cracking, near the hinges, but the lock still held. Then a hand snaked out and tapped her on the shoulder.

Zindi turned and saw Jeevanbhai. She looked at him and she looked at the lock in her hands and her anger vanished and her face began to drip with sweat. Jeevanbhai, she stammered, dropping her hands. I . . . I don't know.

Jeevanbhai nodded politely; he was as sober as a rock in a desert. You should have asked me for the key, Zindi, he said.

No, no, Zindi said confusedly, it wasn't that. I just wanted to make sure you hadn't forgotten to lock it.

Are you sure now? Jeevanbhai smiled, putting his key into the lock. Come in – look around. There's nothing here.

I know that, Jeevanbhai, Zindi pleaded, following him in. It was a small narrow room, with one small window set high in the far wall. There was a camp-bed in one corner, and beside it a rough wooden desk and a chair. A few neatly folded files lay on the floor, next to the desk.

Jeevanbhai flicked a switch and a pedestal fan in a corner began to turn slowly, sweeping the room with gusts of hot, damp air. He sat on the chair and pointed at the bed: Sit down, Zindi.

Really, Jeevanbhai, believe me, I wasn't doing anything, Zindi said, sinking on to the bed. It creaked under her weight. A dimly glowing bulb dangled on a wire above her head.

I know, Zindi, Jeevanbhai said, I know. You didn't want anything. It's just that you're worried about something, aren't you?

A long minute passed while Zindi weighed the significance of the question. Then, hoarsely, she said: What do you mean?

Well – Jeevanbhai looked at his fingers – you're worried about Forid Mian's marriage, for example, aren't you?

Zindi felt the breath rushing out of her. She stared at
Jeevanbhai's impassive face: What do you mean?

I suppose, Jeevanbhai said quietly, it would be nice for you
if he married Kulfi and came to live here and started working
for you? He would be reliable; not like the others? Isn't that
so?

Zindi, watching him, felt her face going stupidly slack, her
mouth falling open.

Zindi, Zindi, he said, chiding her gently, shaking his head.
How could you be such a fool as to plot against *me* with Forid
Mian? You're growing so old and desperate, you're losing your
wits. Did you really think I wouldn't hear about it? Don't you
know? Forid Mian has no secrets from me; he can't have. Do
you know how he came to al-Ghazira? He used to work in a ship
which, in Dhu-l-Hijja, used to carry pilgrims on the Hajj, all
the way from Singapore and Chittagong and Bombay and all
kinds of places. It used to stop here on its way to Jiddah. That's
how I met Forid Mian; he used to carry things for me
sometimes. One year the ship arrived with Forid Mian locked
up in the hold. He'd killed an eighty-year-old woman, a
pilgrim. They found him under the covers of a lifeboat, trying
to file the gold off the corpse's teeth. He'd have hanged for
murder in Chittagong, if I hadn't managed to buy his way off
the ship. But I kept the papers of course. So, you see, Forid
Mian can't afford to have any secrets from me. Did you really
think you could make an ally out of *him*?

Zindi's enormous shoulders sagged, and for a long time she
sat slumped forward, in grim silence. Then, with an effort, she
rose from the bed. She went to the chair and stood behind
Jeevanbhai. She ran her hands over the sides of his face, over
his nose, and over his lips and the edges of his red teeth.

Jeevanbhai, she said, do you remember that time? How you
crawled into this house black with bruises and sweating fear?
Do you remember how I hid you with the geese, and rubbed
your body with oil?

Very deliberately, she undid the first button of Jeevanbhai's
shirt and slid her hand inside. She rolled the coarse hairs of his
chest between her fingers and, slipping her hand under his
vest, she brushed her thumb over his nipples. She could feel
them stiffening. Jeevanbhai's breath became a trace heavier.

Do you remember? Her hand wandered down, past his navel, till they reached the drawstring of his underwear. She bent forward and caught his earlobe in her mouth. Jeevanbhai was shivering now. Remember? She took her hand out of his shirt and rubbed the fly of his trousers. She could hear him gasping for breath. She pulled the button open and slid a finger in.

Jeevanbhai caught her wrist with both his hands and tried to fight it off. She had as much strength in her wrist as he had in both his arms. Zindi, he gasped, stop, you're going crazy. He twisted his body sideways and managed to struggle to his feet. Lowering his shoulders, he gathered his strength together and threw himself against her stomach. She staggered backwards, in the direction of the bed. For a moment she tottered on her feet, staring at his flushed face, and then, covering her face with her hands, she crumpled on to the bed. Her sobs came in short dry bursts, shaking the bed.

Zindi, Zindi, Jeevanbhai said, what's the matter? What's happened? He latched the door and went to the bed. Awkwardly he put his arm around her shoulders.

Zindi, he said, what's happened? What have they done? Tell me.

He brushed her cheek clumsily with the back of his hand. Tell me, he said. I can help you. You know that. I know you want the shop. Why didn't you just ask me? Why did you have to go through this drama?

He took her black scarf off, folded it neatly and put it beside him on the bed. Then he ran his hand gently through her thin, greying hair, and stroked her neck and her arms. His hand brushed her heaving breasts, and he drew it back sharply in embarrassment. Zindi, he whispered, tell me. What have they done to you? Is it something terrible?

Terrible? What could a word like 'terrible' mean for someone who had to spend each day watching her own house slipping out of her hands, watching it turn against her, defying nature, like a horse turning on its rider? What did 'terrible' mean for someone who had to watch the very people she had sheltered, her own children, picking the world apart, hunting for chaos and calling from the rooftops for their own destruction? What is terrible? Is it terrible to find yourself afloat on a whirlpool of madness, to see the currents raging around you, and to be powerless to do anything but wait helplessly for the last wave?

Sometimes broken bones and pain aren't necessary to make things terrible; being a spectator is terror enough.

In the beginning it wasn't so bad; it had seemed as though nothing would come of it. Everyone who had lived in the Ras long enough had seen it swept by bursts of craziness. There was the time someone spread a rumour about the potato liquor that was being sold on the beach, and the men went into a frenzy because they thought their balls were climbing back into their bodies; and there was the year people spent every night for a whole month sitting up and waiting for an earthquake.

This was different; it went on and on and on. There was no end to it.

First, they got Romy Abu Tolba. It was Abu Fahl and Professor Samuel who went to him (Alu never went anywhere; he only sat in Hajj Fahmy's courtyard and wove and wove and wove). They went to Romy with a huge gang and they said: Your shop spreads dirt in the Ras. We won't put up with it. Either join us and we'll run it together, like everything else, or you'll lose your shop.

Romy is one of those people who minds his business and doesn't bother to find out about things. That's madness for a shopkeeper; every good shopkeeper has to stay ahead of the news. Romy didn't know what was happening in the Ras. When they said all that to him, he was so astonished he couldn't think of anything to say. After a long time, he laughed and said: Are you mad? It's all right to drink, but drunks shouldn't go around disturbing honest people.

They said, All right, you'll see, and they left. They were the last people to set foot in Romy Abu Tolba's shop.

The next day Romy opened his shop in the morning and sat down to read his newspaper and wait for customers. He waited and he waited but nobody came into his shop. He called out to people when he saw them going past, but they turned their heads and walked away. He'd stocked watermelons that day, and they began to rot. And still nobody came, all through the day.

Never mind, he told his son Tolba the next day. They'll need things; they'll fall short.

But Abu Fahl and Zaghloul and the rest had already taken one of Hajj Fahmy's trucks and bought stocks of sugar and oil and tea and everything else in the Souq, and they began to give them out in Hajj Fahmy's courtyard, while Samuel noted it all down in his account-books.

There was no shortage of anything, and that evening Romy's stock of eggs began to smell.

Next day, Romy dropped his prices. Still nobody came. That night almost the whole of the Ras gathered around Hajj Fahmy's house and till late in the night they talked about the terrible dirt that shops deal out.

Next morning Romy began to beg people to go in. He needed money now. But nobody even passed by his shop any longer; they skirted fearfully around it as though it were a leper's lair. They were afraid; afraid of the dirt and the germs. Germs! In Romy Abu Tolba the Fayyumi's shop, where everyone had bought everything for God knows how many years!

At the end of the day Romy knew he was beaten. What's the use of a shop without customers? He went to Hajj Fahmy that evening and said: Do what you like with my shop.

They say Hajj Fahmy kissed him on both cheeks and hugged him like a brother.

The day after that they went to the shop and washed every inch of it with carbolic acid. They washed the shelves, the floor, the walls, the counter, even the lane outside. They took away Romy's old iron cash-box, and in its place they put their files and account-books.

That night on the beach they burnt the cash-box and danced around it.

Now everything in the shop is given away and the price is marked down in the files against people's names. There aren't any profits any more. Romy's just a clerk now, in his own shop. He spends the day noting down who buys what in the account-books. They pay him a wage. It's not a bad wage, but you can already see death weighing down his eyelids. Who wants to be a paid clerk in his own shop?

That was just the beginning. After that the flood of carbolic acid started. Every day they send out groups with buckets of carbolic. They wander all over the Ras, washing out lanes and houses as they please. They came to this house, too, but the

door was barred, and Abu Fahl, for some reason of his own, led
them away. But they'll be back, and who'll stop them the next
time? They'll come again and again and again, until they get in.
And what then? Who can live with the stench of that stuff?

Next, they say, they're going to put a stop to the dirtiest of
the dirty – the mugaddams, the labour contractors. Soon, they
say, no one in the Ras will ever work for a mugaddam again.
And after that? After that – no mistake about it – they'll want
the houses; houses which have been held together for years
with sweat and love. They'll want them, too.

Everyone's with them now. They've got so much money, it's
unbelievable, but at the same time they say there's not a note
or a coin left anywhere in the Ras. It's all in their account-books
and files. Every day every person who works outside takes
money for the day in an envelope, and at the end of the day
they burn the envelopes. Every week they bring their pay to
the Professor in envelopes (he's got a kind of office now, in a
shack near Hajj Fahmy's house). He writes it all down in his
books and puts it in the bank. Then, at the end of every week,
he goes to the post office and sends money to all the addresses
in his files. They say the shacks in the Ras are now full of people
who're growing as rich as kings back home in their villages.
They're sending back three, four, five times more money than
they used to before, because they don't have to spend any of it
here, as they used to. But there's so many of them, and there's
so much money in those books, that they still have money to
burn. They began by showing films on the beach every second
day. Now its videos and a new film every day. Then they're
going to hire buses to take them on holidays to the hot springs.
They're not going to go home on ordinary planes any more.
They're going to charter whole planes, and everyone who's
going to Egypt or India or wherever will go together. They'll
save half the money, they say.

And now it's not just the Ras any more. People are getting to
hear of it outside, and they're pouring in. Last week the
Baluchis, who used to sweep the streets of the New Town
during the day and sleep in them at night, started arriving and
they've all been given places to stay.

It's getting worse and worse every day. Now no one will talk
to me any more or let me into their houses or their shacks,

because I'm not fool enough to wear their duster on my arm. They say I bring in germs. Think of it! Zindi at-Tiffaha, without whose consent no shack could be built in the Ras once upon a time, brings in germs now!

Whatever happens, it's the end for me: either they'll get the house or the police will. It's just a matter of time now before the police and the Amirs get to hear of it. No one's gone to them yet, because that's the one thing no one in the Ras ever does. But soon enough someone or other will go, and then it'll be the end of the Ras, the end of our houses, the end of our peace, the end of our luck and our good times.

And where shall I go then?

Jeevanbhai Patel was staring at the floor, his hands clasped between his knees. It was a long time before he spoke. He said: Zindi, you don't have to go very far. What about the shop?

Zindi, still hiccuping with sobs, stopped wiping her face: What shop?

My shop. The Durban Tailoring House. Don't you want it?

Zindi looked him over suspiciously: Yes. Why?

Jeevanbhai smiled and patted her on the shoulder. Tell me, Zindi, he said, why do you want that shop so much?

Why do I want it so much? Can't you see why I want it so much? If I had it, I'd be able to get away from here before the end comes. And who knows? God willing, I might be able to take a few of them with me. They might listen to me if I had something to offer, some alternative. They won't listen to me now, but with that shop who knows? And at least, if I do get it, when the end comes a couple of them will have somewhere to hide.

Jeevanbhai ran his tongue over his teeth. Zindi, he said, I told you before, but you weren't listening. You *can* have the shop.

Zindi rose from the bed and went to the door. All right, Jeevanbhai, she said briskly, tell me what you've got in your mind or I'm going. I know you're not a man who gives away shops for love and sweet words. So just tell me the truth; I'm not a child.

No, Jeevanbhai said quietly, you're right; I'm not the kind of man who gives away a shop for nothing. But I'm *not* going to give it away for nothing. You'll have to pay me half what it would cost on the open market. I know you've got enough money hidden away somewhere. We can talk about the price later. The other half will be my share. We can divide the profits. The place needs a change anyway; it never brings luck if it stays the same for too long. I've been thinking of it myself.

Watching him closely, Zindi said: But that's not all, is it?

Jeevanbhai smiled. No, Zindi, he said, it's true. That's not all. I want something from you, too. But it's a small thing, and it's not very important.

Tell me quickly and no more talk. You know you can have what I've got to give, but *that* you don't want. What *do* you want?

She leant forward and peered at him. Not Kulfi? she gasped in surprise. No, not her?

Jeevanbhai burst into laugher: An old whore's like an old zip – stuck. Can't you ever think of anything else? No, I don't want her or anything like that. You can still marry her off to Forid Mian if you like – if he has the strength to sign the khitba. No, what I want is a very small thing. I just want you to tell me what's happening here, now and then. You know I don't get to hear as much now as I used to and, as you said yourself, nowadays one can't afford to be behind the news. And I may want you to do a couple of things for me sometimes.

What things?

Small things. For example, I've got a couple of friends – Indians, nice people. One of them's heard about Alu and wants to meet him. Maybe you could take him tomorrow?

Zindi leant her head against the door and thought hard for a while. Then, with a quick, regretful shake of her head, she said: Police, I suppose? No, I can't. You know that's one thing I couldn't do to them. Whatever happens in the future, in the past they all ate my bread and salt. They've become part of my flesh. You shouldn't have said that, Jeevanbhai. You know I can't do it.

Zindi, Zindi, don't be a fool. Do you think I'd ask if they were police? Don't I know you well enough? They're not – they're just ordinary people who I met once in India. They're just ordinary people. You'll know as soon as you see this man. He's a boy really, just like Alu. He must be in his twenties. He always looks surprised, like a schoolboy. One of his eyebrows is higher than the other. He's just heard a few things and he's curious, like anyone else. Like you or me. That's all. Believe me.

Zindi hesitated for an instant, and then she shook her head. No, she said, you know I can't do it.

So what about the shop, then?

Zindi turned, swinging her huge bulk sharply on her heel, and took the latch off its hook.

Jeevanbhai spoke rapidly, at her back: Listen, Zindi. God didn't mean you to be a fool. Listen to me. I'll talk to my friend and I'll tell him to wait for you, in the road opposite my office, near the harbour. Don't come into the office. Bring him straight here and take him to Hajj Fahmy's house. Wear a duster if you have to, for once. Give him one, too, if they won't let you in otherwise. Let him talk to Alu if he wants. He may even want to take a few pictures. Afterwards take him out of the Ras, put him into a taxi and send him home. But I want you to tell me what he does and what he says. So come to the Souq the next day – day after tomorrow. Come to the Durban Tailoring House at nine. I'll be there. We can talk safely there. And the very next morning you can start setting up the shop. Do you hear me? Zindi?

Zindi threw the door open and hurried across the courtyard. It was time to feed Boss again.

ι

Chapter Fifteen

Reflections

Zindi knew that today she would have to walk all the way to the Souq. Very few share-taxis or buses passed by the Ras after dark, and those that did never stopped.

 She left her house at a quarter past eight, for she knew it would take her three-quarters of an hour, probably more, with Boss in her arms. At least there weren't any lemon-squeezers to carry. She remembered at the last minute to take her torch; it was very dark in the Ras at night, and even someone who knew its lanes like the lines on her own hands, as she did, stood in danger of tripping over a sleeping dog or stumbling into some newly sprouted shack. As an afterthought she decided to take a stick as well – many of the stray dogs in the Ras were known to turn vicious at night.

 It took her longer than she had expected to reach the Maidan al-Jami'i. She had to stop twice on the way to rest: Boss was growing heavier every day. By the time she reached the Souq it was almost nine-thirty. Most of the jewellery- and electronics-shops had already shut down, but a few of the cloth-shops were still open. She didn't expect to see a light in the Durban Tailoring House. She knew Jeevanbhai would be in the small room behind the shop. Drinking, probably. He could wait: it would do him good; make him drunker. Maybe he'd drink himself to death.

 Zindi wandered into one of the cloth-shops and looked it over. It took her no more than a glance to see that it was all wrong – some shelves were too crowded, some too bare, and there weren't enough sample leaflets on the counter. She left it, nodding to herself. She knew she could do better.

 The Durban Tailoring House was dark, as she had expected; but she could see a sliver of light under the door to the room at the back. She rattled the shop's heavily padlocked steel collapsible gates. The door at the back opened promptly, and she saw Jeevanbhai silhouetted against a rectangle of dim light. He stood there for a moment, fumbling for his keys, his shoulders slightly stooped, his hair neatly combed as always, his teeth an iridescent ruby streak in the darkness. As she watched him unlocking the gate, the helpless, unnameable rage that had kept her awake for two nights suddenly poured into her head and began to throb in her temples.

'*Aish Halak ya Zindi?* he said, smiling politely, as he pushed the gate back along its rails.

Zindi crashed past him into the shop, knocking him aside with her shoulder. Why is it so dark here? she snapped. Spinning around, she slammed the edge of her palm on the light switches. Two neon lights flickered on, filling the shop with their silvery glare.

Zindi, what're you doing? Jeevanbhai protested, sheltering his eyes and groping for the switches.

Zindi blocked his way with an outstretched arm. What's the matter? she said. Why d'you always hide from the light like a cockroach?

She reached over the counter to the shelves and yanked out a roll of cloth. With jerks of her hand she spread several layers of the cloth over the counter. Then, very gently, she laid Boss on the improvised cot.

Yalla, go on, *ya* Boss, she whispered loudly. Piss, shit, do what you like. It's our cloth now – yours and mine. We're buying it tomorrow.

Zindi, Zindi, Jeevanbhai muttered in mild protest. Can't you do all that later? I've been waiting for you. Come into the other room, and tell me. . . .

Listen, Zindi snarled, spraying his face with spittle. I did what you said, for *my* reasons. *Mine*, not yours. I'm not your bought slave like Forid Mian. So don't give me any orders. I'll do what I want, and I'll tell you when I want.

She reached into a pocket in the waist of her fustan and pulled out a tape measure. Laying one end of it at the corner of the shop, beside the collapsible gate, she measured along the wall to the far corner. Then she started at another corner and measured the breadth of the shop.

Just four metres by three metres, she said to Jeevanbhai.

Very small; much smaller than it looks.

It's big enough, Jeevanbhai said.

Have you got the documents ready?

In good time, Zindi, he answered guardedly. In good time.

'Good time' means tomorrow morning, as you said that day. You'll remember that, if you want to keep all your bones together.

Zindi lifted Boss, together with his makeshift cot, off the counter and put him on the floor, in a corner. Then she put her hands and shoulders to the counter and pushed with all her strength. It scratched out a tooth-jarring squeak as it moved across the floor.

Zindi, Jeevanbhai shouted over the noise, what're you doing?

Zindi dusted her hands and leant back to look at the counter. It was now parallel to the far wall. It looks better this way, she said. And it's more convenient. Tomorrow I'll get it painted nicely.

The counter had left behind a long, rectangular plinth of dust near the shelves. Zindi picked a dead scorpion out of the dust and threw it out through the bars of the collapsible gate. Look at this filth! she said. I'll have to get it properly cleaned tomorrow.

All right, she said briskly, looking round the shop. Now I'll do the shelves.

Zindi, Jeevanbhai said, can't you do that tomorrow? Come inside now and tell me what happened.

Zindi smiled grimly at the unfamiliar sight of Jeevanbhai pleading. First, she said, tell me, what time shall I come tomorrow?

Any time.

No, I want a definite time. I'll come in the morning, at eight-thirty, before the other shops open. I want to take the signboard down and shut the place up, while I rearrange it and get new stock and all that.

Jeevanbhai spat disgustedly through the collapsible gates into the corridor. All right, he said, come at eight-thirty, come at seven, stay the night, do what you like. Can't we decide all that later?

No; the important things come first. So you'll be here at

eight-thirty with the documents, then?

Why do we want documents? Can't we just have an agreement, between friends?

Yes, we could if we were friends, but you haven't had a friend since your wife died. So listen, you bastard, you bring those documents with you tomorrow or I'll tear out your cock and stuff it up your arse with a pneumatic drill. Do you understand?

Jeevanbhai backed away from her, licking his teeth. Yes, he said, I'll bring them.

Fine, she said and shoved him towards the room at the back. We'll go inside now.

Before going into the room, Jeevanbhai switched off all the lights in the shop, while Zindi put Boss back on the counter. The only light in the tiny room at the back came from a table-lamp that had been turned to the wall. Jeevanbhai cleared files and papers off a folding steel chair and gestured to it. A half-empty whisky-bottle and a few glasses stood on the desk, weighing down the litter of flapping paper. Jeevanbhai waved the bottle at her. Have a little bit?

Zindi made a face: A little bit.

So what happened yesterday? Jeevanbhai asked, pouring whisky into two glasses. He handed Zindi one of the glasses. She stared at the amber liquid for a moment, and then threw her head back and drained the glass.

A little bit more?

A little bit.

So what happened yesterday? Jeevanbhai asked again, pouring whisky into their glasses.

Nothing very much happened, she said. She took the glass and gazed into it, holding it in both hands. Then she pinched her nose tightly shut and tossed the whisky down.

I met him exactly where you'd said, she began. He was standing in the road outside your office and I went straight up to him and spoke to him in Hindi.

He was absolutely flabbergasted. Who knows what he'd expected? His mouth fell open and his eyebrows shot all over his forehead. He looked as though he was longing to run back across the road into the office. Perhaps he thought there had been some kind of mistake; that he was talking to the wrong

woman. And then, when he understood that it wasn't a
mistake, he began to behave like a schoolboy who'd run into his
headmistress with a cigarette in his mouth. In the taxi he sat
squeezed against the door, as though he was afraid of being
beaten, and began to talk about birds.

Birds!

It seemed as though he wasn't really in his right mind. It
grew even worse when he was trying to explain what he did for
his living. He seemed to be choking on his tongue. In the end
he managed to say: I'm a journalist – but he didn't, for one
instant, look as though he expected to be believed.

The whole thing seemed more and more difficult as the taxi
drew closer to the Ras. How was anyone going to take this tip-
top suited-booted babu into the Ras without people knowing
exactly what he was the moment they saw him?

But it was the Ras itself which solved that problem.

From a long way away it was clear that something unusual
was happening around the embankment. The driver saw it,
too, and he slowed down. There was a crowd at the foot of the
embankment. Even at that distance, they could hear shouts
and a tremendous noise. Then a large part of the crowd broke
away and went up and over the embankment, and disappeared
into the Ras.

They saw then what had drawn the crowd – a car lying on its
side. The taxi-driver stopped the car when he saw the crowd.
He was a Ghaziri and he tried to stay away from the Ras, he
said, when it looked as though there'd be trouble. So they had
to walk the last part.

There was so much confusion, nobody looked at them twice.
They slipped into the crowd and worked their way down the
embankment to the car (she holding him by the hand). It was a
new Peugeot, balancing on one side, with a wheel still
spinning, and a door open in the air, like a trapdoor. There was
a jagged, gaping hole in one side of the windscreen, and what
was left of the glass was all frosted over with cracks.

Someone must have been hurt, she said to somebody.

No, he said, whoever he was, no one was hurt. It must be
true, she thought to herself. There's no blood anywhere.

So how did it happen?

It was all to do with the mugaddams, the labour contractors.

Adil al-Azraq, the blue Moroccan, and his cousin had come to the Ras in their car that evening as they often did. When they reached the embankment, they lit cigarettes, gave the horn a gentle push, and sat back in their seats, expecting people to come running up to them, as they usually did.

But there was a surprise waiting for them. They sat for a full five minutes, which they'd never done before, and there was still no sign of anyone. They blew the horn again, a little less languidly this time. It made no difference. They blew it again, and again, until at the end of twenty minutes, when the setting sun had heated the car into an oven, Adil the Blue had his elbows jammed on the horn. But still they wouldn't get out of the car and go into the Ras – their prestige wouldn't let them.

Then the men appeared – not running, but in a compact, dignified group. There were a lot of them there – about thirty, including Rakesh and Zaghloul. Abu Fahl was in the lead. They'd decided that he'd speak for all of them.

Abu Fahl didn't waste any breath on greetings. He went straight up to them and said: Listen, I have to tell you something. Here in the Ras we've all been thinking a lot about dirt and germs and money. We've managed to do away with almost all the money in the Ras. The big problem is you mugaddams. With you it's money, money, money all the time: take money, hand out money, take back money. It's a dirty system: it spreads germs like a squid spreads ink. We've decided to do away with it. From now on we'll go to the contractors and architects ourselves, all together, and we'll work out our own terms, and we'll carry the money we make safely to the bank, in envelopes. You can join us if you like – you can come and work with us. But – *salli-'ala-n-nabi* – no one here will work for a mugaddam again.

Adil the Blue and his cousin were fuming and steaming all through this, especially Adil, whose burnt blue cheeks had turned purple. He'd have run Abu Fahl over right then, but his cousin stopped him. He saw Zaghloul and twenty-eight others standing around the car, so he squeezed Adil's elbow to keep him quiet and smiled at Abu Fahl and said: Abu Fahl, why not send all these people away, to the bottom of the embankment, and then we'll talk?

Abu Fahl could see no harm in that, so he told Zaghloul to

take the others off, and he went to the side of the road and watched them go down the embankment.

The moment the others had gone Adil the Blue started the car and threw it at Abu Fahl's back.

Abu Fahl spun round, as quick as a top, but the car was just a hair away from his chest. So, instead of running, he jumped at the bonnet and managed to roll over safely on the other side. He picked himself up, ran to the side of the embankment and looked for something to throw, but there was nothing there, except a few pebbles. So he slipped his watch off his wrist – it was a heavy old automatic, not one of those thin quartz things – and hid it in his palm.

Adil the Blue looked back, and he was surprised to see Abu Fahl still on the embankment, waiting for him. He wheeled the car around and went straight for him, steering carefully. Abu Fahl waited until it was almost on him, and then in one movement he hurled his watch at the windscreen and jumped aside.

The watch was thrown with such force that when it hit the windscreen there was an explosion of glass. Adil lost control and the car rolled over the side of the embankment.

The others were already running up the embankment, and they followed Abu Fahl down to the car. Nothing had happened to Adil or his cousin, though they both had a bit of glass in their hair. Soon enough they got over the shock and climbed out through the door at the top.

Abu Fahl would have beaten them to a pulp right there, but Zaghloul and Rakesh stopped him. No, they said, we shouldn't do anything to them ourselves. We'll take them to Hajj Fahmy and see what he has to say. And so they led them off across the embankment and into the Ras.

And it was only a few minutes after that that their driver stopped his taxi and told them that they would have to walk the rest of the way.

In a way it was the best thing that could have happened. In all that confusion and excitement, it was clear that nobody would have the time to notice who was who, and who was wearing a duster and who wasn't. So she decided not to waste any more time and led the Bird-man straight to Hajj Fahmy's house.

There was a huge crowd there already. The news had spread everywhere: Adil al-Azraq had tried to kill Abu Fahl, but Abu Fahl had been too quick for him, and they'd caught Adil and his cousin and taken them to Hajj Fahmy's to be judged.

She had to use all her strength to clear a path for them through the crowd, holding tightly on to his arm all the while so that he wouldn't fall and end up being trampled to death. Once, she wondered how this young bird-lover was taking the crowds and the Ras and the excitement; whether he was frightened or nervous.

He wasn't. The arm she was holding so tightly was perfectly steady, though damp with sweat. He seemed curious, mainly: he was staring all around him, at the crowds, peering into shacks, watching people, looking at the colourful dusters on their arms. It was as though he were watching a film.

Pushing, shoving, thrusting her weight at sharp angles, she managed to clear a way for them right up to the door to Hajj Fahmy's courtyard. By wriggling a couple of tall Baluchis out of the doorway she managed to get a good view of the courtyard. The crowd had formed a huge circle around the courtyard now. Adil the Blue and his cousin were alone in the middle of the circle, squatting. Someone handed them a couple of cigarettes, and they lit them, and puffed away furiously. But that wasn't enough for them. They asked for tea. Hajj Fahmy sent a message into the house, and Professor Samuel made a note in his pad, and soon a tray with two glasses appeared.

Zindi pulled the Bird-man in front of her, and held him tight against her chest, so that she could whisper into his ear without anyone else hearing. And then she pointed them all out to him. There was Abu Fahl, his one eye glowing a livid red, his jallabeyya tied around his waist with a scarf, like it used to be when he went into the fields to harvest rice. There was Zaghloul laughing, that laugh which used to drive the girls in his village mad; and there was Rakesh, worrying about his hair, smoothing his shirt. That was Professor Samuel there, worried, nervously fingering the calculator in his breast pocket. And there was Chunni squatting at the edge of the circle and Karthamma, enjoying herself while Kulfi looked after Boss at home. And of course, over there, sitting gravely on the platform, legs folded, next to the loom was Hajj Fahmy, solemnly counting his beads, for all the world like an elder sitting in council to settle a family quarrel.

And Alu?

She pointed him out, at the loom, weaving, his big head turned away from the crowd, ignoring the noise. And when he saw him the Bird-man stared and stared, like a timid falcon sizing up some unusual and frightening prey.

Hajj Fahmy asked Abu Fahl to speak first since he was the one who had been wronged. So Abu Fahl walked into the circle and, like a storyteller at a fair, he began to speak. He described every moment of it – what he had said, and what they had said, and how they drove at him, and how he shattered their windshield. It was masterful; the whole crowd was enthralled. At the end of it the courtyard rang to shouts and applause and the stamping of feet. Abu Fahl, of course, was as pleased as a new bridegroom: he was smiling and grinning so much you'd have thought he'd be happy to forgive Adil al-Azraq for giving him a chance to tell that story.

All through this, Adil al-Azraq and his cousin were sullenly smoking cigarettes and drinking tea in the centre of the courtyard. By the time Hajj Fahmy called on them to speak Adil was grinding his teeth so loud it was like the rattle of stones in a crusher.

Hajj Fahmy called him to the platform and said: What have you to say for yourself?

Adil stood up, with his cigarette in his hand, and went up to Hajj Fahmy. He blew a cloud of smoke straight into the Hajj's face and said: You'll find out what I have to say soon enough, . you son of a whore. You'll find out when my men come here tomorrow and tear your rotten old teeth out.

Hajj Fahmy was quite unmoved, but the whole courtyard gasped. Abu Fahl leapt on Adil and sent him sprawling across the courtyard. He would have taken him apart right there if Hajj Fahmy hadn't gestured to the others to hold Abu Fahl.

The Hajj was quite angry. He pointed his finger at Abu Fahl and said: Who do you think you are? Who gave you the right to fight in my courtyard? Do you think this is a market? There won't be any fighting in my house.

Abu Fahl was furious, too; there were at least six men

holding him and you could see they weren't finding it easy. He
shouted at Hajj Fahmy: I didn't do anything to them at the
embankment even though they tried to kill me. The others said
we should bring them here, and I let them. But now that
they're here do you think I'm going to let them threaten us? Do
you think I'm going to let them go? Just like that?

Hajj Fahmy looked at him very coldly and said: Since you
can't control yourself, you should let other people think about
these things.

He held up his hand and looked around the courtyard. No
one spoke. The Hajj said: We won't have any fighting or
beating here. But, still, it *is* true – these men are dirty. They've
dealt in dirt so long you can see it caked on their skin. Fighting
and beating won't do them any good. What they need is a bath.

A bath? everyone said.

Yes, said Hajj Fahmy, a bath. A good proper bath, with lots
of antiseptic to kill all the dirt that's clinging to them. They'll
bathe themselves – we won't do anything but watch quietly –
and then they can go.

He sent a message to his wife, and soon she sent out four
buckets. They were all full of water that was milky with
antiseptic. Someone carried the buckets and two mugs to the
centre of the circle and put them in front of Adil and his cousin.
And then the crowd drew back.

Adil the Blue and his cousin were alone now, in the middle,
each with their two buckets of water and a mug in front of him.
The courtyard was so silent you could hear the waves breaking
on the beach, in the distance.

And Alu?

Alu? Alu wasn't weaving any longer, but he wasn't watching,
either. He was looking in front of him, totally bewildered. You
had only to look at him to know that the whole thing was
beyond him now. He could no longer understand what he'd
started.

At first Adil and his cousin looked at the buckets and from
them to Hajj Fahmy, in complete disbelief. Then Adil let out a
loud, sneering laugh and shouted: Do you think Adil al-Azraq,
who's given you all work for the last fifteen years, has suddenly
become a child that you're going to make him bathe in public?

Hajj Fahmy looked straight at him, without blinking and

without speaking. Adil and his cousin turned to their left and to
their right and they laughed again, as though they wanted to
share a joke with the crowd. Look, they said, he's a mad old
man – he's lost his mind.

But their laughter returned to them, echoing hollowly in
that bowl of silence.

They spun around then, appealing to everyone. This is crazy,
they said. What'll you get out of watching us bathe? We'll give
you some money instead. It's true, we shouldn't have tried to
run down Abu Fahl. But it's a simple thing and easily settled.
How much do you want? Just tell us. How much?

No one took their eyes off them, and no one answered. Now
they were running from one end of the courtyard to the other,
like insects in a matchbox, clutching at people's hands, Abu
Fahl's hands, begging, pleading.

Nobody moved, no one spoke.

Trapped in that storm of silence, they circled slowly back to
the centre, looking around the courtyard like caged foxes.
Slowly, as they began to understand the depths of their
humiliation, the disbelief and mockery on their faces faded into
terror. Weighed down by the silence they sank to their knees.
Then suddenly they lifted up their buckets and drenched each
other in antiseptic.

And at that moment the young bird-lover jerked himself
free, and fought his way through the crowd. Once he was out of
the lane, he began to run. He lost his way among the shacks but
he kept on running, in circles, until somehow he reached the
embankment. He stopped there to get his breath back, but also
because he realized at last that he was lost.

Why did he run? Jeevanbhai asked incredulously. His eyes
were glazed now and he was slumped across his paper-littered
desk, with a glass clutched in one hand.

Why did he run? Was he scared?

No, said Zindi, tossing off another shot of whisky. He wasn't
scared exactly. He was shocked: it was as though the world had
suddenly started moving backwards.

What did you do then?

Zindi could feel herself swaying on the chair, and she
gripped the edge of her desk to hold herself steady. I found him
near the embankment, she said. And I walked with him till we

found a taxi. And all the way, like a child in search of a secret, he bombarded me with questions about birds.

Birds! Jeevanbhai snorted, curling his lip. That's all they're good for: birds, and their promotions and their postings. It's no use expecting anything from them. A man has to do what he can for himself.

So, Zindi said, holding out her empty glass, I'll be back at eight-thirty tomorrow. And you'd better have the papers ready, Jeevanbhai.

Wait, Jeevanbhai cried, with drunken petulance. That's not all. You have to tell me more. What happens now?

What do you mean? said Zindi. I'll come at eight-thirty, then we'll sign the documents, and after that I'll start work. And tell me: have you told Forid Mian yet?

No, no, I didn't mean that. Jeevanbhai waved an impatient hand. I meant, what are *they* going to do next?

Zindi repeated with slow menace: Have you told Forid Mian yet? When are you going to tell him?

I'll tell him tomorrow, don't worry. There's nothing to worry about. Now tell me: what are they going to do next?

Zindi poured a finger of whisky into her glass and sat back. Nothing much, she said. They were so happy with what they did to the mugaddams they've decided to celebrate. They're all going to the Star tomorrow evening – half the Ras.

The room was suddenly swimming before Jeevanbhai's eyes. He shook his head fiercely, in an effort to clear it. They're going to the Star? he asked hoarsely.

Yes, said Zindi. They're all going to the Star tomorrow. You know, they lifted the police cordon last week, so there's nothing to stop them going now. They're going to look at the room Alu was buried in. If they find the two sewing machines that saved him, they're going to bring them out and give them to him as a gift. And the Mawali women are going to take fruit and bread and kahk biscuits to distribute at their sheikh's grave, if they can find it in that mess. After that they're all going on a shopping spree in Hurreyya Avenue – in all the foreign shops. Professor Samuel is going to take a briefcase full of money.

Jeevanbhai rose slowly from his chair, gripping the desk tightly. He stood still for a moment, testing his legs. Then he staggered over to Zindi's chair and leant against her back.

I went to the Star once, he said thickly, clutching her shoulders. Only the Star wasn't there then and I had to go by boat. Do you remember, Zindi?

I remember, Zindi said grimly, and brushed his hands away. They came back again, feeling their way unsteadily over her shoulders and neck.

Do you remember? Do you remember how I arrived in your house? Jabal and the Pathans were behind us. Abusa managed to get us on to a horse, and we raced away. Only, I fell off on the dirt path, where the embankment is now. But somehow I crawled into your house. Do you remember?

He bent down and kissed her on the top of her head, where her hair was thinnest. She jabbed her elbow angrily into his stomach. He lurched backwards and then fell to his knees beside her, hugging her arm.

Do you remember how you looked after me, Zindi? Do you remember that one time when you came to me at night and found me writhing in pain?

Zindi pushed him back: Stop this nonsense.

There were tears in his eyes now, and his face crumpled like wet paper. He caught her hand and lifted it to his cheek.

We lost that battle, Zindi, he said, and that war, too. Why did we lose?

Zindi snatched her hand away. Jeevanbhai, she snapped, be a grown man, in God's name.

Jeevanbhai brushed the back of his hand across his eyes. Then he put his arm around her waist as far as it would reach, and sank his head into her lap.

Do you think I'd win now, Zindi, he said, if I tried?

Zindi did not answer and she made no effort to push his head away. He looked up at her. He said: Do you think I might win, once?

Zindi shook her head. Stop this now, Jeevanbhai, she said wearily. There's nothing to win any longer.

Jeevanbhai reached up and pulled her head down. Zindi, he whispered into her ear, once more. Please. Just one more time, like the last one.

Zindi snapped her head back, startled. But where? she cried.

Jeevanbhai waved a hand at the records of his planned

matings. I could spread them out on the floor, he said eagerly.

Zindi laughed: We're too old, Jeevanbhai.

Zindi, he pleaded, just one more time.

She looked at him and saw a spark of hope glinting behind the fog of years of defeat and, despite herself, she drew his face towards her and kissed him gently on his moist forehead. Then she pushed him away: It's too late now, Jeevanbhai.

He caught her hand and sat back on his haunches. As you like, Zindi, he said. But can I tell you something? I can tell you now because we're both drunk and tomorrow's so close. In my own way I've always loved you – as much as I can love, and with as much as I had to spare from my wife.

Zindi ran her hand over his papery cheek. No, Jeevanbhai, she said sadly. You're like all men; what you loved was the reflection you saw of yourself in my eyes.

She rose from her chair and banged her glass on the desk. I have to go now, she said. Boss has to go to sleep; it's very late.

Jeevanbhai darted to one corner of the room and began to rummage around in a stack of files. Wait, he called out after her. I've got another new bottle somewhere here.

Zindi went into the shop and pulled the collapsible gate open. The passageway was pitch dark. She lifted Boss into her arms and pressed him to her breasts.

Listen, she shouted into the inner room, I'll be back tomorrow at eight-thirty. You'd better have the papers ready.

There was no answer. Growling to herself, she left the shop and walked down the passageway, trying to keep her steps even.

Zindi! a shout echoed down the passageway. She turned, pulled her torch out, and shone it towards the shop. Jeevanbhai was leaning against the collapsible gate, holding a new bottle of whisky in one hand. She turned back and hurried away towards the Bab al-Asli.

But his voice followed her: Zindi! Tell them I'll meet them at the Star. Tell them they have nothing to worry about. We'll win this time.

Chapter Sixteen

Dreams

At six in the morning the telephone shattered Jyoti Das's thirty-two hours of sleep. The telephone was on a low table beside his bed. He tried to open his eyes and found them gummed together. Turning over he fumbled blindly around till his fingers touched the cold plastic of the sleek digital telephone, and found the right button. The electronic bleating stopped. He had no idea how long it had been making that noise; the sound had seemed to grow out of his sleep. It could have been hours.

Hullo? he said into the plastic flap which opened out of the receiver. His throat felt like clotted sand.

Hullo? Das? He recognized Jai Lal's voice, crackling with urgency.

Yes, he said. He prised his eyes open with his fingers. The heavy curtains that he had drawn across the plate-glass windows yesterday were glowing, with the first morning light behind them.

Das? Jai Lal said. Listen.

Yes? said Das.

I've got something to do in your part of the town. It's important. I'll stop by your hotel on the way. It might interest you, too.

All right, Das said. Jai Lal disconnected before he could say anything else.

Stretching his arm out to put the phone back, he could feel an almost painful stiffness in his joints. The crumpled sheets of his bed had left their impression on his skin over the last day and a half; his arm was marbled over with wrinkles. He hadn't slept through all of the thirty-two hours, of course. Twice yesterday he had gone down to the hotel's restaurants. He had even thought of going out for a walk once, but when he reached the revolving glass doors which sealed the steamy Ghaziri air out of the hotel his resolution had failed him. He had looked through the glass at the swirling traffic, at the entrails of unfinished buildings festooned across the skyline, and the flow of people with their inexplicable nationalities, and all he had wanted was to get back into bed, back to peaceful, orderly sleep. He had meant to ring up Jai Lal but hadn't got around to it; sleep had claimed him first. Besides, Jai Lal had made it clear that he was busy and wouldn't be able to shepherd him around any longer.

But now he had to hurry to be ready for Jai Lal. He made his way unsteadily to the bathroom.

By the time Jai Lal knocked, he had shaved, changed and even ordered breakfast. Jai Lal, looking grim, forced a smile when he opened the door.

Hullo, Jai, hullo, Das said. Come and sit. I've just ordered breakfast – do you want some?

Breakfast? Jai Lal gaped at him in astonishment. *Yar*, this is urgent; I didn't come to have breakfast.

Das grimaced. Sorry, he said. I was just asking. What's the matter?

Jai Lal glanced around the room. Haven't you got a radio or something? he asked.

Das pointed to a knob set in a perforated panel next to the bed. Jai Lal turned it and the hotel's piped music tinkled out of the panel.

Sorry, said Lal. There's no need really – it's just a habit. I even do it at home sometimes.

There were two low chairs, upholstered in imitation leather, near the window. Das took one and gestured at the other.

What's the matter? he said. What's so urgent?

Jai Lal kept standing. I can't sit now, he said. I just came to tell you: Jeevanbhai Patel has been taken in by the local security people. It happened early this morning – or, rather, very late last night. I don't know exactly what happened, but I may be able to find out soon. One of their security people, a Pakistani who I know a bit, rang up this morning. He didn't say very much except that Jeevanbhai had said, during an interrogation, that I might be willing to stand bail for him. Don't know what gave him that idea, and I don't know what else he's said. It could be quite tricky. He wants me to go there as soon as possible. Of course bail doesn't have anything to do with it; it could hardly be anything bailable. Anyway, I'm going there now to find out. I thought I'd keep you informed, because I think – I'm not sure, but I think – it may have something to do with your friend, the Suspect. Something he said gave me that impression.

Das nodded thoughtfully. So, then, he said, do you think their security knows about the whole thing now?

Jai Lal shrugged: I don't know. Maybe. I thought of taking you along, but the thing is I know this chap, and he might talk to me a little. He wouldn't if someone he didn't know was there, too. Anyway I'll come back and tell you all about it.

Fine; I'll wait here.

Jai Lal went to the door and opened it. I'll be back as soon as I can, he said, and hurried away.

Das sat down to wait. Soon a waiter brought him his breakfast. Das looked at him curiously; he seemed Indian. He was a young man, with sandy skin and very dark hair.

Are you from India? Das asked him in Hindi.

The waiter grinned shyly and scratched his head. Yes, *sahb*, he said.

From where exactly?

From Sundernagar.

Sundernagar? Where's that?

The waiter was surprised: You don't know Sundernagar, *sahb*? How's that? It's a district headquarters. It's in Himachal, at the foot of the Dhauladhar Range.

Das bit his lip, embarrassed by his ignorance. It must be cold there, he said, up in the mountains.

Arre han sahb, he said. It's very cold. There's always snow on the Dhauladhar. All the greatest rivers in the world start there – the Beas, the Suketi. You should see them; they could sweep away a place like this.

Oh? said Das. And where do you live? In the hotel?

No. I and some friends – they're mechanics, electrical, all from Sundernagar – we share a room.

In the Ras al-Maktoo? Das prompted.

No, *sahb*. He was quite indignant. Our room's a long way from that place.

Das was oddly relieved. He called the waiter back as he was going out, and gave him half a dirham.

After finishing his breakfast, he tried to read a magazine, but his feet took him to his bed, and he lay down. Jai Lal would probably take longer than he'd expected, he thought as his eyes closed.

He had hardly shut his eyes, it seemed to him, when a knock woke him. In fact it was almost midday and he had been asleep for more than four hours.

Jai Lal's clothes were crumpled and there were large dark patches under his armpits. Were you sleeping or what? he said sharply, his urbanity a little frayed, when Jyoti Das opened the door. I've been knocking for five minutes.

Sorry, Das said. He almost added 'sir'.

Why's this room so dark? Jai Lal said. He went to the window and drew the curtain back. Das flinched from the sudden burst of light, but Jai Lal did not notice. He sank into one of the chairs near the window and wiped his face with his handkerchief.

Das turned the music on again. So? he said. What happened?

Jai Lal pulled a face: God, it's so hot out there. I was really tired by the end of it. It would take too long to tell you all about it. I'll just sum up the main points. It appears that they've been watching Jeevanbhai Patel for quite a long time now. That's because he was fairly deeply involved in the old regime. In other words, he was quite close to the old Malik of Ghazira. After this regime came into power, they banned him from going to the Old Fort, where the Malik lives. But apparently Jeevanbhai used to get in there every now and then – how, nobody knew. The security people had some idea of his doings, because they had a source placed quite close to him. But they didn't know anything concrete. Now very late last night, at about three or four in the morning, they had information from their source that he was on his way there again. The source thought it was something serious this time.

They picked him up near an old disused gate at the back which they hadn't bothered to guard all these years. He was horribly drunk, and more or less raving (must have been drinking that whisky I gave him). They questioned him a bit last night and again at dawn today. Apparently he raved on and on. They couldn't make sense of everything he said, but the gist of it was this: a massive procession led by your old friend is going to march out of the Ras tomorrow – sorry, today – in the evening. They might even be armed. They plan to march to the Star. The Star is the building which collapsed and buried your Suspect – you remember? The security people aren't quite sure why they're going there; maybe it's some kind of demonstration. Whatever it is, that alone is a serious business. Demonstrations and processions are as forbidden as forbidden can be here, and have been ever since this regime came into power. But, it seems, Jeevanbhai had even grander plans for them and himself. He had some wild idea of getting the old Malik to take advantage of the demonstration and make a show of force at the same time. Perhaps even. . . .

A coup?

Maybe that's not the right word, but something like that, I think. You know, he still has a lot of support among some people here. But the whole idea was crazy of course. The Malik's bedridden and ill. He'd probably have thrown Jeevan-bhai out, or handed him to security himself. Jeevanbhai must have been very, very drunk to think of something like that.

Maybe he wasn't, said Das. I told you – that man was living in a dream. There was no telling what he might do.

Maybe you were right, Jai Lal said.

So what happens now?

Well, they're very concerned. A demonstration by migrant labourers could be quite dangerous. They're going to deal with it very firmly.

You mean they'll go into the Ras al-Maktoo and arrest them?

No, that would take a lot of preparation, and there isn't enough time now. And, in any case, that place is a labyrinth; half of them would be gone before the security people got within a mile of the place. No; they're going to wait for them near the Star, and they're going to take the whole lot in over there.

Oh, said Das. So what happens to our Suspect?

Jai Lal coughed into his fist. Well, he said, I was able to work out an agreement. It's very lucky I happen to know this chap. They're willing to take us along as observers. They'll hand over your Suspect once they've got him, and you can take him back.

They have no interest in keeping him of course but, still, it's very generous, you know, because we don't have an extradition agreement with them. Anyway, be ready at four today. I'll pick you up.

Jai Lal sat back and lit a cigarette. He said: Personal contacts help, you know. No one can work without contacts. That's the only talent a good officer needs, I always say.

But won't you need clearance from your ambassador?

No, not strictly. He doesn't really have jurisdiction over what I do or don't do. It's a matter of courtesy really. But I thought something like this might crop up sooner or later, so only last week I put up a note. HE sent it back marked 'urge fullest co-operation' or something like that. So that's OK.

He looked at Das expectantly. Das inclined his head. That was very far-sighted, he said. Good work. You'll probably get a promotion for this, Jai. Or at least an increment.

Jai Lal shook his head: Oh, I'm not expecting anything like that. It's much too early yet. Let's see how the reports and things turn out first. But it's turned out well for you, hasn't it? You can go back now, with your friend all tied up. I'll send a telex so that they'll be ready for you.

God, yes, said Das. I'll be glad to get back.

Jai Lal got up to go. Jyoti Das was staring at the streets below the hotel and the expanse of white sand beyond the city. He turned suddenly. Listen, he said on an impulse, couldn't we meet Jeevanbhai Patel again before I leave? I'd like to ask him a few things – just personal things. How he ended up here, what he did and suchlike. Meeting him was the only worthwhile thing that happened to me here. Is it possible?

No.

But couldn't you ask this chap in security, since you know him so well? Or else couldn't we visit him in gaol, like ordinary visitors?

Lal shuffled his feet uncomfortably. No, he said, it's not possible. You see, Jeevanbhai hanged himself this morning. With his belt. He was dead when I got there. Must have done it as soon as he sobered up. That's why I took so long. They needed someone to identify the body and sign papers and all that. He had no relatives.

Chapter Seventeen

A Last Look

There was no sleep for Zindi that night. When she got back to her house, she lay on her mattress with Boss beside her and tried to still her pounding pulse and shut her eyes. But it was no use; the metallic sharpness of her excitement worried at her tongue like a brass shaving. Soon she gave up and lay on her back, staring at the ceiling, and to the tune of the snores in the next room she filled the darkness with her plans for the Durban Tailoring House.

She rose a little before dawn, alerted by the stirring of the geese in the courtyard. That was when, she knew, sleep is at its deepest; she could have knocked down a wall without waking anyone in the house. But, still, her every instinct cried to her to be careful. She found her torch, and stealthily, crouching on the floor, she cleared a pile of mats, mattresses and cooking-pots from a corner of the room. Once, a tin tray dropped from her hands. She froze as the clattering echoed through the house. But there was no break in the steady rhythm of snores in the next room. She went back to work, biting her lip fiercely.

When she had laid the floor bare, she counted four handspans from the corner towards the centre of the room, and marked the place with a matchstick. Then she sat back, closed an eye and examined the angle again. She had to get it just right. When she was sure, she removed, very carefully, a section of the thin, cracked layer of cement which served as the floor. There were bricks underneath. She shone her torch over them, squinting hard, until she found the brick she wanted: one with a tiny daub of white paint in a corner. That brick had an almost invisible dent in one side, which provided a grip of sorts for a fingertip. But the bricks were wedged firmly together and it took her a long time and a broken fingernail to pull it out. After that, the four bricks around the empty space of the first came away easily, exposing a large patch of loose soil.

Zindi bent down and dug her hands into the soil. She scrabbled about for a moment, and then, sucking in a long breath, she drew out a large aluminium cooking-pot. Inside, wrapped in cellophane, was a heavy iron box. It was fastened with a huge padlock. She drew her handkerchief-wrapped bunch of keys out of the neck of her dress, found the right key and opened the box.

It was all there, all the money she had saved in her decades in al-Ghazira: the measure of her life. It was a lot of money: dirhams and dollars and sterling in yellowing cash. Enough to pay for the shop *and* lay in an entire range of new stocks.

She shut her eyes and breathed the name of God, the Compassionate, the Merciful.

It took only a few minutes after that to stuff the money into her dress, to put the empty box back, and rearrange the bricks and the cement and the mats and mattresses. Then she stood back and looked at it, pleased with herself; even she wouldn't have known whether anything had been moved.

It was dawn now, and the wads of notes rustling against her skin charged her with an unbearable impatience. But before leaving she had to talk to Kulfi, and Kulfi was still asleep in the women's room. If she went in there to wake her up she might wake the others as well. So instead she decided to wait in the courtyard, for Kulfi was always the first one up in the morning.

Squatting in the courtyard, listening to the hissing of the geese, Zindi suddenly remembered that other day, so many long months ago, when someone else had waited for Kulfi at dawn, and she smiled to herself. Mast Ram was beaten now, at last. She had beaten him. With the shop in her hands, she would wean Rakesh away first, with clothes perhaps. Then Zaghloul. Kulfi was with her anyway, only too timid to say so. Abu Fahl would follow, and then they'd all come, back to the shelter of her house. All of them, hanging their heads and pleading. . . .

Kulfi came out soon, yawning. Zindi gestured quickly to her to be quiet and caught her arm. Don't go anywhere today, she whispered into her ear. Wait for me in the house. I'll need you later today – there'll be work to do. I can't talk now, but I'll tell you about it later. Boss is in the other room. Look after him. Don't go anywhere; don't move. Stay here and wait for me.

But where are you going at this time of the morning? Kulfi asked in surprise.

To the Souq, Zindi hissed, to Jeevanbhai's shop.

Now? Kulfi said doubtfully. She turned and looked at Jeevanbhai's door. A lock hung upon the latch. But, she cried, he's not here. Where is he?

Zindi pinched her arm and Kulfi squealed. Be quiet, Zindi snapped. What does it matter? You know he often passes out in his sleep when he's been drinking. He's there, in his shop, waiting for me. Now, remember: don't go anywhere – just wait for me.

With a last warning tap on Kulfi's arm, Zindi turned and surged out of the house.

It was not yet seven when she reached the Maidan al-Jami'i, and the shops and cafés in the square were all shut. A man was washing the pavement outside the mosque, singing to himself, and in the square there were a couple of figures stretched out on the stone benches. Zindi hurried past them, straight to the Bab al-Asli. She stopped there for a moment, and for the first time that morning a doubt struck her. Would he be waiting after all? She shook her head and slipped quickly through the Bab al-Asli into the enveloping blackness beyond.

She had to feel her way along slowly at first, half-blinded by the sudden darkness. She tried to hurry and stumbled. Muttering to herself, she slowed down again, though impatience and worry were clawing at her scalp now.

She turned into the first lane and a huge sigh of relief gushed out of her lungs. The steel collapsible gates of the Durban Tailoring House were drawn and its neon lights were glowing like beacons in the gloom of the passageway. She stopped and carefully patted the wads of notes around her neck and waist. Then she looked up again, and at exactly that moment a head appeared in the shop's doorway, blew its nose, and vanished into the shop.

It wasn't Jeevanbhai. Even in that brief glimpse she had seen, quite clearly, a peaked cap and the neck of a black uniform.

Her mouth went dry and she had to lean her shaking body against the wall of the corridor. After a while, when her knees

were steady again, she pressed herself against the shop-fronts
and inched forward, towards the Durban Tailoring House,
grateful for the shadowy blackness of her fustan.

An age seemed to pass before she was halfway down the
corridor. The head didn't appear again, but she could hear
muffled voices now. They grew louder as she worked her way
forward, but she could see nothing except the shop's window.
When she was almost opposite the Durban Tailoring House,
she dropped to her knees and half-crawled along the corridor
till she could see inside. Three black-uniformed men were
lounging on stools, laughing and talking good-humouredly.
Files and papers lay piled up in heaps all over the floor of the
shop. Zindi crouched back against the billboards of the travel
agency behind her, shivering. They had only to turn their
heads to see her.

One of the men called out towards the room at the back:
Where's the tea gone, *ya 'ammi*? A moment later the door of
the back room opened and Forid Mian came out, nursing a
kettle in his hands. He put it on the counter, raised his head
and looked straight across the corridor into Zindi's eyes.

For a long moment they stared at each other. Then Zindi
pulled her dress up to her knees and lurched down the
passageway as fast as she could.

Zindi! Forid Mian's voice echoed after her. She stumbled
fiercely on, without looking back. Faintly, through the convul-
sive wheezing of her own breath, she heard other footsteps
ringing through the corridor, and Forid Mian again, shouting
shrilly: Zindi! Stop! Why're you running?

She pressed a hand on the wads of money around her neck
and pulled herself round the corner. A blinding patch of
daylight was shining in through the Bab al-Asli. Gulping in a
huge breath, she flung herself at it. And when she was no more
than a yard from the daylight Forid Mian's hands closed on her
elbow and drew her to a halt. She struggled feebly but her
strength was gone.

She collapsed almost gratefully on the floor, shuddering and
swallowing air.

Why were you running, Zindi? Forid Mian panted. What
was the need?

Zindi cast a frightened glance past him into the passageway.

Why're you afraid? Forid Mian said aggrievedly. They aren't coming. They don't care about you; they have nothing to do with you. They've only come to take away his papers.

What papers? Zindi scoured his face with her eyes. Why?

Forid Mian threw a quick glance over his shoulder and fell to his knees beside her. Don't you know? he confided, his eyes alight. They caught Jeevanbhai last night and put him in gaol. He died this morning.

Zindi gazed at him, trembling. He stroked his beard and pressed his thin, cracked lips together. His mouth twitched, his eyes flickered, and then suddenly his face flowered into a wide, boyish smile.

Zindi! he cried, shaking her shoulders. I did it. I did it at last. I saw him going out and I knew he was going to the Old Fort, so I rang them up just like they'd told me to, and I told them, I told them, and they caught him and put him in a black car, handcuffs and all, and took him straight off to the big gaol and locked him up. Locked him up. That's where he died – killed himself.

He dropped his hands and stared at the floor. He's dead, he whispered incredulously; he's dead at last. And now the shop's mine. They're going to give it to me.

Then he flung his arms around her and hugged her, whimpering with joy and disbelief. He was a bad man, he said. He was a bad, wicked man.

Zindi pushed him away and patted her dress to make sure her wads of notes were undisturbed. He was a bad man, Forid Mian whispered again, shaking his head. A bad, bad man.

He was a better man than you'll ever be, Forid Mian, Zindi said. Despite everything. A thousand times better. At least, while he lived, he was alive.

Forid Mian laughed. You didn't know him, Zindi, he said. I tell you, he was a bad man.

Zindi dusted her dress and turned to go. Forid Mian reached out and caught her arm. Wait, Zindi, he said. Don't be in a hurry.

Zindi stopped. He dropped his eyes and shot her a shy, upwards glance. Maybe I'll feel lonely now, Zindi, he said. Maybe I should have someone to look after me, as you were saying that day. I can afford it, now that I've got the shop.

He looked away modestly and shuffled his feet. The stringy white beard was suddenly incongruous on his glowing face; he looked twenty years younger. Tell me, Zindi, he said, did you talk to Kulfi?

Zindi tried to speak and could find no words. She pushed him aside and looked down the murky passageway into the heart of the Souq. Then her eyes filled with tears and she turned abruptly and hurried out through the Bab al-Asli.

Zindi took a taxi from the Maidan and so reached Hajj Fahmy's house in half an hour. When she arrived there she stood outside the walls of the courtyard and shouted in: Are you there, *ya* Hajj Fahmy? Come out.

A girl peeped through the door and, seeing her, shut it again. She heard the pattering of feet and shrill cries inside the house: It's Zindi, Zindi at-Tiffaha; she's here.

She called out again: *Ya* Hajj, are you there? The door flew open and Hajj Fahmy stood in front of her, beaming: Come in, Zindi, come in, how are you, come in, come in, you've brought blessings, come in.

Zindi stepped reluctantly over the threshold and stood with her back to the door. Alu was working at the loom, at the other end of the courtyard. He looked up and smiled at her. She could see two little girls watching her from the shelter of a door.

Come in, Hajj Fahmy said. I'm glad you've come, Zindi. I hope you've come to join us at last. I knew you would sooner or later; I told the others so. Come and sit in the mandara and have some tea.

No, no, she said urgently, shaking her head. There's no time.

No time? he smiled at her gently. No time for a cup of tea?

No, *ya* Hajj, there's no time. Listen: Jeevanbhai's been taken to gaol. I think he's killed himself.

The Hajj started; his face clouded over. God have mercy on him, he said, laying his right hand on his heart.

But that's not all, Zindi cried.

It's very sad, Hajj Fahmy went on, talking more to himself than to her. But it was bound to happen. He got his fingers into too many things; that was always the trouble with him.

Zindi caught his arm. Listen, she said. Just listen to me now.
There's no time. He knew that all of you are going to the Star
today. I told him so last night. I think that's the reason why he
was arrested. I don't know exactly how, but I'm sure that's the
reason. He was planning something. He was arrested on his
way to the Old Fort.

The Hajj stared at her in astonishment. Because of our trip to
the Star? he said. What are you talking about? We're going on a
shopping trip and on the way we're going to stop at the Star for
a few minutes, to see if we can find Alu's sewing machines. It's
allowed now; there's no police cordon. Why should Jeevanbhai
be taken to gaol for that? He had nothing to do with it.

I don't know, she said, but I think that was why. . . .

She saw him looking at her with a faintly ironic smile, and the
things she had meant to say, all her arguments and phrases,
became a confused jumble in her mind.

What gave you this idea, Zindi? he asked. Have you heard
something definite?

No, Zindi stammered, searching her mind. But I think. . . .

Hajj Fahmy frowned. Is this one of your little tricks, Zindi?
he said softly.

Helplessly Zindi shook her head. She decided to make one
last effort. Just believe me, she pleaded. Don't go today. Take
my word for it; I have nothing to gain. I came straight here, as
soon as I heard about Jeevanbhai – to warn you. I had to. I
didn't think you would believe me, and I can see you don't, but
I had to try. That's why I've come. You'll be taking my whole
house with you, and a woman can't sit by and watch her
children walking to their end. Don't go, for God's sake, don't
go. Don't take the risk.

Hajj Fahmy scratched his cheek. But, Zindi, he said, we're
just going on a shopping trip. What could possibly happen?
Why should the police be interested in a shopping trip? If they
were, they'd be locking up the whole of al-Ghazira every day.

Trust me, *ya* Hajj, she said. *Allahu yia'alam*, this is no trick.
Don't go. Not just because of me or my people. Think of the
Ras. If, just if, something does happen and the police are there
and they catch you all together, it'll be the end of the whole
place. They won't leave it standing – it'll be finished.

Hajj Fahmy broke into a smile. Zindi, he said playfully,

you've been having your bad dreams again.

She dropped her hands hopelessly. So you'll go? she said.

He thumped her on the back and laughed: Come and have some tea. It won't be as good as yours, but it won't be bad.

Zindi turned away from him and went quickly across the courtyard to Alu. She reached up, caught his shuttle strings and said very rapidly in Hindi: Alu, don't go. Don't let them go today. You can stop them if you try. If anything happens, their blood will be on your hands.

Slowly Alu shook his head. There's nothing I can do, he said. You know that. I don't want to go myself. It's not in my hands.

Hajj Fahmy came up and stood beside her. Stop running about, Zindi, he said. Come and have some tea and cool your head a little.

Zindi released Alu's shuttle strings and turned slowly to Hajj Fahmy. She took his hand, and before he could pull it away she bent down and kissed it, formally.

God keep you, Hajj Fahmy, she said. You're a good man.

And then she rushed away, for there was a lot to do and very little time to do it in: providentially she had heard somewhere that a sambuq called *Zeynab* was to sail for the Red Sea that very night.

Chapter Eighteen

Dances

When Abu Fahl stepped through the door, everyone in Hajj
Fahmy's courtyard could tell at once that he had a bottle
hidden under his jallabeyya. His gleefully secretive grin made
it plain; they didn't even really need to look at the bulge under
his arm to make sure.

Though it was only four o'clock, there were already a dozen
men waiting in the strip of shade under the far wall of the
courtyard. Alu was sitting at the loom at the other end, and
Zaghloul was squatting beside him, asking questions and
laughing at the answers, pretending incomprehension. Zaghloul saw Abu Fahl first, so he knew even before the others. He
leapt to his feet and shouted delightedly: Bring it here, *ya akhi*,
fast, before they get their hands on it. But there was a quick
chorus from the other end, too: What have you got there, Abu
Fahl? Show us.

Abu Fahl, swaggering across the courtyard, tried to wipe his
grin away and assume innocence: Nothing, nothing at all – *wala
haja*.

Come on, Abu Fahl, they sang out again. What is it? Potato
stuff? Arrack? Whisky? Anything good?

Nothing, really, nothing at all, Abu Fahl said, demurely
smoothing over the bulge under his arm. He glanced quickly
around the courtyard and at the house: Where's Hajj Fahmy?

Everyone laughed – sympathetically, for they would have
been nervous, too, in his place. No drop of liquor had ever
passed between Hajj Fahmy's lips, and were he to hear that a
bottle had entered his courtyard the man who had brought it
would almost certainly be expelled from his house for all time.
Don't worry, someone said, it's all right. He's inside, sleeping.
But hurry.

Abu Fahl, relieved, winked across the courtyard at Zaghloul

and began to back away from the others. A couple of them jumped indignantly to their feet, crying: What's the matter? Where're you going? Do you think you're going to drink it all by yourself?

Just one minute, Abu Fahl said, begging for patience with a gesture. I have to tell Zaghloul something. You'll get some, don't worry. There's plenty.

He edged back to the loom, with the others still watching suspiciously. Then, very swiftly, he turned, and with his back to them he pulled a green bottle out through the neck of his jallabeyya and slipped it to Zaghloul. Zaghloul tore the cap off and took one long gagging swallow, and then another, The liquor was white and raw, distilled from potatoes, and it burnt like red coals in his throat. The others jumped to their feet, all together, shouting protests. Abu Fahl spun round to face them, pushing the sleeves of his jallabeyya threateningly back. They hesitated for a moment. The bottle passed into Alu's hands and he gulped down a mouthful. Then Abu Fahl snatched it out of his hands and threw his head back, and the others surged across the courtyard.

But by the time they managed to pull the bottle away from him it was a third empty and Abu Fahl was weak with laughter: Fooled you, gang of asses.

And then, with the bottle drained, lit, and thrown away, everyone, as always, was complaining; it wasn't enough, what good was one bottle, and that, too, of this second-rate Goan stuff, what use? There was still an hour or more to kill before they left for the Star, and everyone was tired of talking about what they were going to buy afterwards, and they'd already told all the jokes about Japanese cassette recorders called No and Aiwah, so instead somebody got hold of one of Hajj Fahmy's transistors and found a station playing Warda. But nobody was in a mood to sit and listen quietly, for the potato liquor, which always proved stronger than it seemed, was bubbling pleasantly in their stomachs. Abu Fahl began clapping first, very loudly, with his palms cupped. Soon Zaghloul joined in. Then suddenly everyone else was clapping, too, and some were stamping their feet as well, sending up clouds of dust. The women of Hajj Fahmy's house, his wife, his daughters, his sons' wives and their daughters, came pouring out into the courtyard and stood around the doors, laughing behind their hands and their scarves – all except the Hajj's wife, who was too old to care whether she was seen laughing, black teeth and all, or not.

More people were arriving now, and they began clapping, too, and soon there was so much shouting and noise and laughter that no one could hear Warda any more. So Abu Fahl switched off the transistor and bellowed, Why're we all sitting when we can dance? – and even before he'd finished people were jumping to their feet.

Everyone gathered in the centre of the courtyard and formed a ring. Someone handed Zaghloul a spoon and a disht, a huge circular steel wash-basin. He stood at the edge of the ring with the disht leaning against his knee and began to beat out a ringing, ear-splitting, one, two, three, four, five, six rhythm with the spoon.

Go on, Abu Fahl, the crowd shouted, go on – you're in the middle.

Abu Fahl looked around him as though he was waking from a trance, and saw that it was he who the ring had formed around, that he was alone in its centre, and at once his grin was struck away by shock and he tried to break his way out, pleading: No, I can't – you know I can't. But the ring held firm and pushed him back into the centre: Dance now; let's see what you can do. So Zaghloul took pity on him and began a quick, pugnacious chant, for he knew the best Abu Fahl could do when he tried to dance was mimic a fight. *Khadnáhá min wasat ad-dár*, he chanted; we took her from her father's house. *Wa abúhá gá'id za'alán*, the crowd shouted back; while her father sat there bereft. Then Zaghloul again – *Khadnáhá bis-saif il-mádi*; we took her with our sharpest sword. And the refrain, *Wa abúhá makánsh rádi*; because her father wouldn't consent.

But still, despite Zaghloul, it was pitiful, though funny, for no song could have made a dancer of Abu Fahl. He tried hard, but his shoulders were too broad, his legs too heavily muscular, his waist so knotted that when he moved his hips his whole torso twitched as though he were in a fever. The second chanted refrain dissolved into laughter, and Abu Fahl sank gratefully back into the ring, mopping his dripping purple face and smiling sheepishly.

Then it was Zaghloul's turn. Zaghloul was a real dancer: slim and lithe as a cat. He undid the grey scarf that he usually kept knotted around his skullcap and tied it tightly around his waist. Someone was beating a difficult rhythm on the disht now, slowly to begin with. The first line of a song rang through the courtyard – *dalla' ya'árís, ya abu lása nylo* – and everyone roared their approval, for what better song could there be to sing for Zaghloul with his youth and his fine, bright face than one which told of the joys of bridegrooms?

Zaghloul began slowly, by turning in the centre of the ring with short, quick steps, his arms raised high above his head. Then gradually the pace of the beat increased, and in perfect time Zaghloul's hips began to move with it. The crowd closed in intently around him, the shuffling of so many feet raising a cloud of dust which hung above the ring, encircling him in a golden halo. The claps came in sharp, quick bursts now, as the whole ring threw itself into his dance. In response, the jerking, twitching movement of Zaghloul's hips quickened, too, and in exact counterpoint, as his hips moved faster and faster, the upper part of his body became more and more rigid and still, the tense fixity of his torso framing the driving energy of his waist. The disht was ringing deafeningly now, the beats spinning out in a throbbing, vibrant tattoo. And Zaghloul danced still faster, his face perfectly, stonily grave, his arms flexed above him, his torso motionless, his waist pulsating, hammering, in a movement both absolutely erotic and absolutely abstract, both love-making and geometry; faster still, the claps driving him on, and still faster, until with a final explosive ring of the disht the chant died and he collapsed laughing on the ground.

Somewhere the women were ululating as though it were a real wedding building towards its climax.

. Then someone spotted Rakesh, sitting by himself in a corner of the courtyard, and a shout went up – Rakesh now! – and he was hauled towards the ring, screaming protests. But Abu Fahl saw that he was close to tears because his carefully ironed terry-cotton trousers were being dragged through the dust, so he wrenched him free and sent him back to his corner with a slap on the back. Instead Hajj Fahmy's wife pushed her way into the ring and, without feigning a modesty she was too old to feel, she did an odd little dance mimicking Zaghloul. She ended by tweaking his cheeks and kissing her fingers. In the midst of the laughter and the cheers a thought struck Abu Fahl, and he exclaimed: Where's Isma'il? He's the one who loves to dance!

None of the men around him had seen Isma'il, so he asked one of Hajj Fahmy's grand-daughters: Hey, you, girl, where's your uncle Isma'il?

Covering her face shyly with her sleeve, the girl murmured: He's inside.

Inside? Why?

He's sitting on his bed. He won't get off.

In bed! Abu Fahl exclaimed in surprise. *Ya nahar abyad!* Why in bed?

He's like that sometimes, the girl shrugged and turned away, embarrassed for her uncle.

Abu Fahl ran into the house, and found Isma'il sitting perched on a high bed in his mother's room. Hajj Fahmy was sitting at the other end of the bed. They were watching a wrestling match on television.

What's the matter, *ya* Isma'il? Abu Fahl cried in surprise, putting out his hand. What're you doing sitting here, when we're all outside?

Smiling cheerfully, Isma'il shook his hand without stirring from the bed. I'm watching television, he said.

Tell Isma'il to come out, we're all waiting for him, Abu Fahl said, extending his hand to Hajj Fahmy. And what about you, *ya* Hajj? Why haven't you come out yet?

Hajj Fahmy smiled: There's too much noise outside, and Isma'il doesn't want to go. I'll come a little later. His eyes narrowed and he sniffed suspiciously: What have you been drinking?

Abu Fahl leapt back. Nothing, nothing at all, he said, trying to smile.

I hope so, said Hajj Fahmy, turning grimly back to the television set.

Come on, Isma'il, Abu Fahl exhorted. You can't sit here all day. Come out. Aren't you coming to the Star with us?

No. Isma'il shook his head. I can't.

Allah! Why not?

The germs are out today. They're all around the bed. I can't get off.

Abu Fahl's mouth fell open: Germs around the bed!

Yes, said Isma'il. All the germs are out today. They're all over the floor. Can't you see?

Abu Fahl looked significantly at Hajj Fahmy, but the Hajj was intent on the television programme. Isma'il, Abu Fahl said, gently reasoning, there's nothing on the floor, absolutely nothing. Can't you see? I'm standing here. There's nothing.

They're all over the floor, Isma'il said stubbornly. They're just waiting to bite. I'm not getting off. It doesn't matter to you – your hide's too thick – they'd break their teeth. I'm not like that.

Ya Hajj Fahmy, Abu Fahl appealed, why don't you tell him?

Let him be, the Hajj said. Let him sit here if he wants to. How does it matter?

But what about you, then? Abu Fahl said. Aren't you coming? To the Star and shopping and all that? Everyone's here.

I'll come as soon as the noise stops, Hajj Fahmy said. He looked at his watch. You'd better go out and tell them to hurry up. It'll be time to leave soon.

Be careful, Isma'il called out, gurgling with laughter, as Abu Fahl turned to go. They're everywhere today; even with your hide you should be careful. They might get you in a soft part.

The first person Abu Fahl saw as he stepped back into the courtyard was Professor Samuel. He was sitting on the platform, beside the loom. His briefcase was open on his knees, and he was worriedly counting through a pile of thick white envelopes. Abu Fahl went straight up to him and gave him a bone-jarring slap on the back. At least you're here, he said. And now since you're here we have to see you dance.

Stop that! the Professor snorted, furious. Can't you see I'm busy? I have things to do. I have to count the people here. I have to distribute the envelopes, all the arrangements have to be made. . . .

You're always busy, Professor, Abu Fahl said. But today we're going to see you dance.

Be quiet, Abu Fahl, the Professor said sharply. Go and do

some work instead of wasting my time. Have you handed out your tools and ropes and all that yet?

But Abu Fahl only turned and shouted to the others: Come here. The Professor's going to dance for us. Help me carry him.

A moment later the Professor was hoisted on half a dozen shoulders and carried, kicking and scolding, into the court-yard. They put him down in the middle and imprisoned him in a tight circle. Go on, Professor, dance a little, Zaghloul said, tapping the disht. Just for fun.

But I can't, he cried. I've never done it before.

Go on, go on, just for fun, they urged, and even Chunni joined her voice to theirs: Go on, Samuel, what does it matter? Do anything at all; anything you can.

The Professor looked grimly around him. All right, he said. He kicked off his sandals and, leaping high, he snapped his right arm back, clenched his fist and swung it through the air. He jumped up again, and the first enthusiastic claps wavered and then faded away as everyone looked on in astonishment. He was leaping around the ring now, spinning in the air, flailing his right arm over his head. Zaghloul tried to find the right rhythm on the disht and gave up baffled. The Professor jumped again, faster, and yet again, his face flushed, sweat flying off his forehead. The initial laughter died away and an awestruck silence descended as the Professor flung himself into the air, again and again, swinging his rigid arms over his head in great powerful arcs.

What *is* he doing? someone said. That's how they dance in those parts, a voice answered. Haven't you seen them in films?

Chunni was beside herself. It's the queues, she shrieked. Stop him, Abu Fahl; something's gone wrong. He can't stop; the queues have got him again. But instead everyone backed apprehensively away from the leaping, whirling Professor.

At last the Professor stopped, winded, and looked around, clutching his waist, at the circle of wide eyes and frozen faces. What's wrong, Samuel? Chunni asked anxiously. He looked at her for a moment, so sternly that she edged away. Then he doubled up, laughing uncontrollably, and his spectacles drop-ped off his nose.

What's the matter, Professor? What's happened?

Professor Samuel, holding his sides, face flushed, tears

pouring out of his eyes, managed to say: Nothing. I was just practising my badminton smashes. Nice cabaret, no?

After that it was all confusion, for it was almost time to leave. Everyone was worrying about what they were going to buy now, and they milled around the courtyard, the newly arrived begging advice from the experienced, gathering information on the relative prices of the various makes of calculator they were thinking of buying for college-going brothers at home; of the portable television sets they were planning to take to their village-bound parents and sisters; and of the clothes they were going to buy for themselves (and there Rakesh was in great demand, for there was not a thing he didn't know about all the brands of American jeans and Korean shirts). There was a mild panic when someone claimed to have heard that Professor Samuel hadn't brought enough money for them all, and the Professor was immediately riddled by volleys of anxious questions. But he had no answers to give, because, as he said: How can I know whether I've got enough? First, I've got to count how many people there are here, and how can I count unless you stand still? That only made the panic worse – He admits he hasn't got enough; that's what he said – and everybody milled about even more, and that made counting still more difficult. Then, in the middle of all that, Hajj Fahmy appeared and shouted that it was time to tie on the dusters and get ready to leave, because sunset was no more than an hour away, and there would be no point in going if they got to the Star after dark. That reminded the Professor of something else altogether and he forgot about counting and pushed his way around the courtyard until he found Abu Fahl and cried, worriedly: Listen, Abu Fahl, what are we going to do if we do find those sewing machines in the Star? How will we bring them back? We can't carry them with us into all those foreign shops in Hurreyya. What are we going to do? But Abu Fahl had his own worries now, for he was busy trying to find all the ropes and crowbars and everything else he had gathered together over the last few days in preparation for their journey to the Star, so he merely shrugged and said: How should I know? Why don't you ask Alu? We only promised to present him with the sewing machines. He'll have to think of some way of bringing them back himself. But that wasn't good enough for the Professor, and he rushed off, clicking his tongue in irritation, to look for Hajj Fahmy. The Hajj tried to reassure him: Don't worry, Samuel, it won't be difficult – we can always put them in a taxi if it comes to that. But, said the Professor, there aren't any taxis in that part of the Corniche. And this time the Hajj pushed him away: Don't worry – we'll manage.

There was nothing more he could do, so the Professor went back to his counting, and while he was at it Karthamma ran into the courtyard, sweating and wild-eyed. I can't find Boss, she cried to anyone who would listen. I just went to the house and there was no one there. Zindi's cleared all her things out, and Kulfi's gone, too, and there's no sign of Boss anywhere. But there was too much noise in the courtyard, and everyone had something to do, so nobody had time to listen to her. Frantic with worry, Karthamma found Chunni and, shouting into her ear, told her everything; but Chunni only laughed, saying: Why're you so worried? Where could they have gone? They'll be in the house when we get back this evening, you'll see. Where could they go? There's nothing to be worried about. That heartened Karthamma, for there is nothing so reassuring as having one's fears laughed at, and she went back to thinking about the pram she was going to buy for Boss.

A little later the Professor finally finished counting and discovered that there were fewer people in the courtyard than he had expected – only thirty-two, where he had allowed for forty-five – so there was plenty of money for everyone. He tried to spread the good news, but his voice was too weak, and by that time people had forgotten about him anyway, so he had to ask Abu Fahl instead. But it was some time before even Abu Fahl could make himself heard, and when he did it only made matters worse in a way, for there was a great cheer and people began streaming out of the courtyard, and Abu Fahl had to run out and bring them back, because he hadn't distributed the tools yet. There weren't very many – a few crowbars, a couple of saws, some coils of rope and a pulley, a few shovels, pickaxes, an ancient car-jack, and three powerful torches – but because of the confusion it took a long time to hand them out.

At last, when all the tools had been given out and everything was more or less ready, Abu Fahl remembered Alu and saw him sitting at the loom with his head in his hands. It made Abu Fahl angry to see him sitting there like that. Come down here, Alu, he shouted, we're going now. But Alu hesitated, and sensing his reluctance Abu Fahl went up to the platform and pulled him off it. What do you think? he said, thrusting a coil of rope into his hands. Do you think you're going to sit there like that all day while we do all the work and fetch you your sewing machine?

The others were already straggling out, led by Hajj Fahmy and Professor Samuel. Abu Fahl waited with Alu and Zaghloul till everyone was gone. Then, after making sure that no one was left in the courtyard except the women of Hajj Fahmy's house, they set off through the lanes of the Ras. By the time they reached the top of the embankment the sun had dipped low over the city, and the others were strung out over the road ahead of them. They could see Rakesh, Karthamma and Chunni a long way ahead of them. They stopped for a moment to catch their breath, and when they started walking again Abu Fahl clapped Alu on the shoulder. So, he said, at last you're going to get your sewing machine.

Chapter Nineteen

Sand

The sleek black road on the embankment ran through a kilometre or so of empty sandflats after leaving the Ras behind. Then gradually it sloped downwards till the road was on level ground. A little farther on, stray mud-brick houses appeared on either side. With every step after that the houses crowded closer and closer to the road. Soon the road merged into a narrower and much older thoroughfare which ran along the inlet. From that point onwards the road became a thronged, bustling hive. Fifty or even a hundred men, no matter what they were carrying, could have vanished into that crowded street with all the ease of pigeons in a piazza.

On one side of the road, jostling for space, were tiled Iranian chelo-kebab shops, Malayali dosa stalls, long, narrow Lebanese restaurants, fruit-juice stalls run by Egyptians from the Sa'id, Yemeni cafés with aprons of brass-studded tables spread out on the pavement, vendors frying ta'ameyya on push-carts – as though half the world's haunts had been painted in miniature along the side of a single street.

The other side of the road was comparatively less crowded, for it looked out over the inlet and no shops or stalls were allowed there. That was where the people of the Old City came with their friends and brides in the evenings, to walk and eat and watch the brilliant sails of the sambuqs and booms in the inlet.

The other bank of the inlet rose steeply out of the water into a solid concrete-and-glass cliff of hotels and offices.

The road became even narrower and still more crowded farther on when it reached the wooden jetties and rickety wharfs of the old harbour. There, the pungent muddy waters of the inlet were only a step away from the road, and in places the pointed lateen sails of the sambuqs sometimes seemed to be poised directly above the pavement.

It was there, in a little room above a café, that Jeevanbhai Patel had had his office.

Soon after that the road wound around the inlet, through a huddle of houses and away, straight into the sands beyond, towards the broad sweep of a curving headland in the distance. At that point the road broadened and blackened and became the Corniche.

A short way after the last cluster of houses, the Corniche began to rise gradually, and by the time the sea first became visible on the left, a kilometre or so away, it was a good height above the sand on the seaward side, and still rising. In contrast, on the other side of the road, to the right, the ground fell away only slightly. All along that side of the Corniche the viscera of newly begun high-rise buildings lay scattered in a long, skeletal trail. Soon an outward curve took the road even closer to the sea, and there it rose still higher, till it was about ten feet above the sandy beach on the far side. At its outermost point the road was so close to the sea that its surface was usually moist with spray. At that point there stood a huge, almost-finished airline office. The office had been built to take advantage of the view, and one part of it jutted out almost into the road. There the road turned, angling sharply around the building, so that approaching the building from one end the other side of the curve was blocked out of view. After that the Corniche ran inland for a stretch before curling out again to meet the Star.

When Zindi first spotted the airline office, Hajj Fahmy, Professor Samuel and a knot of people immediately behind them were very close to the building and walking fast. The rest were strung out behind in an untidy dribble, their dusters bright against the indistinct greyness of the twilight. Sometimes, when the road curved, she could see silhouettes; the outlines of crowbars and axes on bent shoulders clearly etched against the sand and the evening sky.

Abu Fahl, Zaghloul and Alu, still bringing up the rear, were only a hundred paces or so ahead of her. That was a stroke of luck for her, for she could not have planned that. Otherwise it had all happened exactly as she had hoped. She had waited in the harbour with Kulfi and Boss, hidden in the little launch that was to carry them to *Zeynab*. She had spotted Hajj Fahmy and

Professor Samuel easily enough despite the crowds, for the dusters on their arms stood out like bright lights. She had waited till they had gone past, all of them, and then, at a careful distance, she had hurried after them to salvage what she could of her fallen house.

It had been a long walk and she was tired now. Her feet ached and the tension of expecting something to happen at every turn had worn her patience away. But nothing had happened. Maybe it was she who was wrong after all, and Hajj Fahmy right. She stopped to wipe her face. She could see the shadowy figures of Hajj Fahmy and Professor Samuel in the distance, very close to the airline office and the blind curve. She shut her eyes and turned to the sea breeze and let it play over her face. She pulled the neck of her dress up with her finger and gratefully felt the coolness of the breeze on her chest.

And while she stood there, with her eyes shut and the wind licking gently at her body, she knew suddenly that it had happened, for she heard something like a shout, and by the time she had turned a whirling cloud of sand had blotted Hajj Fahmy and Professor Samuel from her view.

As she watched, a helicopter rose into the greyness behind the building and swooped down on the road. She had seen it before that evening, twice. It had flown overhead and away, in the other direction. She hadn't given it much thought: rich young Ghaziris were always buzzing the roads in their planes and helicopters. But this time it was coming in very low, sweeping the road slowly. And now it was above her, a high staccato drumming noise, buffeting her with axe-like strokes, pulling at her clothes. Around her the sand was rising in solid walls from both sides of the road to meet it. As it passed above, only a few feet from her head, she saw a pointing arm, the barrel of a gun and a black uniform.

She knew then that this was no young Ghaziri on a joyride, but a part of the machine that she had known to be lying in wait.

It was all sand now, everywhere, like the desert in a Khamsin, wrapping her in layers, sifting into her mouth and into her eyes. She was caught in a sandy fog, hardly able to see the road beneath her feet. She could hear screams in the distance, and odd muffled popping sounds. Then she heard the helicopter again, and in terror she ran blindly along the edge of the road. She heard it swooping low over her and she threw herself over the side and rolled to the bottom of the embankment. As she rose unsteadily to her feet again, she felt an odd stickiness on her eyelids. She drew a hand across her face and it came away covered in blood. She screamed, but the sound was lost, for there were shouts and screams everywhere now, shrilling eerily out of the gritty, golden cloud. Faintly she caught a whiff of tear gas.

Sobbing with fear, she pulled the scarf off her head and wrapped it over her face, covering her nose and leaving only a slit for her eyes. She tried to run but fell and struck her head against the embankment. She struggled up and tried to run again, in the other direction, but she could see no more than a few feet ahead; and suddenly, horror-struck, she realized that she was running *towards* the screams. She stopped in utter, terrified confusion, and then somewhere close by she heard a shout. She looked up and saw two figures tumble off the road and come rolling down towards her, screaming. A moment later another figure came crashing down after them.

When he was almost upon her, she recognized Abu Fahl. He collapsed in a heap hardly a foot away from her and lay there whimpering in shock, blood pouring from a gash in his head. A little way behind him lay Alu and Zaghloul, clinging to the sand in blank terror.

Suddenly Zindi's head was clear again. She pulled Abu Fahl's arm and shouted – Get up, get up – but he lay as he was, inert on the sand. She shook him and then drew her hand back and slapped him hard across his face. His head snapped back, and then slowly recognition filtered into his eyes. She pulled him to his feet and screamed into his ear: What about the others, all the rest, Samuel, Karthamma, Chunni, Hajj Fahmy?

He could only shake his head stupidly. She turned him round and pushed him towards Zaghloul and Alu. Take them with you, she shouted, pointing towards the inlet, and run in that direction. Hurry, we can still get away; they haven't seen us yet and there aren't any of them on this side of the embankment. They were all on the other side so that we wouldn't see the ambush.

She pushed him again – Run – but he clung helplessly to her arm: And you?

I'm coming, she said. But, first, I've got to see if there are any others. She gave him a shove, and this time he stumbled away; and, pulling up her skirts, she scrambled up the side of the embankment.

The tear gas clawed at her nose and eyes as soon as her head was level with the road. For a moment she was blinded. Then, very hazily, through a golden-grey glow, she saw a line of helmeted black-uniforms with riot-shields and batons, charging the milling crowd on the road. She saw Hajj Fahmy prone, screaming under a baton; she saw Professor Samuel and Rakesh being dragged off the road by their feet, and then she couldn't see any more for her eyes were smarting like a salted wound. Blindly she pushed herself back towards the edge of the embankment, and just as she was about to slip down again she heard a familiar shriek across the road.

She fought her eyes open, scraping at them with her nails, and darted across. It was Chunni, kneeling on the ground, tearing at her hair and screaming hysterically, as though she wanted to rip her lungs apart. Zindi crouched low and clutched at Chunni's hand. She caught a bleary glimpse of Karthamma lying beside Chunni and she snatched at her hand, too, and pulled, crying: Come on, quick. But Chunni slapped her hand away, and before Zindi could stop her she had struggled to her feet and wandered off, screaming, straight towards the black-uniforms. Then Karthamma's head rolled limply to one side and Zindi screamed, too, for she saw that Karthamma was dead; that she had fallen on a pickaxe, and that the end of the axe had passed through her back and emerged bloodily from her navel.

Heaving the body away, Zindi turned and threw herself across the road and down the embankment. She rolled to the bottom, her skirts ripped to shreds and splashed with blood. When she managed to push herself up again, she saw three figures, nothing more than shadows, vanishing into the haze. She ran after them and caught up; and together, shielded by the darkness, they hurried towards the inlet and the waiting motor-launch.

And, though she was weeping herself, she comforted them

and helped them and she put her arms around their shoulders and held them up, for they stumbled often on that torn beach: it was not long since that the black-uniforms had driven their jeeps across the same sand, leaving it furrowed and sown with salt.

Part Three

TAMAS: DEATH

Chapter Twenty

Playing to a Beat

And so it happened one day that Dr Uma Verma came upon an odd little group in a roadside café while she was walking down the sand-blown, dusty length of the Avenue Mohamed Khemisti in the little town of El Oued on the north-eastern edge of the Algerian Sahara.

She was on her way to visit a Berber patient of hers, an elderly Acheche woman who had promised her half a dozen eggs from her own chickens. She was walking very briskly; not because she was in a hurry – her patient had assured her, smiling till the tattoos on her face disappeared into her wrinkles, that there would *always* be eggs in her house for the 'Indian doctor' – but partly because that was how she always did everything. That was one of the first lessons her father had taught her. Often, before he set off for school in the morning, the old man would say to her: If you're going to do anything, do it as though you meant to finish it, and finish it well besides. That's what went wrong with this country – nobody ever thought anything worth finishing. Look at those Rajput kings and all those Mughals who sat around in Delhi and *began* things – just began. . . . She could see him now, old Hem Narain Mathur, *masterji*, his bespectacled eyes bright in the gaunt hollow of his face, smiling, sucking his teeth, standing as though for a photograph beside the most treasured of his few possessions, his first bookcase – a few old nailed-together planks of wood which he had clung to somehow through all his years of wandering – three shelves which held all the most beloved books of his college years, the very bookcase which now haunted a corner of her drawing-room in El Oued like some patient, dusty ghost waiting for who knew what? And she could see herself watching him, stiff and starched in her school uniform and oiled braid, hurrying him out of the house – It's time to go now, Ba – out into the almost-Himalayan cool of the Dehra Dun morning; walking hand-in-hand through their gullie, past the Clock Tower, listening to his frayed old cotton shirt and white trousers swishing briskly beside her, trying to keep up with him and wondering why it was that he who walked so briskly and talked so often of finishing – not just beginning – had never finished anything himself.

But there he was, in front of his bookcase again, smiling. She could see his smile clearer than ever now; and today, with the smell of failure already bitter in her nostrils, it stung, for she could see that it was at her that he was smiling, even though his smile was not mocking but melancholy.

And so, with her worries gnawing at her mind anew, Mrs Verma quickened her pace.

Just before leaving her house she had spoken to an acquaintance of hers, an Indian doctor in the hospital in Ghardaia, far to the south-west, deep in the Sahara. He or, rather, his wife was more or less her last hope. All her other Indian acquaintances in various hospitals in Algeria had said no, some rudely, some nicely. The young doctor's was the last name on her list, and now he had said no, too. She couldn't really blame him, for Ghardaia was a long way away and in any case she had got such a bad connection that he had barely understood what she was trying to say. At the end of her long explanation he had shouted: You want a young Indian woman? Why? She had begun to explain all over again, but the phone was crackling wildly, and she couldn't even begin to imagine what he heard, for suddenly he shouted, very angrily: No, we don't have a maidservant, and if you want one you should go back to India, Mrs Verma, instead of asking for my wife.

Then he had slammed the phone down.

So now, despite that unbelievable stroke of luck three days ago, she was back exactly where she had started. It looked as though it was all over.

Mrs Verma pulled the anchal of her sari tight over her head and walked straight on. She was always careful to keep her head covered when she went out into the streets of El Oued; it seemed appropriately modest somehow in that land of cavern-ous hoods.

But she was still conspicuous as she walked down the Avenue, not only because so many of her own and her husband's patients greeted her with deep bows and their hands on their hearts, but also because her sari was brilliantly orange. Otherwise there was nothing at all remarkable about a short, pleasantly plump, honey-complexioned woman in her mid-thirties striding briskly down a dusty avenue in a small town. If there was anything to distinguish her from the thousands of other similar women who were probably doing the same thing in thousands of other small towns around the world, it was something which had no connection with her at all. It was the stark lunar majesty of the immense golden sand-dunes which towered above the avenue.

And so Mrs Verma hurried on down the Avenue Mohamed Khemisti, as strikingly visible as a newly flowered anemone on a beach, walking even faster now, for there was her father again, stooping over his bookcase, smiling, saying in his firm, gentle way: Stop worrying about it; it won't work. It's pointless. Can't you see – the issue is *political*? Haven't I told you? It's the very same mistake that the Rationalists made.

*

Kulfi, who was sitting next to the window, saw her first. Alu, opposite her, was staring down into a glass of thick mint tea; and Zindi, sitting between them, was testing Boss's forehead with the back of her hand, trying to decide whether he was running a temperature or not.

Kulfi spotted the orange sari when Mrs Verma was still a long way down the street. Very slowly, as though she were afraid to trust her eyes, her thin, tired face froze, and then suddenly she shot upright on her hard steel chair and struck the tin table-top with her fists.

Zindi looked up at that, and when she saw Kulfi sitting deathly rigid in her chair, gripping the edges of the table, her eyes feverishly bright, a great tide of weariness washed over her. She knew the symptoms; she could hardly not. In those two months she had watched the onset of Kulfi's attacks of chest pains more than a dozen times. She had always done what she could to help her; but this time, with Boss already ill, in an unknown town in the middle of the desert, with nowhere to spend the day but the sand-dunes, an almost irresistible longing to let go gripped her – a yearning to give up, like them.

But instead she leant forward, saying instinctively: Kulfi, do you want to lie down?

In answer Kulfi turned, eyes glittering, and her arm went up and pointed rigidly out of the window.

Then Zindi saw her, too: a short woman in a bright orange sari, with a comfortable, homely face and a prominent upper lip, walking briskly down the street, smiling and nodding at people as she passed them by.

The men at the other tables, who had watched the two women enter the café with frowning disapproval, were staring at them now. Zindi, suddenly self-conscious, pulled Kulfi's pointing hand down and growled: Be still, Kulfi – people are watching. Let me think. Kulfi pulled her arm free, sprang to her feet and stood poised above the table like a bird about to take flight. Zindi reached out again and this time she took hold of her sari and pulled her down hard. Kulfi crashed down on the chair with a gasp. What're you doing? she snapped. Can't you see? She could help us.

Wait, I have to think, Zindi began, but her voice died in her throat and then she forgot Kulfi altogether as the days-old knots of fear in her stomach uncoiled and something seemed to shoot up her spine in a warm jet, bathing her in a blessed shower of relief. Her cradled arms lifted Boss's head to her cheek and, kissing him, she whispered: Allah! You're saved now; saved in the middle of the desert. They're your countrymen; they'll have to do something for you.

Yes, said Kulfi, swaying on her chair, that's right. I knew something was going to happen today. I could feel it in my heart. I prayed to Bhagwan Sri Krishan this morning, and he told me. He said: Something's going to happen today. It won't go on like this any more.

Kulfi leant forward and squinted into the sunlight. She looks very respectable, she said anxiously. Good family. She smoothed her hair back, ran her fingers through the drapes of her sari and stood up, muttering to herself: What'll she think? Hair all in knots, no powder, nothing . . . in the middle of the desert.

Kulfi, wait, Zindi said quickly. You can't just go like that. What'll you tell her? She looks a proper babu's wife. She'll ask you all kinds of things, she's bound to: Who're you? What're you doing here? and all that.

So? said Kulfi. I'll tell her something.

Yes, Zindi said sharply, but what?

I could tell her something like – we got off the bus. . . .

No. Zindi shook her head. What you'll tell her is this. You'll tell her that you're tourists; that Boss is your son and that you and Alu are married.

What? Kulfi's lips curled thinly back. Married to *him*? she spat, her voice jagged with contempt. Married to that thumbless half-wit? It's no use, she won't believe it. Not when she sees him and his withered thumbs.

Alu's head dropped and involuntarily his hands hid themselves between his legs.

Zindi jabbed Kulfi's thigh with a forefinger. Listen, she said, you'll do exactly as I say or you can go on alone. You'll tell her that Alu is your husband. Never mind his thumbs; he can hide them in his pockets. You'll tell her that he works for an oil firm in al-Ghazira – she'll like that. Babus' wives like people who work for oil firms. Tell her I'm your ayah and you've brought me along to look after Boss. Tell her that you've come sightseeing; that we've arrived here by mistake and Boss has suddenly fallen ill, and that we need a place to spend a night or two. That should satisfy her.

She won't believe me, Kulfi said. She'll know I'm not married the moment she sees me. There's no sindur on my head and there aren't any bangles on my arms. She'll know at once.

Tell her something, tell her you've lost your things – anything, it doesn't matter.

Zindi snatched at Kulfi's arm as she started forward. And listen, she hissed. Not one word about the Bird-man following us. Do you understand?

Do you think I'm a fool? Kulfi glared at her.

The orange sari was passing the window now. Zindi gave Kulfi a push – Go on, tell her – and watched as she darted out of the door. Then she looked up. The stretched white sky seemed to be smiling at her at last, and she smiled back. But a moment

later she picked out a tiny speck, hovering like a mote in the
sunlight, far above, and gazed at it with gathering unease.

Soon her smile faded away, for she saw that it was a vulture.

*

Actually Mrs Verma saw them before Kulfi had reached the
door. She always glanced into that café when she passed it, for
she had once done a series of blood tests on the owner's wife
and ever after he had always come out to greet her when he saw
her walking by.

This time, looking in, she caught a glimpse of an unac-
customed shade of yellow somewhere in the dark interior.
Something unexpected, something vaguely familiar about the
drape of the cloth, lodged in her mind and drew her to a
puzzled halt. She looked again and now there could be no
doubt: it was a woman in a sari.

She started walking again, shaking her head. Miss Krishnaswamy the nurse perhaps; but, no, she'd asked her whether
she wanted to come, and Miss K. had said no, she had to stay
and cook lunch. And not Mrs Mishra, either; she was at home,
too – she'd seen her that morning, across the square.

And neither of them had saris of quite that shade, and in any
case they wouldn't be sitting in a café. Mrs Verma stopped
again and looked back in bafflement, not allowing herself to
believe that it could be true: it couldn't be; it would be too
heaven-sent; too much luck; no one was *that* lucky in this
world.

A moment later Kulfi came rushing out of the café and Mrs
Verma saw that it *was* true; that she was indeed a woman in a
sari, and quite young, too – exactly the right age in fact.

By the time Kulfi caught up with her Mrs Verma was so
elated, so consumed by surprise, that she heard barely a word
of Kulfi's babbled explanations.

The only occasions when other Indians had come to El Oued
in the two years Mrs Verma had spent there were when she and
her husband, or Dr Mishra and his wife, invited some of their
friends and acquaintances from the hospitals in Ouargla or
Ghardaia, or even Tamanrasset in the far south, to come up for
a holiday. Those visits needed months of advance planning;

supplies had to be hoarded, parties organized and leave applied for. Those were the only Indians, as far as she knew, who had ever come to El Oued.

Of course other foreigners, mainly tourists, passed through El Oued every year, in a trickle which varied slightly with the seasons, like the height of the water-table. They were French mainly, with a sprinkling of Germans and a handful of Italians. Sometimes they arrived by bus, with rucksacks on their backs and water-bottles which could have emptied lakes. Or else they came in specially equipped jeeps or vans bristling with compasses to help them find their way south to the Mzab and the Ahaggar – the Heart, they said, of the Sahara. They often turned up at the hospital with upset stomachs or sunburn and talked to her in halting English about the legends of Légionnaires and Mécharistes and the veiled men of the Tuareg; about their childhood dreams of the desert and the promise of dangers and hunger and hardship that had drawn them there. In her first year there she had listened in astonishment and protested, thinking of the lacquered roads and swift buses, the air-conditioned hotels and brimming swimming-pools, the pylons and oil-derricks she had always encountered on her journeys south. But soon, rather than spoil their holidays, she had decided to keep her silence.

Not that everyone merely passed through; many people came just to visit El Oued as well. And there was no doubt about it; it *was* an extraordinary place. At first, she'd taken it very much for granted. But once someone led her and her husband to the top of the minaret of Sidi Salem.

The sight had taken her breath away.

If you looked down on El Oued – the old town, that is – from the top of the minaret or the new tower in the Hôtel du Souf, what you saw was a fine carpet of thousands and thousands of small yellowish-white domes, ringed by a sea of gigantic golden dunes. The houses stretched into that golden horizon like banks of confectionery at a feast. Every house had not one but dozens of tiny domes, perched on walls which sloped away at bewildering angles. If you walked through the lanes of the old town, every few steps you had to stop and marvel at the brilliant blue borders on the limestone walls; at the little sand-roses encrusted on the houses; the lush, vivid green of the doors. And then, beyond that knotted carpet of domes were the date palms, vast basins of sunken, dusty date palms, only their fronds visible above the sand, doggedly fighting the marching dunes.

But she knew that when she left it would not be the domes or the palms or anything like that that she would see when she tried to remember how it had looked. It would be the dunes. Even now, after two years, whenever she looked at them she was beggared, humbled, all over again, just as she had been the very first time.

These were no ordinary dunes: they were the great towering crescents of the Grand Erg Oriental. When you saw them poised above you, stretching towards the horizon in gigantic scalloped arcs, you could only be silent; they were outside human imagination, a force of nature displaying itself in space, like a typhoon or earthquake rendered palpable and permanent.

There were lots of other things about El Oued – fine points of Saharan architecture and archaeology and anthropology. Erudite visitors temporarily humbled by diarrhoea or dysentery often told her about those things. She would listen to them and then send them on to Dr Mishra. He took an interest in that kind of thing.

As for herself, she preferred people.

Mrs Verma tried to listen as the thin, pale woman chattered excitedly on: . . . and, then, you know the firm gives him a holiday bonus, so we thought why not? Everyone else buys VCRs and TVs but we already have all those things and we thought, you know, we should see the world, too, especially since we have an ayah and everything. Of course, it was a problem, you know, our house there is so huge and I didn't know *who* to leave it with, servants are so unreliable nowadays, but if you think of all that you can *nev*-er do anything. . . .

But the one thought on Mrs Verma's mind was: Two years, *two years*, and not so much as a hint of an Indian tourist; and now, in the space of three short days, *just* when we need them. . . .

She saw old Hem Narain Mathur standing beside his bookcase, smiling, and this time she smiled triumphantly back.

*

Raising herself on tiptoe, Mrs Verma stole a look over Kulfi's shoulder and immediately fell back flat-footed. An indescribably vast woman swathed in some kind of immense black tent was bearing down on her, like a migrating Bedouin camp. She had a baby in her arms, and following close behind her, with his hands behind his back, was a man with a strangely distended head, and huge, staring, watchful eyes.

It occurred to Mrs Verma that this was the husband the pale woman had been talking about all this while. Her first reaction was of mild relief: as soon as she had heard about the husband some subterranean layer of her mind had busied itself with calculating whether this new factor would entail an even more dramatic revision of her casting than she had allowed for when she first saw the woman in the sari. But the moment she saw him she knew there was nothing to worry about: her first choice wasn't ideal perhaps, but certainly this husband of hers was no contender for the role of mythological hero.

It occurred to her that she had said almost nothing all this while. Scolding herself for her thoughtless selfishness, she reached out, took Kulfi's hand in her own and smiled. Kulfi broke off in mid-sentence, silenced by the sweetness of her smile. Mrs Verma said softly: I can't tell you how happy I am to see you. My name is Uma Verma, Dr Uma Verma. My husband and I work in the hospital here. He's in ENT and I'm a microbiologist.

She stopped, for Kulfi was brushing her hands across her eyes, and it didn't seem as though she had understood much. I do a bit of gynae, too, she added quickly, though it's not on the contract.

But that didn't appear to make much of an impression, either, so then she said simply: You're very, very welcome.

Next moment Zindi was upon her, her heavy-jowled face blazing hope. You're a doctor? she cried in her guttural Hindi. A real doctor? God be praised.

She thrust Boss into Mrs Verma's arms. What's happened to him, Doctor? she said, her voice honed sharp by days of unvoiced worry. What's happened to him, Doctor? Tell me what's happened to him.

Mrs Verma felt his forehead with the back of her hand. I'm not in paediatrics, she said apologetically, but I don't think it's

anything serious. Perhaps he has a little fever. Has he been like
this for long?

Ten days, Doctor, Zindi said. Ten whole days.

Ten days! Mrs Verma was shocked. She turned to Kulfi: Why
haven't you taken him to a doctor before this?

There wasn't any time, Doctor, Zindi cried, the words
pouring out of her in a wailing, unthinking wave. There just
wasn't any time. First, we were on the ship and we couldn't
take him to the doctor there, though I did give him a few
tablets. Then we had to get off at Tunis. I thought we'd find
a doctor there, and actually we were on our way but then
suddenly something happened and we had to rush off and
that made him worse. Then in Kairouan I thought I'd take
him, but we had to rush off again, and after that it was just a
mess and all we could think of was how to get to the
border. : . .

Kulfi managed to stop her by leaning sideways and giving
her elbow a discreet jog. It's all right now, she said, smiling
brightly at Mrs Verma. God has brought us to a doctor.

Mrs Verma ignored her. To me, she said, frowning, it sounds
rather as if you were running away from something.

For an unbearably long moment she examined their faces.

Zindi held her breath: the doctor looked as though she had
read something on their faces. How? Had the Bird-man's
talons marked them with the scars of the hunted?

Then Mrs Verma shrugged and said briskly: Anyway, he'll
be all right; I don't think it's anything serious. Probably just
needs a little rest and a tonic.

Yes, Doctor, Zindi said eagerly, that's what I thought – just a
little rest.

You can come and stay with us, of course, Mrs Verma said to
Kulfi, ignoring Zindi. We have plenty of room – though it may
be a little crowded now, with so many people. But you won't
have any trouble. We could go right now, but we'd better not
carry your little boy all the way in the heat. I'll ask Driss to let
you rest inside the café. Then I'll go on home and see if we can
get the hospital's land-rover to fetch you.

She made her way through the little crowd that had gathered
around them into the café and talked urgently to the proprietor
in her own argot of French and Arabic. When they followed her

in, she smiled: It's done. The proprietor found them a table next to a fan and went off to fetch a mattress for Boss.

I'd better go now, Mrs Verma said. Would you like to come with me Mrs . . . Mrs . . . ?

Bose. Mrs Bose.

Oh! exclaimed Mrs Verma in surprise. You're Bengali, too, then? You speak Hindi very well.

Kulfi let out a trill of high laughter. *He* is, she said. I'm from . . . from Jamshedpur. Then she paused, puzzled: What do you mean – Bengali, *too?*

Oh, we have another visitor in our house, Mrs Verma said, but never mind that. She turned to Alu: So you're Bengali?

He nodded.

I see, she said. Well, you might be able to help me a little.

How? said Alu nervously.

I'll explain later, she said. It's a small thing, a translation. A thought struck her, and she clutched at Kulfi's hand. I hope you can stay for a while? she asked anxiously. You're not in a hurry or anything, are you? You must stay at least a week. At the very least. I won't let you go before that.

Kulfi, surprised, said: Yes, we can stay a week, I'm sure.

Good, Mrs Verma said, patting her hand. Very good. She thought of what Dr Mishra would say when he heard and suddenly she was smiling radiantly, tasting for the first time the full flavour of the victory which now seemed within her grasp.

*   *   *   *

So, sighed Zindi, it looks as though we're safe from the Birdman at last.

There's only one way to be sure of that, said Alu.

What?

Don't ever say 'We're going west' again.

As quick as she could Zindi slapped her hand over his mouth. But it was already too late. You've said it, it's done now, she whispered, trembling, her eyes searching the corners and shadows of the café. They were empty to all appearances, but that meant nothing. It's done now, she whispered again. Now it's just a matter of time.

It was nothing less than a certainty; like a sorcerer's incantation those words could conjure a presence out of emptiness.

When she first said it she could not have imagined that words could leave a trail like an animal's spoor. Even if she had, there was nothing else she could have said then; there was no other direction they could have taken. For that was the day they reached her village and her brothers' wives barred their doors on her and shrieked till the roof of the very house she had built for them shook: The whore's back from al-Ghazira – Fatheyya, who's given herself some fancy whoring name. She's come to take our daughters for her brothel.

It was more a hamlet than a village – a little 'izba, near Damanhour, perched on the casuarina-lined banks of a canal – a few mud-walled dwellings and one big house: the house that Zindi's brothers had built with her Ghaziri dirhams. The way there was all dust and drying cotton fields and barking dogs, but when they arrived they were cheering – all five of them, Zindi, Abu Fahl, Zaghloul, Kulfi and Alu – screaming like children waiting at a circus. For this was no ordinary hamlet: it was the dream which had kept them alive while they dragged themselves across oceans, seas and half of Egypt; it was a promise of deliverance, of refuge, of a new life. They were cheering so loud when they drew up in their hired pick-up truck that it was a long while before they noticed the eerily empty lanes, the barred doors and the screeching chorus of voices.

When she heard those voices at last, Zindi looked around her at the mud walls of the lane, glowing treacherously in the morning sun, and she knew that if she were to live in that narrow pathway, jostled with hate on every side, she would not live to see another year.

It was all over then.

But she had a revenge of sorts. Abu Fahl battered down the door and they loaded their truck with furniture, jewellery, bales of newly harvested cotton – every movable object of value they could find. But those were paltry things; they could make no difference to a woman who had lost her nephews, nieces, land, even the magic of the name she had chosen for herself (who knew from where?). She was a different Zindi now, stripped, revealed as nothing but Fatheyya, plain old Fatheyya, Fatheyya *Umm*-nobody, mother of nothing, poor, simple, barren Fatheyya who was once abandoned in Alexandria by a child-hungry husband. Nothing she took with her could shut her ears to the cries of her brothers' wives, the roar which shook the dead cotton bushes in the fields and creaked in the canals with the kababis: Fatheyya the whore is gone at last, *shukr Illah!*

That was when, teeth gritted, eyes rolling, she said to the driver of the truck: We'll go west.

At first she had meant nothing farther away than Alexandria. She filled the first part of their bumpy ride with plans – she still had money left, and there would be more now with that truckful of goods. It could lead to anything – a new house, a shop, even a factory. But, at the crossroads near ad-Dilinjat, Abu Fahl and Zaghloul spotted the fine two-storey houses their fathers and Abusa's father had built with their Ghazira-earned money. They looked down the road at distant, difficult Alexandria, and then back again at their fields and the houses with their crenellated pigeon-towers; they saw their lands growing, brides smiling and children playing naked in the canals as they had done themselves. And then there was no holding them.

After that Zindi talked to the half-empty Datsun about her plans not because she believed in them any more, but because she could not bear the silence.

It happened that very evening in Alexandria. Zindi and Alu saw him while Kulfi was away buying a comb at a shop in Tahrir Square. He was standing on the Corniche, leaning on the parapet with his back to them, watching the gulls as they scavenged in the harbour.

Two days later they heard that an Indian was asking about a huge woman called Zindi and a potato-headed Indian. Zindi decided then that Alexandria wasn't safe. Next morning she dug out the passports she had had made for them in al-Ghazira and went off to a friend in Muharram Bey who dealt in currencies and visas, and she had them stamped for every country she could think of.

He asked: Where are you going, Zindi? And she answered: We're going west, where the sewing machines are.

It happened again. This time Alu saw him alone. Zindi had raced off to the harbour because the wind had brought news that Virat Singh, the great pehlwan of Bareilly, had turned sailor and arrived in Alexandria in a Greek freighter. So Alu, with Kulfi snarling at him, and nothing else to do, wandered off to the Mohattat ar-Raml; and there, just as he was about to cross the street to the tram station, the door of a Greek restaurant opened and the Bird-man stood opposite him, staring him in the face. He ran, managed to lose him, but only just, by barging through the crowds on Safia Zaghloul Street and doubling back down Nabi Danial.

Later he discovered that at that very moment Virat Singh had asked Zindi: And where are you going next? And Zindi had answered: Westwards.

But it turned out well, for it so happened that Virat Singh's ship was going west, too, to Lisbon. So naturally he decided to take them with him: balls to the captain.

So the ship it was and plain sailing, with the four of them safely hidden away below deck, until Alu asked: What after Lisbon, Zindi? Absent-mindedly (for she was tending to Kulfi, who had just had an attack of chest pains) she answered: Westwards still; where the sewing machine sets.

Sure enough, at dawn the next day, when the ship docked at Tunis, soon after Zindi first detected Boss's fever, Virat Singh came scrambling down to tell them that there was an Indian on the bridge, some kind of policeman, who was insisting that the ship be searched for stowaways.

With the help of a few friends and a little money Virat Singh smuggled them off the ship and through the port, to the vast football-field width of the Place d'Afrique. Where now, Zindi? he asked, before turning back.

Zindi covered her face and sobbed: Westwards, where else?

It broke his great pehlwan heart to see her like that. He put a huge corded arm around her shoulders and barked, tugging fiercely at his moustaches: I've got to go now, before they find me missing. But I'll be back. The ship will be in Tangier exactly three weeks from now, on its way to Port Said and Bombay. If you need help, meet me there.

Inevitably, that day they saw the Bird-man again. It happened while Zindi and Alu were wandering along the

Avenue de France trying to find a doctor for Boss. They shot across the Avenue with his claws almost digging into their shoulders. They managed to lose him in the maze of the Medina and later, somehow, they dragged themselves to the Souq al-Attarine where Kulfi was buying perfume. That was the end of Tunis for them. But there he was again at Kairouan. This time it was he who spotted them, Alu and Zindi, bargaining at a taxi-stand, and he chased them all along the city walls, shouting.

What was he shouting? Zindi asked Alu later.

Alu said: He was shouting – Come back, I only want to talk to you.

Yes, snorted Zindi, come back to be tear-gassed.

After that Zindi would hear of nothing, stop for nothing – fever, chest pains, anything short of death. But mysteriously, just then, chance began to play at puppetry with them; trains left moments before they arrived at the station, buses were full up, taxis had flat tyres. . . . And no sign of the Bird-man all that while. Where was he? Where was he waiting? Or had he flown away at last?

Never again, Zindi swore, would she say those words, those deadly, poisonous, son-of-a-bitch words. There was only one hope now: the border. The border it had to be; safety lay on the other side, in the vast welcoming emptiness of the Sahara.

So there they were, ten days after they left Virat Singh, sitting in a café in the desert. And now?

And now, said Zindi, you've said it again.

She looked up at the sky and a flash of hope sparked in her eyes. Perhaps, she said, we *are* safe after all. There aren't any birds in the desert.

But a moment later she saw the vulture again, circling patiently above.

*

As they walked down the Avenue, Kulfi was still wondering, with gnawing apprehension, what exactly Mrs Verma had meant when she remarked: It sounds rather as if you were running away from something. She couldn't help shooting a few quick sidelong glances at her.

Mrs Verma saw Kulfi looking at her and instinctively her hand rose to cover her protruding upper lip. She knew what her profile was like. She tried to think of something to say, but nothing occurred to her. It was always like that: since her girlhood she had never had the defences to cope with those particular looks.

It would have been different if her father had listened to her while she was still at school. There was still a chance then. She knew, because when she was twelve two girls in her class had had braces fitted by the Parsi dentist who had his clinic near the Odeon. Their cases were much worse than hers; their teeth fell like weighted curtains over their lower lips. But six months after they got their braces you could see the difference, and after a year you could hardly tell.

She talked about it to her father, all the time, hinting, hoping. He had prominent front teeth as well; she got hers from him. It gave her a right to hope that he would understand; after all, he had suffered the name Dantu through all his college years. Surely he had once felt something of what she went through every time the teacher told her to stop staring and cover her teeth, and the whole class exploded into laughter? It wasn't the money; she knew that. It didn't cost much; he could have raised the sum if he'd wanted. It was only a question of making him understand. He had always listened gravely and attentively to everything she had ever had to say. But when it came to this subject he never seemed to notice.

Actually, of course, he did notice; had noticed all the time. She discovered that when she couldn't bear it any more and said to him, weeping: Ba, if you don't take me to that dentist I'll die. I know it. Even if I don't die right now, no one will marry me so I'll die as soon as I grow up.

There was a strong practical streak in her even then, so she added: And think of all the trouble you'll have trying to find me a husband.

He took her into his lap then and dried her cheeks with the hem of his kurta. My love, he said, do you think I don't know what it's like?

Then, take me to that dentist, she sobbed.

I can't, he said helplessly. I can't – not for this. Don't you see:

it's not important. If it was to do with your health, we'd go this very minute. But this is just a thing of appearances.

But it's important to *me*. And it would be so easy.

No, my love; it wouldn't be easy at all. What do you change if you change your face? Those are things of the outside; if we wanted things like that, where would we stop – jewellery, cars, money, houses? That's not how I've lived, and that's not how I want you to live. As for marriage, if no one wants you, why, you'll be free. Anyway you're going to be a microbiologist, a scientist; you'll be too busy with your experiments to think about such things.

I *will* think about it, she cried. I think about it all the time – in school, walking down the road, everywhere. It's the only thing I think about.

Then, he said, that's the best reason for not doing anything about it. As you grow older, it'll matter less and less. You'll see. And the day it doesn't matter at all you'll know you're a woman at last.

She shrank back, frightened by the finality of his tone. Then, choking on her sobs, she pounded on his chest: It'll always matter; it'll always matter. How can you know? You don't have to live with it.

He caught her hands and kissed them. I'll show you, he said. He turned and pulled a book out of his old bookcase. I'll translate something for you. When I read it to you, you'll see that things like these don't matter.

She pushed herself angrily out of his lap and didn't talk to him for a week. A translation. What difference would a translation make to the laughter in her classroom?

But the old man had been right about one thing: almost imperceptibly every passing year dulled the wounding edge of those glances. Nowadays it took her only a few minutes to recover.

So, after a while, almost cheerfully, she said to Kulfi: It's a small town, isn't it? One day I'll take you to the top of a minaret and you can see it all spread out below you. Actually we've been here just two years ourselves. We're leaving soon. Our children won't let us stay away any longer. They're back home in Dehra Dun.

Oh, said Kulfi, glad to have the silence broken. So you've

come here with only your husband, then? I suppose there aren't any other Indians here?

Oh, no, Mrs Verma laughed. There are five of us. There's Miss Krishnaswamy – she's a nurse. Then there's Dr Mishra. He's the seniormost among us. He's a surgeon. He's very good; some people say he's brilliant. He looks it; you'll see when you meet him. Then there's his wife, but she's not a doctor. They're both from Lucknow.

It must have been lonely, Kulfi said thoughtfully, coming to a foreign place; having to work with people you didn't know. You know, in al-Ghazira, I must say, in the beginning, though there were all his colleagues in the firm, I really—

People I didn't know? Mrs Verma interrupted her. You mean Dr Mishra? Yes, I suppose it's true that we didn't know him, but it didn't feel like that. You see, I'd heard about him for years. My father knew his father quite well once upon a time, and he talked about them quite a lot. So in a way, when we first met him at the interviews in Delhi, it was like meeting someone we'd known for a long time. Besides, he talks a lot. . . .

Her voice trailed off. You'll see, she added lamely. You'll meet him this evening. I'll ask them over so that we can make arrangements for. . . .

She stopped and looked intently at Kulfi. Kulfi stopped beside her.

Tell me, Mrs Bose, she said, can you act?

*

Perhaps, Zindi said hesitantly, she could do something about your hands, too. After all, she's a doctor.

Alu jerked his head quickly from side to side and his hands slid behind his chair. Much later she saw him sitting with his hands in his lap, staring at his fingers. The thumbs had stiffened and the skin had sagged over the bones, like a shroud on a skeleton. He tried to move them and he couldn't. The bones were as rigid as a corpse's; she half-expected them to clatter, dice-like. Then Alu caught her looking at him, and at once his hands disappeared under him and he went back to staring vacantly ahead of him.

That was the only time she had referred to his thumbs. She

first saw them long after they had slipped past the frowning heights of Perim, through the Bab al-Mandab, into the Red Sea. They had already been at sea for – it seemed like months, with months left to go.

Somewhere on the journey, soon after *Zeynab* had swung through the Red Sea in a great arc and tacked close to the coast between Dhofar and Makalla, a very old man appeared in the ship. Nobody saw him arrive; he was just there one day. Nobody wondered, either, for there were boats enough drawing alongside *Zeynab* on that stretch of the coast, though always under the cover of darkness. He was a small man, with a gritty, hollowed-out face. He wore a string vest, a hat like in American movies, and khaki trousers many sizes too large for him (there were plenty of British soldiers in those parts, some dead). Nobody knew his name, for he couldn't talk. His tongue had been torn out from the roots; he would wag the stump for anyone who cared to look. Nobody needed to ask how it had happened: there were more wars than villages along those shores.

Fikry, the dark, towering nakhuda of *Zeynab*, was said to know all about him. But despite Zindi's efforts he never gave anything away, not even his name.

In the end the old man was named by the half-dozen boys of various ages who manned *Zeynab*. His one possession happened to be a Japanese umbrella, a thing of great mechanical beauty, which grew at the press of a button from a foot-long stump into a vast canopy, as shady as a banyan tree. It was dubbed, naturally, the Japanese Miracle, and it gave him his name: Abu Karamat il-Yabani.

He of the Japanese Miracle never lost his smile, all through the days after Makalla when they swung out again towards the open sea and their barrels of fresh water were found to be empty; nor even afterwards when they ran out of food somewhere in the Red Sea, along the Eritrean coast, and not one of the boats Fikry waited for in three different places turned up. Even then he kept smiling, though for everyone else it was nothing less than torture to have to watch the fires of the fishing villages on the coast and smell the delicious warmth of cow-dung smoke on empty stomachs.

Provisions reached them soon after, but then they had to suffer a torture of another kind. Fikry decided one evening that a coastguard or some other busybody had sniffed their trail. So with a few powerful bursts of her engines (rescued from a Centurion tank somewhere in Iraq) *Zeynab* lost herself in the basaltic maze of the Dahlak Archipelago. For the next few days they had to pick their way through hell. While two boys hung over the prow examining the colour of the water and shouting instructions to Fikry, at the wheel, they had to sit motionless as those tortured, jagged anvils of rock flung themselves at the boat's side; watch while the magnificent, muted colours of the coral reefs leapt up without warning to scrape *Zeynab*'s prow.

It was somewhere there that a tail of sharks attached itself to *Zeynab*. No one knew what drew them: perhaps it was the sight of those two boys hanging so close to the water. It couldn't have been the meagre remains of their rice-and-lentils meals.

No, said Fikry, they hang close because they like the smell of human shit. And, certainly, it was under the holes in the stern that they usually hung, jaws snapping, waiting for fresh turds.

All through those days the old man never once stopped smiling. He and Alu were drawn to each other by their silences, and soon they were spending the days sitting together on a little ledge near the stern, silently meditating under the banyan shade of the Japanese Miracle.

Things grew a little better after the Dahlak Archipelago. But their progress was still slow; for Fikry, in his keenness to stay safely away from the main shipping lanes, kept them close to the mangrove-encrusted shores where they had to pick their way through unpredictable sand-shoals. In the stretch between Trinkitat and Suakin they swung out towards the main shipping lanes again, to avoid Port Sudan, and somewhere there Fikry sniffed the air one morning and said: Big ships ahead – I can smell them. He laughed at the alarm his announcement caused: Nothing to worry about – these fish are too big to stop for shrimps like us.

Soon they saw it: like a city in the sea; so vast that it took a full half-hour to climb over the horizon, emerging gradually, in layers, until even at that distance it was like a marine skyscraper, dwarfing the little flotilla of destroyers in its wake. It grew vaster and vaster as it ploughed towards them. They could see planes on its flat deck now, and tiny men in uniform, and towers and turrets.

Those are guns, said Fikry, not these water-pistols we're selling.

They were all crowded along the sides of *Zeynab* now, watching in silent awe. As it drew closer its flat deck became part of the sky above them and they could only see the curving black steel of its side. Even its bow wave was higher than the tallest mast in *Zeynab*. When it was almost level with them Abu Fahl let out a great yell and Zaghloul tore off his scarf and waved it in the air. Next moment the tiny *Zeynab* erupted into shouts and whistles and cheers.

He of the Japanese Miracle was watching, too, but he had ducked down and was squinting over the railing, his face screwed small like an angry boy's. Then suddenly he leapt to his feet, gabbling incoherently in bellowing grunts and snorts, and waved the Japanese Miracle in the air. As the aircraft-carrier drew level with *Zeynab* his gabblings rose to a frenzy. Before anyone could stop him he threw one leg over the railing, swung his arms back and hurled the Japanese Miracle at the vast ship.

And just then, while his hands were still in the air and his leg was hanging precariously over the side, the aircraft-carrier's bow wave hit *Zeynab* and tossed her up. The old man tottered and clutched wildly at the rail. But the timber was wet, his hands slipped, and with a last terrified grunt he fell.

Even before he struck the water it had erupted with the thrashing of sharks' tails.

Alu was closest to him and he shouted: He's gone over. He whipped round and reached for a rope. But no sooner had he picked it up than it slid out of his hands. He tried again; and again, like water, the rope poured out of his hands. So he stood there frozen, staring at his hands in helpless horror.

Do something, Kulfi shrieked. Throw him the rope.

He looked up then, and said: I can't.

Instead it was Abu Fahl who ran there and flung a rope over the side. They could still see the old man, though the water around him was already frothing with blood. A shark rammed into him and dived but an instant later it was snapped in half by its own kin and its severed head floated grotesquely to the surface with a khaki-clad leg still clamped between its jaws.

The old man's head was still above water, his fear-crazed
eyes crying for help. Abu Fahl flung the rope out and the old
man lunged with the last reserves of his strength, but the rope
danced past his hands on a wave. Abu Fahl threw it out again
and this time it went straight to him. They saw his fingers
clawing, closing on the rope. Abu Fahl heaved and Zaghloul
caught hold of the rope, too, and they hauled it in together, as
quickly as they could. They saw his hands, his shoulders, his
head, rising safely from the water. Then two sharp fins scythed
through the water and afterwards, when the foam cleared, the
head, the torso and the shoulders were all gone but the hands
and arms and bloody, ragged stumps were still clinging to the
rope as though the old man had willed them all his dying
strength.

Abu Fahl and Zaghloul covered their faces and prayed.

Later Kulfi went up to Alu, and in front of the whole ship she
hissed: Why didn't *you* do anything?

In answer he held up his hands and they all saw that his
thumbs had gone rigid and the skin had begun to sag on them
like the fuzz on fallen apricots.

Kulfi spat on the deck, and held his hand up for everyone to
see. Look, she said, you're looking at the most useless thing in
the world – a weaver without thumbs.

She pulled his hand back and slapped his face with it. Hold
them up in front of you, she said. They'll remind you that you
can never *do* anything again. All you've got left now are your
eyes.

*

This is how it had happened.

Dr Mishra brought up the matter first, giving Mrs Verma an
initial tactical advantage.

Verma, he said, addressing himself to her thin faded
husband, as he always did when he wanted to say something
important to her. Do you have any ideas for this celebration
they're planning at the hospital?

Startled, Mrs Verma almost spilt the dal she was ladling into
Mrs Mishra's plate (for Mrs Mishra would have nothing to do
with the meat curry; vegetarianism was the only issue on which

she had ever dared to go against her husband's declared wishes).

Not that Mrs Verma was surprised: a couple of their Algerian colleagues had already dropped a few hints to her about a get-together. She had expected it, for at about the same time last year they had organized a small celebration to mark the second anniversary of their arrival in El Oued. Since they were to leave in a few months she had taken it for granted that they would do something of the same kind this year; on a larger scale, if anything. But she had taken great care not to mention the matter in Dr Mishra's hearing. She knew it was going to be a long battle, and she had no intention of hampering herself by choosing her ground first. And now Dr Mishra had conceded her the advantage.

Her husband, following his instructions, said nothing. Instead, Mrs Verma, choosing her words carefully, said: Well, Mishra-sahb, why don't you tell us what *you* have in mind?

She knew perfectly well of course: what he had in mind was a repeat of last year.

Last year all the doctors, nurses, and even a few patients, had gathered in a large room in the hospital. First, a couple of their Algerian colleagues had said a few nice things. Then Dr Mishra, with the help of an interpreter, had made a speech.

He began by talking matter-of-factly about how happy he and all the other Indian doctors were to have had this chance to live and work in Algeria for a while – and to earn plenty of money, he added in an undertone (that raised a laugh). He commented on the good sense of the Algerian government in compulsorily repatriating half their salaries to India in foreign exchange. It showed, he said, a genuine understanding of the needs of developing nations (tactfully he said nothing about how the French doctors in Algeria were paid much more than they were, simply for being French). But, then, he went on, it was only to be expected, for they had all seen for themselves how, almost alone among the oil-producing nations, Algeria had forsworn ostentation and concentrated on bettering the lot of the common people; how, in such marked contrast to some neighbouring countries he could name, in Algeria one sensed everywhere an energetic purposiveness, a belief in the future.

But it was only after that, when he began to talk about the

Algerian revolution, that he spoke with real emotion. He talked of how he had followed every event in the course of the revolutionary movement in the fifties and sixties; of his great admiration for Ben Bella (causing more than a little embarrassed foot-shuffling in the audience). With a softly confiding wonder that seemed very strange in a man usually so trenchantly cynical, he told them how moving it had been to work in a country that had literally risen from ashes; how it still staggered him to think that this very country had survived one of the most savage wars of this century; that it had lived through the whole wretched catalogue of technology-taught horrors – concentration camps, organized genocide and all the rest – that had been inflicted upon it by the French. It was nothing less, he said, than a testimony to the strength of the human spirit that a people who, of their meagre sixteen millions, had lost one whole million, had yet gone on to face the future without bitterness.

As a socialist, he ended, his voice breaking, it had filled him with pride to work in such a nation.

His emotion was very real. He had meant every word he said, and his audience was moved, despite the falterings of the translator. For months afterwards everybody they met talked about Dr Mishra's speech.

It was not that she objected to what he said, for of course it was all true. But, still, at the end of his speech she had had to stifle a laugh.

Maithili Sharan Mishra a socialist! Even while he was saying it, she had heard old Hem Narain Mathur's voice in her ear, telling her how bright young Murali Charan Mishra had come back to Lucknow in the thirties with a degree from the London School of Economics in his pocket, the Indian Masses on his lips, and a Scottish pipe in his mouth. That was the kind of socialist he was.

His son, too, for all Lucknow had known that young Maithili Sharan's one ambition was to follow his father into politics. Only, by then, old Murali Charan knew better, and even though his decades of fancy footwork in various legislatures had earned him more money than people could even begin to guess at he had ultimately forced his son into the safe certainties of the medical profession.

It was not that Mrs Verma was self-righteous politically; her
father had talked to her too often about the ugliness of socialist
in-fighting. But certainly, if anyone had a right to point his
finger at Murali Charan Mishra, it was old Hem Narain
Mathur. For he was a *real* socialist, as true as the new-
ploughed earth, and he had died in unsung obscurity while
Murali Charan Mishra was still fattening himself on minister-
ships. It was a debt which had to be paid some day.

In 1933, a few confused months after he left Presidency
College, Hem Narain Mathur gave up a fine job with a tea
company and plunged into Bihar's villages with Swami Saha-
janand and the reactivated Kisan Sabha movement. Often it
was a forlorn and lonely life: in the villages he battled vainly to
explain his theories, the glories of science, and his vision of the
future (which he only half-understood himself); and back at the
innumerable party conferences and congresses he battled no
less vainly to explain to Murali Charan Mishra and the party
theoreticians that people were not atoms to be dealt with in
formulae.

And while he was away, organizing that movement or this, at
some conference or the other, the party was always splitting
and splintering. At the centre of it all was Murali Charan
Mishra, his pipe hidden under his various man-of-the-people
disguises, reading out his evolving theses – first, on the
Uneven Development of the Economy; then on Progressive
Bourgeois Nationalism; and finally on the need for a Guiding
Hand at certain stages of history, and the absolute necessity for
an immediate tactical alliance with the classes and parties in
power.

And so, while Murali Charan Mishra climbed his way up the
political ladder on the rubble of the crumbling socialists, Hem
Narain Mathur grew old before his time, torn between
certainty and history. He wasted away with the obscurest of
diseases, bewilderment, as he watched the world spinning
beyond his grasp; as old comrades began to out-scoundrel
scoundrels once they had been given a whiff of power; as
fledgeling peasant unions withered inexplicably away or
simply vanished in puffs of smoke as the membership was
roasted alive by landlords. He had one final surge of energy in
the fifties when Ram Manohar Lohia kindled the last spark of

hope in the socialists. But by that time he was already too ill
and too tired to carry on long; all that he really longed for was
the solace of his bookcase, of J. C. Bose and Huxley, of
Tagore and Darwin, Hazlitt and *Science Today*, and of course
of that beacon which still lit those unsteady shelves – the *Life
of Pasteur*. His mind was made up for him when his wife died
suddenly of meningitis, leaving him with a daughter to bring
up on his own. It was then that he took a job in a small
government school in Dehra Dun. And there he lived out the
rest of his time – a tired old man who, as he said so often, had
only one worthwhile thing left to do. And that was to
introduce his two redeemers, his old bookcase and his
growing daughter, to each other.

But right till the very end he had stayed a socialist; never
once was he tempted by the simple-minded attractions of
cynicism. Lying on his deathbed with the spoonful of holy
water from the Ganges already at his lips, he had found the
strength to place his daughter's hand on his bookcase and say:
My love, make my failures the beginning of your hopes.

If anyone had a right to object when Murali Charan Mishra's
son called himself a socialist, it was her father's daughter.

* * * *

To tell you the truth, said Dr Mishra, I thought it went off quite
satisfactorily last year. He was a short, stout man in his early
fifties, with a round face and a bushy, unkempt moustache. His
head was shinily bald, except for a crop of curly hair which ran
along the top of his neck to his eartops. He was never still: a
crackling, restless energy coursed incessantly through him,
sparking out of his bright, bespectacled eyes and keeping his
hands continually busy.

Some more meat, Mishra-sahb? Mrs Verma said, emptying a
spoonful into his plate.

So, Verma, what do you think? Dr Mishra said, a little too
loudly. I don't see the need for a change. Shall we just have the
same kind of thing again this year?

Dr Verma did not look up from his plate; nor did he by the
slightest gesture acknowledge that the question had been
addressed to him. Mrs Verma busied herself with the rice: she

had to be careful now; she could tell that he had already guessed something; that he was trying to draw her out. She laughed briefly: It was very nice last year, Mishra-sahb, really wonderful. And, of course, if you feel strongly. . . .

She left the sentence strategically unfinished and turned to Mrs Mishra: No more rice, Manda-bahen? Then have some prickly-pear custard – we got them from our own cactus. It tastes just like mango really, if you don't worry about the smell too much.

Dr Mishra was ripping a chapati into minute pieces. So, then, Verma, he barked, you *do* have some other idea, do you?

Not exactly an idea, Mrs Verma said smoothly, but, yes, I did think that this year we could have something a little less cerebral . . . something lively. . . . Of course, we must have your speech, too; we can't possibly do without it. But in addition, if we could have something on the stage maybe, just something small to give everyone a glimpse of our country and our culture, our village life. . . .

So *that's* your idea, is it, Verma? Dr Mishra snorted.

Dr Verma sleepily mopped his plate with a chapati.

So you want to give them a glimpse of 'our culture', do you? Dr Mishra said. What exactly did you have in mind, Verma, could I ask? A pageant of the costumes of Indian brides perhaps, like the bureaucrats put on for foreigners in Delhi? We could dress up our elderly Miss K. and our own shy little brides, and you and I could be the bright young grooms, couldn't we?

No one suggested that, Dr Mishra, Mrs Verma said sharply. She could feel her temper rising.

Oh, no, you didn't suggest that, Dr Mishra snapped. What did you suggest, then, Verma?

Dr Verma quietly collected a few plates and went into the kitchen.

Can *I* suggest something, then? Dr Mishra went on, talking at the empty chair. Why don't we give them a more realistic picture of 'our culture'? Why don't we show them how all those fancily dressed-up brides are doused with kerosene and roasted alive when they can't give their grooms enough dowry? Why don't we show them how rich landlords massacre Untouchables and raze their villages to the ground every second day? Or how Muslims are regularly chopped into little bits by Hindu fanatics? Or maybe we could just have a few nice colour pictures of police atrocities? That's what 'our culture' really is, isn't it, Verma? Why should we be ashamed of it?

Typical! Mrs Verma exploded. Absolutely typical! Just like 1936.

1936? Dr Mishra turned to her at last, in bewilderment. Why 1936? You weren't even born then.

So what if I wasn't born then? That doesn't mean I don't know about it.

About what?

Mrs Verma's face was suffused with blood now. She pounded her fist on the table. Don't lie, she shouted. You know perfectly well what: 1936 – the second socialist conference in Meerut. Don't think we've forgotten, for we haven't. What was your little crowd doing there, do you remember? Do you remember how you lectured us about revolutionary theory and class struggle; about historical necessity and Leninist party organization? Do you remember how you talked about technology and the Scientific Temper and building a new rational world by destroying the superstitions of the peasants? And then, when we said surely there was more to socialism than just that, that in the villages we talked of socialism as hope, do you remember how you laughed? You laughed and said: Comrades, leave your villages for a while; peasants can't lead peasants; go and study your theory. And, after all that, where were you when the crunch came? Who fell over themselves in their hurry to join the Congress in 1947 so that they wouldn't have to waste any time in getting their fingers into all that newly independent money? Who broke the Praja Socialist Party when the real socialists were away, struggling in the villages? Who sabotaged Lohia? Don't think we've forgotten. We've forgotten nothing. We know your kind inside and outside, through and through: we've heard your sugary speeches *and* we've seen the snakes hidden up your sleeves; we've seen you wallowing in filth with the Congress while High Theory drips from your mouths; we've heard you spouting about the Misery of the Masses while your fingers dig into their pockets; we've watched you while you were snarling over bribes with your Congress gang-mates, so we know exactly where your cynicism comes from. It comes from the rottenness within: those who've been dipped in pitch see nothing but blackness everywhere. So please don't give *me* any clever lectures about India and Indian society, Dr Murali Charan Mishra, for my father gave me the measure of your kind when I was still a schoolgirl.

Dr Mishra laughed. It was a frightening thing about him that, though he often seemed to be on the verge of losing his temper, he never actually did so.

Murali Charan Mishra was my father, he said.

Same thing, she snapped, her chest heaving.

Dr Mishra smiled: Anyway, it's all much clearer now. What you really want to do is climb on to the sand-dunes and let the Algerians know about your father's Lohia-ite socialism. But to come back to the point: what do you want to put up for this get-together? Some kind of village festival perhaps, since you're so enamoured of rural socialism? Or maybe one of those song-and-dance plays about gods and demons and mythological heroes?

Mrs Verma shook her head.

But, please, do remember, Dr Mishra went on, that your audiences will be made up of your own Algerian colleagues, who are rational, scientifically trained people. I, for one, wouldn't like to give them the impression that the *whole* of India is still in the Middle Ages, still wallowing in ghosts and ghouls and demonology. I'd like them to know that some of us at least are in the modern mainstream.

Mrs Verma smiled secretly across the room at Hem Narain Mathur's dusty old bookcase. She had her answer ready.

*

Mrs Verma settled back in her chair and rested her hands demurely on the rim of her plate. Please, forgive me, Doctor-sahb, she said. I shouldn't have shouted at you like that.

He watched her suspiciously: Yes?

The fact is, she said, looking at her nails, that I do have a plan.

Wonderful! Dr Mishra exclaimed. He broke a matchstick in half and began to pick nervously at his teeth. A village masque, I suppose. Some kind of Ram Li la. Why, we can clear out a

stage on a sand-dune and put up a few idols and images and give
them a full-scale puja with chanting Brahmans, mantras and all
the rest of it. I'm sure your fellow rural socialists will be
delighted by a nice, gaudy spectacle of medieval superstition
flaunting itself on a sand-dune. But, please, Mrs Verma, you're
welcome to dance about on the sand scattering holy water on
the date palms, but don't ask me to do it. I'm too old.

I wasn't really thinking of anything like that, Mishra-sahb,
she said. I was thinking of something else.

What? He was suddenly wary.

Well, she paused for a moment. What do you think of
Tagore? I know you don't much care for medieval villagers, but
you can't have any objection to Rabindranath Tagore. Apart
from everything else, he got all the most modern literary
awards in all the most modern cities, you know.

Dr Mishra laughed: Very good, Mrs Verma; you're learning.
Go on.

Well, people here do sometimes ask about Tagore. Surely it
would be appropriate to give them a glimpse of his work? You
can't object to that, after all.

What exactly did you have in mind?

Chitrangada. Mrs Verma allowed herself to smile: My father
did a translation from the Bengali. I still have it.

Dr Mishra reached into his pocket, though his hands were
still unwashed after the meal, and pulled out his pipe.
Chitrangada? he said, twisting the stem. Could you just
remind me what it's about?

It's a dance drama.

That's nice, said Dr Mishra. A dance drama. Of course
there's no shortage of dancing girls here – you and old Miss K.
and my own bouncy young wife. Go on.

To tell you the truth, I don't really remember it very well
myself now. My father read it to me when I was a girl. It's based
on a legend from the *Mahabharata* I think. Chitrangada is the
king of Manipur's daughter; she's been brought up like a man,
and she's a great hunter and warrior and all that, but she's not –
well, very pretty. Then one day Arjuna goes to Manipur and
she sees him – handsome, a great hero and warrior – so
naturally she falls in love with him. She goes to him and
declares her love, but he turns her away. Then she gets very

depressed because she thinks he can't possibly love a woman who looks like her. So ugly, you know. So she goes to the gods and asks them to give her the gift of beauty for just one year. They do, and Arjuna falls in love with her, and they sort of get married, I think, but she doesn't tell him who she is. But as the year passes Arjuna hears more and more about the heroism of Chitrangada, and he longs to meet her and is half in love with her, though he doesn't even know who she is. Chitrangada sees all this and she learns finally that appearances don't matter, so at the end of the year, when her beauty is gone, she stands before him and says something like: I'm no beautiful flower, I'm not perfect, my clothes are torn and my feet are scarred and so on, but I can give you the heart of a true woman. Then Arjuna, too, sees that beauty is only deception, an illusion of the senses.

Well, said Dr Mishra sardonically, that makes it much clearer. I can see now why you want to play Chitrangada, but who did you have in mind for Arjuna? Verma? Do you really think it would suit him to dress up as a hero, in a sort of mini-dhoti, and dance around with bows and arrows? He's short-sighted, you know; he might hit Chitrangada with those arrows.

Mrs Verma turned quickly away, blushing furiously. Of course I wasn't going to play Chitrangada, she said. We could ask some of the younger doctors and their wives to come up from Ouargla or Ghardaia.

She looked him over appraisingly. Actually, Mishra-sahb, she said, there's a part that'll be perfect for you.

Which?

Madana, the God of Love. I can just see you – hovering above the dunes, showering love on the Sahara.

Dr Mishra rose and paced the floor while she watched apprehensively. All right, Mrs Verma, he said at last. I'll take up your challenge. I'll play Madana if you can fill the other roles. But there's a condition: since it's we who are putting it on for our Algerian colleagues, you'll have to find Indians to play the parts.

Mrs Verma nodded.

Have you thought of the other problems? Who's going to sing? Who's going to dance? Where are you going to get the

music? And it must be a very long play – are you going to stage
the whole of it?

That's easy, said Mrs Verma. We won't do the whole thing;
just a few scenes. And don't worry about the music; that's an
advantage with this play really. My father gave me a record
years ago. We can just play that – we won't even have to talk.
We don't have to dance, either; we can just mime the scenes.
We can explain the plot beforehand through an interpreter.
I'm sure Miss K. and Mrs Mishra will help me make the
costumes. Even you could do something; you could help me
choose the right scenes. I'll give you the script.

You mean your father's Hindi translation?

Yes, she said. I'll lend it to you, but you must be very careful
with it. To me that's the most precious of all the things he left
me.

Tell me, Mrs Verma, Dr Mishra said curiously, how did your
father learn Bengali?

Oh, he learnt when he was in college in Calcutta. He loved
Tagore's poetry.

Dr Mishra gestured to his wife to get up. When they were at
the door, he turned to Mrs Verma, smiling grimly. All right, he
said, the bet's on, then. If you do somehow manage to put it
together, I'll admit defeat and you can give a speech instead of
me. But if you *don't* you'll have to apologize in public for
everything you've said tonight.

Yes, I accept, Mrs Verma said at once, looking directly into
his eyes. I have nothing to worry about.

But soon she was very worried; it didn't seem as though she
would ever be able to find a cast. And every morning at the
hospital there was Dr Mishra, solicitously asking after the
progress of her plan, grinning, like a school bully gloating over
the break-up of a rival gang. She had come perilously close to
accepting defeat simply to put an end to those questions and
those grins.

Then one morning there was Arjuna, lying unheroically on a
hospital bed, his oddly irregular eyebrows raised at her in
surprised inquiry.

That was encouraging enough to hold a rehearsal and start
work on the costumes. But, as Dr Mishra had said while he was
being measured for his halo, it's no use without a Chitrangada.

She had had no answer.

And then, like a gift from Madana. . . .

*

So do you think, Mrs Verma asked Kulfi anxiously, you'll be able to do Chitrangada? It won't be difficult at all really – all you'll have to do is dress up in a nice sari and pose on stage. You won't have to say anything because the record will be playing off-stage. It'll just be a set of tableaux really.

They turned left, and a broad square ringed with low bungalows sprang up and hung before them on a pall of dust.

Kulfi tossed her head: It'll be easy. I haven't acted before, but I do see a lot of films and, I must say, I don't know why but in al-Ghazira my husband's colleagues used to keep telling me, at every party I went to, Why, you look just like Hema Malini, Mrs Bose. I don't know why you say that, I used to tell them. . . .

And luckily, said Mrs Verma, you'll have a nice Arjuna.

I hope so, Kulfi said, frowning. Who is he?

You'll meet him in a minute.

Mrs Verma pushed open a steel gate. That's our house, she said, waving proudly at a thick-walled colonial bungalow, surrounded by tenaciously green patches of garden. She led Kulfi down a brick-lined path, past dusty casuarinas and doggedly blooming bushes of bougainvillaea to a low, deeply shaded porch. Then her eyes fell on a snapped clothes-line at the other end of the garden and she rushed off with a cry to rescue the scattered clothes from the dust.

Peering at the veranda which led on to the porch, and the darkness of the rooms beyond, it was evident at once to Kulfi that Mrs Verma took good care of her house: the veranda was spotless, the curtains in the windows were clean and bright, and there were calendars on every wall. She took a step towards the veranda and caught the sound of a muffled voice somewhere inside. Craning forward, she squinted into the shadows.

The darkness rippled and a moment later Kulfi sprang back, shrieking.

A short, stout man dressed in a scarlet knee-length dhoti had appeared on the veranda. Bits of tinsel were dotted about his chest and there was a white flower entwined in the sacred thread of his Brahminhood. Above it, like a rainswept rock framed by the setting sun, his bald head shone against a noisily spinning halo that seemed to grow out of the back of his neck.

Poised to run, Kulfi stole another quick look. He was peering at her in short-sighted confusion, his narrowed eyes hugely enlarged by his thick glasses. Kulfi choked back a scream.

Folding his hands, he bobbed his head and at once the halo slipped, grazing his glistening scalp. *Namaste*, he said, wincing, and pushed the halo hurriedly back into place. Don't pay any attention to all this – he waved a deprecating hand at his clothes – it's only because I'm Madana.

Madana? Kulfi whispered hoarsely.

Yes, he said, hitching up his dhoti and advancing upon her, the God of Love. And you?

Kulfi began to back away rapidly, watching his every move. Then, to her relief, Mrs Verma was beside her, her arms full of clothes.

So Madana's found Chitrangada? she said, laughing. That old curtain really suits you, Dr Mishra; you should wear it more often.

Dr Mishra was suddenly acutely self-conscious. Never mind, he growled, crossing his hands over his tinselly chest.

What? said Mrs Verma. I can't hear you.

Will you please make me known to this lady? Dr Mishra shouted over the whirring of his halo.

Mrs Verma smiled and waved, magician-like, at Kulfi. This, she said, is my Chitrangada.

Dr Mishra stared, and Kulfi lowered her head shyly. Did you create her, Mrs Verma? he said. Or did Madana drop her from the sky?

Actually, Mrs Verma said, she appeared out of Driss's café. She and her husband are passing through – they're tourists.

I see, Dr Mishra said, examining Kulfi suspiciously. Well, I suppose we should take our touring Chitrangada in and introduce her to her Arjuna.

Led by Dr Mishra they went into a large cool room which had its twin functions unmistakably indicated by a dining-table at one end and a circle of sofas at the other. Otherwise, except for a few calendars and a papier-mâché Taj Mahal, the room was clinically bare. But it was that very bareness which seemed to shine a spotlight on a far corner of the room where a battered old bookcase stood propped against the wall, reigning, some-how, in spite of its rickety shelves and frayed dustcovers, over every other object in the room.

As they entered Dr Mishra gestured at a young man who was rising awkwardly from a sofa. Well, Arjuna, he said drily, here's your Chitrangada.

Turning on his heels, his arms spread out, he said: May I introduce you to our very own avatar of Arjuna? Mr Jyoti Das.

Jyoti Das had not seen them yet, but his hands were already folded and he was smiling in polite expectation. Then his eyes found Kulfi, and the smile vanished from his face and he swallowed and clutched at his throat.

Mrs Verma dropped her armful of clothes on a chair and bustled forward. How are you feeling now? she asked him kindly. He shook his head in an effort to take his eyes off Kulfi, failed, and sank wordlessly back on to the sofa.

He's not been well, you know, Mrs Verma confided to Kulfi. We met him quite by chance a couple of days ago, when he was brought to the hospital with a mild case of heatstroke. He'd been here a few days already and apparently he'd spent all his time at the bus station watching the buses from the border come in, and on the dunes, where he was looking for a vulture. Just imagine – a vulture! Are you a corpse, I said, that you're looking for a vulture in this blazing sun?

Jyoti Das moistened his lips mechanically and, without taking his eyes off Kulfi, he said: Not any old vulture, Mrs Verma. I thought I'd spotted a lappet-faced vulture. I had to find it – none has been reported from these parts for decades.

Mrs Verma shrugged: A vulture's a vulture, whatever its face. Anyway, you'd better get up now; you have to go to Miss K.'s for lunch.

But Jyoti Das stayed as he was, his eyes riveted on Kulfi.

Kulfi tossed her head. She swept past Mrs Verma and went across to the bookcase, swaying her hips. She saw him turning, following her with his eyes, his young boyish face contorted with the clumsy, painful longing of a virgin rebelling too late against his condition. Inclining her head slightly, she gave him

a tight little smile and with his gaze lapping thirstily at her back
she began to flip languidly through a calendar.

I see good things, Dr Mishra said, watching them shrewdly
from the other end of the room. It looks as though Madana's
going to have some success at last.

*

While Mrs Verma rang the hospital, her husband began
dismantling Dr Mishra's battery-operated halo.

Can't you make it a little quieter? Dr Mishra said. They'll
think Madana is a kind of helicopter if it goes on like this.

Mrs Verma put the phone down and clapped her hands. All
right now, she said. We all have to hurry. There's a lot to do
today.

What? said Dr Mishra.

Mrs Verma nodded at Jyoti Das and said: The two of you
have to go to Miss K.'s for lunch. She's expecting you; she's
saved up a whole cauliflower, and she borrowed a tin of
pineapples from me this morning. And after that you have to
come back here for a rehearsal. We can do it properly, with
costumes and everything, now that we have our Chitrangada.

Do you think, Dr Mishra growled, that I don't have anything
better to do on a holiday than spend all my time dressed up in
an old curtain?

Mrs Verma laughed: It's too bad, Dr Mishra. You'll have to
come, holiday or not. It was a fair bet and you can't let me down
now, when I'm so close to winning.

She beckoned to Kulfi. Come, let me show you the room
you'll be staying in, she said, leading her to a room at the back.

When they came out again Jyoti Das was standing beside the
door, rigidly still, waiting. Mrs Verma bustled past without
noticing him, but Kulfi hung back. As she stepped out of the
door, she lurched and fell sideways. Her hands brushed against
the front of his trousers and flew back as if scalded.

Shaking with nervousness, falling over himself, Jyoti Das
managed to catch her in his arms. She leant against his
shoulder, eyes downcast. I hope I didn't hurt you, she said.

He stared at her tongue-tied, his forehead filming over with
sweat. She could feel his groin quivering against her thigh. She

swayed, and her breast brushed against his arm. A spasm seemed to shoot through him and he clutched helplessly at her blouse. Oh God, he breathed hoarsely into her neck, oh God. . . .

Then there was a rustle in the corridor as Mrs Verma came hurrying back, and Kulfi shook herself out of his arms. Where did you disappear, Mrs Bose? Mrs Verma cried. She looked from Kulfi, gazing demurely at the floor, to Jyoti Das, standing frozen beside her, and a tiny eddy of suspicion stirred in her mind.

The land-rover's come, she said to Kulfi. Shall we go to the café now?

She saw Kulfi glancing at Jyoti Das and, turning to him, she said sharply: You have to go out for lunch now, Mr Das. Dr Mishra's waiting for you. Don't waste time.

Jyoti Das went quickly back to the other room.

So, Mrs Bose? she said. Shall we go now? Of course, if you're *very* tired you can stay here and rest.

To her surprise Kulfi nodded eagerly. Yes, she said, raising her hands to her temples. I'm very tired and I have a headache. I think I'll rest here.

Achchha, Mrs Verma said doubtfully. But before leaving the house she went back again and handed Kulfi a crimson sari and box from her dressing-table. While you're waiting, she said, you may as well try on your costume.

Later, in the land-rover, she said to her husband: These people are so . . . so strange. Do you think they're all right?

He said nothing.

That Mrs Bose doesn't seem, she carried on, at all like a married woman. And I must say she was behaving very strangely a little while ago. Mr Das, too. . . .

Mrs Verma stared silently at a ration-shop.

They're not like anyone I've ever met: that husband and that ayah – so strange. I just can't place them. She fell silent. But just before they reached the café she added: Still, I suppose she'll make a good Chitrangada.

On the way back she and her husband took turns at examining Boss, while Zindi heaped them with information about his symptoms.

He'll be all right, she said, handing him back to Zindi. I'll

give you some medicine for him when we get back. She
glanced at Alu, thinking of starting a conversation, but he was
sitting so dourly hunched up, with his hands under his legs,
that she thought the better of it and looked ahead.

When the land-rover drew up, she jumped out, relieved to
be back, and led them quickly into the house. Come, she said,
I'll show you the way. But when she reached their room she
found that only Zindi was following her; Alu had disappeared.

She found him crouching in the middle of her drawing-
room, staring at Hem Narain Mathur's old bookcase in startled
confusion.

What are you doing here, Mr Bose? she said in surprise.
Come and look at your wife. You won't recognize her – she's
Chitrangada now.

Alu had snapped upright as soon as he heard her voice. He
stood staring at her uncertainly, shifting his feet, with his hands
behind his back.

Come on, she said briskly. Follow me.

But at the door she stopped, puzzled, and looked at the
bookcase and then at him and back again. Why, Mr Bose, she
said at last, when I came in you were staring at my father's old
bookcase as though it had just spoken to you.

*   *   *   *

Kulfi! Zindi shrieked. What're you doing to your face? Stop it.
You can't go out looking for customers here in the desert; you
gave that up when you left India.

Swathed in a zari-spangled sari, corseted by the heavy gold
thread of the fabric, Kulfi was sitting stiffly upright before a
looking-glass, powdering her already paper-white face. Zindi
snatched the powder puff out of her hand. Stop it now, Kulfi,
she cried. What d'you think you're doing?

Don't you know? Kulfi flashed her a brilliant smile. Today
I'm a princess; I'm Chitrangada.

Chitra . . . what? Zindi gasped. Listen, you bitch. Today
you're no different from what you were when I first met you.
You're Kulfi the small-time callgirl whose MA-pass husband
turned her to whoring when he lost his fancy job; you're pale-
faced, unemployed old Kulfi who came to me in Bangalore

and said, Take me to al-Ghazira and give me some honest work.

No, Kulfi hissed, her voice quavering on the edge of hysteria. Today I'm Chitrangada, princess of Manipur.

Zindi's mouth dropped open: Princess of what-place? You're a princess, are you, you two-pice whore?

Just listen to that! Kulfi trilled with laughter, and the bangles that covered her arm in a sheen of plastic armour tinkled in counterpoint. *I'm* a whore? *You* dare say that to me when you've got the Grand Trunk Road between your legs and no toll-gates, either?

Still laughing, she dipped her fingertips into a small lead pot of sindur and filled her parting with a gash of bleeding vermilion. Today, she said, smiling at her reflection, I'm Chitrangada, princess of Manipur. You can go and ask Mrs Verma if you like. She's an educated woman like me, not a gutter-slut like you. She'll tell you. I'm Chitrangada and I'm going to marry Arjuna, hero of heroes.

Zindi's eyes narrowed: You're going to marry who?

Arjuna. He's fallen in love with my beauty.

Zindi shot a quick worried look at Alu. Then she laid Boss on the bed and stood over Kulfi. Look, Kulfi, she said quietly, don't give me any more of this *phoos-phas* or I'll knock the teeth out of your mouth. Tell me quickly: who is this Arjuna?

He's a man who's staying here, said Kulfi. He's Arjuna and I'm Chitrangada.

Zindi took hold of her shoulders and shook her till her bangles began to clatter. Who is he, Kulfi? she said. Tell me quick.

Kulfi slapped angrily at Zindi's hands. Let me go, she said. I've told you what I know. Why don't you go and ask him if you're so curious?

Grinding her knuckles against her teeth, Zindi sank on to the bed. Kulfi, she said, drawing a breath in a long, whistling gasp. Is he the Bird-man?

Kulfi's hands froze in the act of raising a tin tiara to her head. The Bird-man? she whispered. I don't know. I haven't ever seen your Bird-man, remember? I'm the only one. And he hadn't seen me before, either.

Then she remembered how he had looked at her when she first entered the room, how his eyes had followed her, and she

pealed with delighted, girlish laughter and crowned herself.
Don't worry, she said. Even if he is the Bird-man, I'll manage
him. You'll be safe.

What did he look like, tell me, quick? Zindi said.

Before Kulfi could finish the first sentence of her answer,
Zindi knew. It's him, she wailed, it's him. He's got us now.

Yes, it *is* him, Kulfi said. I remember now; he said he was
looking for a vulture.

A vulture? Zindi breathed. He's come with a vulture?

Stop moaning, Kulfi snapped. Didn't I tell you it'll be all
right? Aren't you listening or what?

As she got up to leave, Zindi snatched at her arms: You can't
go with him waiting out there. I won't let you.

Kulfi snorted contemptuously: Why don't you try to stop
me? Her eyes fell on Alu, standing by the door, and she
stopped dead. Listen, you, she snarled at him, if you go
anywhere near that bed I'll tear your rotten thumbs off. She
peeled away the bedcovers and flung them into a corner. You
can make your nest there, she said and stormed out of the
room.

Alu hesitated, then backed away towards the door.

Where are you going? Zindi snapped at him.

To look at the books, Alu said.

Books? Is this the time for books? Zindi snapped at him.
Come back here. It's your fault. You've brought him here – it
was you who said it first.

But he was here before I said anything, Alu said. How did he
know, Zindi? How did he follow us here?

God blind me for not thinking of it, she said. It must have
been the easiest thing in the world. After he saw us in Kairouan
he had only to look at the road-signs to know that we would
head this way. Where else could we have gone? He must have
known that with our kind of passport we wouldn't risk any but
the most remote of border posts. And once you're across the
border there's nowhere you can go but El Oued if you're
heading west. He knows all that; he's like a bird – he hears us
every time we say we're going west.

Maybe, said Alu, he's only going west himself.

Do you think so? Zindi said eagerly, suddenly hopeful. Do
you think it's possible?

If he really wanted to do anything to us, said Alu, he'd have done it already. He must be here somewhere.

It's possible, she muttered, but the ripple of hope had already trickled out of her voice. It makes no difference, she said. That man carries death with him wherever he goes. He can't help it; it's in his eyes. Think of what happened to Jeevanbhai; think of Karthamma and all the rest. And this time he's come with a vulture.

For a while she stared blankly at the wall. We should never have come, she said at last. We should never have left Egypt. I can smell death in this house: it's there in writing – one of us isn't going to leave this house alive.

She lifted Boss into her arms, very gently, and kissed him as though she were bidding him goodbye.

As long as it's not him, she whispered. Let it be me, but not Boss. Not him, Allah. . . .

*

As soon as he could, Alu slipped back into the drawing-room. It was empty and curiously still; more than ever the bareness of the walls seemed to thrust the bookcase directly at him. For a long time he stood still, staring at it across the room, wondering why his skin was tingling with recognition. Then he began to inch his way forward, biting his nails, scanning the dusty brown-paper covers of the books for a visible sign.

When he was less than halfway across the room, Mrs Verma came bustling in. He stopped guiltily and began to edge away. Ah, there you are, she said. I've just given your ayah some medicine for your son. He'll be all right soon.

He nodded, looking away, and hid his hands in his pockets. Mrs Verma cleared her throat. Mr Bose, she said hesitantly, you remember I was telling you that I might need your help? Well, as your wife has probably explained, we're going to put on a small production of *Chitrangada* – I'm sure you're familiar with it – for our colleagues. We have the record, luckily, so we won't have to sing. But instead we're going to explain the scenes we're doing through a translator. I've been trying to put together a few notes but unfortunately I've run into a little trouble, and that's where I need your help. You see, I have a

Hindi translation of the original done by my father, but there are a couple of places where I can't read his handwriting. He copied the original down along with the translation, but the trouble is I can't read Bengali. Mr Das helped, but there were some bits he couldn't read, either. So, if you could just help a little . . .?

Reluctantly, Alu nodded. Mrs Verma sank on to a sofa, next to the bookcase and began to look through the shelves. She noticed Alu bending over, looking intently at the bookcase. She patted the sofa: Sit down, Mr Bose. He seated himself next to her with his hands under his thighs, but his eyes stayed riveted on the books.

She found what she was looking for and drew it out: a tattered hardbound exercise-book that had been lovingly wrapped in brown paper. She flipped through it, showing him the smudged sections, and with the help of his glosses of the Bengali text she wrote down suitable Hindi substitutes. After half an hour she snapped the exercise-book shut. I'm very grateful to you, she said. I think that's all that needs to be done. She put the book tidily back in its place and straightened the row with the back of her hand.

And then Alu saw it.

It bore no outward clue to its identity for it was wrapped in a cover like the others. Yet, the moment he looked at it, he knew. He tried to control himself, tried to say something polite, but the words died in his throat and he fell to his knees and snatched the book from its shelf.

He didn't even need to look at the title-page. The fading print smiled at him like an all-too-familiar face. His eyes brimmed over with tears.

It's the *Life of Pasteur*, he said quietly, looking up at Mrs Verma.

She had been watching him with some alarm, but when he spoke she laughed. Yes, she said, have you read it?

He nodded dumbly.

It was one of my father's favourite books, she said. He loved it. A close friend of his gave it to him when he was in Presidency College.

Who? What was his name? Alu was already thumbing through the stiff, crackling leaves, fumbling for the title-page.

Somehow it kept slipping past his fingers. He broke into a sweat, stopped, closed the book between his palms and opened it again, gently.

He saw Balaram's handwriting on the first page, in red ink, sprawled across the corner: To Hem Narain Mathur, Rationalist and friend, from Balaram Bose; Medical College Hospital, Calcutta, 1932. Another hand had inscribed beneath: To remember Reason.

He could not bear to look at it. He shut the book and hugged it to his chest.

Why, Mr Bose, Mrs Verma said in surprise, you seem to be very fond of that book?

Mrs Verma, Alu said, this book is the only real brother I ever had. I'd lost him and now I've found him again – here in the desert, of all places, and in your house.

Mrs Verma listened gravely, picking at the frayed threads on the fall of her sari. Then she said: That's very sad.

Sad! cried Alu. How can you call it sad?

I can see that you love that book, Mr Bose, and that's very sad, because you can love a book but a book can't love you. That's what I used to tell my father, but he could never understand. He would look at the world whirling around him and he would look at his books, and when they told him different stories, like a man caught between quarrelling friends, he wouldn't know which side to take. But in the end, even though it meant shutting himself away, the books won. They ruled over him: for him that bookcase had all the order the world lacked. I used to think it was love, but I know better now. He was afraid; afraid of the power of science and those books of his; afraid that if he disowned them they would destroy him.

That can't be true, Alu cried. What could a book like this one have done to him? You're wrong; you must be.

She smiled: You may be right – I'm often wrong. She took the book from him and flipped through it gingerly, holding it at a distance. Do you know, she said, looking at it in wonder; it's because of this book that I'm a microbiologist today? My father told me that microbiology was Pasteur's heritage, and that I was to keep it alive.

She took a deep breath and held the book out to him. Take it, she said. I've always wanted to get rid of it. Only I've never dared; I'm too much my father's daughter.

Alu hesitated: How could I take it? It was your father's. . . .

Take it, she insisted, almost angrily. Now that I've found the courage to give it away I won't take it back. Keep it with you. Take it outside to the dunes if you like, and read it in peace there.

Yes, he said eagerly, holding out his hand. I'll do just that. I can always bring it back.

She dropped the book into his hands. He fumbled and it slipped and fell open on the floor. A paragraph underlined heavily in red pencil stared up at them from the open pages.

Read that bit out, she said quickly. What does it say? It always means something when a book falls open like that.

It's about death, Alu said. It says that without the germ 'life would become impossible because death would be incomplete'.

Smiling nervously, Mrs Verma looked around the room. I wonder who it was pointing at, she said.

*

By the time Dr Mishra and Jyoti Das returned, just before sunset, Mrs Verma had already cleared a space for the rehearsal in the drawing-room, and she and Kulfi were busy making a garland – of bougainvillaea, for lack of jasmine – to go with Arjuna's costume. It was dull work, and Mrs Verma would have been glad of another pair of hands, but Zindi was busy watching over Boss's drugged sleep behind a locked door, Alu was still away at the dunes and, as for her husband, she knew from experience that flowers always fell apart in his hands.

Mrs Verma was alarmed the moment Jyoti Das stepped in. His eyes were feverishly bright, his face tense, strained with suppressed excitement. With deep misgiving she saw how his eyes scanned the room, how they came to rest hungrily on Kulfi's lowered head.

Come on, Mr Das, she broke in quickly. Come on, Mishra-sahb. Change into your costumes; we have to get started now. She waved them ahead of her, and when Jyoti Das hung back she herded him relentlessly on: Come on, come on now. . . .

Jyoti Das came back first, dressed in a dhoti and kurta. He was stooping with his shoulders painfully hunched up, for the kurta was Mr Verma's and therefore two sizes too small for him, and its starched seams were biting unpleasantly into his armpits. Pinched between his fingers, as though it were a dead rat, was a small bamboo bow.

No sooner had Mrs Verma stifled a laugh than she saw his eyes stray beseechingly towards Kulfi. She saw Kulfi rewarding him with a smile of approval, and at once, tapping the chair next to hers, she rapped out: Come and sit down Mr Das; you ought to study your scenes now.

Then Dr Mishra appeared, scarlet below the waist, glittering with tinsel above, mouthing soundless curses. Isn't this funny enough for you? he said to her. Do I have to put on Verma's contraption as well?

Yes, she said, you look much better with a halo. And I have something else for you, too.

What? he said suspiciously.

She held up a cone of cardboard and gold paper. It's a crown, she explained. It's a kind of symbol of your reign over the realm of Love.

Don't lie, he said, looking at it scornfully. It's to cover my baldness.

Mrs Verma, undeterred, jammed it on his head. There, she said, and now you won't catch a cold, either. But when her husband strapped on the halo and gave it a trial spin the crown hurtled off Dr Mishra's slippery scalp and flattened itself on the floor. Mrs Verma pushed the tip up and tried to fit it on again, with a rubber band this time. Halfway through she happened to look up. Next moment the crown fell from her hands and Dr Mishra howled as the rubber band snapped back, catching him on the tip of his nose.

Kulfi was bending over Jyoti Das with the garland of bougainvillaea in her hands, smiling with coy bridal modesty. Mrs Verma started forward, but before she could reach them Kulfi had slipped the garland over his head and pirouetted away.

Jyoti Das rose to his feet, breathing hard, his eyes dilated, but before he could take a step Mrs Verma was in front of him.

No, no, Mr Das, she said sharply, pushing him back on to his chair. No more of that; sit down now.

After that she looked up every two seconds while strapping on Dr Mishra's crown to make sure that they hadn't moved. Dr Mishra was immensely amused. Love-game for Madana, he hummed. Three cheers for rural socialism.

Soon Mrs Verma was ready to begin. A quick look at Jyoti Das's flushed face persuaded her to start with a scene which needed only Chitrangada and Madana.

The first part of the scene, in which Kulfi only had to kneel before Dr Mishra and suit her expression to the song of supplication that was playing on the gramophone, went off without a hitch. But when Dr Mishra pulled her to her feet as he had been told to a gust from his whirring halo caught Kulfi's tiara and blew it off her head. Kulfi's hands shot up. She patted her head with gathering dismay, and then she turned upon Dr Mishra with such unbridled rage blazing out of her eyes that he cowered back in fear.

Mrs Verma had to dart in between them. I think this scene's done now, she said hurriedly. We'll go on to another one.

She fetched a shawl and draped it around Kulfi's shoulders. This shawl, she explained, represents the ordinariness of Chitrangada's real appearance. You'll have to wear it now, because we're going to do the last scene, in which Chitrangada reveals her real self to Arjuna and he cries out in wonder: *Dhanya! Dhanya! Dhanya!*

She led Kulfi and Jyoti Das to the empty space at the far end of the room and explained their parts to them. While they took up their poses – Chitrangada with her hands dramatically outflung before a wonder-struck Arjuna – she stood beside them, watching narrowly, making sure that they stayed a respectable distance from each other. It was a long while before she was satisfied. But finally, apprehensively, she backed away and turned the gramophone on.

Ami Chitrangada, the record lilted softly, *ami rajendronon-dini. . . .*

Jyoti Das edged slowly closer to Kulfi. Louder, please, he called out to Mrs Verma. We can hardly hear it over here.

Reluctantly Mrs Verma turned the volume up and carried the needle back to the first groove. The voice rolled sonorously

*out of the gramophone: I am Chitrangada; daughter of
kings. . . .*

Jyoti Das stole a glance at Mrs Verma and the others. They
were well out of earshot now, cloaked securely behind a screen
of music. He leant forward as Kulfi gestured at her shawl with
sweeping flourishes of her hands.

I am Chitrangada. . . .

Are you, he whispered, the one they call Kulfi-didi?

*

Jyoti Das knew, from the sudden jerk of her head, that she had
heard him. He glanced at Mrs Verma. She was leaning forward
in her chair, watching them anxiously.

I am Chitrangada. . . .

Kulfi whirled around and came to rest on her knees. He fell
to his knees, too, as he had been instructed.

I am no goddess. . . .

I know who you are, he whispered, trying not to move his
lips. Don't be afraid of me, I beg you. I know you're Kulfi-didi.
I know who the others are. There's nothing to be afraid of and
there's nothing to hide. I won't harm you or them. Listen to
me, Kulfi, please. . . .

And nor am I an ordinary woman. . . .

Kulfi, please. . . .

The sweat was pouring down his face now, but his mouth was
curiously dry; his viscera, his loins, were straining against an
invisible, unbearable constriction.

Kulfi, please. . . .

She raised her lowered head. Her eyelashes fluttered and
she gave him the briefest of smiles.

His head swam drunkenly. He groaned: Oh, Kulfi. . . .

If you keep me by your side. . . .

He leant forward, shielding his face with the bow. Kulfi, he
said, I know you're not married. I know he's not your husband. I
know all about him. I know you're a free woman. Kulfi, please, I
beg you, we can't talk here. I beg you, come out into the garden
tonight. Later, much later, when everyone's asleep.

She looked up at him suddenly. He cut himself short,
reading a reproach in her widening eyes and trembling lips.

No, no, Kulfi, he said, swallowing convulsively. Nothing like that, really. I swear. I promise you. I won't touch you. I swear it. We'll just talk; it's impossible to talk here. Please, Kulfi, please. . . .

Her eyes flashed and she rose unsteadily to her feet.

If you let me share your trials. . . .

Anything, Kulfi, anything, he said, rising with her.

Suddenly she stiffened and looked him full in the face.

Today I can only offer you. . . .

He no longer cared whether anybody saw him or heard him. Kulfi, he cried, I can't bear it. I'll marry you, if only tonight, just once. You see, I've never. . . .

I can only offer you. . . .

Her eyes had grown huge now. She shuddered and her hands rose to her heart. He started forward in a great surge of joy. But then he caught a glimpse of Mrs Verma, watching, frowning, and he checked himself. Don't say anything now, Kulfi, he whispered hastily, jabbing his thumb at Mrs Verma. They might hear you.

Kulfi's moist lips fluttered. She moaned and stretched her arms towards him, imploring, beseeching.

I can only offer you Chitrangada; daughter of kings. . . .

Not now, Kulfi, he whispered urgently. Just wait a little; till tonight. What's the hurry?

Dhanya! Dhanya! Dhanya!

Kulfi crashed to the floor, clutching her heart. In a trance, Jyoti Das watched her go down.

The first person to run across the room was Dr Verma. He pushed Jyoti Das back, undid the top buttons of her blouse and felt for her heart.

Jyoti Das covered his eyes and tried to steady himself. When he looked up again Alu was standing opposite him. For an interminable moment they stared at each other across Kulfi's body. Then Dr Verma rose to his feet between them.

She's heavenly, he said in English. Absolutely heavenly.

Her fathers have gathered her to their heavenly abode.

Chapter Twenty-One

Curtain

Very gently Mrs Verma closed Kulfi's eyes. For a moment she looked into her pale, rigid face and then her lips began to quiver and she had to tilt her head to keep her tears back. Three of us, she said, three doctors sitting right in front of her, and there was nothing we could do. Nothing.

We're not to blame, Mrs Verma, Dr Mishra said gruffly. There was nothing we could do. Especially since her husband didn't bother to warn us that she had a heart condition.

Mrs Verma ran a consoling hand over Alu's back: It's not his fault, poor man. What could he do? She was so keen to do the part. How was he to know that she would get so carried away?

She glanced reproachfully at Jyoti Das, squatting beside her on the floor. If anything, she said, perhaps Mr Das could have behaved with a little more restraint. I won't say any more.

Jyoti Das flinched and buried his head in his knees.

Anyway, Mrs Verma continued, there's only one thing we can do for her now, poor woman.

She went into the kitchen and returned with a brass bowl and a spoon. Kneeling beside the body, she said: Go on, Mr Bose. Even though it's too late now, you should wet her lips.

A quickly stifled snort of laughter checked her as she held the bowl out to Alu. She looked up, startled: What's the matter, Dr Mishra?

Sorry, he muttered contritely, slapping a hand over his mouth. The sudden movement jolted his halo back into motion. Ignoring it, he said loudly: That's a strange thing you're doing, Mrs Verma.

What? she said. I can't hear you.

Sala! he swore, taking a swipe at his halo. He yelped and snatched his hand back as the whirling blade skimmed the skin off his knuckles. *Sala, bhain* . . . sorry. Verma, he roared, can't you get this thing off my neck? Dr Verma ran to help him.

What were you saying, Mishra-sahb? Mrs Verma said.

I was just asking, he snapped, whether you've managed to connect your kitchen tap to the Ganges? Or do you keep your own private stock of holy water for these occasions?

What do you mean? she said puzzled.

Maybe I should explain to you, in case you don't know, that the water in that bowl has never been anywhere near the snows of the Himalayas or the Gangotri. It's from a million-year-old water-table that lies under the Sahara. It's never flowed past Rudraprayag or Hardwar or Benares or any of your holy cities. In fact it's never flowed anywhere. It's been pumped up by an artesian well.

Mystified, Mrs Verma looked from Dr Mishra to Alu and back again. So? she said.

In a word, that's not Ganga-jal. You can't give it to her.

She shook her head impatiently and turned her back on him. Go on, Mr Bose, she said, prodding Alu. Give it to her.

Wait! Dr Mishra cried. You can't do that.

But, Dr Mishra, she said, where do you think we're going to get Ganga-jal here in the Sahara? This is all we've got. What's the point of arguing?

There is a point. First, I think you should ask yourself whether you as a rational, educated woman wish to encourage anyone in the belief that a bit of dirty water from a muddy river can actually do them any good when they're already dead.

This is hardly the time for a debate, Mrs Verma said. We can only do what we think is right. Go on, Mr Bose.

Wait a minute! Dr Mishra leapt to his feet. If you are going to do this, you have to do it properly. You can't just pour water from an artesian well down her mouth and pretend it's Ganga-jal. You can't. There are certain rules.

Never mind the rules, Mrs Verma said. We'll just do what we can.

She put the spoon into Alu's hands and helped him slip a few drops of water through Kulfi's dead lips.

*

When she saw the body Zindi sank to the floor slowly, like the crust on a loaf of cooling bread. She straightened Kulfi's outstretched arms, and then suddenly, like a scolded child, she began to rock from side to side, sobbing. She was pointing at me, she sobbed. Did you see her? She thinks I did it.

Alu put his arms around her. Zindi, he said, whispering, so that the doctors at the other end of the room would not hear him. Zindi, it's not your fault; there was nothing you could do.

How do you know? Zindi whispered back. Her death won't be on your soul. You've done nothing but stare at your thumbs ever since we left al-Ghazira. It was *I* who decided everything; *I* who brought her to this house of death; it's *I* who'll have it hanging over me on the Day of Judgement.

By why, Zindi? She came of her own will.

But I allowed her to stay on here, even after I smelt death in this place. If I'd done what I should have and we'd left, she would have lived.

But, Zindi, Alu said, you know we couldn't have left. Boss is ill; and anyway where would we have gone?

She elbowed him angrily away. I don't want your hugs and your explanations, she hissed. I'll have to live with this for every day of what's left of my life. Leave me in peace. What can you ever understand of this?

A hand touched her shoulder and she turned. It was Jyoti Das, his eyes bloodshot and swollen, his mouth open. He was trying to say something.

It's the vulture, she cried.

It's my fault, he stuttered. He reached out to touch her feet.

Zindi jerked her legs back. Don't touch me, she snarled. Keep your murdering claws away or you'll kill me, too.

Jyoti Das stared at his hands in despair. What could I do? he said. She came in out of the desert like a mirage and I. . . .

Take him out, Alu, Zindi sobbed. Take him away. Don't let him get his claws into me. . . .

She was still sobbing as they helped each other up and limped out of the room like a pair of grieving cripples.

*

What do we do now? said Mrs Verma.

You don't do anything, Dr Mishra said. You have no

connection with the whole business except that it happened
under your roof. What you should do now is ring up the
hospital and the police. They'll come and take the body away.
Then it's out of your hands. Maybe they'll do an autopsy; they
may have to, for the death certificate.

And then?

What do you mean, 'and then'?

I mean, said Mrs Verma, what will they do with the body?
They can't keep it in the morgue for ever.

Dr Mishra shrugged: They'll do whatever they usually do
under these circumstances. I suppose they'll hand it back to
the next of kin. Whatever it is, it has nothing to do with you or
me or any of us.

Mrs Verma thought hard, with her chin cupped in her
hands. That means, she said, that they'll hand the body back to
Mr Bose. But what will *he* do with it?

How does it *matter* to you? Dr Mishra said brusquely. He
can do what he likes. It's none of your business. You don't even
know them. They just turned up today and you gave them
shelter. For all you know, they may be international criminals
or something. I think you should be very, very careful. Don't
get mixed up in this business.

Let's see, Mrs Verma said, counting the possibilities on her
fingers. He could take the body to Algiers. But how, and what
for? Or he could fly it back to India. But how? He'd have to take
it to the airport at Hassi Messaoud, and who knows whether
there's a plane tomorrow – and anyway the body would never
last. Or else he could just leave the body with the authorities
and let them . . . dispose of it.

Her eyes widened as she thought out the implications of that
last possibility. What do you think they'd do with it? she said.
Involuntarily she clenched her fist and raised it to her mouth.
What do you think they'd do?

Dr Mishra chuckled: What's another corpse to you, Mrs
Verma? You've been seeing dozens every day ever since you
first went to Medical College. You've chopped them up, pulled
out their gullets, pickled their hearts in alcohol. Don't you
think it's a bit late to start weeping over a bit of dead tissue?

It's not the same thing, she said confusedly, when it happens
in your own house.

It's exactly the same thing, he answered, tapping the table with his pipe. Surely you don't need me to tell you that. There's nothing there that you wouldn't find in any morgue or any textbook.

But only a few hours ago I offered her a room in my house because she had nowhere else to go. Don't we owe her anything now; now that she's dead?

We owe her nothing, he said sharply. We didn't even know her.

But what will her husband do? Where will he go with the body?

He can go, Dr Mishra said gleefully, back to wherever he came from.

Mrs Verma rose from the table, her hands clasped determinedly together. There's only one thing to do now, she said. We shall have to cremate her ourselves, properly, somewhere among the dunes.

Dr Mishra slumped back, stunned. After a while, his voice hoarse with shock, he murmured: How can we do that? There's no crematorium here. What will the authorities say? We can't do it. There's a proper procedure for these things.

That can be worked out very easily, Mrs Verma said, clearing the table. After all, the authorities know us and we know them. We can explain the circumstances. I'm sure they'll be sympathetic.

Mrs Verma, Dr Mishra said softly, recovering himself. When you said 'a proper cremation' what exactly did you mean?

Well, like we've seen it being done for our fathers and mothers, I suppose.

Say it, Mrs Verma, don't be afraid. What you mean is a proper Hindu cremation.

It doesn't matter what you call it.

Dr Mishra leant forward with all the aplomb of a chess-player about to signal a checkmate. But, Mrs Verma, he said smiling, what makes you think she's *eligible* for a proper cremation?

*

How could Jyoti Das explain, especially with Alu's expectant, unblinking gaze clamped on him like that, what she had looked like when she first came through the door, how he had seen her then? It was an image with too long a past; it had appeared so suddenly, like the last photograph in a hastily riffled album, out of the haze left by pages of blurred pictures.

There was, for example, that final interview with the Ambassador in al-Ghazira, when he had said, with a sarcasm which could have sliced silk: Tell me, is it true, Mr Das, that you were away shopping when your so-called 'extremists' made their getaway? And before he could deny it the Ambassador was off, reminiscing pointedly about the incompetence of all the cloak-and-dagger men he had ever known; about the grudge they bore against the world because they hadn't qualified for the more prestigious services in the examinations; about the 'extremists' they concocted to wangle trips abroad at government expense.

Mr Das, do you really think, he asked softly at the end, that we believed all this business about 'extremists'? We know quite well why they send you people to visit embassies every now and then; they send you to watch *us*.

Then later there was Jai Lal sitting beside him, telling him how a First Secretary in the embassy had confided to him that even a small part of the report the Ambassador had sent to headquarters would be enough to stub out young Jyoti's career like a half-smoked cigarette. And then Jai Lal again, telling him how there was only one way of retrieving something of his once bright future – and that was to find the Suspect.

After that, grey, sour days, waiting for his permission to proceed Cairowards to be cleared. And more grey days even after the permission arrived, for nobody in the embassy in Cairo would meet him. His contact said: The news is spreading fast; everyone's heard about the business in al-Ghazira and your, your. . . .

Failure? prompted Jyoti.

Inability to fulfil your commission, corrected his contact. Nobody wants to get involved.

But there were two flashes of light in Egypt as well: one the encounter in Alexandria when he knew that he had sighted the right flight-path; and the other a letter from his engineer uncle in Düsseldorf with a hint about a job for him in Germany as well as a draft for a few hundred dollars.

The money bought him a ticket to Tunis, but once there it was all darkness. When he rang the embassy a voice asked him for his name, designation, rank, business, and then informed him gleefully that they had received a telex from the Ministry notifying a Shri Jyoti Das to show cause why he should not be suspended for dereliction of duty.

Luckily there were a few more hundred dollars from Düsseldorf, waiting poste restante. What could he do, but put them in his pocket and set off to look for the only people he knew in that continent?

So there he was, in the desert, lying on a sofa, terrified of the future, without a past, aware only of the prickings of his painfully virginal flesh, and there, suddenly in the doorway, was Kulfi.

There I was, he said to Alu, lying on a sofa thinking of a vulture, and I looked up and there she was in her yellow sari, framed in the doorway, like an oriole in a Mughal miniature.

*　　*　　*　　*

You can't give her a proper cremation, Mrs Verma; your own scriptures won't permit it.

Why not? she demanded.

Well, Dr Mishra said, I can think of two perfectly good reasons. To begin with, I think I could undertake to persuade anyone who's interested that her death was largely accidental – sudden shock, etc. Do you agree?

Mrs Verma nodded uncertainly: How does it matter anyway?

There, he cried. You see how you pay the price for your well-intentioned ignorance? Don't you know that, strictly speaking, someone who's died accidentally is not entitled to a proper funeral? If you don't believe me, have a look at the *Baudhayana Dharmasutra* – you can see for yourself. The argument, if I recall correctly, is that someone who dies accidentally can't enter Pitrloka anyway, so why bother? I can't quite remember offhand, but I think in scriptural times the bodies of people who died accidentally were thrown into rivers or left in forests. That should give you something to go on, except that, as you'll notice if you look out of the window, there aren't many forests here, nor rivers, and it's possible that the Algerians might be a little upset if we dumped her in an artesian well. So maybe we can just leave her on a sand-dune somewhere and give some of Mr Das's vultures a nice meal. What do you think?

Dr Mishra burst into laughter. Poor Mrs Bose, he said chuckling. She didn't do anything right. Didn't she know that she ought to have made a gift of a cow to a Brahmin before dying? It would have been so easy, too. All she had to do was call out for me; I've always wanted a cow. And now she'll have to answer for it, poor thing. She'll be stuck on the banks of the Vaitarani, with no cow to lead her across it into the underworld.

Mishra-sahb, Mrs Verma said, do you think this is the right time for your jokes?

If you think I'm joking, he said evenly, why don't you go and take a look at the Smritis yourself? The trouble is you can't, of course, because you don't know any Sanskrit.

Tell me, Mrs Verma said curiously, where did *you* learn?

From my grandfather, he said. What do you think I was doing all those years when my father was away in England? My grandfather was a real old Kanyakubja pandit; he used to give me vivas till the day he died. But, to come back to the point, there's another reason why you can't give Mrs Bose a proper cremation: I think you could see quite as well as I could that she was within hours of adultery. It can't have been the first time, either. You ought to see what your law-giver Manu has to say about giving funerals to adultresses and fallen women.

Gazing at him in wonder, Mrs Verma said: Do you really believe in all this, Mishra-sahb?

All what?

Manu and the Smritis and everything?

Of course I don't believe it. You know that quite well – I don't believe a word of it. Dr Mishra stabbed a finger at her: But *you* appear to believe it, so you ought to know what your beliefs imply. I think it's time someone showed you, Mrs Verma, that ignorance is a poor foundation for belief.

You shouldn't have bothered. I know quite well how ignorant I am.

That's not the point. I think you're old enough to learn that you can't just do what you like on impulse. There are certain rules.

Rules, rules, she said softly. All you ever talk about is rules. That's how you and your kind have destroyed everything – science, religion, socialism – with your rules and your orthodoxies. That's the difference between us: you worry about rules and I worry about being human.

*

Alu had little interest in Jyoti Das's visions of birds. Never mind all that, he said. Tell me what became of the others.

The others?

Hajj Fahmy, Professor Samuel, Chunni, Rakesh and all the rest. What happened after you ambushed us at the Star?

Jyoti Das had to think hard to put a face to every name. They were questioned, he said shamefacedly, mainly about you and Zindi at-Tiffaha and all the rest of you who got away. I wasn't there then; they wouldn't let me stay. I only saw them the next day. They were taken straight to the airport next morning to be deported – sent back to India or Egypt or wherever they had come from. I only saw them from a distance. They had plainclothesmen all around them, and no one was allowed to go close. Many of them looked as though they were in a bad way. Only Professor Samuel seemed calm. He even seemed to be trying to quieten some of the others. When they were being taken out of the lounge to the plane, he turned and saw me. I think he recognized me – I don't know. But, whatever it was, he stopped and shouted: This is not the end, only the beginning. Why? I shouted back. I couldn't think of anything else to say. The plainclothesmen were pushing him then, but he managed to hold them off for a moment. He smiled at me and shouted, even louder: How many people will you send away? The queue of hopes stretches long past infinity.

It was some time before Alu spoke again. He said: And what will happen to them now?

I don't know, said Jyoti Das. They might be tried or they

might be allowed to go straight home. Anyway, nothing serious
will happen to them – no one worries too much about things
which happen far away. And it's you they wanted – not them.

And what happened to Hajj Fahmy?

He died the same day, Jyoti Das said. Of shock, the Ghaziris
claimed.

A little later he added: When they took Hajj Fahmy's body
home the next day, they found that his family already knew.
They were waiting, dressed in mourning. His widow said that
her son Isma'il had told them the moment it happened.

*

So what will you do now, Mrs Verma? Dr Mishra asked. Will
you clean the body for the cremation? Do you know how to do
it?

After a moment's hesitation, Mrs Verma nodded. She said: It
shouldn't be too difficult for a doctor.

But you've always had nurses to stand between you and any
real pain, Mrs Verma. Not that a corpse feels pain, of course.
But what have you ever done to a corpse other than cut it up
anyway? No corpse has ever presented you with anything
which wasn't in *Gray's Anatomy*. This is a little different, isn't
it?

I'll manage, said Mrs Verma.

It's not quite as easy as you think, Dr Mishra said with relish.
You'll have to reach into the bowels and clean out all the dead
faeces. You'll have to scrape the insides of the rectum and the
anus to make sure that they're absolutely clean; that not the
faintest trace of mortal shit remains to defile the sacred fire.
Are you sure a well-brought-up woman like you will be able to
do it, Mrs Verma? I'm not.

Mrs Verma cast a quick, uncertain glance at the corpse and
wiped her forehead with the fall of her sari. I don't know, she
said.

You see, said Dr Mishra, it's not as easy as you think.

Then Zindi rose to her feet and plodded slowly to Mrs
Verma's chair. She put her hand on her shoulder and glowered
across the table at Dr Mishra. Don't worry, she said, her
tongue tripping indignantly over the Hindi syllables. I'll help

you. We'll do it together. I've often done it: we clean out the bodies of our dead, too.

Dr Mishra lowered his head, momentarily embarrassed. Wonderful, he said, under his breath. Now we can have an international feast of love over our adulterous corpse.

Mrs Verma stood up and took Zindi's arm. Come on, she said, we'd better start now.

Not so soon, Mrs Verma, Dr Mishra called out. You can't do anything to the corpse yet. You have to contact the authorities first. They may want an autopsy.

Mrs Verma stopped abruptly. That's right, Dr Mishra smiled. In the meanwhile all you can do is lay the body out properly. I don't suppose you know how to do that, either, Mrs Verma? Well, let me tell you. First, you have to find a clean place on the floor somewhere and you have to purify it with Ganga-jal. If I remember correctly, you're meant to cover it with cow dung, too. But since you're not going to find much cow dung on the sand-dunes, I suppose you could always use camel dung instead and do a few penances when you get back. However, personally I feel compelled to advise you strongly to leave that step out altogether. After that you have to lay the body out straight, with the head pointing south and the feet north.

Mrs Verma dusted her hands briskly. We can lay her out on the veranda, she said to Zindi. That'll be the best place. But first we have to clean it out properly.

They went into a bathroom and came back carrying buckets and mugs. When the first few mugfuls had splashed over the veranda Dr Mishra began to sniff the air suspiciously. Then, throwing back his head, he burst into laughter. Mrs Verma, he gasped, tell me, is that carbolic acid in those buckets?

Yes, of course, Mrs Verma said.

He nodded weakly. The world has come full circle, he groaned. Carbolic acid has become holy water.

Mrs Verma dropped her bucket, went up to his chair, and stood over him, arms folded. What does it matter? she cried. What does it matter whether it's Ganga-jal or carbolic acid? It's just a question of cleaning the place, isn't it? People thought something was clean once, now they think something else is clean. What difference does it make to the dead, Dr Mishra?

For a microbiologist, Dr Mishra said, wiping his eyes, you're not very rational, Mrs Verma.

Mrs Verma pulled her sari tight around her waist. Shall I tell you something? she said. I hate microbiology. I hate it.

*

Is a microbiologist who takes a bit of someone's piss or pus and runs tests on it really so different from a mechanic who takes a crankshaft or a spark-plug out of a car and checks it to see whether anything's gone wrong: whether the steel's rusted or the porcelain's cracked; whether there's grime or dust somewhere in the machinery?

The specimens even come to you in bottles, labelled with names or numbers, like so many dirty spark-plugs. It's not even like being a surgeon: at least the surgeon sees the whole machine, even though it's all shrouded and chloroformed, face covered and weeping mothers hidden away, every trace of its humanity blanketed. The microbiologist has only her test-tubes. At least the surgeon can see how the parts mesh, how the crankshaft connects to the gear-box. And at the end of it, after he's done all his oiling and his tightening and his replacing, he can, if he wants to (though he doesn't, of course) go and take a look at the entire contraption lying dead in the morgue, or ticking away in its room. What does the microbiologist do? Where does she go to see whether all her shelf-fuls of piss are clearing up or dripping blood?

And when you do find something in a specimen can you really help wondering sometimes where all those microbes and bacteria and viruses come from? Whether they can really, all of them, be wholly external to our minds?

And just as you let yourself wonder whether sometimes they are anything other than a bodily metaphor for human pain and unhappiness and perhaps joy as well you cut yourself short, for it dawns on you yet again that ever since Pasteur that is the one question you can never ask.

Then you feel exactly as you did when you once helped in a general practice and found people straying in, all through the day, with nothing wrong with them – nothing that a mechanic could have repaired at any rate – complaining: I have this pain,

Doctor, and that pain, Doctor, and I think this or that has gone
wrong here or somewhere else. Then, too, you almost began to
speak till you realized yet again that the tyranny of your
despotic science forbade you to tell them the one thing that was
worth saying; the one thing that was true. And that was:
There's nothing wrong with your body – all you have to do to
cure yourself is try to be a better human being.

*   *   *   *

The phone rang an hour after the police had come and gone,
when Mrs Verma and Zindi had almost finished with the
cleaning of the corpse.

Dr Mishra managed to get to it first. It's the police, he hissed
at Mrs Verma with his hand on the mouthpiece. You'll see,
they'll never allow your cremation. I told you, there was no
point wasting your time explaining to them. Why should they
allow it? Why should it make any difference to them whether
some passing Indian tourist happens to die here? Why should
they agree to bend the rules?

Mrs Verma smiled: Why don't you hear what they have to
say first?

They all gathered around to watch as Dr Mishra listened to
the voice at the other end. He said nothing beyond an
occasional *oui* and startled *mais peut être*. Gradually his face
fell and when he put the phone down it was with a grimace,
half-rueful, half-angry.

What did they say? Mrs Verma demanded.

I don't believe it, he said, shaking his head. They're not in
their right minds. They've made a mistake.

Tell us what they *said*, Mrs Verma cried.

They said it's all right; they're willing to look the other way.
Only, we have to cremate her quietly, somewhere in the
dunes, and quickly.

Mrs Verma bit back a cry of delight. You see, she said, *they*
know how important it is to die properly. Haven't you heard
how during their war of independence the French used to blow
up the bodies of the Algerian dead to demoralize the guerillas,
because they knew how important it is to Muslims to be buried
with their bodies whole and undesecrated? I knew the

Algerians would understand: if there's one thing people learn from the past, it is that every consummated death is another beginning.

*

And wood? Dr Mishra cried suddenly, when Mr Verma was about to leave the house to fetch a land-rover from the hospital.

Where are you going to get wood from? You have to have wood if you're going to cremate her. Or do you think her body's so pure now that it'll go up like a lump of phlogiston when you put a matchstick to it?

Mrs Verma fell into a chair. That's true, she said, biting her lip. That's going to be a problem.

Delightedly, Dr Mishra called out after her husband: Stop, you don't have to go now. It's all called off.

But Mrs Verma waved him on. Nonsense, she said. Of course we can find the wood if we try. Go on, get the land-rover; we'll arrange for wood somehow.

All right, so what's your plan now, Mrs Verma? Dr Mishra said. Are you going to send us out to chop down date palms?

Mrs Verma laughed: No, no, Dr Mishra, you won't have to do anything. Mr Das and Mr Bose can do it. It's quite simple: there's that old table in the kitchen – the top's plywood, but the legs are good, solid wood. Then there's that huge crate-like thing the refrigerator was packed in. I'll ring up Manda-bahen, too; there's bound to be lots of wooden boxes and things lying about your house, considering all those expensive things you're always buying. I know old Miss K. has some termite-ridden old boxes she wants to get rid of.

Dr Mishra shook his finger violently in her face. You can't do it, he cried. You just can't do it. I won't let you. You can't put that poor woman on some termite-ridden bonfire and set her alight. That's not a cremation; that's like roasting a tandoori chicken.

I don't see what's wrong with it.

There's everything wrong with it. You can't do it like that. You have to have the right wood.

What wood?

I don't know, Dr Mishra snapped, flinging up his hands impatiently. There has to be some sandalwood; I remember that.

Sandalwood? Mrs Verma said. Come with me.

She led him across the drawing-room and knelt beside Hem Narain Mathur's old bookcase. Reaching into the gap behind the books she drew out two battered sandalwood bookends, carved like elephants. One had no trunk and the other lacked a leg.

Since they can't be used for beautification purposes any more, she said, they might as well be added to the pyre.

Dr Mishra stormed out of the room without another word.

Mrs Verma rang Mrs Mishra and Miss Krishnaswamy and then sent Jyoti Das and Alu to their houses. Over the next couple of hours the two men carried a number of crates and several pieces of old furniture into Mrs Verma's garden and chopped them up. When Mrs Verma went out into the garden later, there was a sizeable pile of wood chopped up and ready.

That's plenty, she said. We won't be able to fit any more into a land-rover. She noticed Alu standing beside her, shuffling his feet awkwardly. Yes, Mr Bose? she said.

He began to say something, but his voice sank into an inaudible mumble. What's the matter? she asked a little impatiently. Do you want to say something?

I don't want your book, he said in a rush, holding it out to her. The *Life of Pasteur*. . . .

Oh, she said, pushing it back, that's a problem. I don't want it, either. What do we do with it now?

I don't know, Alu said.

She took the book from him and turned it over in her hands. Then she gave it back to him.

Maybe we could give it a funeral, too? she said.

She left him staring at it in silence. After a long while he raised it high in both his hands and placed it reverently on the pyre.

*

Dr Mishra decided to play his last card soon after his wife and Miss Krishnaswamy had arrived in Mrs Verma's house to help with the arrangements for the cremation.

All right, Mrs Verma, he said. You've managed all right till now. But there's one thing you seem to have forgotten.

She sensed the elation simmering beneath his smooth tone and was on her guard at once. What thing?

The ghee, he said. What about the ghee?

Mrs Verma stared at him blankly: The ghee?

Yes, the ghee. You have to have ghee for a cremation. You have to pour it over the wood so that it catches fire. You can't very well use kerosene, you know.

Frowning with concentration, Mrs Verma whispered: If only I had some butter, it would be so easy to make ghee. But we finished all our butter last week.

Then, eagerly, she cried: But what about that nice soya-bean oil I bought in Algiers?

Soya-bean oil? Dr Mishra said faintly.

It was very expensive.

Mrs Verma, he said, you're cremating her, not pickling her.

Mrs Verma's head sank on to her hands: Where can I get ghee now?

So that's that, then, Dr Mishra said, rising jubilantly to his feet. We can call it off now. I'll go and tell Mr Bose.

Wait! Mrs Verma reached out for Mrs Mishra's hand. Manda . . . Mandodari-bahen, she appealed, don't you have any butter?

Like a frightened bird, Mrs Mishra cocked her head at her husband. Mrs Verma brushed her hand angrily across her swimming eyes. For God's sake, Mandodari, she said, surely you won't let him tell you what to do in a situation like this? Can't you see how important it is?

Mrs Mishra swallowed and then, with another frightened glance at her frowning husband, she said: Yes, I can give you two kilograms of butter. I stored them away last month.

Mrs Verma clasped her hand between her own and kissed her on her greying hair. So Mishra-sahb, she said. What do you have to say now?

So you're really going ahead with this? he said. You're going to broil her on rotten wood and baste her with rancid butter? It's shameful. It's a travesty. Can't you see that?

The times are like that, Mrs Verma said sadly. Nothing's whole any more. If we wait for everything to be right again, we'll wait for ever while the world falls apart. The only hope is to make do with what we've got.

*

There's only one small thing left now, Mrs Verma told Alu. And that is you have to bathe and shave your head. I'll heat some water for you if you like. And I've told my husband to shave your head. He has an old razor; he can do it easily. Of course Miss K. could probably do it much better, but I thought you would prefer—

But, said Alu, why do I have to do all this?

Of course you have to; you're her husband. You have to perform the last rites – the kapalakriya, lighting the pyre and all that. Who can do it but you? Your son's hardly the right age. And to do it you have to shave your head.

I can't do it, he said, a sudden fear knotting his stomach. I won't be able to.

You have to, Mrs Verma said firmly. Even Dr Mishra says so. It's not really very much, Mr Bose; having your head shaved isn't at all painful, you know.

No, no, he said. You don't understand. Of course I'll shave my head. But I can't light the pyre. I simply can't.

Why not? said Mrs Verma.

It's because. . . . The words seared his throat like a gush of bile: It's because of my hands, my thumbs.

Is something wrong with your thumbs?

Alu caught his breath, shut his eyes and thrust his hands in front of her. Look, he said.

Yes? said Mrs Verma mildly. What's the matter?

Look, he repeated. I can't do it. I can't move my thumbs.

She laughed: But you just did.

He opened his eyes and stared blankly at his hands.

There's a little muscular atrophy, Mrs Verma said, but nothing serious. Look, you've already chopped all that wood. Your thumbs are all right, Mr Bose. Really. You can do whatever you like as long as you want to.

*   *   *   *

Zindi hardly recognized Alu when she first saw him with his head shaven. He was changed, diminished. It was as though the clouds had lifted from some perpetually misted mountain; without his hair his head looked plain, ordinary, even smooth.

You're another man today, she said. I've never seen you before.

But he was thinking of something else. I'm afraid, Zindi, he said, kneading his hands. I have to light the fire, and I don't know whether I'll be able to do it.

They left just before dawn when the dunes were glowing with the first amber streaks of the eastern sky. Zindi stood in the veranda with Boss in her arms and watched them drive away. Though Miss Krishnaswamy and Mrs Mishra had stayed behind and only five of them had gone, they had still had to take two land-rovers, because of the wood.

When she couldn't hear the land-rover any more Zindi went back to her room and began throwing her things into her small suitcase. Hours and hours seemed to pass before she heard them driving back. She snapped her suitcase shut and hurried out to the veranda.

The moment she saw Alu jump out of the land-rover and walk towards her she knew it had gone well. She didn't need to ask; she could see it in his step.

It was he who said: I did it, Zindi. Then he held up a sealed brass box.

What is it?

It's a bit of her ashes.

Zindi backed away hastily. Don't bring it close to me, she said. We don't believe in cheating the Day of Judgement by burning our bodies like that. You can keep it for yourself. What are you going to do with it?

Alu turned the box around slowly, looking at its aged joins. He said: Mrs Verma gave it to me to take back. She said it would give me a good reason to go home.

*

Dr Mishra adjusted his spectacles, explored his pockets, shuffled his feet and, because he had still found nothing to say, he coughed.

Mrs Verma studied her watch. It's very late, she said, looking meaningfully at her husband. She was thinking of everything she had to get done before they left for the hospital. But Dr Mishra was still standing in front of her, wriggling a little, as though he had something to say but didn't know how.

Everything went off very well, she said brightly, to help him. Don't you think so, Dr Mishra? Now we can just forget about it.

He kicked a pebble and followed its trajectory intently till it vanished into a bougainvillaea bush.

Mrs Verma raised her voice: I wonder what the time is?

Well, Verma, Dr Mishra said at last, still looking at the bougainvillaea bush. It looks as though your *Chitrangada* is not going to get very far now.

No, Mrs Verma said, prompting her husband. That's all finished with now. We can just have what we had last year.

But this year is not last year, is it, Verma?

What do you mean, Dr Mishra? she said. Her husband stared sadly at a cactus.

Dr Mishra turned to her: This year you'll have to make the speech.

Why me?

Dr Mishra tried to smile, but instead his mouth twisted awkwardly sideways. Because you've won, Mrs Verma, he said. You've beaten old Murali Charan Mishra at last.

*

Alu looked from Zindi's locked suitcase to his own bag lying in a corner with clothes spilling out of it.

What's the matter, Zindi? he asked in surprise. Why . . .?

Zindi, rocking Boss in her arms, didn't answer.

Zindi? he said again.

Zindi hid her face in Boss's hair. I don't know, *ya* Alu, she said. We've travelled so far together. It seems just the other day that we were in *Mariamma* with me worrying about Karthamma and Boss. . . . And you sitting there with all those boils, catching fish. . . . Who would have thought . . .?

He knew then what the packed suitcase meant. But still he

wanted to be sure, so he sat down beside her and took her hand in his: What is it, Zindi?

She would not look at him. I'm old, Alu, she said, and every day I get older and older. I won't last much longer; I've only got a few years left now. And today, when you people took Kulfi's body – God have mercy on her – away, I wondered; I wondered what would happen to me if I died in a desert in a foreign land, without a house or friends to help me. I don't think I would find a Mrs Verma, Alu – not everyone is as lucky as Kulfi – and what would become of me then?

Like a pebble sliding down a mined mountainside, a tear ran down the deep ridges of her cheek. I can't go on any longer, Alu, she said. I'm too old and Boss is too young.

Alu nodded slowly: So what do you want to do now, Zindi?

You're all right now, Alu, she went on. You'll manage. You'll look after yourself somehow. You don't need me any more, so you'll forgive me soon enough. Boss is all right, too, now. So there's no reason to wait any longer here.

What is it, Zindi? he cried. Tell me.

He felt the warmth of her hand on his shaven, shrunken head. She said: Boss and I are going back home, Alu. Boss is going to build me a house some day.

*

Standing apart, Jyoti Das watched as Alu carried Zindi's suitcase and his own bag to the veranda. He listened as Zindi poured profuse, tearful thanks on Mrs Verma, as Alu mumbled his gratitude, as Mrs Verma (looking at her watch, for she was already very, very late) bade them goodbye.

He caught up with them when they reached the gate. Where are you going? he asked Alu.

We're going home, Alu said.

How?

By ship. So we have to get to Tangier first.

Tangier? Jyoti Das rolled the name around his tongue. With Gibraltar on the other side?

Alu nodded.

Jyoti Das looked up at the sky and said: It'll be autumn there now!

He looked past them at the great silent dunes and suddenly he saw a sky alive with Cory's shearwaters and honey buzzards, white storks and steppe eagles, Montagu's harriers and sparrowhawks circling on the thermals; all of them funnelled, like clouds driven to a mountain pass, into that point where only one narrow strip of water lies between Europe and Africa, like a drawn sword.

My God! he said. The whole sky will be migrating over Tangier now.

He saw Zindi's face cloud over with suspicion, so then he said: I'm migrating myself – to Düsseldorf. I've got nowhere else to go. Can I come with you, too?

Chapter Twenty-Two

Tamám-shud

There is little left to tell.

Travelling slowly, because of Boss, it took them nine days to reach Tangier. They found a cheap pension in the rue des Postes and took two rooms on the second floor from which they could, if they craned out of the window, glimpse the winding tumult of the Petit Socco. Next day Jyoti Das rang his uncle in Düsseldorf and later he bought a ticket for the ferry to Algeciras in Spain.

Next morning they went down the Avenue d'Espagne and, while Jyoti Das watched the flocks of swift-flying birds in the sky, Alu and Zindi gazed across the sparkling blue water at the hint of Spain shimmering in the distance. When the time came, they walked with Jyoti Das till he had to turn off into the quays. As he walked away, they waved and waved at his back and the single airline bag slung across it.

When he was through the gate and walking away, he seemed to remember something. He spun round suddenly and ran back.

Alu, he shouted through the bars.

What? Alu shouted back.

He cupped his hands around his mouth: Don't worry about the sewing machine; they make them better at home now.

He laughed. Alu waved, and he waved back. Jyoti Das's face was radiant, luminous, as though a light were shining through him. He waved again and walked jauntily away.

By the time the sleek Spanish ferry drew away, churning up the harbour, Jyoti Das was already on deck, waving. He was sure he could see them among the trees of the Avenue d'Espagne, so he kept waving as the lovely white town cradled in its nest of hills shrank away. Then he looked down and saw a humped back caracoling through the water. Then he saw another and another and suddenly there was a whole school of dolphins racing along with the ferry, leaping, dancing, standing on their tails. He looked up at the tranquil sky and gloried in the soaring birds, the sunlight, the sharpness of the clean sea breeze and the sight of the huge rock growing in the distance.

It was very beautiful and he was at peace.

When the ferry entered a bay and turned away from the rock of Gibraltar towards the shiny oil-tanks of Algeciras, Jyoti Das turned back to wave for one last time. But all he saw there was a mocking grey smudge hanging on the horizon, pointing to continents of defeat – defeat at home, defeat in the world – and he shut his eyes, for he had looked on it for too many years and he could not bear to look on it any longer.

And so he turned to face the land before him, now grown so real, and dizzy with exultation he prepared to step into a new world.

*

Alu and Zindi, with Boss in her arms, walked up through the steep, narrow streets of the Medina to the high battlements of the Kasbah. From there they could see the ferry clearly, cutting swiftly across the Straits, towards the Mediterranean. But Boss was looking the other way, towards the Atlantic, and soon they were looking there, too, scanning the waters. They saw nothing except sleepy, crawling oil-tankers. So, drowsily warmed by the clear sunlight, they settled down to wait for Virat Singh and the ship that was to carry them home.

Hope is the beginning.

F
GHO

Ghosh, Amitav.

The circle of reason

DATE			